ALIENS™

INFILTRATOR

THE COMPLETE ALIEN™ LIBRARY FROM TITAN BOOKS

THE OFFICIAL MOVIE NOVELIZATIONS BY ALAN DEAN FOSTER:
ALIEN
ALIENS™
ALIEN 3
ALIEN: COVENANT
ALIEN: COVENANT ORIGINS

ALIEN: RESURRECTION BY A.C. CRISPIN

ALIEN: OUT OF THE SHADOWS BY TIM LEBBON
ALIEN: SEA OF SORROWS BY JAMES A. MOORE
ALIEN: RIVER OF PAIN BY CHRISTOPHER GOLDEN
ALIEN: THE COLD FORGE BY ALEX WHITE
ALIEN: ISOLATION BY KEITH R.A. DECANDIDO
ALIEN: PROTOTYPE BY TIM WAGGONER
ALIEN: INTO CHARYBDIS BY ALEX WHITE

ALIEN 3: THE UNPRODUCED SCREENPLAY BY WILLIAM GIBSON AND PAT CADIGAN

THE RAGE WAR BY TIM LEBBON:
PREDATOR™: INCURSION
ALIEN: INVASION
ALIEN VS. PREDATOR™: ARMAGEDDON

ALIENS: BUG HUNT EDITED BY JONATHAN MABERRY
ALIENS: PHALANX BY SCOTT SIGLER
ALIENS: INFILTRATOR BY WESTON OCHSE

ALIENS VS. PREDATORS: ULTIMATE PREY
EDITED BY JONATHAN MABERRY AND BRYAN THOMAS SCHMIDT

THE COMPLETE ALIENS OMNIBUS, VOLUME 1 BY STEVE AND STEPHANI PERRY
THE COMPLETE ALIENS OMNIBUS, VOLUME 2 BY DAVID BISCHOFF AND ROBERT SHECKLEY
THE COMPLETE ALIENS OMNIBUS, VOLUME 3 BY SANDY SCHOFIELD AND S.D. PERRY
THE COMPLETE ALIENS OMNIBUS, VOLUME 4 BY YVONNE NAVARRO AND S.D. PERRY
THE COMPLETE ALIENS OMNIBUS, VOLUME 5 BY MICHAEL JAN FRIEDMAN AND DIANE CAREY

THE COMPLETE ALIENS VS. PREDATOR OMNIBUS, VOLUME 1
BY STEVE PERRY AND S.D. PERRY

ALIEN: 40 YEARS 40 ARTISTS
ALIEN: THE ARCHIVE
ALIEN: THE BLUEPRINTS BY GRAHAM LANGRIDGE
ALIEN: THE ILLUSTRATED STORY BY ARCHIE GOODWIN AND WALTER SIMONSON
ALIENS: THE SET PHOTOGRAPHY BY SIMON WARD
THE ART OF ALIEN: ISOLATION BY ANDY MCVITTIE
THE ART AND MAKING OF ALIEN: COVENANT BY SIMON WARD
ALIEN COVENANT: THE OFFICIAL COLLECTOR'S EDITION
ALIEN COVENANT: DAVID'S DRAWINGS BY DANE HALLETT AND MATT HATTON
THE MAKING OF ALIEN BY J.W. RINZLER
ALIENS—ARTBOOK BY PRINTED IN BLOOD
ALIENS VS. PREDATOR REQUIEM: INSIDE THE MONSTER SHOP
BY ALEC GILLIS AND TOM WOODRUFF, JR.
AVP: ALIEN VS. PREDATOR BY ALEC GILLIS AND TOM WOODRUFF, JR.
THE PREDATOR: THE ART AND MAKING OF THE FILM BY JAMES NOLAN

ALIEN NEXT DOOR BY JOEY SPIOTTO
JONESY: NINE LIVES ON THE NOSTROMO BY RORY LUCEY
ALIEN: THE COLORING BOOK
ALIEN: THE OFFICIAL COOKBOOK BY CHRIS-RACHAEL OSELAND

PREDATOR: IF IT BLEEDS EDITED BY BRYAN THOMAS SCHMIDT
THE PREDATOR: HUNTERS AND HUNTED BY JAMES A. MOORE
THE PREDATOR BY JAMES A. MOORE & MARK MORRIS
PREDATOR: STALKING SHADOWS BY JAMES A. MOORE & MARK MORRIS
THE COMPLETE PREDATOR OMNIBUS BY NATHAN ARCHER, SANDY SCHOFIELD

ALIENS™

INFILTRATOR

A NOVEL BY WESTON OCHSE

TITAN BOOKS

ALIENS™: INFILTRATOR
Print edition ISBN: 9781789093988
E-book edition ISBN: 9781789093995

Published by Titan Books
A division of Titan Publishing Group Ltd
144 Southwark Street, London SE1 0UP
www.titanbooks.com

First edition: April 2021
10 9 8 7 6 5 4 3 2

A CIP catalogue record for this title is available from the British Library.

Printed and bound by CPI Group (UK) Ltd, Croydon CR0 4YY

To the fourteen-year-old boy and his date who saw
the original movie in theaters and was
blown away by the experience

1

PALA STATION LV-895
JANUARY 12, 2202

He dreams of storms and flames, the heat of a thousand suns turning everything into molten nightmare. He screams, but the roar of the superheated beast drowns out his cries. His mother, his father, everything he ever knew consumed by something so hungry it cannot be stopped. Even as far away as he is, the heat blisters his face and burns away the hairs on his head. His tears prism his vision until his small universe is a kaleidoscope of fire.

The shuttle jolted him awake.

"Welcome to Pala Station," the pilot announced as the shuttle landed. The announcement could not have been delivered with less enthusiasm. Still, the welcome was a punctuation to a long journey for Dr. Timothy Hoenikker, who'd traveled too many light years, all at the chance of investigating a cache of newly discovered artifacts.

Alien artifacts.

For a theoretical archaeologist, who up until now had

depended on modeling in order to advance his research, examining *actual* components of an alien race's past was beyond remarkable. This could be, he hoped fervently, the opportunity of a lifetime.

Wiping the dream from his eyes, he shoved the familiar fiend to the back of his mind.

His shuttle partner sighed heavily.

"Back to the shit," the man said. He'd introduced himself earlier as Logistics Specialist Steve Fairbanks. His eyes were haunted, his gaze far away, and he had the world worn look of someone who'd been in the thick of it, and still hadn't found a way out. Probably just short of thirty years old, he was average height and had black hair cut close to his bullet-shaped head. His nose was too thin for a flat face, but that wasn't his fault.

"Can't be as bad as all that," Hoenikker said hopefully, hiding his discomfort at being spoken to, and with the information.

"Just wait, sir," Fairbanks replied. "You'll see what Pala is about in no time."

The station was out on the edge of the known systems—but then, weren't all the places where new discoveries were possible? When Hoenikker had been recruited, he'd convinced himself that leaving the luxury of his cushy Weyland-Yutani corporate job was going to be worth the effort. Before leaving, he'd researched the jungle planet LV-895 and marveled at its exotic life. Sure, the living arrangements might not be what he'd been used to, and the day-to-day luxuries might not be there, but the payoff would be to lay hands on that which he'd only previously imagined.

This could be the opportunity, he knew, to become one of the foremost experts in alien anthropology. His pulse quickened as he imagined the data he could provide to those who would come after, his name synonymous with the greatest archaeologists of all time. Layard. Carter. Jones. Leakey. Evans. Schliemann. Navarro.

Hoenikker.

"Pala Station personnel should be waiting for your arrival," the pilot announced over the intercom. "One minute until doors open."

The thrill Hoenikker felt was tempered with a sick feeling that everything was going to go terribly wrong. He'd always been this way—feeling the desire to experience new things, yet dreading that reality wouldn't live up to his expectations. As had happened all too many times before, was he going to be disappointed, or would this be the greatest adventure of his life?

His friend Stokes, who he'd probably never see again, had argued long and hard for him to take this assignment.

"You might never get this opportunity again," Stokes had said. *"Sure, you could stay here at your nine-to-five, going out for dinner on Fridays, seeing your therapist on Wednesdays. Or you could travel to the edge of the known universe, discover wonders no man has ever seen, and be better for it. Be boring and stay here. Or be dangerous and travel far."*

Stokes always did the dangerous. He'd been a Colonial Marine, then a scientist traveling for the company. Always the center of any conversation. Even Hoenikker looked forward to listening to the outrageous stories the man continually shared—assuming they were all true. This was his chance, Hoenikker knew, to walk in the footsteps of his friend. But in reality, he could never be the person Stokes was capable of being.

The red flashing light switched to green. The rear door of the shuttle opened, revealing a single man waiting for them, holding a pad. He had dark skin, bald, about forty. Part of his right arm was a prosthesis.

Fairbanks was first off.

"Fairbanks. Steven," he said to the man. "Log. Back from emergency leave."

After making a few marks on the digital pad, the man nodded, but didn't say a word.

"Best of luck," Fairbanks said over his shoulder, then he hefted his duffel and disappeared around the corner.

"You must be Dr. Hoenikker," the man said. "I'm Reception Tech Rawlings, Victor, and I'll be inprocessing you. Is that all your luggage?" he asked, nodding to the single large bag on the deck.

Hoenikker nodded. Rawlings stepped over and grabbed the bag.

"This way please."

Hoenikker followed, noting that the air in the hangar was humid. But that was soon replaced by the cool forced air of the interior, the buzz and hum of environmental equipment immediately making him at home. Facilities he knew. Jungles he did not.

"As you know, Doctor, Pala Station's existence is classified," Rawlings said. "I've been here a little over a year, and things don't hardly change. We prefer it that way. So, you're with the scientists?"

"Yes." Hoenikker didn't know how much he could reveal.

Rawlings laughed. "What you all do isn't a secret to those of us on the station. What with the black goo and all. We just don't like when your research subjects get loose. You understand."

"Does that happen often?"

"Once is too often," Rawlings said. He held up his prosthesis. "I've seen enough action. I'm just trying to get my retirement creds now."

There was the sound of rapid footsteps and three men rushed around a corner. As they did, the third knocked

Hoenikker roughly into the wall. The man grunted, but kept going without saying a word. They all held long wooden rods.

"Sorry about that." Rawlings steadied Hoenikker. "We have a rat infestation. Station commander has us on a schedule for extermination duty, and no one is particularly happy about it." He nodded toward where the men had disappeared. "Their turn."

"Rats?"

Rawlings shrugged and gave a good-natured smile. "We're on the edge of nowhere, on a godforsaken jungle planet. Rats are the least of our worries."

They continued on their way, and Rawlings indicated several doors as they passed the various staff sections. Staff Section 1—or S1—was Manpower. S2, Security. S3, Engineering. S4, Logistics. S5, Med Lab. S6, Communications. And S7, Fabrications. He counted them off as they passed.

"Being as far out of system as we are, we can't just order a part. So S7 is in charge of producing everything we need to operate, from a knob, to a screw, to a laser-guided ass missile."

Hoenikker balked. "Laser-guided ass missile?"

"That was a joke. Sorry, military humor. Just know if you need something, they can make it. Anyway, you'll be dealing a lot with S7. Just don't get in the way of their feud with S3. It can get vicious."

They passed through a door and entered an office like many others he'd seen. The setup was familiar. A desk. Two chairs. A camera attached to a terminal.

"Sit there, please." Rawlings gestured. "We'll take your picture, retina display, biometrics, fingerprint, and DNA. Need to make sure you are who we think you are, and give you access to where you need to be later."

Hoenikker sat in the chair across from the camera, eyeing the cradle made for his hand. He could see several dozen minute needles, almost invisible to the eye, and didn't relish the idea of embracing it. Still, bureaucracy. He sighed.

"I think it started two years ago," Rawlings said, oblivious to his hesitation, "when Fabrications ran out of materials and there were no supply shuttles for six months. They were forced to take what they needed from everyone else. It wasn't that bad really, but Engineering—who feel self-important because they keep the lights and air running—began calling Fabrications by all sorts of names, to get under their skin. 'Acquisitions,' 'Infiltrations,' 'Reparations,' 'Thieverations,' and my favorite, 'Mastications.'"

Rawlings pointed. "Eye here, please. Thanks."

Hoenikker placed his right eye in front of the reader, and stared into the light.

"I know. I know," Rawlings continued. "It seems like a small thing, but all day every day for six months became too much. That's it. Thanks, Doctor."

Hoenikker leaned back.

"So, when Fabrications had the chance to turn the tables, turn them they did. Engineering needed Fabrications to create a water pump for the commander, which they did—but they put everything in backward so the pump exploded, and then they blamed it on Engineering. Even pulled out instructions they had clearly fabricated—pun intended—to imply a design flaw. Meanwhile, Engineering is completely overwhelmed, dealing with the effects the environment has on the station, not to mention the rats that are getting into the wiring.

"We're so far away from any supply depot, Fabrications is constantly fixing things that medlab needs, or producing the special glass used in the containment areas for your experiments." Rawlings rolled his eyes, and Hoenikker thought he detected a note of resentment in his voice. "I could tell you about the other staff sections, but we don't have that sort of time. Your fellow brainiacs will have to brief you up."

He gestured at the hand cradle. "Now for this. It won't hurt at all. I promise. Each needle is coated with a local anesthetic. You just have to press firmly."

Hoenikker held out his hand, but hesitated.

Rawlings reached out, gently but firmly grasped Hoenikker's hand, and placed it in the cradle. The reception tech's prosthesis was cold against his skin.

Hoenikker sucked in air, ready to shout out.

The tech was right. No pain.

Rawlings maintained his grip as he made a few selections on the display with his left hand.

"And don't get me started on the commander," the reception tech said, and this time his ire was obvious. "He's completely useless, spending more time trying to get the hell out of here than trying to do his job." He glanced over, and nodded as if Hoenikker had said something. "I know. I know. The deputy should step up, but he's oblivious—too in love with the flora and fauna outside to pay attention to what's going on." He sighed. "It's our own fault, really. We're all professionals—if we weren't, the place would *really* fall apart. The fact is, each section operates on its own, without supervision. It's not like this is brain science, you know? But no one's paying attention to the big picture."

He released the hand, and Hoenikker hoped it meant he could go. So much gossip…

"Alright. You checked out, and you're checked in." He handed Hoenikker an ID badge on a fob. "Wear this at all times, and Security will leave you alone. Same goes for the synths, but I doubt you'll even see them."

"Synths?" Hoenikker asked, realizing upon hearing his voice that he hadn't spoken in a long while.

"Sure. You know, 'state-of-the-art,'" Rawlings said, delivering air quotes. "Special Security Chief Wincotts maintains them, but we've never seen them in use. No need, I guess. Probably stacked in a closet somewhere, covered in glass with a big sign that says, *Break In Case of Emergency*." He laughed.

"It all sounds a bit intense," Hoenikker said.

"Oh, no—not really," Rawlings said, standing and urging Hoenikker to do so as well. "I've been in units where the tension is so thick you're worried someone's going to pop off a pulse rifle. Or we could be crawling in mud, on patrol on a new LV. Hell, I could be on sentry duty! No thank you, sir. I'll take the politics of Pala Station anytime." He looked Hoenikker square in the eye. "Just know where you are and who you're talking to before you say something you can't take back." He patted Hoenikker on the shoulder. "But hell, that's the same everywhere, no?"

Hoenikker nodded as he felt himself being guided gently out of the room.

"Now, let's get you situated."

They passed several more doors and went down enough corridors that Hoenikker lost track. Then they came to a door with his name on it.

"Only you and Security will have access. Just place your palm on the access panel." Hoenikker did so and realized the numbness had already passed. The door slid open, revealing a room that was large enough for a desk and chair, a bureau, and a narrow bed.

He turned to Rawlings. "Bathroom?"

The tech pointed across the corridor. "Communal. For brainiacs only. Sorry, Doc. If you wanted a private bathroom, you should have applied to be the commander."

Hoenikker sighed.

"Listen," Rawlings said. "Unpack. Get situated. I'll be back to get you in an hour."

Then he was gone, leaving Hoenikker alone. All he could hear was the pumping and hissing of forced air.

The silence was blissful.

2

When Rawlings returned, Hoenikker was sitting on his bed, hands in his lap. He had folded and refolded his sparse collection of same-color shirts, pants, and lab coats and placed them in their appointed places in the bureau. Pulling out his personal display he had placed it in the middle of the desk, hooking up to the station's comms so he could have access to news, vids, and mail. He'd stripped the bed to check the state of cleanliness, then had remade it.

Now he was ready to get to work.

During the short walk from his quarters to the area that housed the labs, he heard three arguments, saw four rats, and witnessed a man yelling something that sounded like, "I've had it up to here with this shit!" So, when he arrived in the quiet contemplative reception room that led to the labs, detecting the familiar antiseptic smell, he grinned inside. It felt more like he'd escaped from the streets into a house of worship.

For Hoenikker, a lab *was* a house of worship—a place to worship facts, critical hypotheses, and discovery.

A narrow man approached, wearing all black with a

severe Mandarin collar. Somewhere between sixty and seventy, he had a white goatee and white hair that ran into a ponytail. He held both hands behind his back, and his chin was slightly raised.

"Dr. Timothy Hoenikker, I presume."

Hoenikker stood straight and nodded. He didn't like shaking hands, and assumed by the man's posture that the sentiment was mutual. The man in black nodded to Rawlings, who returned the nod and walked away, leaving the two men staring at each other. Despite the awkwardness, however, if anywhere was home, this was it. Whether it was in the center of a city or on the edge of the known universe, all labs were alike.

"I am Mansfield," the newcomer said. "We expected you a week ago."

"B-but..." Flustered, Hoenikker couldn't help but stutter. "But I, I have no control over transportation. Weyland—"

A hand suddenly appeared and cut him off by chopping the air. "You will find, Doctor, that we don't care for excuses around here. We care about results. Now," he said pausing for dramatic effect, "are you checked in and ready to assume your duties?"

Hoenikker gritted his teeth and nodded. Then he softened. Perhaps the man had trouble dealing with new people. Hoenikker could easily understand this. He had the same problem. So instead of responding with anger, he tried another tactic.

"Thank you, Dr. Mansfield," he replied. "When you recruited me, offering an opportunity to work with verified alien artifacts, I dropped everything and came as fast as I could. I'm eager to begin..." He cleared his throat. "...and I apologize for being a week late."

There. That should ameliorate his new boss.

"You are incorrect, and on two accounts, Doctor Hoenikker. To begin, I am not a doctor, although I am the person to whom you will report. And you will not be working on alien artifacts. We have other tasks in mind for you."

Hoenikker tensed, but tried not to show it. He didn't want to argue with his boss on the first day, but working with alien artifacts was the primary—the *only*—reason he had taken the job.

"There must be a mistake," he replied. "The reason I left my previous position was the promise of working on genuine alien artifacts, to compare them with my archaeological modeling." Despite the attempt to maintain his composure, his words became louder. "If you knew that I wasn't—"

Another hand chop.

"Lower your voice, Dr. Hoenikker," Mansfield said. "I am well aware of the promises that were made. They will be kept. Alien artifacts are closer than you think. However, our mandate is threefold." He began ticking them off on his fingers. "One, create technology with which to defend against the Xenomorphs. Two, to create related tech which the military can use to actively combat any opponents, including the Xenos. And three, discover the nature of the pathogen to determine if it can be used in a positive manner—for example, to cure disease in humans. As it now stands, we've scored some notable successes creating acid-resistant armor. We're also optimistic about the prospects of Leon-895."

Hoenikker had heard rumors about strange things happening at LV-895, but no hint of a biological substance that was the focus of their efforts. Before Mansfield could elaborate, however, a thirty-something woman approached. She had brown hair tied into a bun, and a pleasant face. Mansfield gestured in her direction, but she didn't say a word.

"This is Dr. Erin Kash. She will be your team lead, and will bring you up to speed." Mansfield stepped back. "Is this all clear, Dr. Hoenikker?" He spoke in a way that didn't invite an answer.

Hoenikker understood indeed. Bait and switch. He should have known. And this Mansfield was a real piece of work. He pictured Stokes in his mind, and asked himself what his friend would do.

"Move on," Stokes would say. *"Do your best. Be famous."*

Hoenikker nodded once.

Mansfield turned and walked away. When he was out of earshot, Dr. Kash finally spoke.

"Did he ask you why you were late?"

Hoenikker nodded.

She grinned and glanced behind her. "He does that to everyone. It's his way of establishing the upper hand. Ignore it. He's simply a bureaucrat Weyland-Yutani put in place to ensure that we create something they can sell. In this case, armor to protect Colonial Marines against the exigent threat of the new Xenomorphs."

"Xenomorphs?" he said. "Are those the creatures the rumors speak of?"

"You've never seen one?" She clapped her hands. "Doctor, you're in for something special. We don't have any at the moment, but are due for a new shipment. That said, we *do* have some interesting experiments currently under way. Come. Allow me to introduce you to the rest of the team." She led him through a door.

The lab was larger than Hoenikker had anticipated, given what he'd seen of the tight confines of Pala Station. After the reception room came a central area boasting distinctly top-of-the-line lab equipment—though none that he hadn't seen before. Besides digital testing devices, there were the usual old-school beakers, flasks, and test tubes. Old friends.

Two men worked at the central station, injecting something into a tabletop containment device. One had to be pushing three hundred pounds, while the other couldn't be half as much.

"We call this central area Grand Central," Kash explained. "Étienne, Mel, allow me to introduce my new lab partner."

The pair turned and regarded Hoenikker with good-natured expressions. Reaching out with his hand, Hoenikker introduced himself, as did they.

Biologist Étienne Lacroix was the thinner of the two, and spoke with a French accent. About fifty, his skin was olive and he exuded the confidence of three men.

Chemical engineer Melbourne Matthews was the larger man. Even when Étienne was speaking, Hoenikker noted that Mel muttered to himself and had trouble making eye contact. He was younger than his associate, balding, and white.

"What we're doing here, Dr. Hoenikker," Étienne said, "is trying to determine the nature of the pathogen—that's what we call the black goo—and its effects on various Old Earth diseases. Fun stuff like Ebola and smallpox and shingles."

"Please, call me Tim," Hoenikker said. "Or if you must, just Hoenikker."

"I do like Hoenikker," Étienne said, making a fist. "It's quite a robust name. You must be quite proud of it."

Mel muttered something that sounded agreement.

"Aren't you afraid you might create a super bug?" Having spent his entire career doing computer modeling, Hoenikker thought it was an obvious question to be asked. To his astonishment, Étienne clapped.

"We can only hope, *mon ami*."

Hoenikker pointed to the box. "But I mean, what if—"

Étienne shook his head quickly. "That would never happen. One press of this button—" he gestured, "—and the experiment goes *poof*."

There was a cough, and all three men turned.

"Thank you, Étienne," Kash said. "Thanks, Mel."

"*Mon plaisir*, Erin." He turned back. "Welcome to the team, Hoenikker." Then he clapped Matthews on the back, and they returned to their experiment, Étienne peering through a lens while Mel input notes on a display.

Beyond Grand Central, through an open doorway, there was a single corridor with what appeared to be two containment areas on each side. Each was roughly ten-by-ten-by-ten and had a floor-to-ceiling glass front. A portion of each front could be opened, to allow personnel to enter and leave, and some of the rooms had doors between them. A workstation stood at each containment area, with a keyboard and various knobs and buttons.

"We call this Broadway," she said. Then, seeing the look in his eyes, added, "We had a scientist working here early on, a guy named Deneen who had minored in Old Earth History. New York City was a favorite of his. As far as I could tell, these are the names of landmarks there." Continuing on, she gestured. To the left, nearest them, stood a tall, muscular dark-skinned man who wore his hair in an Afro.

"Here we have Dr. Mark Cruz, testing environmental effects on a pathogen-infected rat." Inside what was labeled as Containment Room One was a creature that Hoenikker guessed had once been a rat, probably from the station itself. While he had always found rats to be arguably cute, the goo's effects on this one were unmistakably arachnid, creating a furry beast with gnashing teeth and six two-foot-long spidery legs.

"Dr. Cruz, allow me to introduce Dr. Timothy Hoenikker. Cruz is one of our xenobiologists, and the staffer who's been here the longest." Cruz didn't turn. He seemed to be focused on making entries into the workstation.

"I heard what Étienne said. 'Robust.' Gotta love the French." He shook his head, then his voice went serious. "If you're going to get along around here, Hoenikker, you need to find something you enjoy doing. I'm not talking about playing cards or whacking off, but something that contributes—that's beneficial to society."

Hoenikker didn't know how to reply. Before he could, Cruz continued.

"Fire and ice. Watch this," he said, in a way that Hoenikker could tell the man was grinning. He tapped a couple of the controls, and water cascaded onto the creature, causing it to twitch. Then he turned a knob, and the water quickly iced over. The gnashing teeth slowed until they didn't gnash at all. Frozen.

"Cruz—" Kash said.

"Easy, Kash," he replied, cutting her off. "It's still alive. This is the sixth time I've done it. The pathogen allows the creature to survive temperatures ninety below zero, maybe more, without cellular deterioration. I'll warm it up in a few moments, and we'll re-examine." With that, he focused on his notes again. Kash guided Hoenikker further along, to a man standing in front of Containment Room Four.

"You might have noticed that Cruz enjoys his work a little too much," she whispered, her mouth conspiratorially close to his ear.

"I heard that," Cruz shouted.

"I figured you would," she shouted back. "Still, it's true."

"Remember, Hoenikker," Cruz said. "Get your pleasure where you can."

The new man was the youngest one yet, probably early thirties. He was bald and fit like an athlete, with high cheekbones and bright blue eyes. He turned and grinned when they approached.

"I see you've met the welcome wagon," he said.

"Mansfield?" Hoenikker said. He thought *a real piece of work,* but bit it back because he didn't yet know the politics. The man laughed.

"I meant our resident psychopath, Cruz."

"I'm actually more of a sociopath," Cruz shouted, still without looking up. "It's not psychopathic if the creatures you enjoy torturing want to kill you."

"There's got to be a better word for it," the young man replied loudly. Then he shoved out a hand. "Mark Prior. I'm the other xenobiologist."

Hoenikker stared, and almost didn't respond, but at the last moment shoved his own hand out. He was immediately disappointed in himself when he wet-fished it, rather than returning the strong, confident grip that Prior had presented. When they released, he glanced into the containment room and saw that it was empty.

Prior pointed. "Do you see it? Can you find it?"

"What? Where?" Hoenikker asked.

"Leon-895. It's in there, I promise. See if you can find it."

Hoenikker had been curious since Mansfield's previous cursory mention. Squinting as he examined the ten-by-ten-by-ten-foot room, he saw nothing but the gray interior. Then something shifted, almost imperceptibly. A slightly lighter shade of gray. He blinked and adjusted his position, but in doing so he lost it. Shaking his head, he grinned self-depreciatingly.

"You saw it," Prior said.

"Only for a moment, and I didn't really see it. I saw the outline of something."

"Here. Let me see if this helps. The one problem with Leon-895 is the inability to change color at low temperatures."

He turned the same knob on his workstation as Cruz had used when lowering the temperature in his containment room. The creature's outline began to form, then the rest of it as it returned to its natural color. It was hairless, and the size of a housecat, but that's where all resemblance stopped. It also had six legs and a mouthful of razor-sharp teeth.

"Hoenikker, meet Leon-895. It has the same ability to change color as many of its Earth-origin cousins. This xeno-chameleon has a superficial layer of skin which contains pigments, and under that layer are cells containing guanine crystals. Color change is achieved by altering the space between the guanine crystals, which changes the wavelength of light reflected off the crystals, thus affecting the color of the skin."

"So, this is one of the Xenos," Hoenikker said.

"Yes and no." Prior turned to him. "There's Xenomorph with a capital X, and xeno with a lowercase x. Big-X Xenos are the gnarly beasts that bleed acid. We don't have any of them right now, but we expect a delivery soon. Small-x xenos are any creature not of Earth origin. Leon-895 is a small-x xeno." Recognizing the questions on Hoenikker's face, he added, "You'll see the difference when we get our first face-huggers down here."

"Prior is doing important work," Kash said. "He wants to see whether the ability to change color increases or decreases with the application of the pathogen. If we could harness the color-changing effect and marry it with the acid resistant armor we've already produced, we might have soldiers who are invisible to the human eyes."

"Where did you get the pathogen?" Hoenikker asked.

"No one knows for sure." Prior grinned tightly. "It came down from corporate."

"Rumor has it that it came from a ghost ship," Cruz shouted. "Found floating in space and of unknown origin."

"Or it could have come down from corporate," Prior said, rolling his eyes.

"Or both," Cruz persisted.

Placing a hand on Hoenikker's arm, Kash showed him down a side corridor, then another bordered with multiple containment rooms. Other creatures of unknown origin resided in different rooms, scratching at the impenetrable glass, trying to get out. Seeing the monstrosities, he began to realize that he was as trapped as the creatures. He was in a closed environment where there were a lot of things that could kill them. Things that came from outside Pala Station.

He wondered how far he'd have to go in order to finally get hold of the alien artifacts he had been promised.

He wondered if he'd live to see them.

3

Night. Everyone who should have been was in bed, except Cruz. He couldn't sleep. He'd been having more and more flashbacks recently, and rather than lie there staring at the ceiling, he decided to work a little.

No one could ever accuse him of not working. He'd grown up in a ghetto of storage containers on a Weyland-Yutani distribution planet that doubled as an intergalactic trash dump. Most of the residents of LV-223 were destined to search the dump for rare metals or, if they were lucky enough, get a job hauling product into awaiting containers bound for out-system LVs.

Cruz wanted none of that. At the time he'd been proud. Too proud. He'd laughed at his father and mother as they struggled to feed him. He'd told them they were lazy and should have found a way to get off planet, so he'd have a better future. When he became old enough, he managed to stow away, only to be discovered and jailed at his destination. He'd been given a choice then to either remain in prison or join the Colonial Marines.

Not really a choice.

At marine training he'd discovered what it was like to finally work hard, sweating and bleeding in equal amounts. He'd relished turning his body into a killing machine and learning how to use a weapon—a pulse rifle. He'd enjoyed his first and second deployments, each one bringing down an insurrection from a planet just like his own, and people just like his own. He'd seen from the other side the squalor in which they were forced to live, realizing for the first time that they *couldn't* leave. They had no means of changing their destinies.

They'd been given their lot and had to make the best they could.

He tried to reach out and speak with his family, to apologize to his father and mother, but all efforts at contact failed.

Then, on his third deployment, he encountered xenos.

He shook the memory away and donned his lab coat. As he entered the lab, the lights came on automatically, attuned to movement. He went immediately to Containment Room One. Cruz wanted to increase the amount of black goo he'd been injecting into his current specimen—what he'd come to call Rat-X. It scowled at him, the front two of its six legs held in the air. He needed to immobilize it, so he turned the temp all the way down.

The others thought he was crazy. Probably even the new guy, Hoenikker. Perhaps Cruz *was* a little crazy. Anyone who'd seen combat was changed by it, something his fellow doctors had no way of understanding. They'd grown up entitled.

Through a hardscrabble life and being the agent of his own actions, Cruz managed to parlay military service into a collegiate opportunity and finished with a graduate degree in xenobiology.

Crazy? No, what he was doing with Rat-X was as

important as anyone else's experimentation, including Prior's specimen-of-the-moment Leon-895. Pala team still had a lot of questions, including how to freeze Xenos so their blood was no longer acidic. Would the nature of the acid change with thawing? Could they create a freeze weapon that would make Xenos easier to kill with conventional weapons, while preventing the blood from dripping through a ship's hull? They were fresh out of big-X Xenos, but they had the rats and they had the goo and they had the time.

Once Rat-X was frozen, he turned off the temperature controls. Before it thawed and awoke, he'd have more than enough time to do what he had planned. Grabbing a biopsy needle from a nearby drawer, and a clamp, he toggled open the containment room door. There was a click, then he stepped inside. A residue of cold made him shiver for a moment. He attached the clamp to a spot along the back wall, then lifted the frozen creature and put it into the clamp, which actuated. Four padded arms enveloped the creature, holding it fast.

Cruz held onto one of the long chitinous legs and shoved the biopsy needle into the abdomen. What he sought was more of a core sample than a blood sample. If he'd wanted the latter, he would have put the Rat-X to sleep using gas. But this was easier and, frankly, made him feel better.

Suddenly, he's back in the wretched darkness—a darkness to which he's returned, over and over. A darkness that won't leave him. One that lives inside of him and somehow forever avoids the light.

Pulse rifles light up the night, turning the events into an old-time movie. Reality flickering from light to dark to light again over and over as the pulses from the rifles strive to save them. They'd been assigned settlement protection on LV-832. Carnivorous moose-sized creatures with tentacles charge their position. Their hooves the sound of thunder. Their howls like musical horns. Pulses from the rifles illuminate the creatures in nightmarish flashes. The forward observer dies first.

Back in the lab, he snaps off a chitinous leg.

The lieutenant tries to be a hero. No one wants a fucking hero. They fire and fire until their rifles choke. Still the creatures come. Trampling.

Snap!

Snyder hurls into the air, propelled by the tentacles wrapped around his torso.

Snap!

Schnexnader screams as his right arm is bitten off. Blood spurts on all of them as he spins madly.

Snap!

Correia is grabbed and slammed repeatedly against a tree until blood and organs explode from his body.

Cruz screams, then cries.

Back in the lab, he realized he was holding a leg in each hand, ripped from the creature's body. He was making a low sound like a continuous groan, felt incredibly drowsy, and wanted to lie down.

The rat began to move, then cried out in pain, the sound of a cat caught in a vice. Rat-X writhed and squirmed. Twisting, it freed itself from the clamp and, with its remaining three legs, latched itself onto the front of Cruz's lab coat.

Cruz madly knocked it off.

It careened to the floor, righted itself, then scrabbled toward him.

Cruz backed away, but the Rat-X grabbed his pants leg. In a spastic one-legged dance as he tried to shake the creature free, Crux made it back toward the containment room door. Rat-X lost its grip and flew against a wall. Then Cruz spied the biopsy needle. He'd dropped it during his blackout. Realizing he still held two of the creature's legs in each hand, he threw first one, then the other at the creature, which backed away.

Diving for the needle, Cruz managed to grab it, but Rat-X surged between his legs toward the open door. From his knees Cruz reached out and grabbed the monstrosity from behind. The creature gnashed its teeth at him, but Cruz managed to narrowly avoid being bitten. He jerked the creature over his head, slamming it into the back wall. The motions threw Cruz to his knees, and he crawled frantically through the door. Twisting onto his back, he kicked the door closed just as Rat-X faceplanted on the glass.

The creature stared daggers at him as it slid to the floor.

Cruz climbed wearily to his feet, and placed the biopsy needle in a drawer. He'd take care of it later. Pulling aside a button cover, he revealed a big red ABORT button. He pressed it, and the containment room filled with flames from top to bottom. Rat-X squealed for a second, then folded in on itself as it first turned to cinders, then ash. When the flames died, Cruz searched the room for any other debris that might represent the legs.

He thought he'd got them all.

Wearily, he headed back toward his sleeping quarters. The night had almost been a disaster.

4

An hour before first shift, everyone else was asleep—but not Logistics Specialist Fairbanks.

Ever since he'd returned to Pala he'd been a nervous wreck. His blood pressure had to have been through the roof. His head ached from the constant pounding, and he couldn't get his hands to stop shaking. He'd thought that maybe he would have been searched when he returned from emergency leave, but Security hadn't so much as glanced at him. That had been an immense relief, but still he couldn't help but wonder if he wasn't being watched.

Although he knew from his work as a logistics tech that there were only a few instances of internal surveillance, his paranoia made him wonder if perhaps Security had planted some devices without him knowing. Just the thought of it made him want to hyperventilate, so before he was able to do what he'd planned on doing, he had to sit and try to control his breathing.

Finally, he was able to stand, his legs still a little shaky. He believed he'd feel better once the deed was done, yet couldn't help but feel as if he was doing something terribly wrong. Just the thought of it made him sit again. He wasn't really an infiltrator, was he? He wasn't a bad guy. He was a victim—a victim of corporate greed. He was a bullet fired from one corporation to the other.

In this case, Hyperdyne firing at Weyland-Yutani.

What they wanted him to do wasn't so bad, he supposed. After all, it wasn't like he was going to hurt anyone. It wasn't as if someone might die because of what he was being made to do.

Yes. He was the victim. He'd been given a part to play in the Corporate Wars and he'd play it then move on with his life. It wasn't as if he had a choice, either. He'd threatened to go to Security, to tell them what had happened while he was away. His blackmailer's response was to remind him how long an arm Hyperdyne had, and how they knew where his family resided—especially his mother. Had it been a threat? Most definitely. So, they had him. There was nothing he was capable of doing except follow through.

Fairbanks stood, reassured about what he was going to do. He nodded to himself, straightened his spine, and strode toward his dresser. Opening the top drawer, he reached toward the back. Beneath his underwear and socks was a thick package. He pulled it free, peeked inside, then closed it.

Still alive.

Good.

Grabbing a pack off the side of his desk, he shoved the thing inside. He slung it over his shoulder, opened his door, and glanced up and down the corridor. Clear. Stepping outside, he closed his door and headed quickly to his left. Three turns later he was in the right corridor. He hurried to the end and stopped alongside an access panel about three feet tall. Checking left, then right, he pulled out a tool and opened the panel, letting it come to rest on its lower hinges.

Inside were several wires and an opening in the ductwork. He slouched out of the pack and rested it on the open panel, pulling free the package and opening it. Inside were three dozen specially designed baby rats provided courtesy of Hyperdyne Corp. He shepherded them into the ductwork, watching as they scampered madly away, probably elated to be free of the dark confines of the package.

Once the last had gone, he put the empty package back in his pack and pulled out a vid display unit. He attached it to some wires, then hammered out a message—code he'd memorized that Hyperdyne would pick up. They'd ensured him that they'd already hacked station comms.

His task complete, he wedged the vid display behind a cluster of wires, used the tool to close the access panel, and placed the tool back in his pack. He was about to leave when a security specialist turned the corner. She stopped and stared in his direction.

"Identify yourself." She had a hard face and short-cropped blonde hair. Her muscles were twice the size of his. Even if he thought he might try and escape, there was no way he'd be able to get away from her. "I asked your name."

He stood at attention, his back against the wall.

"Logistics Specialist Fairbanks."

"What are you doing here?" she asked, eyeing the access panel, then his pack.

Enabling Hyperdyne Corporation to spy on you. He blinked. His mouth was a desert. His head pounded and he wanted to pee. "I thought I heard something in there." He glanced toward the access panel. "Maybe rats?"

She shook her head. "We have rats everywhere. I mean, what are you doing in this corridor? You have no reason to be here. This leads to the underground."

"I—I was trying to get some exercise, prior to shift. I wasn't paying attention to where I was."

"And the pack?" she asked, pointing to it.

"Uh, have some trash in there. Going to dispose of it after exercise."

She held out a hand. "Let me see."

Just his luck to get the most thorough damned security specialist in all of Pala Station. He shrugged out of the pack. She opened it and pulled out the package, checked inside and saw it was empty. Shoving it back in the pack, she pulled out the tool.

"And this?"

"I'm a log specialist." He shrugged and tried to laugh, but it came out as more of a bark. "I use it every day."

She tapped it against her hand a few times then, frowning, placed it back in the bag. She handed it back to him. He accepted it with two hands and held it.

"You were the one went on emergency leave, right?"

"Uh, yeah." He felt his eyebrows raise. "I had to get to a place with better comms."

"So you could call home?"

He nodded.

Her face softened. "That's the main problem with being out so far. That, and the knowing that you'll probably never see your family again." She stared down the corridor and millions of miles farther. Then she turned back to him. "How was it you were allowed to go? What was it, seven weeks' travel?"

He thought of Rawlings, and how the reception tech had hooked him up. Just a few fake signatures and a compelling narrative.

"Lucky, I guess."

She frowned, "I don't believe in luck." She stepped close

and poked him in the chest. "Now, get out of my section and go exercise somewhere else."

Just then the sound of something rustling came from inside the access panel.

She shook her head. "Fucking rats everywhere."

He nodded, then backed down the corridor. When he reached the intersection, he hurried down the new direction, eventually finding his way back to his room. Stepping inside, he closed the door and fell against it, breathing heavily. He hurled his bag onto his bed, then bent over double. He'd never make a good criminal.

Hell, he barely made a decent infiltrator.

5

Reception Tech Rawlings entered his office, sporting a grin and a cup of coffee. He took a sip as he sat behind his monitor.

Any day at the ass end of the universe is better than being in the suck. That was his motto for pretty much every occasion. Glancing at his prosthesis, he chuckled. Some do it for the medals. Some do it for the money. *"Come. Join the Colonial Marines. See the universe."* Shoot things and break things and we'll pay you for it. While his left hand ached with arthritis, his prosthetic right one felt nothing at all. The bright side of a dark day.

He took another sip, then dialed up the dailies.

Staff sections had reported a hundred percent. As it should be. If someone went missing, it meant something bad had happened. Pala Station was a closed station. No one was allowed to go anywhere without the station commander's approval—except of course the deputy commander, who seemed to spend more time off station, hunting and exploring, than he did on duty. Even built a lodge out there. Not many people knew about it.

Nicoli was already at her desk. She was in charge of personnel management and would soon be forwarding the daily accountability to the commander. She also had some disciplinary notes to attach to several personnel folders. It seemed as if the good folks over in Engineering had made their own hooch. Such a thing normally wouldn't have been a problem, but when one of them coded the station lights to flash on and off to the beat of an old rock song, they went a bit too far.

Brown was also at her desk. Her function was readiness management. It was getting to the end of a cycle, and she had to ensure that team leads entered their employee progress reports into the Weyland-Yutani database. Corporate was always about the lure of promotion. Do well, rat on your peers, use their backs for your own stepping-stone, and we will promote you.

Rawlings, meanwhile, had to prepare for the incoming specimens about to be delivered to the scientists and their personnel. The *San Lorenzo* had towed *Katanga* refinery into orbit, and soon they'd have some visitors. It was Rawlings' job to ensure that all inbound had the correct security clearances and personnel files. This caused him to have interaction with Security, which he didn't mind at all. Several of them were former Colonial Marines, trading in their knowledge of infantry operations for security operations.

Rawlings spent an hour at the terminal preparing digital paperwork, then once he was finished, he stood.

"You leaving us again?" Brown asked.

"Going to Security, and then to Fabrications."

"You do know you can just call them, right?" Nicoli asked.

Rawlings grinned merrily. "I prefer the personal touch. No offense to you two ladies, but I do like to see other faces in the flesh, now and again."

Brown shook her head, returning to her screen.

Nicoli shook hers as well. "I just don't understand you, Rawlings."

He smiled wider. "Nothing to understand. What you see is what you get." He saluted her with his empty coffee cup and exited the office.

Cynthia Rodriguez was security chief, and a Wey-Yu corporate troubleshooter. Her deputy for internal security was Randy Flowers, a relatively new addition to the station, still finding his footing. Rawlings had known Randy in the service. Captain Flowers had been a solid no-nonsense marine. They'd deployed together on the mission where he'd lost his hand.

It was less than a five-minute walk to the Security offices. When Rawlings arrived, he found Flowers and coordinated the transfer of personnel, ensuring that there would be follow-on files for him to peruse and store. He grabbed some of their coffee and headed out the door. Right before he left, Sec Specialist Reyes approached him.

"What does a girl gotta do to get off station?" she asked.

He'd always liked her. Although never a Colonial Marine, she had the square jaw of a tough person. He could imagine her in uniform, firing a pulse rifle at some incoming enemy.

"Only the station commander can authorize off-station travel," he said.

"Word has it he'll sign whatever you give him."

"Is that so?" He sipped at his coffee, wondering where she was going with this.

"I bumped into Fairbanks this morning," she said cryptically.

Rawlings nodded slowly. "He had a family emergency."

"Is that so?" She grinned.

He grinned back and sipped his coffee. "Company policy

is that if you have a compelling need, you can have up to ten weeks LWOP—leave without pay. It's just finding the compelling need."

She stared at him thoughtfully.

"Is that all, Security Specialist Reyes," he said, "or are you going to frisk me."

"Yes. I mean no. I mean, yes, that is all."

Rawlings saluted her with his coffee. "Compelling need."

"Compelling need," she repeated, gaze turned inward as if she was trying to figure out exactly what need was compelling.

Next stop was Fabrications. When he entered, they were playing a board game. Something having to do with logistical supply lines to spaceships. Fabrications was the smallest staff section. Tom Ching and Brian Mantle were the specialists, while Robb King was in charge. When he entered, all of them groaned.

"You do know that you eventually have to work, right?" he said.

"We've spent three days on rat duty," King said. "That's work enough."

"How would you like to do *real* work, like actually fabricating something?"

"Don't tell me," Ching said. "The brainiacs need more glass for their containment rooms."

Rawlings saluted the smaller of the three. "Got it in one try."

"How come they need so much of the special glass?" Mantle asked. "It's not easy to blend it with tungsten, and still make it transparent. Why not just use tungsten walls and have a video camera on the inside?"

"Ever seen those things they work on—the ones sent ahead from *Katanga*?"

All three of them shook their heads.

Rawlings offered them a grim smile. "It would rip that camera down in a second. Plus, I'm told it bleeds acid."

All three of the men mouthed the words, *it bleeds acid*.

"Knowing the why is nice, but you fabricate because it's your job." Rawlings nodded. "If I were you, I'd get ahead of the game and see if you can prepare some glass. Plus, if you have work orders, you can't really be rat hunting, now, can you?"

All three of their faces lit up.

"That's true," King said. "That's very true."

Rawlings saluted them with his coffee cup, then went in search of Comms. Three minutes later he was saying hello to Comms Chief Vivian Oshita. Inside the section HQ were three workstations, each occupied by a comms tech. Buggy, Brennan, and Davis. It was Buggy he was there to see.

"Bugs. Share a cup of coffee with me?" Rawlings asked.

"What is it you want?" the tech asked suspiciously. He was about fifty, bald, with pockmarks on his cheeks. Rawlings knew he had a prosthetic right leg, lost during his tour in the marines.

"I'm trying to get a bunch of us together to form a group of… common concern," he said.

"A group of common what?"

"A group of common concern," he repeated. "A club, sort of. One that's filled with former Colonial Marines."

Bugs shook his head. "I don't want to be in any club. I've put the marines behind me."

Rawlings laughed and nodded as he poured Bugs a cup of coffee. He passed it to him. "It's not that kind of club. We don't have parties or dues or wear funny uniforms. We did all that before in the marines, right? No, this is just about us getting together to… to be there for each other." He glanced at Bugs, who was taking a sip of his coffee. "I don't know about you, but sometimes I need to talk about shit, but none of these civilians would understand." He waited for that to sink in. "Plus, in the event that things go bad, we need to stick together."

"What do you mean, *in the event things go bad*?"

"You're in Comms. You know what kind of fucked-up creatures they have on *Katanga*. They're bringing more of them down soon. Have you ever thought what would happen if they got out?"

Bugs gave him a swift glance.

"Wouldn't be something I'd care to happen," Rawlings said without waiting for an answer. "Want your life to depend on station security? Or do you want to depend on guys who went through the same things you did?"

Bugs eyed him as he sipped coffee. "You're making more sense than I thought you would. How many of us are there here?"

"Less than ten. Not a lot of us, but I've managed to get with Logistics and stash away an emergency supply of weapons, just in case."

"Aren't those tracked?"

"Sure they are," Rawlings said, grinning.

"Oh, I see."

"You know that any Colonial Marine worth his or her salt would have a Plan B."

"And *we're* the Plan B," Bugs said. He stared into his coffee for a long minute. "You know, I really thought I wanted to put all my military time behind me. I lost more than people know. But can we really do that? Isn't it who we are?"

Rawlings held up his prosthesis. "I know what you're saying. Every time I do anything with my hands, I'm reminded of what I lost—but then I remember what I've gained. I remember the comradery we had. I remember the highs I had while serving and fighting with my mates."

Bugs absently rubbed his prosthetic leg. "Yeah. It's easy to forget the good times. Sometimes the bad times just outweigh everything. So, what is it you propose? Do we have meetings? Do we have a secret sign?"

Rawlings laughed. "Maybe get together every now and again. We'll play it by ear. I just wanted to see if you were up for it." A moment later he added, "My gut tells me we need to stick together."

"Well, if I can't trust the gut of a Colonial Marine, I don't know what I can trust."

"That's what I was hoping you'd say." Rawlings nodded. He began to back away, saluting Bugs with his coffee cup. "Until next time." Then he turned and was out the door.

6

Hoenikker spent the morning helping the other scientists clean the lab and check the integrity of the containment rooms. Several of them needed replacement windows. Fabrications said it would be a day or so before they could make them. Mansfield, to his credit, ordered enough to replace all of the glass, based on the upcoming delivery of capital-X Xenos.

After a thirty-minute lunch of questionable substances in the mess hall, Hoenikker returned to the laboratory and began to shadow Kash. He'd found her a dedicated professional. One who should be emulated. He'd enjoyed his association so far, and looked forward to more interaction.

As a primer for what they'd be doing later on, she'd arranged the lab table so she could show him firsthand how the pathogen interacted with living matter. While they worked, he eyed Cruz down the corridor, sitting in front of Containment Room Two.

"What's his story?" he asked in a low voice.

"Cruz?" she said. "He's efficient." She withdrew a sample

of black goo from a secure container. "A little sadistic, but then, he was a Colonial Marine."

"How did he go from being a Colonial Marine to being a scientist?"

"Education. Not everyone wants to spend their life in the military."

"I know, I was just..." He glanced at her. "I don't know what I wanted to know. He just seems like a different sort of person to be in a laboratory."

"He's definitely not what you'd expect, but he has an amazing mind. He was the one who made the breakthrough that enabled us to develop the acid-resistant armor. That alone would enable him to run any Weyland-Yutani lab in the known systems."

"Yet he stays here."

"You know how it is. In the central systems, everything is safe. It's all modeling and algorithms—but out here you get to work on live specimens, in an environment that pushes the boundaries. Rules aren't necessarily rules. They're more guidelines, which promotes more out-of-the-box spectacular thinking."

"Hence the breakthrough."

"Hence the breakthrough. Even Mansfield leaves him alone."

"Mansfield," Hoenikker said, the word more of a sigh.

"Typical Weyland-Yutani bureaucrat. He's a constant reminder that we work for a corporation, and not for ourselves."

"How bothersome is he?"

"Not as much as you'd think. As long as we're producing and following security protocols, he leaves us alone." She glanced at him, smiling. "After all, he really has no idea what we're doing."

"Seems like an interesting mix of scientists," he said.

"All are at the top of their game. Étienne is more than what he seems. He's all suave, but he's extremely serious. As is Muttering Mel."

"There's one of him in every lab," Hoenikker said.

"Yes, but what he lacks in social ability, he more than makes up for in concentration. He's best doing repetitive experiments, or creating algorithms to prove or disprove a supposition. He can do those on the fly. Eerie the way he's able to just lean in and do the math."

"Prior seems to be a good guy."

She glanced down the corridor to where Prior was working. "He is, but he has a back story no one really knows. All I could gather is that when I came on board, Mansfield felt he had to inform me that Prior had once been in prison, and asked if I'd be comfortable working with him."

"Prison?" Hoenikker stared at the man, who seemed to be so nice and polite. "What was he in for?"

"Murder, if you'll believe it."

"Murder?" Hoenikker whispered. "Who did he murder?"

"His wife, but there were extenuating circumstances, I'm told. He was released after an appeal."

"Extenuating circumstances?" he whispered. "If he murdered her, then what could those have been?"

"Your guess is as good as mine," she said. "I'm curious as well, but it's not something that comes up in casual conversation."

Hoenikker couldn't help but stare at the man. Prior looked up. He grinned and waved, then went back to what he was doing.

As quickly as he could, Hoenikker looked away. The man knew they were talking about him. Hoenikker felt like an idiot. Still, a murderer? If anyone had asked him who was the murderer in the lab team, he'd first deny that any of them were capable of it. Then, if pressed, he'd have nominated

Cruz. That seemed so obvious, but it was clear that what seemed obvious was anything but.

"They lured you here for alien artifacts."

Hoenikker snapped out of his internal dialogue and nodded vigorously. "They promised me I'd be able to investigate them firsthand. Indicated that they had an extensive collection." He looked around. "But I don't see anything like that, unless it's covered by the jungle canopy."

"I wouldn't be surprised," she replied. "There's definitely more going on here than I know. Did they tell you about the synths?"

"I heard mention."

"Let me just say that they're spooky. When you see them you'll know what I mean."

"Where are they?"

"That's the thing. I don't know where they keep them. It's as if they have another wing that we don't know about."

"I haven't walked the whole station, but it doesn't seem to be that big."

"It isn't. Which begs the question, where are the synths?" she asked, her blue eyes wide. He considered that, and vowed to himself to walk the corridors and get a better lay of the land. After all, he might need it some day.

"How long have you been at Pala Station?" he asked.

"Six months. Previously I worked at a hospital. I also have a medical degree."

"Medical? As in eye, ear, nose, and throat?"

"More trauma surgeon. We were near a mining rig, and there were a lot of crushing injuries." She sighed and looked away. "You couldn't imagine the number of amputations I've had to make. I needed a break—needed some pure science. Weyland-Yutani was looking for an epidemiologist, and I was looking for a change of scenery." She spread her arms. "So here I am.

"What's your story?" she continued.

He sighed. "I'm probably one of the most boring people you'll ever meet. Never been married, no brothers and sisters. I was an orphan who had good enough marks to get a full ride at university."

"You were really an orphan?"

"Yes." An image of fire tried to roar to life, but he stomped it down. "Which is why I suck at relationships." He glanced at her. She raised an eyebrow.

"I didn't mean it that way," he said quickly. "What I meant was that I never really had someone to love, and I was never really loved, so I don't think I understand the concept." He blushed, feeling his face turn hot and red.

"Timothy Hoenikker, are you blushing?" she asked, a smile forming on her face.

He was furious at his traitorous body. Why was he even talking about love? He was worse than "Muttering Mel."

"I don't know what's going on," he replied. "I don't know why I told you that. It's not as if you asked."

"I did ask," she said. "I asked what your story was, and you told me part of it. We all have these things that make us who we are. I was married once. My husband found that he had a better time with nurses than he did with a fellow doctor, so I let him have it his way."

"You were married to a doctor?"

"I thought we'd have something in common. As it turned out, we had too much in common."

A cry went up to their right, and he peered down the corridor. Cruz was backing hurriedly away from the containment room window.

"Protect yourselves," he shouted. "It's going to go!"

7

Rather than running away from the problem, Hoenikker ran toward it, and he didn't know why. He found himself beside Cruz, both of them breathing heavily.

He was just in time to see the glass melt as the Rat-X inside continuously pelted it with acidic spittle. A hole formed. Hoenikker backed away as the creature's chitinous forelegs grasped the opening and it pulled itself through.

The creature landed on the floor. About two feet tall and three feet wide because of the legs, it was a formidable little beast. Not big enough to intimidate, but not small enough to ignore. If one didn't know it could spit acid, they might take it for granted and approach it.

Kash went to hit the alarm button.

"Don't do that," Cruz shouted. "We can take care of it here."

She paused.

The creature saw her, and began to scuttle toward her, propelling itself with its chitinous rear legs while holding up its forelegs in a menacing fashion.

"We combined DNA from a local spider to see what the interaction would be," Cruz said. "Hence the legs, but the acid was an unpredicted result brought on by the pathogen."

Kash circled around the other side of the central table, putting it between her and the creature.

"Are you going to do anything, Cruz?" she asked, eyes wide, looking ready to bolt.

"Just don't let it get near you," he responded. "I have an idea." He dove for a closet and began to pull something out.

Rather than follow her around the table, the creature jumped onto it. It spit a wad of acid at her, but she was able to dodge. The wall behind where she had been standing began to melt in the spot where it hit.

"Cruz! You need to do something now!" she said, edging her way toward where they were standing. Cruz exited the closet wearing something with a tank, a hose, and a long metal nozzle.

"Flamethrower," he said. "I put it here in the event a xeno escaped." He passed Kash. "Get behind me," he said, ushering her back with his arm. He held out the nozzle and was about to fire when the door to the lab opened.

Mansfield stood in the doorway staring at the Rat-X.

"What the hell is going on?"

Before he was able to move, the creature leaped off the table, spit acid at his leg, and scurried out the door. Mansfield screamed as the acid ate away at his clothes and skin. Kash ran toward him, grabbing a med kit from the wall as she did.

Cruz ran out the door and disappeared to the right.

Against his better judgment, Hoenikker followed him. Out in the corridor, he was ten feet behind Cruz as they chased the creature. It hissed and raised its front legs whenever it saw a threat, but seemed more intent on fleeing than harming. His eyes went wide as it jumped onto the wall, and then onto the ceiling, running with as much an ease as it had on the floor.

They began to encounter other people in the corridor. Each time Cruz seemed about to fire, Rat-X would jump down or around something or someone.

They approached a corner, and a clique of people appeared, chatting together. The creature seemed to have decided it had done enough running, and leaped onto the face of a young man in the middle of the group.

The rest screamed and fled, leaving their comrade on the ground, kicking with his legs, trying to pull the thing from his face. It punctured the man's face and neck with the spikey ends of its legs, over and over.

He tried to scream, but the creature spit acid into his mouth.

His legs and arms danced along the ground.

Cruz fired the flamethrower and a jet of fire encompassed both the man and his assailant. The burning creature tried to flee, scrambling up the side of a wall, but Cruz was on it. He fired again, this time hitting it squarely.

It fell to the ground, its legs curling on themselves.

Hoenikker looked on in appalling fascination as the man still rattled the floor with his arms and legs, even as he was on fire, his face melting onto the hard-composite surface beneath him. The image fanned the flames of his own memories, and he found himself backing away.

Cruz turned and opened a gout of flame onto the man's face, and kept firing until his legs and arms stilled.

Hoenikker fell to the ground. He pushed himself back until he was against the wall. Then he turned, hiding his face, but feeling the heat of the burning figure. When it was all over, Cruz slumped against the opposite wall.

"Jesus H. Christ," was all he said.

Security ran up, shadowed by a med tech. One look at the man, however, and they knew there was nothing that could be done. Someone doused him with flame retardant until the fire was out.

The stench of burning hair and human flesh was one of the most horrible scents Hoenikker had ever encountered.

"Is that the only one?" a security officer asked.

Cruz nodded. "Just this one."

Hoenikker shook, peeking through his hands as if he were five, and barely alive. Cruz reached down and grasped him gently by the elbow.

"You okay, Hoenikker?" he asked. "Did you get hurt?"

Hoenikker realized he'd been crying, and wiped his face with his free hand. He allowed the bigger man to pull him to his feet and gently guide him back to the lab. The taller man was shaking, almost imperceptibly—he could feel it through the grip.

When they got back into the lab, Cruz shrugged out of the flamethrower and set it heavily on the chair. He held out his hands and saw they were shaking. He crossed his arms and put his hands under his armpits, and rocked back and forth.

Prior came up and put a hand on his back.

"Wasn't your fault, brother. Was the glass. It's just not made for what we have in there."

Cruz nodded. "I know. It's just—it's just it took me back to where I didn't want to be." Hoenikker looked on but didn't know what to say. It had taken him to such a place as well.

Kash brought Cruz a glass of water, which he drank in one long shaking gulp.

"The PTSD has been bad lately," Cruz began. "I know I can be rough around the edges." He stared solidly at the middle of the table. "But until you've lost all your friends in a battle, you'll never know what it's like." With still-shaking hands, he pulled up the sleeve on his right arm, revealing names tattooed there. "Snyder, Bedejo, Schnexnader, Correia, Cartwright.

They all died. We were trying to protect a settlement, and these giant four-legged xenos with tentacles and way too many teeth attacked. We fired and fired until our pulse rifles locked up from the heat. They killed all my friends."

"How did you survive?" Hoenikker found himself asking. Cruz jerked his attention toward him. He stared hard at Hoenikker. When he spoke, each word dripped with disgust.

"I fucking ran. I saw that all my friends were dying, and I fucking ran. I've always been the fastest, and I used that to save myself."

"Your rifle wasn't working anymore," Kash said. "What could you do?"

"I could have *not* run," he said, staring off into the distance. "I could have stayed with my friends."

"You would have stayed and died," Prior said.

"So what? At least I could live with myself."

"Uh, you mean you'd be dead," Hoenikker said.

Cruz stared at him again. "You say that as if it's a bad thing."

Étienne and Mel rushed in.

"Is everything okay?" Étienne asked. "We heard one got away."

"As good as it could be," Kash responded. "One of the glass fronts failed."

"Damned Fabricators," Étienne said, punching his hand.

Mel went over to examine the hole. As he did, Mansfield returned, fuming. His leg had been wrapped in a bandage.

"What the *hell* did you do?" he roared. "You almost had me killed!"

Cruz took one look at the man, and lunged. Prior and Étienne grabbed him to keep him from pounding Mansfield.

"He saved lives," Kash said. "Without his quick thinking, the creature would have killed more."

"He let the thing escape!" Mansfield said, still red in the face.

"He did no such thing," Prior said. "It's the glass. It's worn out. The Rat-X burned a hole in it, and escaped on its own."

"As if it knew how," Mansfield spat.

Cruz shrugged out of the grip that held him.

"I'm fine. I'm fine." He brushed at where they'd held him. To Mansfield he said, "Make sure that before you accuse someone of something, you know what the hell you're talking about." Then he turned and left.

8

Two hours later, everyone was commanded to be present in the lab.

Security Chief Flowers and Deputy Station Commander Thompson called them to attention. To Hoenikker, Flowers was the image of an old-school retired Colonial Marine general with a face as lined as a topographical map. He wore his hair in a high and tight, and stood ramrod-straight. Although he'd never heard him speak before, he could imagine it as the sound of gravel being chewed in an echo chamber.

Thompson, on the other hand, was the direct opposite. As Hoenikker had heard it, the man had never served in the military. He slouched as he stood, staring at his manicured nails. All of his clothes were tailored and had an expensive sheen to them. He seemed bored, as if he wanted to be somewhere else.

"I understand that yours is the core mission for Pala Station," Flowers said to the group in a voice like Hoenikker had imagined, "but you've put everyone at risk, and the very idea is unacceptable. As it stands, Weyland-Yutani now has to explain to a family why their loved one was bitten by a creature, and then set on fire. You have security protocols in place. You knew you were to sound the alarm. You've practiced regularly, for just these circumstances. So why didn't you follow the protocols?" When there was no answer, he continued, "Clearly there has been a breakdown at all levels."

"If I may interject—" Mansfield started.

"You may not. I place the blame at your feet, Mr. Mansfield. That death is on you. Had you practiced shutting down the lab and locking it down enough times so that it was muscle memory for your scientists, this never would have happened. Did you expect your team to get it right the first time?"

Mansfield shook his head and stared at the floor.

"I'd fire you on the spot, but there's no one to replace you." Flowers turned to Thompson. "Sir, is there anything you want to add."

Thompson nodded. When he spoke, his voice was rich and polished and bored.

"If you're seeing me, then something terrible happened. You should *never* see me. You shouldn't even know what I look like. I certainly don't want to know what you look like. Frankly, I'm too busy to deal with your messes. There are larger problems that demand my attention. We need food for the infes— the creatures on *Katanga*." He paused. "Someone has to lead the hunt for local fauna. Incidents like this take away from the time I need to accomplish what needs to be done." He gave them a disgusted look, then started to leave.

"So inspiring," Cruz said under his breath.

"Wait a moment, Deputy Commander."

Kash stepped forward.

The man stopped and turned, glaring.

"We need better support from the station," she said. "This isn't a fault of the lab. If we had better containment room maintenance, this never would have happened."

Thompson stared. "You're saying it's the station's fault?"

"We sure as hell didn't build these." She pointed at the containment rooms. "They are the tools we use. We take as good care of them as we can, but it's up to Engineering and Fabrications to make sure they're new and functioning."

"So it was a failure of equipment, rather than the personnel." He looked dubious. "Is that what you're saying?"

"That's *exactly* what I'm saying," Kash said.

Thompson flicked his gaze over to Mansfield. "Get a status report on my desk ASAP." Then he left.

Kash breathed a deep sigh.

Hoenikker hadn't been on the station long, but he could tell she'd broken protocol. Yet of all the scientists, she probably had the best chance of not getting her head ripped off, perhaps because of her gender. It seemed like a patriarchal system, as backward as that was.

"She's right, of course," Mansfield said to Flowers. "We could have a hundred protocols in place, but if the equipment fails, then there's nothing we can do about it."

"If you had followed your protocols," Flowers growled, "the creature never would have escaped into the corridors."

"And we would have died," Cruz insisted. "I feel for the family of the deceased, but would you rather lose one or two station personnel, or all of your scientific staff?"

Hoenikker held his breath.

Flowers gave Cruz a hard stare. "That's a pretty cocky statement, Dr. Cruz."

"Remember, we are the reason you are here," Étienne said. "You are here to support us. If we are dead, you have no mission."

"You say that as if it's a bad thing," Flowers snapped, echoing Cruz's earlier comment. To Mansfield he said, "Your team is quite talkative."

"When you have the smartest people in the station, and they have something to say, you tend to let them say it," Mansfield replied. "It's also best to listen."

The bureaucrat's stock rose in Hoenikker's mind.

Flowers nodded. "Get that status report ASAP, Mansfield." Then he was out, the door sliding closed behind him. Everyone let out a sigh of relief.

"Why is it they have to be such assholes?" Cruz asked.

"Not so fast," Mansfield said. "Flowers was right about one thing. What about the security protocols? Why weren't they followed?"

"I wasn't able to press the abort button," Cruz began. "It just happened so fast."

"I was trying to get to the lockdown button by the door," Kash added, "but between Rat-X chasing me around the table, and you entering the lab, I just wasn't able."

"I can vouch for that," Hoenikker said. "It was a perfect storm of unlikely events."

Mansfield listened, then pointed his finger at each of them in turn.

"Remember your security protocols. I don't want you to have to practice them over and over, treating you like a bunch of bad kids. You're adults. You're scientists, for God's sake. But you should know them and be able to apply them." He looked up, as if past the ceiling. "We have new Xenos coming from the *San Lorenzo* and *Katanga*.

"I'm going to get Engineering and Fabrications in here to fix the problems. Kash, Étienne, I want both of you to inspect everything, and make a list of anything we need repaired or replaced. I need it in two hours. I'm going to attach a service request to the status report, to put Deputy Station Commander Thompson on the hook for everything we need."

Kash and Étienne nodded.

"On more thing," Mansfield said. "No new experiments without proper approval."

"Wait. What?" Prior asked.

"Yeah," Cruz said. "*Now* you're treating us like children? No offense, boss, but there's not a scientific bone in your body. You don't know what we're doing here."

"Then school me," Mansfield replied. "Tell me your plans, and explain the benefits."

"So you can decide if the experiment is necessary or not," Kash countered.

"That's my job. You are the brains. I'm in charge. Had Weyland-Yutani felt that a scientist would be a better chief, they would have assigned one. Instead, you have me." Seeing the looks on the scientists' faces, he added, "You could do worse."

"I don't know how," Cruz murmured.

Mansfield stared at him a moment, then turned to leave.

"Two hours," he said over his shoulder. "I need that service request."

As soon as he was gone, Kash and Étienne partnered up and began to check the serviceability of everything in the lab. Cruz left, saying something about he'd be in his room. Prior and Mel began to clean up.

Hoenikker decided it was time to figure out the security protocols. He didn't know what they were, so he moved to his desk, spooled them up on the display, and began to read.

9

Three hours later, with the service request turned in, they were once again hard at work in the lab.

Étienne, Prior, and Mel stood at a table screening a new collection of station rats that had been captured. They needed to confirm that each had a clean bill of health before it was injected with goo. Any infection present in a rat could affect the interaction with the pathogen, and skew the results of an experiment.

Hoenikker and Kash stood behind Cruz, who'd signed out a rifle from Security. Since Containment Room Four was no longer functional for its stated purpose, they used it as a rifle range. As it turned out, the hole created by the xeno's acid was large enough to aim through. They'd affixed the new acid-resistant armor to the back wall, and were currently exposing it to various temperatures for testing.

Cruz fired again, while Hoenikker and Kash recorded the results.

"Looks like you're enjoying that," Hoenikker said.

"Never underestimate the medicinal value of the simple act of firing a weapon."

"I've never fired one," Hoenikker said. "Is it difficult?"

"You've never… get over here," Cruz said.

"I wasn't asking to, I was just—"

"No excuses. The last thing we need is for you to need to use a rifle, having never even fired one."

Hoenikker wished he hadn't said anything, but there it was—he had. Against his better judgment, he handed his tablet to Kash, who gave him a conspiratorial grin.

"Go ahead. It's fun," she said.

Hoenikker stepped next to Cruz, who held up the rifle. The weapon seemed twice the size it had just a few moments ago.

"Now, you don't need to know every detail about the M41 Pulse Rifle, just know this. It fires ten times 24mm caseless ammunition. The stock is the big end and it goes in the pocket of your shoulder. You hold it like this." He demonstrated. "Note my finger. This is called trigger discipline. I never put it in the trigger well unless I'm going to shoot. Do you know why?"

Hoenikker thought for a moment. "So I don't accidently shoot someone in the back?"

"So you don't accidentally shoot someone in the back. Yes. You got it on the first try. Well done. Now, look at the carry handle. You'll never need to touch it. The battery that operates the electronic firing system resides there. Now, look at the barrel. Note that underneath is a grenade launcher. We're not going to use any grenades, or even load it. We're inside a station. Grenades should *never* be used inside. On the right side of the barrel you'll note there's a charging handle. You pull it back to either clear a breach, eject and empty a shell, or to load ammo. Watch me."

Cruz placed the stock snugly into his shoulder, then moved his right hand to the trigger housing. His left hand gripped the rifle underneath the mounted grenade launcher. He aimed through the hole, slowly moved his finger into the trigger well, then slowly depressed the trigger. His shoulder flexed as the rifle fired with a loud report.

"Easy as pie." Cruz held out the weapon. "Now it's your turn."

Hoenikker took a step back.

"Don't be afraid of it. It's nothing more than a tool. Are you afraid of a scalpel?"

Hoenikker shrugged, then shook his head.

"Sure, you're worried about the blade. You don't want to get cut, right? So, do you hold it by the blade?"

Hoenikker shook his head again, beginning to feel foolish.

"Here." Cruz held out the rifle. He grinned. "Just don't hold it by the blade."

Hoenikker grasped the rifle as if it was made of something breakable. It was both heavier and lighter than he'd thought it would be. He turned to grin at Kash, but Cruz stopped him. Hoenikker noted that the barrel was now pointing directly at Cruz.

"Oh. Sorry." He turned back.

"Always take care where the working end of the rifle is pointing. Here, it should always be pointing into the containment room, or what we call 'down range.' Now, sink the stock into the pocket of your shoulder."

Hoenikker did, and Cruz helped him adjust. Then he moved his right hand to the trigger housing and grasped the barrel with his left. Cruz adjusted his grip on the barrel. As it turned out, Hoenikker had grabbed it on the top but Cruz wanted him to hold it from the bottom. It certainly felt better. Probably offered superior stabilization, as well.

"Aim down the barrel and line up the groove in the carrying handle, pointing it toward the target."

Hoenikker noted the groove and lined it up so it was piercing the air between the center of the armor and the barrel. He moved his finger into the trigger well, blindly found the trigger, and pulled it back. When it fired, Hoenikker was surprised at the noise and at the recoil into his shoulder. All that said, he also realized he was grinning. Releasing the trigger, he pulled it again. This time he was ready for it and he was able to tense his shoulder to take more of the recoil. He grinned wider and fired again. He was about to fire a fourth time when Cruz tapped him on the back.

"Okay, killer. That's enough for now."

Cruz reached out and grabbed the rifle gently by the barrel. For a second, Hoenikker didn't want to give it back. He now understood what it was like to fire a weapon. It was actually fun. Reluctantly, he relinquished it.

"Thank you," he said. "I never knew."

"Most folks don't. Less than one percent of people ever serve in the Colonial Marines, and with gun restrictions—unless you are a marine or know one—there's no way you're ever going to be able to fire an M41."

Hoenikker nodded. "I hope I never *need* to fire one, but I'd like do so again someday."

Cruz held the rifle with his left hand and clapped Hoenikker on the shoulder. "After this next round of Xenos, we'll all get together and I'll see if we can't try out a real rifle range. I know Security has one. We'll see if we can borrow it for a day."

"Hey, guys," Prior said. "Get over here. We've made an... interesting discovery."

Cruz leaned the rifle against the workstation at the front of the containment room. They all gathered around the table, where the rats were segregated into six small glass boxes with holes for them to breathe.

"What have you got?" Kash asked.

"MPDTs. In the rats. All of them." Hoenikker didn't know what MPDTs were, but he hoped they weren't contagious—at least not transferable to humans.

"All of them?" Kash asked.

"Who would put them in rats?" Cruz asked.

"Are they signed?" Kash pressed. "Were you able to find a copyright on them?"

Prior shook his head. As did Étienne.

"What is an MPDT?" Hoenikker asked, more uncertain than ever.

"Micro-personal data tracker," Kash said. "We all have them in our badges, and in our shoulders."

Hoenikker remembered when he'd first been assigned to Weyland-Yutani and he'd had to have a tracker surgically implanted. They hadn't called it an MPDT—just a "chip"—and it was so long ago he'd forgotten all about it.

"Every weapon has one," Cruz added. "It's to track them and make certain we know their location at any given time."

"And the rats have them?" Hoenikker asked.

"Yes, miniaturized versions of them, and we don't know why."

Mel muttered something. No one else picked it up.

"He's right," Hoenikker said. "They must be for mapping. The rats are being used to map the station."

"Why would anyone need to do that?" Étienne asked no one in particular.

"I think we need to get the security chief down here, now," Cruz said.

Five minutes later, an impatient Security Chief Flowers, accompanied by Security Specialist Wincotts, stood peering at the rats. Mansfield stood off to the side, looking none too happy.

"These are state-of-the-art trackers?" Wincotts asked. Short and dark-skinned, he was in charge of "special security," which according to Kash meant the synths.

"Yes, sir." Prior said.

"How long has this been going on?" Flowers asked.

"Has to have been recent," Prior said. "We didn't pick this up before."

"Have you found the locus of access for the rats?" Hoenikker asked. Both security chiefs looked his way, and shook their heads.

"There's no way to determine how they're getting in," Flowers replied.

"Maybe if you hack the signal of the trackers," Hoenikker suggested. "I assume they are transmitting data. The trick would be to get your own data, and see if perhaps the trackers have memory storage, then see where they all started."

Everyone was looking at him now and he didn't like the feeling.

"Of course, you could also try and determine where the data is being received." He felt his face turning red because of the attention. "That wouldn't be too hard, I'd imagine, if you have some comms personnel with up-to-date training."

"That makes perfect sense," Wincotts said. He turned to Flowers. "Let me handle this, Randy."

Flowers nodded. "Have at it."

Wincotts rubbed his hands together. "Our rat infestation just became an infiltration. Can't have that," he said, leaving the lab. "Can't have that at all."

10

Communication Specialist Brennan was bored out of his mind. He'd been tasked with deciphering the model and type of MPDTs they'd found on the rats. It was a job anyone could do. Buggy and Davis got the cream job.

They were assigned to hack the devices so that they could get the log history of the data contained in the memory. Brennan would have loved to do that, but he'd been on Oshita's shit list for a long time. So, out of spite, Brennan ignored his assignment and returned to playing his Colonial Marine first-person shooter. He'd played this before. Hell, he played it every day—it was the only thing keeping him sane in a station at the ass end of the universe.

Brennan was on level forty-three of a fifty-level game when his screen blinked red. He had no choice but to pause his game in progress.

Checking the warning, he noted that there was an unauthorized signal going out. He'd seen it before, but had been unable to pin it down. Now that it was live, he would be able to trace it. He actually grinned as he realized the envy Buggy and Davis would have when he solved this one himself. It didn't take five seconds to see that the signal was coming from a comms closet at the end of a dead-end corridor.

Brennan saved his game, grabbed his portable display, and headed out. He passed Rawlings, who saluted him with his coffee cup. That guy was never in his office. Plus, he was far too nice. There had to be something the man was hiding—but then, Brennan thought that of pretty much everyone.

Four corridors later and he was at the access panel. Pulling a tool from his belt, he removed the top two screws and let the panel fold open on its lower hinges. Rats immediately poured out of the wiring and onto the floor, causing Brennan to back away, almost tripping, wondering where the hell the rats were coming from. He began shooing them away with his feet, landing a couple of solid kicks. When the way was clear, he approached the access panel and quickly noted a vid display unit secreted behind the wires. Pulling it out, he tried to access it, but it required either a code or a fingerprint to enable. Common security practice.

Whoever had been sending out the signal had definitely used this terminal. Which meant that this vid display was probably used to send either a burst or an encrypted transmission. If he could determine whose device it was, then he'd know the perpetrator. He grinned as he came up with the word *perpetrator*.

Buggy and Davis were going to be *so* envious.

He hurried back down the twists and turns of the corridors.

Five minutes later Brennan was in the entryway for Logistics, standing at the counter that separated him from the staff. Fields, Fairbanks, and Chase each sat at a terminal.

"Still playing the game, Brennan?" Fields asked. He'd been an actual Colonial Marine, and liked to make fun of Brennan's pretending.

"That old thing?" Brennan said. "Quit that a long time ago."

"It's not too late to join the real corps, you know," Fields persisted. "You're still young enough."

"What, and give up all of this?" Brennan widened his arms to take in the room.

Fields laughed and shook his head.

Fairbanks eyed Brennan and came over to the counter.

"What can I do for you?"

Brennan held out the vid display. "I need to figure out who this belongs to."

Fairbanks stared at it. "Where did you find that?"

Brennan's eyes narrowed. "Doesn't matter. I need to know who it belongs to. It's locked so I can't log in."

"Then I don't know if we can help you," Fairbanks said, still not touching the device.

"What do you mean? Don't you have inventory control numbers?" Brennan asked.

"Maybe whoever owns it is looking for it. Have you considered putting it back?" Fairbanks asked.

"Putting it back? What?"

"Wish I could help you," Fairbanks said.

Chase came over. "What's going on?"

"Guy took a vid display from where someone left it, and doesn't want to put it back," Fairbanks said.

"Guy? Who are you calling 'guy'? It's Brennan, Fairbanks. We've known each other five years. What the fuck's going on?"

"Why don't you put it back?" Chase asked.

Brennan had thought this was going to be easy. It was anything but. If he had to guess, he'd think they were trying to make it harder.

"Listen," he said slowly, trying to calm himself down. "I can't get into the security details, but this vid unit was used to contact someone outside the station. I need to know who it belongs to."

"Why didn't you say so in the first place?" Chase nodded.

Brennan wanted to choke someone.

"Hand it over," Chase said. "I'll check the inventory control number."

That's what I said in the first place, Brennan thought, but he handed it over without saying so.

Chase took it to his workstation, sat down, and pulled out a micro reader. He focused it on a rear corner of the device. After a moment it beeped and a number appeared on the micro reader screen. Chase pulled up a document and compared the numbers.

"Found it, but you won't like this."

"What do you mean I won't like this?" Brennan asked.

"This unit isn't assigned to anyone. It's extra, and should have been in storage."

Brennan thought about that for a moment, noting that Fairbanks was still standing behind the counter, staring at the device.

"Who was the last one to inventory it?" Brennan asked.

Chase punched at his own screen. "That'd be you, Fairbanks." He turned to look at his fellow log specialist. "That would be you."

"I just listed it in the inventory," Fairbanks said. "Anyone could have taken it."

Chase glanced again at his screen. "It was supposed to be in Supply Room Six. That's dedicated to high-value long-term supplies. We keep it locked."

Brennan couldn't help but feel that Fairbanks looked as if he was going to jump out of his skin.

"Someone must have broken in," Fairbanks said.

"I don't think so." Fields swiveled his chair around. "I was just in there yesterday, and there was nothing wrong with the lock. What's the access log say?"

Chase tapped the screen a few more times. "It says that you accessed the room, and before you it was Fairbanks, the day he came back from leave. Why'd you go into the supply room, just when you returned, Fairbanks."

"I… I…"

Brennan's eyes narrowed. Could it be that simple?

"Fairbanks?" Fields stood, holding out the unit. "What did you do?"

"I… I…" Fairbanks gulped. "I swear to you, I didn't do anything. I took a display with me when I went on leave. I know I wasn't supposed to, but I needed something to do on the shuttles. I was just putting it back."

"You know you can't use station equipment for personal use," Fields said. "What if we had a surprise inspection?" He stood and approached his coworker. "Next thing you know, you'll be playing first-person shooters and pretending to be a Colonial Marine." He laughed and patted Fairbanks on the back.

Chase rolled his eyes.

Fields went back to his workstation and sat.

Fairbanks made eye contact with Brennan, but quickly looked away. Brennan stood in his spot for a moment, then shook his head and turned to go.

"What are you going to do now?" Fairbanks asked in a hushed voice.

What *was* Brennan going to do? What was there to do? He guessed he'd report it. Maybe go back and track down the signal again, and see if he couldn't decipher it. Brennan shrugged.

"I don't know," he said without turning. "Maybe nothing."

Then he walked out the door.

11

Shit. Shit. Shit.

It was all Fairbanks could think.

All the effort. All the worry.

And it was Brennan. Fucking gamer Brennan, who never did any work, who'd found him out. How could that even have happened? What had he done to the universe to deserve such a thing? And now Brennan was probably going to make a beeline to Security, and turn him in.

"Fairbanks, what's wrong?" Chase asked.

"If you're worried about us turning you in to Section Chief Jamison, forget about it," Fields said.. "We got your back. Just don't do something that stupid again."

Just don't do something that stupid again. Famous last words.

"I got to go," he mumbled, and headed to the door.

"You got cleanup tonight," Fields said loudly. "Don't forget. Come back from wherever you're going, so you can clean up."

Fairbanks waved his hand to acknowledge and almost ran out of the office. He went down one corridor, then another, searching for Brennan. He didn't know what he'd say when he found him, but Fairbanks needed to stop him, or things would get out of hand.

"Looking for me?" Brennan asked. He was leaning against a wall when Fairbanks turned the corner. Fairbanks halted, eyes wide, breathing heavy. What was he going to say? What *could* he say? That he was committing industrial espionage? That everything would be fine? *"There's nothing going on here. Please run along."*

"It was you, wasn't it?" Brennan looked him up and down.

Fairbanks didn't know what to say, so he merely nodded, blinking rapidly.

"What is it?" Brennan's eyes narrowed. "Who are you communicating with?"

"I can't say," Fairbanks said.

Two security guards turned the corner. A man and a woman. They were chatting, but stopped when they saw the two men. All four eyed one another as the guards passed. Brennan waited several seconds, long enough for them to get out of earshot.

"You have to say something," Brennan whispered. "What happened, Fairbanks? I thought you were a standup guy?"

"I am a standup guy. I just… I just—"

"You just what?"

"I just got in the wrong place at the wrong time." He felt a sob pushing free and he swallowed it. No way was he going to cry about this. "What are you going to do?"

"By all rights, I should go to Security." Brennan shook his head.

Fairbanks felt his stomach sink. He didn't want to go to prison.

"In fact, that's what I'm going to do." Brennan turned and left.

Fairbanks tried to speak, but nothing would come out. So instead, he returned blindly to his quarters. He was almost to his door when he felt the bile rise in his stomach. He ran to the bathroom across from his room, hurled the door open, and spewed into the toilet. The door shut behind him, leaving him on his knees as yellow bile swirled against the metal. The smell of it made him retch again, his back arching with every heave until nothing came out.

After a few moments, he reached out and used the toilet to help him get to his feet. He washed his face and hands, but didn't have the courage to look at himself in the mirror. After wiping his hands and face, he exited the bathroom, used his handprint to enter his own room, and slouched onto the bed.

He wasn't sure how long it would be before they came for him. Five. Ten. Fifteen minutes.

Three knocks.

He glanced up and stared at the door.

Hyperdyne Corporation had given him a vial. They said to take it if he was caught. It was a way out. He stood and shakily pawed through the clothes in the top of his dresser.

Three more knocks.

Just as he was about to give up, his hands curled around the small glass vial. He removed it and placed it in the palm of his hand. It wasn't any longer than a section of his middle finger, and held an amber liquid.

Three more knocks. Insistent.

Try as he might, he couldn't bring himself to take it. He shoved it into his pocket, then went and opened the door, ready to accept his fate.

To his surprise, it wasn't Security.

Brennan stood in the doorway. He pushed his way past Fairbanks and into the room.

"I thought you went to turn me in," Fairbanks said, closing the door.

Brennan walked to the back of the room and turned. The foot of the bed was to his left. The small desk and chair were to his right. He grabbed the chair, spun it around, and sat on it cowboy style.

"Sit down," he said, gesturing to the bed.

Fairbanks glanced at the door. "Are they coming here?"

"I said sit down." Brennan rolled his eyes. "I didn't go to Security, okay? Jeez, relax why don't you?"

"Then what..." Fairbanks sat down slowly, never taking his eyes off the other man. "I don't understand."

"It's simple, really." Brennan spread his hands. "We're going to make a... a transaction. I don't make an issue about this with Security, and you'll be around to provide me with whatever I want. I'm tired of living like a prisoner. I know you have backups for all the swag the section chiefs and the station commander have. I want some."

"You want some—wait. You're blackmailing me?" Fairbanks asked. His fear evaporated as if it had never been there. It was replaced by an equal amount of anger.

"Call it what you want." He shrugged. "Just so long as we come to an agreement."

Fairbanks stood. "What if I went to Security and gave myself up, and told them about the blackmail?"

Brennan grinned. "That's easy. I'd tell them that you tried to offer me a bribe, and I refused. But you could wait until you give me stuff, and then I *couldn't* go to Security. I'd be culpable."

"Or by the time I give you stuff it's too late," Fairbanks said, "because you can say it's a bribe that you didn't want to take, but were forced to." His mind was racing.

Brennan's grin grew wider.

Fairbanks wanted to slap it away.

"That's pretty smart of you, Fairbanks," Brennan said. "You'd make a good criminal. Correction, you *are* a good criminal. That's probably why they picked you."

"I am *not* a criminal." Fairbanks took two steps forward.

Brennan stood. "Sure you are… or do you prefer the word 'spy,'" he said with air quotes.

"I'm neither." Fairbanks balled his fists.

"Then what are you?"

Fairbanks thought of the way Hyperdyne was blackmailing him. He thought of what Brennan was trying to do to him. He knew what he was, and he said it out loud.

"I'm a victim."

"Oh, please." Brennan snorted. "Save it."

That was it.

Fairbanks brought his right fist around and slammed it into the side of Brennan's face. The man stumbled with the blow.

Fairbanks hit him again.

Brennan fell to his knees beside the desk.

Fairbanks grabbed his head and began to slam it, over and over, against the side of the desk. Blood splattered the wall. A moment later pieces of gore began to litter the desktop. At first Brennan tried to speak, but all he could do was grunt each time his head slammed against the hard surface.

Five more times until the grunting stopped, then Fairbanks let go of the man's hair. Brennan slumped to the floor like a bag of meat. Fairbanks stared at his hand, then at the body.

What had he done?

He'd killed the man.

But his anger still fueled him. He'd do it again if he had to. He was tired of being a pushover. He was tired of being forced to do things that he didn't want to do.

He heard a groan.

Was he still alive?

Brennan's hand twitched. His fingers moved like the legs of a dying spider. He tried to roll himself over, and just managed to do it. His eyes were crossed. Teeth had broken through his cheek.

Fairbanks shuddered. Had he done that? The enormity of it hit him like a brick. He stumbled back. He should get help. Maybe they could still save him.

Brennan spit out several teeth along with a bubble of blood.

Fairbanks shoved his hand into his pocket and felt the poison vial. He pulled it out and stared at it. A small glass filled with amber liquid. Really just the size of a tooth. Without thinking it through, he opened the stopper, knelt, and poured the syrupy fluid into Brennan's open mouth.

The dying man choked once, then swallowed to clear it. An eye found Fairbanks and seemed about to cry.

Then everything went still.

Fairbanks hurriedly pushed himself back so he was sitting with his back against his bed, and buried his face in his hands. He sat there for a long moment, then he began to chuckle. Just a titter at first. Then actual laughter. Soon he was giddy with the moment, as full-blown guffaws rocked the inside of the room. He realized two things.

One, Security wouldn't be looking for him anytime soon.

Two, he needed to find a place to hide the body. When he thought about it, he laughed harder. *Hide a body*. He'd never once thought he'd have to think those three words, much less carry through with them.

Hide.

A.

Body.

Life was so hilarious.

12

Cruz shuddered beneath the sheets.

The tentacles are wrapped around Snyder's torso. Surprise and terror battle on his face. The tentacles squeeze, and the sound of ribs snapping is like gunshots. Blood shoots from Snyder's mouth in a waterfall of red that only a dream could create. Blood and more blood and more blood until it covers everything, the world a red-dripped Rorschach.

Cruz begins to gasp, then choke.

He's drowning. Can't breathe. The blood covers all but his reaching hand. Then he breathes it in, becoming Snyder, enwrapped by the tentacles, feeling the impossible strength of the monster as it squeezes out everything it means to be alive.

Cruz shot up to a sitting position. Consciousness returned, and he slid his legs off the bed. He dropped his head between them as he began to hyperventilate. Sweat dripped from his face, falling to the floor. His heart was galloping as if he'd just completed a run. What the hell had just happened?

Damn dreams. Damn Snyder.

It was the marine's own damn fault for not following orders. Cruz realized that it was more than sweat dripping to the floor. He wiped his eyes, then furiously shook his head. Standing, he opened his door and strode across the corridor into the common bathroom. Found a sink and dashed water on his face.

Behind him came the sound of someone flushing. The door to a stall opened and a bleary-eyed man staggered out. When he saw Cruz, he stopped cold.

Cruz turned around. The man wasn't saying anything, just standing there.

"What the fuck do you want?" Cruz said.

The man blinked.

That was when Cruz realized he'd forgotten to put clothes on, and was completely naked. He shook his head.

"Never seen a naked man before? Get back to bed, you." Then he turned back to the sink and stared at himself in the mirror.

His almost-black skin hid many of his wounds, but he knew every scar and pock. He could trace the lineage of the wounds as if he'd inflicted them himself. To a point he had, by joining the Colonial Marines. Back then, when the drill sergeants saw him, they knew he'd be an effective killing machine.

He picked at his Afro. He really needed to get it cut, but there wasn't anyone qualified on the station. Soon he'd have to settle, and probably shave it. The hair was getting knappy.

Throwing water on his face, he headed back to his room, where he pulled on clothes, used a pick to fix his hair as best he could, then donned his white lab jacket. He was on his way to the lab before he knew what he was going to do. He passed two security specialists making the rounds, nodded to them, and they nodded back. When he entered the lab, the motion sensor turned the lights on.

Cruz immediately went to work. The effort of combining the radioactive plutonium with the pathogen wasn't difficult, but because of safety protocols it was time consuming. Not only did he have to make sure that he reduced his exposure to the radiation, but also to the lab itself. So, it was all black box work, the radiation kept inside a lead-lined box with video sensors that allowed him to manipulate arms that were doing the work for him.

Mansfield's voice rang through his mind, reminding him that there were to be no experiments without his permission.

Fuck Mansfield.

The man wasn't even a scientist. All he wanted was for them to toe the line. Didn't he know that it was the mavericks that made the best scientists—that it was the mad geniuses who effected the greatest advancements? The Mansfields of the world would have stopped the discoveries of penicillin, and nuclear fusion, and antimatter, and faster-than-light travel. The Mansfields of the world would have humanity still landlocked to a single planet, instead of out in space going cutting edge.

Yeah. Fuck Mansfield.

Cruz pressed a button, and a syringe with the irradiated pathogen ejected from a side drawer on the black box. Donning lead-lined gloves, he took it and moved to the containment room where Leon-895 was kept. So far, the effects of the goo had been impressive. The size of the creature had increased fivefold, as had the appearance. A new set of legs had appeared, giving it a new and strange presence.

At the containment area, Cruz didn't even try to locate it. Instead, he immediately lowered the temperature. The creature appeared in the top left corner, and he watched as the image of it solidified. Once a coat of frost covered it, he entered the containment room, injected the creature with the irradiated pathogen, then exited again. He wasn't about to have the same problem he'd had last time, when he'd allowed his PTSD to get the better of him.

Once back outside the room, he removed the gloves and returned them to where they belonged. He placed the syringe back in the black box, to dispose of it later. Irradiated as it was, he couldn't just throw it away. There was a process. There were the sacred protocols. Then he returned to the containment room, raised the temperature to normal again, and sat back.

They'd installed a prismatic light system to measure the speed of Leon-895's ability to change color. So far that ability, while impressive, had been slow. Cruz hoped that the irradiated pathogen might cause it to autocorrect sooner. Now, all he had to do was wait.

An image of Snyder returned to him. Not dying, but living. They'd been preparing to go to a cold-as-hell planet for guard duty. The day before, they'd let loose. Snyder had brought his girlfriend and they'd all begun drinking yards of beer—an old German tradition to which his family still adhered. Snyder had always fancied himself a drinker, but he was really just a lightweight.

They'd all been at Sgt. Bone's quarters. Cruz, Snyder, Erica—Snyder's girlfriend—and Foxie, an old buddy of Bone's. It was the usual bout of drinking games and blowing off steam prior to setting off for a nearby LV. Everyone was having a good time until Erica challenged Snyder to a drink-off.

Cruz had come to believe that it was premeditated.

Snyder wasn't about to let his girlfriend get the better of him. So he matched her yard for yard, drinking down an impressive—by anyone's standards—amount of beer. Cruz didn't know from what alcoholic DNA Erica had been spliced, but she seemed impervious to the alcohol. She drank and drank and the only way to know she'd drunk so much was her need to pee. It was on the eighth yard that Snyder spewed the contents of his stomach all over Sgt. Bone's kitchen, then proceeded to pass out on the bathroom floor. Cruz had taken care of his friend as best he could, then cleaned up the mess.

Meanwhile, Erica, none the worse for wear, started cuddling up to both Sgt. Bone and Foxie, laughing and acting as if she wasn't anyone's girlfriend. Once the mess had been cleaned up, Cruz grabbed Snyder and carried him back to the barracks.

They'd left the next morning without ever seeing Erica again. The cherry on top of the memory was that Snyder hadn't packed before he'd gone out drinking, so he only had one extra sock in his 'go bag.' He'd ended up getting trench foot during the mission, and almost had to have his feet amputated.

All because of a girl.

Once Cruz had left the Colonial Marines and taken up his education, he'd learned that there were substances that could render the alcohol of a liquid into pure sugar. Upon discovering that, he'd become certain that was how Erica had beaten Snyder. Cruz wondered if it was just to make her safe from an alcohol overdose, or if it had been a ploy to get next to Sgt. Bone. He'd never know, because Erica had never been seen again and Sgt. Bone had died in a shuttle explosion reportedly caused by a faulty fuel wire.

Cruz sighed. Such were the symptoms of living two lives. The other scientists didn't have his problem. They'd grown up, gone to college, and become scientists of their own accord. They didn't have a life before this one. But Cruz did. In spades.

He checked the temperature of the room and the temperature of Leon-895. Both had achieved stasis. He toggled a switch on the control station, and watched as a light in the containment room slowly began to cycle through three primary colors.

Leon-895 remained visible without any change.

Damn. Had he used too much radiation? Please say that he hadn't used too much. Please show that the creature wasn't dead. Mansfield would have his ass.

Checking the creature's vitals, he noted that they were slightly lower than usual, but not drastically so. It should be attenuating. He waited a few tense minutes, then Leon-895 began to cycle slowly through the three colors—red, green, blue… red, green, blue… red, green, blue.

There.

At least he hadn't killed the damned thing.

He began to cycle slightly faster, and was joyed to see Leon-895 skip a beat, then match the speed of the color change. Then he added three more colors—yellow, brown, and black. A beat skipped again, then Leon-895 began to adapt. Cruz watched for several minutes as the creature changed color with the change of light, pleased at its progress.

Finally, he dialed up a dozen variations, then a hundred, then a thousand. Hell, *two* thousand. Each flash of light, Leon-895 changed, conforming to its new colored reality as easy as if it was breathing.

Cruz turned up the speed so Leon-895 was changing in three-second intervals. He pulled a chair over from the central table and placed it in front of the containment area. For the next two hours he sat and watched his own personal disco as the creature flashed color after color after color, while images of Snyder being squeezed to death *rat-a-tat-tatted* through his mind.

13

Security Specialist Wincotts convinced Mansfield that their experiments should be put on hold, so they could focus on the MPDTs. The scientists were far from thrilled with the turn of events. They each had their own projects, and were loath to stop.

Hoenikker hadn't yet been assigned an individual project, and was seconding several of his peers. Although he didn't have as much emotional or intellectual investment as his fellow scientists, he still felt the frustration and the pull of real science.

Cruz had been the most vocal.

"We've developed a brand-new species here in Leon-895—one that could change the nature of how a Colonial Marine goes to war. And what do they have us doing? Dissecting rats."

"There's nothing to do about it," Mansfield responded. "We rely on the goodwill of the station so that we can operate freely—*especially* after one of your experiments got loose and killed station personnel."

"That's likely to happen again," Cruz countered. "Where's Fabrications? Why haven't they replaced the windows?"

Mansfield nodded. "They claim that they're short on tungsten, and don't have enough to replace all of the glass."

"Then at least replace the worst ones." Cruz stood from the chair he'd been sitting in, and pointed toward the containment rooms. "Jesus, there's so much infighting on this station it reminds me of primary school. Everyone taking sides. Engineering won't talk to Fabrications. Fabrications won't talk to Logistics. Can they just fucking do their jobs, so we can get back to business?" No one responded, and he lowered his voice.

"Sorry for yelling," he said. "I'm… passionate."

Mansfield just nodded, folded his hands behind his back, and left the lab.

"Don't you get tired of all that yelling?" Étienne asked.

"It's part of his personality," Prior said, flashing a smile toward Cruz. "It takes all sorts of us to effectively science. Take Matthews here," he said, putting his arm around the bigger man's shoulders. "He doesn't say much, but he sciences hard."

Mel muttered something that sounded like a thank you, then went back to his microscope.

"Why isn't Comms working on this?" Étienne asked.

"Oh, they are," Mansfield said. "We're working in tandem. So far, they haven't found anything."

Kash clapped her hands together loudly, and Hoenikker jumped. She moved to where everyone could easily see her.

"Let's get to this, so we can return to our experiments," she said. "What's the one thing every piece of tech has?"

Prior and Cruz glanced at each other. Both shook their heads.

Mel didn't look up.

Étienne chewed a fingernail.

Hoenikker had no idea where she was going with this.

"Okay, let me make it easier. What does every piece of art have on it?" she asked.

Étienne was the first to answer. "A signature."

"Right." Kash nodded. "A signature. Tech doesn't have signatures—"

"—but it does have inventory control numbers," Hoenikker said, finishing her words. She snapped her fingers.

"Yes. Or something similar. Weyland-Yutani doesn't make anything without slapping its name on it. They want the world to know that the products they're using were made by their favorite corporation."

"Wouldn't the size of the trackers make that hard to do?" Cruz asked.

"If they can make a device that size, then they have the technology to sign it." She pointed to Hoenikker. "You will run Team B. This is where your theoretical modeling comes in handy. Prior and Cruz will work with you. You're going to find out *why* they are being used." She pointed to Étienne. "You are in charge of Team A. Myself and Mel will be part of your team. We're charged with determining where the MPDTs came from."

"Why aren't *you* in charge of Team A?" Étienne asked. "Don't get me wrong, I love being in charge. I do bossy well."

"Let's try and minimize the bossiness," she said. "I chose you because of the way your mind works. I think you're the right solution for this problem." She turned to everyone and said, "Right. So, let's get to work."

Hoenikker turned to Cruz and Prior. "We don't need to be here to discuss this. Let's carve ourselves a corner in the mess hall and discuss it over coffee."

Cruz nodded. "Finally, a good idea."

* * *

Ten minutes later they were ensconced in the mess hall. Cruz and Hoenikker blew on hot black coffee. Prior drank soda through a straw. Because it was midmorning, the place was almost empty. Only one other was working there. Hoenikker recognized him as Reception Tech Rawlings. He was on the other side of the room, drinking coffee from a portable mug and going over something on his vid display. When they'd entered, he'd saluted them with his coffee, but hadn't tried to get into their space.

The mess hall was pretty rudimentary. On one side of the room was the drinks table that offered everything from tea to coffee, soda, soymilk, and water. The other side of the room held the buffet, currently empty, and the entrance to the kitchen. There were a dozen tables. The gray walls were adorned with posters from Weyland-Yutani regarding security warnings, the need to respect your fellow workers, and the infamous, "SEE A PROBLEM, FIX A PROBLEM."

"So, what are we doing?" Cruz asked.

Hoenikker had become more and more impressed with the man. Where at first he'd felt that Cruz had been someone who gleefully heaped abuse on his specimens, it was clear now that he had multiple layers.

"We have the simplest job, frankly," Hoenikker said. "That's why I wanted us out of there."

"You've solved the problem?" Prior asked.

"I believe I have—and if you think about it, you could solve it as well."

Prior sipped loudly through his straw and gave him a dubious look. Hoenikker took a sip of his coffee.

It was hot and terrible.

"Let's pare it down to the basics," he said. "Each of us has a PDT implanted in our shoulder. What are they used for?"

"To keep track of us good little Weyland-Yutani employees," Cruz said.

"And how do they keep track of us?" Hoenikker asked, raising an eyebrow.

"Reception nodes placed around the facility. We walk by them, it logs who we are, along with a time-and-date stamp," Prior said. "Everyone knows that. And like Cruz said, it's how they keep track of all their good little employees, while making sure we don't go to places we shouldn't go."

"Then what good would the PDTs be on the rats if they were from another company? If this is some sort of industrial espionage, then how could they log the rats as they passed a reception node?"

Cruz sat up. "Unless they hacked the system."

"They'd have to have a man on the inside," Prior said.

"I'll bet if we went to Comms, they could find the signal," Hoenikker said.

"They might have already found it and ruled it out as a glitch," Cruz offered.

"Interesting hypothesis, but it doesn't have any legs," Hoenikker said. "Come on now. Let's keep with the scientific method."

"Why is it you went straight to industrial espionage?" Prior asked.

"What else would the rats with MPDTs be good for? If I'm right, they're being used to map the station, and the results are being broadcast to someone on the outside."

"Might be a hostile takeover," Cruz said.

"You do realize that you were the most recent person to come on station," Prior said to him. "Which makes you suspect *numero uno*." He grinned and sipped at his soda.

"While that may be," Hoenikker said, "why don't we run on over to Comms, and ask them about outgoing signals?"

His associates nodded, and all three stood. They exited the mess hall, leaving Rawlings behind.

Five minutes later they were chatting with Buggy and Davis. The third comms workstation was empty.

They'd been able to hack the MPDTs and found the information logs. The rats had been everywhere, strengthening Hoenikker's supposition. He told them what he believed was going on, and they agreed that it made the most sense. When asked if they'd discovered any outgoing signals, they both shook their heads.

Hoenikker asked them to check.

Davis went to his workstation, and after a few minutes came back. As it turned out, Brennan had flagged two occasions. Both had been burst transmissions, the last one taking place only a few hours earlier. Only Comms and Security had access to the employee PDT log system. Hoenikker asked where Brennan was, so they could question him about it.

When they queried Brennan's location, it showed him in his room. Buggy commented that he was usually playing first-person shooters, even at work, which had earned him a spot on Oshita's shit list.

Together with Buggy, Hoenikker, Cruz, and Prior, they went to Brennan's room. They knocked, but there was no answer. After repeated attempts, Buggy used his override code to enter the room.

It was empty.

"But the signal said he was in here," Cruz said.

Prior glanced under the bunk.

Buggy checked in the closet.

Hoenikker stared at the pillow. It had been fluffed, but was off center. Why would someone take the time to fluff it and not make sure it was straight? He went to straighten it and noted a spot of red on the white sheet. He lifted the pillow, then dropped it and backed away. His heart rate immediately went through the roof as the blood left his face.

"What is it?" Cruz asked. "Looks like you've seen a dead man."

"The pillow," Hoenikker managed. "Look under it."

Cruz grabbed the pillow and lifted it. Beneath it lay an identification fob and a section of skin with a small rice-sized piece of metal embedded in it.

A personal data tracker.

Brennan's personal data tracker.

Which meant that more than likely, Brennan was dead.

Either that, or he's *the infiltrator*, Hoenikker thought, *and removed his own PDT so he couldn't be tracked.*

He voiced the possibility, and they called Security. Each of them was interviewed in turn, to give a thorough account of how they had arrived at their macabre discovery. Once they were allowed to go, Buggy returned to Comms to brief Section Chief Oshita, and the others returned to the lab.

Mansfield was already there. He'd heard through the command channel what had happened. Hoenikker briefed him on their discovery and suppositions.

Étienne's team had continued their work, to a degree of success. They'd discovered where the MPDTs originated. Each MPDT, Étienne explained, had its own inventory control number. Without any information regarding the origin of the device, however, the number was useless.

Under normal circumstances.

Matthews observed a pattern in the placement of hyphens on the MPDT IDs, distinctly different from the inventory control numbers used by Weyland-Yutani. A quick search of the lab yielded equipment produced by other manufacturers, and Kash noted that one of the microscopes was a Hyperdyne product. Its numbering convention matched those of the MPDTs.

Even with this epiphany, they didn't know who had brought the rats into the station, used them to map it, then sent communication bursts to a nearby receiver. Nor were they any closer to finding Brennan… or his body.

There was one thing they did know.

Only two people had come to the station recently, and Hoenikker had the feeling he knew what was certain to happen.

They sent Security the results of their investigation, and not fifteen minutes later a pair of officers entered the lab. With hardly a word they cuffed his hands behind his back without trying to be gentle about it, while the rest of the scientists looked on.

Cruz began to protest, and moved toward the officers and their prisoner, but Kash stopped him with a hand on his shoulder. She didn't look any happier about it than he did, though.

14

To say that he was pissed-off was an understatement. Hoenikker knew he was innocent, and expected everyone else to see it as well. It was *obvious*. He'd always followed the rules—well, *almost* always—and what rules he'd failed to follow had been inconsequential.

The very thought that he was being accused of espionage turned his face red, and caused his skin to prickle. As he was marched down the corridor, however, he wondered what would happen if he wasn't able to *prove* his innocence? He'd heard of innocent men and women who had been incarcerated, their fates based on their abilities to convince someone—the *right* someone—of their innocence. People who'd probably already made up their minds.

The thought was chilling.

"Faster," the officer said, pushing him hard in the center of his back. They propelled him down a hallway he'd never seen, and through a door marked SECURITY. The long room had office cubicles along the sides, and a large conference table in the middle. Guards and other staff members occupied the cubicles, and some sat at the conference table. They did more than glance up when he entered.

They stared, each gaze an indictment—a judgment.

Hoenikker was marched through the office and down an interior corridor, passing several doors with heavy locks and no windows. At the end of the corridor stood an open door, and he was pushed inside. The room held a table and four chairs. One chair was already occupied. It was the other guy who had been on the shuttle.

What was his name? Fairbanks?

The door slammed behind him.

A large glass mirror faced him from one wall. He'd seen enough vids to know it was a one-way glass window. Security personnel were probably on the other side taking notes and recording his activities. Judging him.

"They grabbed you, too," Fairbanks said. "Remember when you said Pala Station couldn't be as bad as all that?" He spread his hands. "What do you think now?"

"I think once I explain myself, they'll let me get back to work," Hoenikker said, almost believing his own words. He began to pace.

"You might as well sit down. They're going to let you steam and cool for at least thirty minutes." When Hoenikker shot him a quizzical look, he added, "I used to date a security guard. He ran me through the steps. Said it makes us more malleable, because we spend all of the time running back and forth in our own minds, either trying to find out what we did to get caught, or trying to figure out a way to talk our way out of the room—or both."

Seeing the logic in his advice, Hoenikker took the seat next to Fairbanks. He assumed that the two empty chairs on the other side of the table were reserved for his interrogators.

He remembered what Stokes had said.

"Be boring and stay here. Or be dangerous and travel far."

If there was a moment he wanted to be boring, this was it. He didn't want to be dangerous. Not to *anyone*. He just wanted out of this room. And out from under any judgmental observation so he could go back to his modeling. He wondered, if he hadn't solved the MPDT problem, would he still be free? Then another part realized that one of the other scientists could just as easily have worked it out, so the result had been inevitable.

He could almost hear Stokes in his ear.

Just relax, everything will work out. You're a good guy, Hoenikker. Nothing bad is going to happen to you.

Nothing indeed.

Like being detained for espionage.

The door snapped open and he jumped. Two security personnel entered. One man. One woman. The square-jawed woman wore her hair short, and looked as if she could gut punch a landing shuttle. The man was lanky, and wore a smirk as if he knew the universe's private punchline.

Rather than taking a seat, the woman leaned against the wall in the corner, crossed her arms, and gave him a death stare. The man sat across from them and introduced himself as Mr. Tacker. His voice was pitched lower than Hoenikker would have expected from someone so thin.

He asked for Hoenikker's full name and employee ID.

Hoenikker gave it.

Tacker did the same for Fairbanks.

He gave it.

Then the man did nothing. He merely sat and smirked at the two of them until what must have been ten minutes had passed. All the while, Hoenikker felt his nervousness increasing, which in turn made him angry. The effect they desired, sitting silence, and he hated himself for falling for it.

"You're angry," the man said finally. "Angry at being caught?"

Hoenikker shook his head. "Angry at being a part of this. You know very well that I had nothing to do with it. In fact, I was the one who figured it out."

"The easiest way to influence the information is to be close to the investigation."

"Influence the information?" Hoenikker snorted. "I *broke* the case." At least he thought that was the terminology. "You wouldn't even know about the espionage if it wasn't for me."

"Broke the case," Tacker said. "Interesting choice of words. Do you like detective fiction, Mr. Hoenikker?"

"*Doctor* Hoenikker."

The smirk widened. "Do you watch the criminal vids, *Mister* Hoenikker? Are you a fan of docudramas? Have you invented your own, so you can have a starring role?"

Hoenikker had never wanted to punch a man in the face more than he did at that moment, and Hoenikker had never punched anyone in the face. He probably couldn't even make a proper fist. Still, he wanted to punch this man in the face.

"Listen," Hoenikker began, "I don't know what you're trying to accomplish here. We both know you have access to station logs, and you can track my movements anywhere. You've probably already been over them. If you want to question me about that, feel free. Better yet, why haven't you tracked Brennan's PDT? After all, we know someone cut it out of him. Where did that occur?"

Ha! He thought. *Answer me that!*

Tacker listened patiently the entire time, giving Hoenikker a heavy-lidded stare. Still, his smirk never wavered. Without answering, he turned his attention to the logistics specialist.

"And you, Fairbanks," he said. "You had a convenient trip off planet."

"Nothing convenient about it," Fairbanks said. "Unless you like shuttling back and forth, and experiencing short-term cryosleep. I don't."

"Was it you who brought back the rats? Was it you who started the infestation? Sec Specialist Howard here said she saw you near the comms access panel—the one that was used to send a signal outside. You were wearing a backpack. What was in the backpack, Fairbanks?"

Suddenly, Hoenikker wanted to know what was in the backpack as well. Was Fairbanks the spy? Was he the infiltrator? He hadn't seemed like one, during their shared trip. But then, how could anyone tell?

Fairbanks glanced at Howard, then back at Mr. Tacker.

"Nothing. Just bullshit."

"Sec Specialist Howard, what was it Fairbanks told you?"

"He said he was out for some exercise, and that the pack was full of trash."

"Was there trash in the pack?"

"Just an empty package, and a tool."

"Could that package have contained the rats?" Tacker asked.

"It could have," she said.

Even to Hoenikker it sounded fishy. Tacker pulled a vid display unit out of his pocket and dialed something up.

"Know what I'm looking at, Fairbanks? I'm looking at your PDT tracking logs since you returned to the station. There's only one time you were up before everyone to *exercise*. Once."

"I pulled a muscle," Fairbanks said. "Should have stretched more."

"'Should have stretched more,'" Tacker repeated. He stared at his vid for some time. "I have you in your room yesterday afternoon, when you were supposed to have been on shift."

"I had some personal issues to take care of."

"Were they personal issues with Brennan?" Tacker asked. "We tracked him into your room at the same time."

Fairbanks glanced at Hoenikker, and then Howard, before staring at his steepled hands balanced between his knees.

"That's personal."

"Personal? You gave up having a personal life when you signed your company contract. I'll ask you again, Logistic Specialist Fairbanks. What were you and Brennan doing alone in your room?"

Hoenikker realized he'd been leaning forward, and sat back in his chair. He understood. He could see it in Fairbanks' eyes. He was sure that Tacker understood as well, but clearly the man wanted Fairbanks to admit it. Hoenikker felt embarrassed for the young man, and looked away. His gaze met Howard's.

She looked as if she was ready to pounce.

"Fairbanks, I'm talking to you," Tacker pressed.

"Listen," Fairbanks began, his voice hoarse and low. "Brennan wanted to be together with me. He wanted to have a relationship. I—I didn't want it." He licked his lips and closed his eyes. "He got mad and stormed out. Maybe he took off? I don't know."

Tacker sat silently for a moment. "You're saying that he left your room of his own accord?" he said. "More likely he spurned you, and you got angry."

Fairbanks shook his head. "It was nothing like that. As I said, he left. He called me terrible names. He was angry. I stayed in my room."

"We have a record of you following him," Tacker said.

Fairbanks stared with tears rimming his wide eyes. "Fine. I followed him to his room. We talked some more. I tried to make him feel better, but… but he wouldn't listen. So I left."

"You left." Tacker's smirk grew again.

Fairbanks nodded, unwilling or unable to meet the interrogator's gaze.

Hoenikker wondered if they'd forgotten he was there.

Fairbanks cleared his throat. "Come on, Tacker. My personal life has nothing to do with this. Plus, if you had anything on us, we'd be in a cell by now. Can we just get back to work?"

Hoenikker nodded. That added up. Tacker was fishing. He must not have any evidence against them. He just figured because they were the last two persons brought to the station that it had to be them.

"How do you know it's not station security personnel who did this?" Hoenikker asked, breaking the silence. He regretted it immediately, but there it was.

"Why would security personnel do this?" Tacker sat back in his chair. "For that matter, what *is* 'this'?"

"I don't know," Hoenikker answered. "You tell me. Why would a scientist who begged for an assignment here, *begged* to study alien artifacts, come here and put everything he had in jeopardy?"

"Maybe you work for someone else," Tacker said. "Maybe you were blackmailed, or *very* well paid. Do you have any evidence that station security was involved?" The smirk was still there, yet Hoenikker knew he had to choose his words carefully.

"As much evidence as you have against me," he said. "Maybe more. After all, there must have been security personnel who were away from the station repeatedly in the last few weeks, with the *San Lorenzo* on the way. They could have met up with another corporation, and been given a bag of rats with MPDTs to bring back into the station."

"What do you mean 'away from the station'?" Tacker asked.

Hoenikker leaned forward. "When Deputy Station Chief Thompson goes on his hunting trips, does he go alone?"

Tacker's smirk died a thousand deaths.

As childish as it seemed, Hoenikker wanted to jump up and point, saying, *I got you!* Instead, he fought to control his facial features and just stared. He wondered how proud Stokes would have been for this moment.

Tacker slid his vid display back into his pocket and stood. "We're done for now," he said. "Be prepared to make yourselves available."

"It's not like we have anywhere to go," Fairbanks said.

Then Tacker and Security Specialist Howard left the room.

They left the door open.

15

The next day Hoenikker was relieved to get back to the lab. Being in custody had soured him enough that he'd considered putting in his transfer packet. What with the absence of the alien artifacts he'd been promised, and the sheer state of paranoia on Pala Station, he'd feel much more comfortable back in a corporate cubicle, working nine-to-five, creating models based on his own theses.

The argument convincing him to stay had an unlikely source.

Cruz. The man was operating on a combination of caffeine and excitement. He hadn't slept much and had come to the lab for some distraction. And he got it.

As Hoenikker stood before Leon-895, he was sure the creature had grown to at least five times its size since he'd last seen it—what he *could* see of it. Cruz had the lights flashing through a prismatic color sequencing and the creature matched it with barely a pause. It was in that pause that Hoenikker noted spikes jutting from its top and sides, like an old-world porcupine.

"I haven't yet tested the effects of temperature fluctuation on color attenuation, but the fact that it can change so fast is absolutely incredible," Cruz said, more than a little giddy. "Imagine if we had armor that could allow our Colonial Marines to blend into any surface. They'd be virtually invisible. Combat efficiency would skyrocket, as would the survival rate. This is groundbreaking."

"It's a great first step, Cruz." Hoenikker could appreciate the man's excitement—but they were scientists, and far from any viable conclusions. "Next we need to replicate your findings with other Leon-895s, to identify the new standard. Then devise a method of copying the creature's modified guanine crystal cell structure, and apply it to armor."

"Of course. Of course." Cruz nodded. "But isn't this fantastic?"

"It is," Hoenikker admitted.

Off to the side the lab door opened, and Fairbanks stepped in, followed by two log specialists Hoenikker didn't know. Kash stepped away from her station, approached one of the specialists, and began to speak. Hoenikker moved closer to hear what was being said.

"—from *San Lorenzo* soon. I'd like Engineering to inspect the integrity of each of the glass fronts, to determine which ones need replaced, then get Fabrications working on them ASAP."

"I've checked the inventory, ma'am," Fairbanks began, glancing at Hoenikker, then quickly away. "I'm not sure we have enough tungsten to replace all the glass fronts. We may have to triage."

"Why on earth wouldn't you have enough tungsten?" Kash asked. "Who else uses tungsten in any quantity?"

"Well, Deputy Station Chief Thompson has been creating his own ammunition for his hunting rifle. He uses nothing but station tungsten."

"My God," she said. "How many bullets does the man need?"

Fairbanks stared at the ground. "I'm not sure, ma'am."

Kash placed a hand on his shoulder. "Of course you aren't. We'll just do the best we can. Please, take the team to the back of the lab and work your way forward. Don't interfere with any of our experiments, though, and do not—I mean do *not*—touch any controls on the workstations."

"Yes, ma'am," he said. He and the other two slid past Hoenikker and headed toward the back.

"What's that all about?" Hoenikker asked, sidling next to her.

"We're retrofitting as best we can before more Xenomorph samples arrive. They should be here within forty-eight hours, and I'm not convinced the glass fronts can contain them."

"I've never seen the Xenomorphs—not firsthand," he said. "Are they that bad?"

"Take every nightmare you've ever had, mold it into a ball, and sculpt the worst thing you can imagine. The Xeno won't be it, but it will eat what you imagined. That's how bad they are."

Hoenikker gulped.

Mansfield entered, his hands folded behind him.

"I heard you were questioned."

Hoenikker frowned. "The entire experience was ridiculous."

Mansfield nodded. "That's the thing about knowing there's an infiltrator on station. It could be anyone. Leads to paranoia."

"I didn't see them questioning *you*?" Kash said, coming to Hoenikker's defense.

"Mark my word," Mansfield began, "if they don't identify the guilty party soon, all of us will have a turn. It's not something I relish, and I didn't relish it for you, Dr. Hoenikker. I would have stopped them if I could."

Hoenikker stared at the bureaucrat.

Was that empathy?

"Now for what I came here to do," Mansfield said, his voice suddenly hard. He marched past Kash and Hoenikker until he was standing behind Cruz. "Dr. Cruz, may I please have a moment?"

Hoenikker and Kash eased forward a little.

"I've made a breakthrough, Mansfield." Cruz turned, his smile still firm. "You see, I couldn't sleep last night, so I—"

Mansfield held up a hand. "Dr. Cruz, did I or did I not place a moratorium on any new experiments? Did I or did I not indicate that *any* new experiments had to be cleared through me?"

"But you've got to see what I've done. You need to—"

"I don't need to see anything, Dr. Cruz. *Did you not understand me?*"

Cruz straightened. His smile fell. His eyes went dead, like those of a Colonial Marine who knew how to play the game.

"I understood you," he replied, all excitement gone from his voice. "Did you understand me when I indicated that I may have had a breakthrough that could substantially increase the survivability of Colonial Marines in combat?"

"Dr. Cruz, you cannot be trusted," Mansfield replied. "You are relieved. Return to your quarters and stay there."

The bigger man blinked as if he'd been slapped. "What did you say to me?" Cruz growled, stepping toward Mansfield.

"I told you to return to you—"

Hoenikker surprised himself, and leaped to grab Cruz, as did Kash—who put herself between the scientist and Mansfield.

"What did you say to me?" Cruz shouted, muscles jumping in his arms and shoulders. Hoenikker wanted to be anywhere but where he was. Still, he held the bigger man as best he could.

All eyes were on Cruz.

Prior's.

Matthews'.

Fairbanks'.

The two specialists stared, as well.

Mansfield didn't move. He stared into the face of a man who could beat him to a pulp. Hoenikker admired his bravery, though he questioned his good sense. Cruz looked dangerous when he was mad. Hell, Cruz looked dangerous when he was happy.

"I believe I gave you an order, Dr. Cruz," Mansfield said evenly.

Cruz stopped, tensed, and tossed off Hoenikker's hands as if they were nothing. He backed away, chewing the inside of his cheek. Then he turned and marched out of the lab. Mansfield eyed both Hoenikker and Kash. After a moment he spoke.

"Isn't there something you should be doing?"

"Come on." Kash grabbed Hoenikker. "Let's go help Prior and Matthews with the inventory." Hoenikker allowed himself to be pulled away, as long as it was away from Mansfield.

So much for empathy.

16

They found the body the next morning.

All of a sudden the medical lab became the popular place to be. In addition to Dr. Erikson and the body, it hosted Security Specialists Howard and Tacker, Reception Tech Rawlings, and Casualty Operations Specialist Edmonds. Slight and introverted, Edmonds wasn't at all suited to looking at a dead body. Rawlings, on the other hand, had seen plenty of dead bodies from his time in the Colonial Marines.

Brennan lay naked on the table. From the neck down, the only damage was the ragged hole in his shoulder from where the PDT had been removed. The body bore the same white flaccid complexion to be expected from a lifetime of working inside various stations.

His head and face were another thing altogether. It looked as if someone had beaten him to death. Pieces of his skull were missing. Teeth poked through ruined cheeks. An eye had hemorrhaged. His nose was a twisted mess.

Rawlings drew an imaginary line down the center of Brennan's face and noted that one side hadn't been hurt at all.

Rawlings had been in enough fights to know that Brennan's head had been immobilized, probably by someone grabbing his hair in a tight-fisted grip.

"The damage is extensive," Dr. Erikson said, even though it was obvious to everyone in the room. "I removed metal shavings from inside of his mouth and skull. My techs reviewed them, but they're from the common composite used in the fabrication of the station, and much of the furniture."

"Was there anything on his clothes that might have indicated where he was?" Howard asked.

"He was found naked, his clothes already removed," Rawlings said, having seen Brennan *in situ* where he'd been stashed. The body had been found in a rarely used supply room.

"We'll need to do a search for the clothes," Tacker said, "but they've probably already been put in the incinerator. We'll do a tracker pull to see everyone who had access to it in the last six hours or so."

Howard nodded. "Then we can determine if Hoenikker or Fairbanks was anywhere near where the body was found," he said. "It seems convenient, finding the body right after we released them from custody." She pulled out her vid display unit and began to punch up information.

Rawlings considered her logic. Not finding the body might have been better. Whoever had killed Brennan, if they could have made it to Fabrications, they could have used the section's industrial-sized incinerator. That would have predicated them carrying a body through corridors teeming with people—much easier to spot in the video record. No, if Rawlings had to guess, Brennan hadn't moved far. His body had been stuffed in that room for convenience. Most likely the killer waited for a time during the night when the corridors were emptier, to move the body as quickly as possible.

"Hoenikker was in his lab the entire time," Howard said. "But Fairbanks fell off the grid again." She eyed Tacker, who nodded.

"I think we have a suspect," he said. "Do you think it was a lovers' quarrel?"

"If what Fairbanks said was true," she began, "then yes, it could have been a crime of passion."

"Wait a moment," Rawlings said. "Are you saying that Brennan and Fairbanks…" He laughed. "Can't possibly be."

"Fairbanks told us that Brennan came to his room so they could hook up," Howard said.

"I don't know why Brennan went to his room, but I can tell you that Brennan wasn't inclined that way. In fact, Brennan is—was—pretty much asexual. He spent every waking hour playing first-person shooters, video games. His file is full of reprimands from Comms Chief Oshita."

"How do you know about his sexual orientation?" Tacker asked. "It's not something we keep in personnel files."

"I just know," Rawlings said. "Small things. Phrases used. Words used. We're close units in the Colonial Marines. We know each other's inclinations. Not that it matters, but we know it. It's the same here." He stared straight at Howard. "I know everyone's inclinations. I pay attention."

She broke his gaze to stare at the body.

"Let's pretend you're right," Tacker said. "Then why? Why is this body so battered?"

Rawlings shrugged. "I'm not Security. I just know the people in my station."

"Where's Fairbanks now?" Tacker asked. "Or is he off the grid again?"

Howard attended her vid display. "No. He's on the grid. We have him currently in the laboratory, providing support to a Fabrications team." She paused again. "Looks like they're replacing some of the glass fronts on the containment rooms."

"Put security outside the lab. No reason to go in there if we don't have to. The last thing I need is Mansfield complaining to Flowers," Tacker said. "Let's go take a look at Fairbanks' quarters. And get someone from Logistics to join us."

"One more thing," Dr. Erikson said, holding up a hand.

Tacker stepped from foot to foot. "What is it?"

"Comms Specialist Brennan was poisoned."

"Poisoned?" Tacker stopped moving. His eyes narrowed. "How?"

The doctor turned Brennan's head. "Note the blackening of the tongue and the petechia of the eye. Nothing else could cause this. What type of poison it is? We're not sure at this point, but it's not anything we have on the station."

"Why would someone poison a guy they just beat to a bloody pulp?" Howard asked.

Rawlings wanted to know the same thing. It made no sense.

Tacker chewed on his cheek for a moment, then nodded slightly. "Perhaps the beating was out of rage, but then when the killer realized he hadn't completed the job, he used poison." He leaned over to stare into Brennan's mouth. "That's the only explanation I can come up with. But where did the poison come from?"

"Why not just choke him, or beat him some more?" Howard asked.

"Maybe the killer didn't want to be a killer. Poison is a lot less hands-on," Tacker said. Then he turned toward the door. "Come on. Let's go to Fairbanks' quarters."

Once outside the medlab, Rawlings realized how tense he'd been. Dealing with bodies always took him back to his days in the Colonial Marines. He held out his hands. The one on the right, metal, emblazoned with a Weyland-Yutani stamp. The one on the left, flesh and blood, trembling slightly as his nerves flared, memories of the bodies, his friends, dead and in ditches on a far-away LV.

Looking up, he noted that the others had already reached the end of the corridor and turned the corner. He wanted to be with them and see this through. So, he hurried after them, arriving at Brennan's room just as Tacker and Howard did. They were joined by Buggy from Logistics.

Tacker entered the room first. He went to the middle of the room and stood. Not touching anything. His gaze raking over everything.

From the doorway, Rawlings could see a perfectly made bed on the right. On the left were a metal bureau and a small desk and chair. A room like any other. A room like his own. So mundane. It would have been difficult to believe a murder had taken place here, had he not seen similar scenes before. Like the church they'd found sitting serene in a forest glen. A place of worship, a center for gathering, the church had been a locus for community and religion for three decades. Then they'd opened the door and found the missing villagers inside, bloody, draped across the pews, dead where they had been shot, bodies ravaged by the M41 Pulse Rifle used by an AWOL Colonial Marine.

He shook his head to chase away the memory.

Tacker sniffed the air. "Smell that? Disinfectant."

Howard stepped into the room. She sniffed as well. "Heavy duty cleaner." Stepping over to the desk, she pulled on plastic gloves, bent down, and touched the edge. She straightened. "This desk is new."

Buggy bent down, and ran a scanner over the inventory control sticker underneath the desktop. He read the results.

"Nope. This is the one assigned to the room."

"Can't be." Howard shook her head. "Know what I think? I think Fairbanks put his old inventory control tag on a new table, and put the new one on his old table. It's probably been put back into storage. Maybe even cleaned up. He'd have wanted to make sure there wasn't any evidence left on it."

Tacker knelt down, peering at the wall beside the table.

"Is it me, or are those spots?" he said, pointing.

Howard joined him. "We can have those tested."

"Let's do it," Tacker said. "Meanwhile, let's go have a chat with Fairbanks. I think we have a better understanding of what went on here." Both he and Howard strode out of the room, leaving Buggy and Rawlings alone.

"Did you see the body?" Buggy asked.

Rawlings nodded. "It was pretty bad. Face bashed in and all that."

"How you holding up?" Buggy asked.

"A little anxious. Brought back memories." He grinned as the interior of the church was superimposed on the room, the body of an elderly woman twisted and staring at him, the unasked question, *why did you let him do this to us*, hanging in the air. "To be expected, I suppose." He turned toward the door. "What I need is some coffee. Want to join me?"

Buggy hesitated, then grinned as well. "Sure. I'll join."

They left the murder scene behind and headed to a better place.

17

Fairbanks was in a personal hell.

He never should have let Hyperdyne Corporation blackmail him. He should have informed Security the moment he returned to the station. That would have been the proper thing to do, but his cowardice hadn't let him. Instead, he hid and did their bidding and installed software into the system until even the most inadequate and incompetent comms specialist had tracked him down.

And then instead of turning him in like he should have, the guy had the temerity to try and blackmail him again. How could Fairbanks have allowed that to happen? Once was bad enough, but to let himself be blackmailed two times…

How could he look himself in the mirror?

Yelling began at the front of the lab.

Fairbanks spun to the sound, but it was only the large black-skinned scientist, screaming at his boss. Fairbanks watched in fascination as the smaller man just stared into the face of the violent man, until, with barely a few words, the larger of the two was storming out of the lab.

That was the kind of strength Fairbanks appreciated. Strength from silence. Strength from a perceived position of weakness. Fairbanks had never been a big man, nor would he ever be, but to be in a position to know people and have people do your bidding—that was an envious position. Like Rawlings. Sure, the man had been a Colonial Marine; and sure, he'd lost a hand. But he knew everyone and everyone knew him. If he were to ask around, he doubted there was a single person who had a problem with him.

Fairbanks wanted to be someone like that. He didn't want to be a traitor. He didn't want to be an infiltrator. He just wanted to be someone good, whom others respected.

"Get your head out of the clouds, Fairbanks," Glover said. "Are you taking notes or what?"

Fairbanks jumped, and attended his vid display.

"This is another one that needs to be replaced. We have pitting and scoring in three of the four quadrants."

Fairbanks looked nervously inside the containment room, at the rat with large spider legs. He shuddered as he imagined the creature crawling over him.

"Fairbanks?" Glover said. "Are you with me?"

"Uh, yes. That, uh, makes seven out of the nine we've checked, and we still have six to go."

The third specialist spoke up. "No way are we going to be able to provide that many fronts. Do you realize the process?" His name was Ching, and he worked in Fabrications.

"Don't you recycle any of the tungsten from these fronts?" Fairbanks asked. "Can't they be recovered?"

Ching sighed and looked as if his lunch wasn't sitting well. "Recovery is a long procedure. Even if we did recover the tungsten, the degradation would be too much."

"But added to what I can supply now," Fairbanks pressed,

"if you recovered what's in these, would it be better than what we have?"

"Yes." Ching nodded grudgingly. "Marginally."

"If 'marginally' is the best we can do, then I say we do it," Fairbanks said.

They moved to the next containment area, where lights were strobing in different colors, for no apparent reason. This unit appeared to be empty, but just as Fairbanks was going to dismiss it, he spied the spiky shape of a large creature that was blending into the background.

The door to the lab opened and Security Specialists Tacker and Howard entered. Fairbanks caught them in his peripheral vision, and turned away. The last thing he wanted was for them to notice he was there. So far he'd been able to steer clear of them. If he could just keep it up—

"Fairbanks," Tacker said. "Can we have a word?"

He looked into the eyes of Ching and Glover. Both of the men had the odd combination of curiosity and accusation. Was it that easy to accuse a fellow worker? They didn't know what he'd done. He shouldn't be thought of as being guilty, just because of an accusation. Where was the brotherhood?

"Fairbanks. I'm talking to you," Tacker said, closer.

Ching backed away.

As did Glover.

Without turning, Fairbanks said, "I'm in the middle of an inventory. If we can do this when I'm finished—"

"You are finished," Tacker said.

Howard appeared next to him and gently but firmly removed the vid display from his hands.

Fairbanks turned.

Everyone was staring at him.

His face burned red.

"What is it you want?"

"You're accused of the murder of Comms Specialist Brennan. You will come with us."

"Come with you?" he asked, his voice rising several octaves. "I don't know what you're talking about."

"Fairbanks, we've been to your room. We found the table you replaced. We've scanned the blood you failed to clean up. You killed Brennan, and now you need to be held accountable."

In that moment, everything he'd ever dreamed of accomplishing died, and he let out an awful groan.

Tacker sighed. "Howard. If you will?"

Howard reached for his elbow.

Fairbanks panicked. He punched her in the face—to no effect except to hurt his hand. He backed into the workstation in front of the containment area. He looked down and saw several buttons.

"Don't touch anything," one of the scientists warned.

One button said ABORT.

The other said RELEASE.

He glanced up, and everyone seemed to be moving in slow motion.

"Don't do it," Hoenikker cried.

Fairbanks punched the RELEASE button and dove.

The door sprung open but nothing seemed to happen.

No one moved for a good ten seconds.

Then Ching went to close it, and as he reached for it, his arm disappeared.

A creature came into existence—large, four legs, the front two as striking claws. Tentacle-like protrusions from its mouth chewed at Ching's arm, then spit it to the side. It blinked at everyone as if seeing them for the first time, then leaned back and let out an awful roar.

Then it disappeared.

"It's Leon-895," someone shouted. "The idiot let it out."

Mansfield backed toward the door. "I'll seal the room," he shouted.

Howard tried to pull her weapon, but was decapitated before she could complete the move. Her head rolled to Fairbanks' feet and he screamed like a child, even as the woman's blood fountained into the air.

Two of the scientists were hurled to the floor.

The "Leon" materialized above one of them, the fat one, ripping at the scientist's chest with its claws. He fell to his knees, grabbing his chest.

Another of the scientists, Hoenikker, ran toward the exit. The creature could barely be discerned chasing after him, knocking things and people down as it loped.

Mansfield tried to escape through the door. He hit the button and the creature was on him, ripping great gouts of meat and muscle from his small boney frame. Blood flew and covered part of the beast, and even as it chameleoned to the colors of the laboratory behind it, the red swath marked it as a killer.

The door opened and Hoenikker ran through it.

The creature followed.

Fairbanks saw his opportunity. He bolted from the room and took off the other way.

18

Hoenikker paused to catch his breath. Had that really happened? Had that dumb shit really opened one of the containment rooms? The one that contained Leon-895?

A scream sounded from behind him.

Hoenikker spun and watched in terrible fascination as a specialist had his throat ripped out by the Leon. The only parts of the creature he could discern were those covered in blood.

For one brief dreadful instant, the creature materialized. No longer did it blend into the background. Now it was merely the horrific creature Cruz had helped create. Almost the size of a human, with four legs, the center one propelling it forward while the outside legs helped it to maintain balance. It began to move toward Hoenikker with a slow, steady gate.

“Shoo,” he said. “Shoo!” He batted the air with his hands as he backed away. Why was it following him? What had he done to deserve its attention?

“Out of the way!” A security guard ran up and pushed him aside.

The woman held up a pistol.

She fired but missed.

The Leon winked out of sight.

Hoenikker could track it because of the blood, but the security guard didn't know what had happened. She straightened and looked around.

"Where did it go?"

She flew against one wall.

Then the other.

Then the ceiling.

Then the floor.

Her face condensed upon itself as a great muscular weight was applied and the head was crushed into a parody of itself.

The smell of her death hit Hoenikker in the face, the distilled essence of blood and offal and brains. His back arched as he retched. Just the sight of her face being crushed was enough to change him. But he had to get away. Hoenikker turned to run, and crashed into a group of people.

"Hey, now."

"Watch where you're going."

He picked himself up off the floor and tried to push past, but they held him firm.

"Looks like he's running from the devil," one said, laughing.

"Let me go," Hoenikker begged. "It's coming."

All eyes turned to stare down the corridor.

"There's nothing th—" The speaker was snatched forward, then slammed into the wall.

Suddenly the alarm sounded.

"I don't see it," someone said. Then he too was thrown back.

Hoenikker managed to push past, then was knocked into the side of the corridor as the others turned and fled, jostling him with their urgent need to survive. He fell to one knee, but hurriedly struggled to his feet. He had his own urgent need to survive.

Another security specialist appeared. This one was a man carrying a pulse rifle. As deadly as the weapon seemed, Hoenikker knew it wouldn't be enough.

"Run," he said, voice cracking.

"I got this," the man said, suicidally obtuse.

But there was nothing to get.

No target.

Only a corridor with dead people.

Still, Hoenikker backed away.

The Leon materialized above the security specialist.

Hoenikker was about to shout for the man to look up, but it was too late. The Leon grabbed the man by the neck, lifted him up, and snapped a bite out of the top of his skull, the brain bleeding like it was the top of a man-size ice cream cone.

The smell hit Hoenikker again. He was so used to the disinfectant aroma of a lab. Even outside of the work area, the station had a clean metallic smell, despite the rats and the close proximity of humans. It was the air scrubbers and the filters that did the job. But here, next to a hunter, the smell of the dying combined with the new scents of internal organs and sweetbreads made him want to vent everything that was inside of him.

Another alarm sounded, this one higher pitched. This one was matched by the sound of running feet.

Five guards turned the corner, only they looked different. Their faces, all identical, were devoid of emotion. Their bodies were the color of the walls and floor—their own form of chameleonism, he supposed. Each held a pistol in his right hand. Their movements were too fluid. Too neat.

Synths.

One grabbed him and put its arms around him. Like a hug, but one he couldn't escape. Hoenikker wasn't sure if the gesture was meant to protect him or detain him. He struggled briefly, but found it almost impossible to even move. The synth spun and pinned him against the wall, shielding him with its back. Hoenikker craned his head to watch.

The remaining four synths fanned out in the corridor, looking back and forth, trying to find a target.

"Switch to infrared," he shouted. "It's invisible to the naked eye."

All heads swiveled to him, then each other, then to a spot near the corner of wall and the ceiling. Hoenikker saw the swatch of red just as the synths opened fire.

The Leon materialized like static, as each round found a home. It backed away and they chased after it, around a corner in the corridor. Now was the time Hoenikker should have been trying to run, but he wanted to know what was happening. The science part of his brain fought with his need to survive.

Two synths crashed back into sight, against the wall, as if thrown. The synth that was holding him let go and rushed around the corner, immediately opening fire with its pistol.

Hoenikker heard a dozen shots as he crept forward.

He was about ready to turn the corner when a great invisible beast rushed past him, knocking him to the ground. It held him there, its terrible maw and gnashing teeth mere feet from his face. All the creature had to do was lean down and take a bite, and Hoenikker's life would be ended.

Three synths turned the corner, raised their pistols, and fired.

Leon-895 took off.

They ran after it, chasing it down the corridor and around the corner.

Hoenikker lay on his back, trying to gather enough sense to stand. He'd been inches from death. He didn't know *why* he'd survived. Was the creature interested in him? Was there a sentience inside Leon-895 of which they'd never become aware?

Kash appeared above him.

"Hoenikker? Tim?" she said breathlessly. "Are you alright?"

He felt himself. Somehow, he'd gone unscathed. The creature had seemed to fixate on him. Why was that? Why had it followed him, or had Hoenikker just been unlucky enough to have been in the way of its retreat? Had it been pure coincidence? Would it have followed him had he turned left instead of right?

"Tim," she said, kneeling and gently shaking him by the shoulders. "Are you alright?"

"Yeah," he said, softly. Then with a little more strength he repeated, "Yeah. I think I am."

He sat up.

"What about the others?" he asked.

She shook her head. "Dead. So many. Dead."

19

The number of dead was unimaginable. All from a single Leon-895, something no one on the station knew existed until now. To think that a simple creature captured from the jungles of LV-895 could have wrought so much havoc.

Rawlings made his usual rounds, exchanging coffee for gossip, and could detect fear circling the edges of every conversation.

It was only going to get worse.

He also had it on good authority that the next day would bring not only wholesale changes to the way Pala Station was being run, but more of the Xenomorphs on which the scientists had experimented before. He'd only ever seen one of the adults, but that had sent chills through him as he watched it chase down a sample of local fauna, its jaws extending from its body to rip the creature in half.

Which was why he'd called the meeting. He hadn't anticipated needing one so soon. When he'd first divined the idea of creating a group of common concern among the station's veterans, he'd thought they might benefit from a group of close comrades, to vent about various issues that only they could understand. As a group they were all older than their peers, and age brought with it a certain worldliness and weariness.

Now it was more than that. His gut told him that they might need the group to survive.

They met in the mess hall, gathering between breakfast and lunch. A few workers were refilling some of the drinking containers, but other than that, they were alone. Buggy from Comms sat across the table from him, sipping soda loudly through a straw. Flores and Dudt sat beside Buggy, both from Security, and both new to Weyland-Yutani corporate, so basically fresh off the boat.

McGann from Engineering sat beside Rawlings, with Chase from Logistics. They were only waiting on Dr. Cruz to arrive to establish their quorum.

"Any news on Fairbanks?" Chase asked the two security specialists. Flores shook her head and glanced first at Dudt before answering.

"It's like he disappeared. There's no pings from his PDT. Nothing."

"I bet he ripped it out," Dudt said. He had red hair and skin so white you imagined he'd never been in the sun. "That's what he did to Brennan."

"There are ways to hide the signal," Buggy said. "In special services, we had devices that adhered to the outside of the skin where the implant was. That blocked the signal, and it scrambled it so even if something leaked, nothing could read it."

"What are they saying in Log about Fairbanks?" Rawlings asked Chase.

"We're all pretty stunned," he replied. "Fairbanks was a standup guy. We never knew he was into espionage. I mean, why would you even do something like that—and then to kill Brennan? I heard Fairbanks did a number on his face."

"It wasn't pretty," Rawlings said.

Chase's eyes brightened. "You were there?" Then he nodded to himself. "Of course you were. You go everywhere."

"I just try to pay attention." Rawlings sipped from his cup of coffee. "What about you, McGann? Heard anything?"

A thirty-something, acne-faced woman with a dark ponytail, she shrugged. "We're always hearing things. Seems the rat problem is finally under control. We haven't had to pull any extra duty." She knocked on the table for luck. "But there's some talk about the incoming Xeno specimens. Between us and Fabrications, we're concerned about containment."

"Yeah," Chase said. "Don't those scientists have any security protocols? I mean, that Leon should have never gotten out. The lab should have been locked down immediately."

"Security has an answer for that," Flores said. "They're putting two synths in the lab, so if there's another problem, they can take care of it before it gets out of hand. Word has it that there will be no more breaches. Before that happens, the station commander will order all the specimens killed."

"Not that we've heard from the station commander at all," Chase said.

Rawlings took a sip of his coffee. "He's on the outs. It's the incoming commander who said that. We get to meet him tomorrow. Get ready for an ass reaming."

"We've already been warned down in Security," Dudt said. "The ass reaming has begun by remote control."

"Do you think that's going to be enough?" McGann asked, her eyes as hard as flint. They were surrounded by laugh lines that seemed seldom used.

"It's going to have to be," Cruz said, entering the room. He grabbed some iced tea and a straw and pulled up a chair to sit at the head of the table. Rawlings nodded to him.

Rawlings had been the highest ranking when they were in the Colonial Marines, rising to the rank of warrant officer. But here on Pala Station, the scientists were the big men on campus. The station staff were all about supporting them. So, Cruz was *de facto* in charge of their little group, even though it was Rawlings who'd created it.

"How are you guys recovering?" Rawlings asked. He'd helped process the bodies, so he knew of the decimation the scientific staff had experienced.

"Not good," Cruz said. "I feel like shit that I wasn't there to help."

"I heard Mansfield relieved you," Rawlings said carefully. Cruz glanced at him for a sharp-eyed second, then shrugged. "Difference of opinion. You know the deal. Fucking civilians."

The others all nodded. Each had experienced their own run-ins. Each one knew what it was like to be in the shit. They might all be fucking civilians now, but their muscle memory was still as marines. For a moment everyone had a faraway look, as if remembering another time and another place, when things were different.

"Mansfield isn't going to be relieving anyone soon," Rawlings said.

"We also lost Prior and Matthews. Matthews was a thumb-sucker," Cruz said. "Don't know how he got the job, but Prior was a solid scientist. He knew his shit."

"I heard Matthews wasn't touched," Chase said.

"He wasn't. Heart attack. Mind you, I might have had one too, had I seen Leon in action," Cruz admitted.

"And they still haven't found it," Dudt said. "It's still somewhere on the station."

"What about the synths?" Rawlings asked. "I heard they were doing patrols."

"Even with their advancements, they can't seem to find it," Flores said.

"I fucking hate that it killed people," Cruz said. "I know there are those who blame me, because I was the one who experimented on it. But can you imagine if we can harvest the chameleon ability of the beast onto power armor?" He smiled and leaned forward. "Imagine going into combat being invisible."

"All in the name of science," Chase said, rolling his eyes.

Cruz gave him a hard look. "Yes. In the name of science. Listen, people die. Shit happens. We're not here at the edge of the known universe to fuck around. We're here to develop technology that will save marines."

Rawlings held up a finger. "That, and something else, my friend. We're here to develop technology sold by the Weyland-Yutani Corporation, for a handsome profit."

"The man's got to get paid," Cruz said. "That's for sure." He leaned back. "Enough of the small talk. Why did you bring us together? I mean, I'm all up for a group of 'common concern,' but I wasn't planning on having weekly meetings. I have a laundry list of things to do, not to mention seeing if we can fix the damage done by Leon-895."

Rawlings looked around the table. Everyone was staring at him, waiting for a response.

"Here's the deal," he began. "We all know there's been two containment problems with the lab. We also know that the containment fronts aren't what they should be. Log, and Fab, and Engineering are working on it, but there's only so much they can do—and now we're about to bring down the second round of specimens from the orbital mining facility *Katanga*. It's been in space for more than twenty years, and has been the station's source of Xenomorph specimens. These are the real deal. As bad as Leon-895 was, these are far worse. Do you remember that feeling you got in your guts before a mission, when you knew for certain you were going to be shot?"

Everyone nodded their head.

"I have that feeling now," Rawlings said. "I can't quantify it, I can't science it, I can't prove it, but I know some serious shit is about to go down, and I want to make sure we at least have a chance at surviving it."

"What do you think is going to happen?" McGann asked.

"Murphy," Rawlings said flatly. "Murphy's Law is going to happen. We're going to have all the protocols in place, we're going to have plans for how to mitigate problems, and still bad shit will ensue, and we won't have any control over it whatsoever."

"Murphy," mumbled Cruz.

The rest did the same.

"So, what is it we can do?" Flores asked.

"Be aware of what's going on. Constantly check your six," Cruz said. He glanced at Rawlings, then at the others. "I've had the same flutters in my stomach, as well. We need to be careful. Who here has personal weapons?"

No one raised their hands.

"Come on. No bullshit," Cruz said. "I have body armor, a pulse rifle, and a flamethrower—don't ask. What about the rest of you? No Colonial Marine, current or former, would let themselves be caught dead without a weapon. So, give."

"Dudt and I each have a full complement of weapons we were issued, that we store in our hooches," Flores said.

"Can you get more if necessary?" Rawlings asked.

She glanced at Dudt, who nodded, then nodded to the group.

"I have two pistols," McGann said.

"I have a pulse rifle, but hardly any ammo," Chase said.

"What about you, Rawlings?" Cruz asked.

Rawlings sipped from his cup of coffee.

"I have three pulse rifles and five thousand rounds of ammo."

"HFS," Chase said.

"How'd you get so much?" Flores asked, suspiciously.

Rawlings grinned and shrugged. "I just asked for things. People gave them, and sometimes when people leave, they leave stuff that hasn't been inventoried. No big deal. I'm not looking to overthrow anything.

"I'm just looking to survive."

20

All the essential staff were packed into the mess hall. The tables and chairs had been removed so everyone was standing shoulder-to-shoulder, butt-to-butt, uncomfortable in the indescribable way that can only be understood by being in that situation.

Security personnel lined the walls. Although they didn't carry weapons, their demeanor was deadly serious. The scientists—or what was left of them, at least—had been placed in the front row. Étienne, Kash, Hoenikker, and Cruz, whose suspension had been negated by the death of Mansfield. Ironically, because of his seniority, he'd been put in charge.

Hoenikker didn't care who was in charge, but it seemed to him a little like the fox guarding the henhouse.

The section chiefs were lined up at the head of the room, silently facing out over the crowd, and they didn't look happy. Several heads were down. Conspicuous by their absences were Station Chief Crowther and Deputy Station Chief Thompson.

Finally, a newcomer—a man—entered wearing a white uniform. He stopped in front of each chief, shook hands, and said a few words the rest couldn't hear.

"Let the ass reaming begin," Cruz said under his breath.

"Anyone know about this guy?" Étienne asked.

"Not a word." Kash shook her head.

The man turned and centered himself in front of the section chiefs. He had piercing blue eyes and the chiseled face of someone who spent a lot of time at the gym. His figure beneath the uniform seemed to tell the same story.

"Men and women of Pala Station, I am your new station commander," he said so all could hear. "My name is Vincent Bellows. Station Chief Crowther has been relieved for cause, and will be taking a long voyage back to headquarters." His words were neither angry nor endearing. They were delivered in a flat, businesslike manner to be expected of a senior Weyland-Yutani executive.

"Deputy Station Chief Thompson has also been relieved," he continued. "He will be joining Crowther on his journey. But that's irrelevant, as far as you're concerned. I'm here to point out to all of you that the mission of Pala Station is research. Everything we do here, everything *you* do here, is to advance Weyland-Yutani capabilities, and to increase corporate profits.

"Every time someone dies, we have to pay out death benefits. Every time something breaks, it needs to be replaced. Our job is not one of dying and breaking, it is one of discovery.

"To date, we have managed to develop acid-resistant armor technology which we can sell the Colonial Marines," Bellows said. "As briefed by Dr. Cruz, we also have another opportunity to improve armor through the creation of biological stealth technology, although that specimen seems to have disappeared. I have been informed by Security Chief Rodriguez that motion sensors are being positioned in order to try and track the creature. If you see it, do *not* engage. Note the location, get to safety, and inform Security."

He paused, likely for effect, Hoenikker guessed.

"Up to now, it seems as if your greatest single shared asset has been incompetence. Let me assure you that this will cease. If I relieve you from duty, I will ensure that you are on the slowest ship back to corporate, and that any bonuses you've earned during your time here will not be paid. Pala Station needs to produce. To do that, I need everyone's very best. From Logistics to Personnel. From Fabrications to Engineering. From Security to Medical. I need everyone to know their job, and perform it perfectly.

"As for the scientists, I need you to follow scientific safety protocols. If any more specimens escape, I will hold you personally responsible. I will shut down research until I can get more qualified scientists. Certainly, corporate will be mad at me, but I'm used to people being mad at me. If there's one thing I know it's Weyland-Yutani policies, and trust me when I say that I have enough policies in my back pocket to ensure my own continued survival. So, do not—I repeat, do *not*—tempt me to shut something down, or kick someone off the station.

"I'll do it in a corporate minute.

"Finally, there will be no more hunting trips outside of the station, and no need to maintain an external facility. We have enough work to do without leaving to find something else." He placed his hands behind his back as he leaned forward. "Now, are there any questions?"

Silence.

"Any questions? Come on. Now is your chance."

No one responded.

"Alright, I can see that the lot of you are nervous," he said. "So, I will answer the most obvious concern. What is happening next. The *San Lorenzo* arrived in orbit two days ago. That's how I got here. Right now, synths are acquiring specimens from *Katanga*. They'll be shuttling them down later this afternoon.

"As you know, these specimens are some of the most dangerous creatures we've ever encountered, which is why Pala Station is in the middle of nowhere. We don't want any of the specimens getting into population centers. What does that mean? It means they are dangerous. They are *beyond* dangerous. To that end, I will be posting extra security in the lab, in order to protect station personnel."

He stared at the assembled mass, nodded once, then turned on his heel and left. The moment he was out the door, the room let out a collective sigh. Everyone began to move toward the exit.

The section chiefs left first, single file out the door, heads still down. Hoenikker wondered if they didn't have another, more private meeting where they would each be told in explicit terms what was expected of them.

Cruz and Kash headed out the door, and Hoenikker would have followed, but Rawlings stopped him.

"A moment," Rawlings said.

Hoenikker stared into the scarred black face of the reception tech. The man's smile always seemed to be in place. Perhaps the way he went through life. Certainly better than frowning, he supposed.

"Sure," Hoenikker said. "How can I help you?"

"I just wanted to let you know that things are going to get a little bit jumpier around here."

"Jumpier?" Hoenikker said. "Than what?"

The smile faded a bit. "Folks are going to be quicker to get angry, and quicker to react. What with our new station chief and a new group of specimens, the staff are going to be worried. They know what these things can do if they get out, and what they don't know, they make up."

"I'm not sure why you're talking to me about this," Hoenikker said, glancing back to the doorway and freedom.

"It's just that you will be closest to the action. Closer to the danger. You're going to be one of the first ones to know if something isn't right."

Hoenikker nodded.

"So, if you find yourself needing a place to run, or needing to tell others it's *time* to run, I'm that person. I can keep you safe in the event…" He didn't finish.

Hoenikker frowned. "In the event of what, exactly?"

Rawlings' smiled widened again. "I don't rightly know, but my guess is that when it happens, you'll know."

Then he left, leaving Hoenikker standing in a room that had quickly emptied.

Two times specimens had gotten free, just since he had arrived. Would the same happen with the Xenomorphs? *Could* the same happen with Xenomorphs? He was so lost in the possibilities of it, he didn't notice the mess hall staff trying to put the room back together and prepare for dinner, until one of them came up to him and politely asked him to leave.

21

Cruz was in charge, and he wanted everyone to know it, making Hoenikker feel vaguely like a Colonial Marine instead of a scientist. They'd been waiting for him, and he felt this heat from Cruz's gaze as he entered the lab, the last scientist to do so.

While Hoenikker hadn't exactly liked Mansfield, at least the Weyland-Yutani bureaucrat knew how to keep things organized. Now Cruz was the boss. Cruz—the same person who enjoyed frosting and roasting specimens. Hoenikker glanced at the others as he took his seat.

No one was looking at Cruz. They'd all found their own horizons at which to stare.

"Now that we're all present," Cruz began, clearing his voice, "here's how things are going to be. Prior and Matthews are gone. It sucks, but that's the way it is. Their… departure makes it harder on us."

Hoenikker watched Étienne mouth the word *departure*.

"Now we have to perform the functions of six scientists with only four. While it's easier to replace Prior, because

I'm a xenobiologist, replacing Matthews—no matter his individual eccentricities—will be much more difficult. His chemical engineering skills will be missed. So, we're all going to have to buck up and take on more responsibility. Frankly, if the rest of the station was run the way we're going to be running the lab, starting immediately, we'd all be in much better shape."

Étienne formed the words *better shape*. This time, Cruz saw him.

"Is there something you want to share with the group, Étienne?"

"No." Étienne shook his head, and stared at the floor. "I'm fine."

Cruz sneered. "You don't look fine. It looks like you have something you want to say."

Étienne sighed, then glanced up. "Don't you think you're taking this 'being in charge' bit a little too seriously?"

Cruz's face hardened. "Too seriously? People have died, Étienne. This is *very* serious."

"You might have died, had you not been sent to your room for malfeasance," Étienne replied. "You were just lucky enough to have been kicked out of the lab."

"Malfeasance?" Cruz quickly rose to his feet. "Who the hell do you think you are, you little French cocksucker?" He moved toward where Étienne sat, but Kash stood and placed a palm on his chest.

"Dr. Cruz? Is this really the way you wanted the meeting to go?" she asked, her voice low and level. He tried to push past her, but she kept in his way, gently but firmly pressing her hand into his chest, trying to lock eyes with him. Finally, he looked at her. "Let's all sit down and apologize, okay? After all, we're scientists, not brawlers."

Cruz glanced from her to Étienne, then seemed to sag.

"You're right of course." He returned to his seat, smoothed down the front of his lab coat, and smiled the sort of smile someone might wear if he or she were disemboweling a cat and enjoying it immensely. "I'm sorry that I called you a French cocksucker."

Étienne smiled as well, his the sort Hoenikker would expect an enemy to provide at the funeral of their rival.

"I accept your apology." He paused a moment, then said, "And I'm sorry I've been thinking you're an overbearing psychotic windbag who shouldn't be in charge of yourself, much less a team of scientists. I'm sorry that I know we're pretty much all going to die because of your need to self-medicate your PTSD by killing specimens. And finally, I'm sorry you weren't in here when Leon-895 escaped, because I'm sure either Matthews or Prior would still be alive."

His eyes going wide, Hoenikker turned to watch Cruz as Étienne spoke, waiting for the bigger man to launch himself across the table. But the reaction was anything but what he expected. Instead of getting angry, Cruz began to laugh. Full-out guffaws that made Kash look at Hoenikker with eyes that asked, *Is he crazy?*

"That's good, Étienne," Cruz said. "That's rich. You reminded me what it was like back in the barracks when we used to exchange *your* mama jokes. You've got to learn to get as good as you give." Cruz glanced around the table. "And you're right about Leon-895. It probably would have come for me, so in a strange way, I owe Mansfield my life. That said, I'm still in charge, and we need to pull together.

"Speaking of Leon-895," he added, "has there been any news?"

"Security is doing a search, and placing the motion sensors," Kash said, "but their number one priority is to make certain the specimens from *Katanga* arrive safely." She glanced at Hoenikker. "Wait until you see them. Going to make you wished you'd stayed in your office."

Hoenikker swallowed hard. He really just wanted his alien artifacts. After all, they couldn't bite back.

"I'm putting Kash in charge of the Xenomorph experimentation," Cruz said. "We're already aware of their morphology, so we need to make certain we experiment during all phases. Hoenikker, this is all new to you, so keep your eyes open and your hands in your pockets. Don't do anything unless Kash gives you the go-ahead."

Hoenikker nodded, feeling a bit like he'd shown up three weeks late for kindergarten.

Cruz had a few more words, then directed Étienne to supervise the insertion of the new glass fronts for the specimen containment areas. As it turned out, Engineering and Fabrications had put their heads together and determined that they did, indeed, have enough tungsten, as long as they spread the mixture more thinly than before. They assured Cruz, however, that the barriers would still be within safety protocols.

Cruz left to meet with Security about the specimen transfer.

Which left Hoenikker and Kash alone.

Then the engineering staff arrived, accompanied by a pair of synths. The two scientists watched as the fronts to the empty containment rooms were removed, one by one, and replaced with new ones. The process was laborious, made even more so by Étienne's insistence that everything be just right. Hoenikker didn't mind it at all, though. The safer they were, the better he felt. After they'd watched the removal and installation of two fronts, Hoenikker turned to Kash.

"What's the story about *Katanga*, anyway?" Hoenikker asked.

"It's been hanging over our heads like the Sword of Damocles for more than twenty years," Kash said. "It was originally created as a facility for a terraforming planet. The problem was that the colonists encountered Xenomorphs on the planet, and were forced to flee to the mine. Then, of course, the mine became infested, and all was lost."

"By the same creatures that were on the planet?" he asked.

She nodded. "Appears so. These particular Xenomorphs like to use human bodies to gestate. When it's time to give birth, they just about ruin everything on their way out."

Hoenikker shuddered, trying not to picture what he'd just been told.

"So, then they built Pala Station."

"No. Evidently," Kash said, "Pala Station was already here. They transported the mine from another solar system to this one."

"I thought it was purpose built for the Xenomorphs?"

"Nope," she said.

"Then why put Pala Station here? What makes this planet so important? I thought Pala was built to support research into the Xenomorphs on *Katanga*? But if Pala was already here, then it had to have been built for a different reason."

Kash shook her head. "I can't tell you for sure. But every now and then Mansfield would bring in an artifact covered in strange glyphs." His pulse quickened at her words. "There are also areas of the station that are off limits to everyone but Security. I mean, if the station was built for a purely scientific reason, then why wouldn't they allow us full access? Cruz believes there's an entire other crew doing side-by-side experimentation in the part of the station we aren't allowed to enter."

"That seems a little far-fetched," he said. "But he seems the sort who would buy into conspiracy theories."

"I agree, on both counts, but there's something they aren't telling us," Kash said.

Hoenikker scratched his head. "So, for the past twenty-plus years the *San Lorenzo* or some other ship supplies us with specimens?"

She nodded. "I heard that they originally sent scientific teams to try and collect specimens, but that didn't end well. Since then, they've had military research teams that collect Xeno specimens in their egg form, and cryochamber them to us at regular intervals. My predecessor said that they only had one delivery during his tenure at Pala Station. So far, this would be my third."

"I thought there had been only one other," he said.

She made a sour face. "Security protocols forced us to kill them all before we could really begin testing."

He eyed the two synths standing against a wall, almost blending into the machinery. Having seen them in action, he knew how fast they could move. Yet as fast as they were, they'd been unable to capture the Leon. He hoped they'd fare better with the Xenomorphs.

The scientific part of him was interested in their morphology. The human part of him was scared shitless.

22

The next morning the scientists were in the lab before sunrise. They checked the integrity of all the glass fronts, as well as the workstations at each containment room. Rawlings brought them all coffees, with the exception of Kash, whom he brought tea. He hung around, watching and nodding occasionally as one of the scientists passed. The arrival of the Xenomorph specimens was like Christmas, and he wanted to be in the center of it all.

Security was abuzz. Word had spread that Bellows had lit into them, promising each and every one that if there was a security incident during the transfer, they'd be on that long journey back to Weyland-Yutani, *without* cryosleep. Rawlings wasn't sure the commander had the authority to do such a thing. Anyone traveling without cryosleep would age accordingly. But the threat of it seemed to put a spring in Security's steps. The ones he could usually chat up were close-mouthed and all business.

So, he posted himself in the lab, hoping no one would notice him and kick him out. He wasn't let down.

They came two-by-two from the loading docks. Each pair of security personnel carrying a cryosealed container about three feet by three feet by three feet. Hypercold air leaked from the seams of the containers in a dull hiss, creating a ground fog that swirled and danced as they moved through it. The personnel wore special gloves that insulated them from the cold. Each team placed a specimen inside a containment area.

Étienne Lacroix made certain the doors were sealed and security locks were set. Once all twelve containment rooms had been filled, the security persons went away.

With the exception of the two security synths. Although they seemed to blend into the background, Rawlings knew they could activate in a split second.

He took a sip of coffee.

This was getting good.

Cruz and Étienne went to separate workstations and, using articulated arms, began to open the cryosealed containers. As the tops came loose and were placed to the side, an egg-like shape could be seen in each container.

"They're called Ovomorphs," Kash said. "This is the first stage of a Xenomorph's existence—essentially an egg laid by the queen. They're still cryo'd until we remove the lower case. After that, they'll 'wake up,' so to speak.

"They're kept in stasis during transit," she continued, "because studies have determined that the eggs have the ability to detect biological organisms around them. Inside each Ovomorph is a stage one Xenomorph."

"Go ahead and call them by their real names," Étienne called over his shoulder as he removed yet another container lid. "Stage one Xenomorph sounds so boring by comparison."

"They call them face-huggers," she said, nose scrunched at the word. "Imagine two giant skeletal hands," she said, putting her wrists together, locking her thumbs, and waggling her fingers. "And a spine-like tail. The tail wraps around the victim's throat and the stage one Xenomorph essentially hugs the face until it can implant the highly mutagenic substance known as *plagiarus praepotens*. We're going to work with this substance and try and determine the effects of the pathogen on it. Mutagenic substance vs. mutagenic substance."

"It's going to be lovely," Étienne called.

"How does the er… face-bugger stay in place?" Hoenikker asked.

"Once over the mouth of its target, the *face-hugger* controls the host by rendering it unconscious using a cyanose-based paralytic chemical similar to dimethyl sulfoxide, administered simply through skin contact."

"It's also been able to suppress the host's immune system," Étienne added, "so that the body can't fight against the invasion. Once the mutagen is set, the 'face-bugger' releases, having done its job of delivery. Then comes the fun part," he said. "Stage two." He made a fist near his chest then opened it dramatically while simultaneously making the sound of an explosion. "Chestbursters."

Hoenikker shook his head.

Rawlings took a sip of his coffee to hide his expression.

"But we're not going to have to worry about that," Kash said. "We're going to focus on the Ovomorphs and try and entice mutagens from them without face-huggers."

"About that," Cruz said. "There's been a change of plan."

"What do you mean?" Kash asked. She turned, hands on her hips. "The plan has been in place for months."

Cruz finished removing his last container lid and stood, straightening his lab coat, then wiping his brow with a sleeve.

"Bellows has other ideas. He wants Xenomorphs. The acid-resistant armor is a game-changer. We need more tech like that, and he thinks that testing the mutagenic effects of the pathogen on the various stages of a juvenile and adult will give us the best results."

"But he isn't a scientist," she said. "What did you tell him?"

"I told him I'd do what he said."

"You what?" Étienne cried out. "You didn't even stand up for our agenda?"

"What was I supposed to do—on my first day? Disobey a direct order? We'll have other chances to do things the way we want. For now, we need Xenos."

"But that requires..." Kash looked around. "Oh, no, we are *not*."

"We are not what?" Hoenikker asked.

Rawlings knew exactly what her concerns were, and he had the same problem with the sudden change of plan.

"Bellows has a cache of criminals," Cruz said. "Don't worry, they've all signed waivers, and it's perfectly legal. He assured me of it."

"Do you hear yourself speaking?" Étienne said. "A cache of *people*? People can't be cached."

"Don't get all high-and-mighty, Dr. Lacroix," Cruz said. "Weren't you the one just now dramatizing the chest bursting to Hoenikker here?"

"That was before I thought—" He glanced at Hoenikker. "He's right. I shouldn't have been joking. It's a terrible thing to watch."

"Have you seen it?" Hoenikker asked.

"Only in videos," Étienne said. "Say, can we send these back, and get fully formed Xenos?"

"Do you want to lead the team to try and capture them?" Cruz asked.

"What happened last time?" Hoenikker asked.

"We received several infected humans who were purportedly 'explorers.' Our containment areas weren't as secure then, so we never saw the actual chest bursting," Kash said.

"Another time, we received several adults in cryogenic stasis," Étienne said.

"And now we have twelve Ovomorphs," Hoenikker said. "Which means we'll need—"

"Stand aside," Bellows commanded as he entered the room. Behind him came a flow of civilians dressed in dirty gray jumpsuits, accompanied by security personnel.

"You going to do this now?" Cruz asked.

"We don't have the capacity to keep them anywhere else." Bellows glanced at the other scientists, then planted himself in front of a containment room so he could admire the Ovomorph. "Might as well begin testing, or whatever it is you do here. I count twelve eggs, and we have twelve volunteers."

"Wait a minute," Étienne said, his voice rising. "Just wait a minute. I didn't sign up for this."

"Nor did I," Kash said.

"Nor did I," Hoenikker echoed, looking like he might be sick.

The twelve humans stood with their heads down. Three were women—two in their mid-thirties and one near sixty. The rest were men of various ages and ethnicities. All of them shared the same look of world-weary rejection, as if they just wanted to be done with it all.

"Oh, look, the new scientist has an opinion," Bellows said without turning around. "Listen and listen good, people. You will all perform your functions as per your contract with Weyland-Yutani. Any ideas you might have not to work will be met with the severity only a corporate giant can impose.

"Dr. Hoenikker," he continued, "we are aware of your sister and her troubles. These can either be exacerbated or corrected. Likewise, Dr. Kash. You were unhirable when you came to us. Do your partners in science know that you were once called the Angel of Death? And Dr. Lacroix. You are a very happy scientist to not be in prison. Prison isn't a luxury for anyone. Just look at the twelve volunteers we have here.

"I do not threaten anyone. I merely provide realities. Right now, your realities are as scientists aboard Pala Station. Those realities can change if you feel they must, but for the moment, you have jobs to do and I expect them to be performed to perfection."

He turned, hands folded behind his back, and regarded the three scientists. Then he turned to Cruz.

"Doctor? I expect a report first thing."

Cruz nodded. "Yessir."

Bellows left the room, walking stiffly past the doomed. Cruz nodded to the security personnel, who walked each one of the humans into a chamber that contained an Ovomorph. One man and one woman had to be physically restrained as they began to shriek, and begged not to be put in the room. But to no avail. Ultimately, Security managed to get them where they were supposed to go, closing the doors.

The shrieks became muffled.

When the security personnel left, Cruz turned to his team.

"To your stations," he said, his jaw tight.

Hoenikker had a look of horror on his face.

Kash held a fist to her mouth.

Étienne's focus was more precise, anger curling his lip.

"I said *stations*," Cruz said.

Étienne whirled on him. "How can we just do this?"

"What do you want me to do?" Cruz asked. "You heard the man. You heard what he said. He talked about realities." Cruz pointed at one of the containment rooms where an older man sat in a corner, hugging his knees, staring at the egg in the middle of the room. "They volunteered. They want to change their realities—the realities of their families. Don't ruin it with sentimentality."

"Sentimentality?" Étienne asked. "It's not sentimental, not wanting someone to die."

"They're going to die so that others may live," Cruz said. "The Colonial Marines who benefit from this might never know, but each of you will know what they've given—what they've sacrificed."

"I think I'm going to be sick," Hoenikker said.

Kash put her hand on his back.

Cruz continued his monologue. "As a former marine, I can tell you that the sacrifice will not go unappreciated."

"That's not something we can grasp," Kash said. "It's hard for us to get past the idea that these people are going to die, and we can't stop it." She paused. "It—it just feels wrong."

"You're going to have to get past it, Kash." Cruz nodded in turn at each of the scientists. "All of you are going to have to find a way to get past it. Now, get to your stations. We need to inject the pathogen while we're still able."

The scientists remained in place for a moment. Then one by one, each of them moved to their station.

Cruz noticed Rawlings.

"You? Do you have a place to be?"

Rawlings nodded.

"Then get there."

Rawlings was glad to leave. Part of him wanted to watch the process, intrigued by what that was about to happen. But another part knew there were some sights that couldn't be unseen. An alien bursting out of the chest of a young woman was one of them.

He hoped he'd never see such a thing again.

The coffee tasted weak in his mouth right now.

He needed something stronger.

23

The last time Rawlings had been this drunk before noon, he'd just been fitted with his second prosthesis. The reason he'd needed a second prosthesis was because in a drunken fit, he'd thrown his first mechanical arm into traffic, and it had been run over.

He'd forgotten the reason he'd hurled it into traffic, but thought it might have had to do with his girlfriend of three years taking off with all his stuff and leaving him with a dead plant, a fishbowl with dead fish, and the trash strewn all over the room.

He'd forgotten why she'd taken off as well, because he'd been on a four-day bender.

They'd forced him into detox after he received his second prosthesis, and he hadn't really drunk much since then. He'd been happy to partake of coffee and contemplate the good qualities of a life outside of the Colonial Marines—even with a corporation such as Weyland-Yutani.

But that was before he'd watched a group of human beings trade their lives for what was the most gruesome experience possible. Rawlings had seen it happen.

Hell, he'd almost fallen victim to it himself.

Pouring the rest of the bottle of whiskey into his coffee cup, he screwed the top in place, took a sip, stumbled, then straightened. Wouldn't be right if anyone saw him stumbling around the station. Wouldn't be right at all. He managed to hug the walls all the way to the Comms section before stumbling a little as he entered the office.

Brennan's desk was still empty, as was Davis's, but Buggy was still there, which was good because that was why Rawlings came.

One look at Rawlings and Buggy was out of his chair and helping the reception tech back the way he'd come. When he got Rawlings to his room, he eased him onto the bed and closed the door.

"What the hell, Vic?" Buggy asked, taking away the cup, smelling it, then wincing at the smell. "Anyone see you drunk on duty, and Bellows is going to have your ass."

"Do you know what they're doing here?" Rawlings asked.

"Everyone knows. It's not our business."

"Why not? Isn't it our job to protect those who can't protect themselves?"

"Easy there, Vic. You're not a Colonial Marine anymore."

"Who says?" Rawlings shouted. "Once a marine, always a marine!"

"Easy, now. Keep it down. Listen, I'm going to get the others."

Rawlings began to hum cadence he hadn't marched to in a dozen years. Buggy made a few calls on the wall communications panel. Within minutes, McGann and Chase had joined them.

Rawlings watched it all through amused eyes. He wasn't as drunk as he could be, but he was definitely impaired. He'd wanted them together anyway, so this was as good a way to accomplish that as not.

"What is it—a flashback?" McGann asked, checking the bottle.

"How'd he get the booze?" Chase asked.

"You'd be surprised at the sorts of things I have," Rawlings said. "When people leave here they don't always take everything." He clapped his hands together and pounded the bed beside him. "Have a seat. We need to make plans."

"Plans?" Chase asked. "What plans?"

"He thinks he's still a Colonial Marine," Buggy said.

"Once a marine, always a marine!" Rawlings shouted.

"What the hell, Rawlings?" McGann said.

Chase went to the desk and picked up the cup. He smelled it first, then took a tentative sip. Once he was sure what it was, he took a deep draw.

"Easy there, Chase," Buggy said. "You don't want to end up like Rawlings."

"Not enough in here to end up like him. Just enough for a stiff drink." He took another, then held it out. "This is some good shit."

McGann took it and slugged back a mouthful. She sighed after she swallowed, then held out the cup to Buggy.

Buggy stared at it for a moment, then grinned. "What the hell. You only live once." He held up the cup and said, "Semper fi," before kicking back the last of the whiskey.

The others repeated it back to him.

"Semper fi!"

After a few moments of silence, Rawlings spoke. "You know what that means, right? 'Semper fi.' *Semper fidelis*. It means, 'always loyal.' Like us. Always loyal to the corps. But it's more than that. It's also always loyal to your friends. Your fellow humans, even."

"Fellow humans?" Chase glanced at McGann. "What's he getting at?"

"The alien eggs and the twelve people who are going to get infected," Buggy explained. "It's messing with his head."

"Wait. What?" McGann asked. "No one said anything about infecting humans. Who could force someone to do that?"

"They've volunteered," Buggy said. "Some had life sentences commuted, so they could die early."

"I heard one of the women is doing it to get her husband out of prison," Chase said. "She has some disease, and doesn't have long to live, or something like that."

"It's still fucked up," McGann said.

Chase nodded hurriedly. "Definitely fucked up."

"So, what are we going to do?" McGann asked.

"What is there to do?" Buggy said. "Just do your jobs."

"We need to be ready," Rawlings said. "Bad shit's coming, and we need to be ready."

"You can't know that," Chase said.

Rawlings stared at him. "Know that feeling in the pit of your stomach before a battle? Know that itch on the back of your neck when you're on patrol? What about that catch at the back of your throat, or the snap of your teeth together, unable to release them because they're more ready for an impact than you are?"

The others nodded, looking to their own memory horizons.

"I ever tell you how I lost my hand?" Rawlings asked.

They shook their heads.

"Just another LV. Just another patrol. You know how it goes. They send you into space and you're sent to keep someone or something from killing settlers, or miners, or agro-farmers. In this case it was a mining colony. People were dying mysteriously, so they sent for the marines. Same-o, same-o."

"If I had a hundred credits for each colony I'd gone to, I could vacation for a year," McGann said.

"Exactly," Rawlings said. He nodded toward the cup. "Any left?"

Buggy shook his head.

Rawlings sighed, and lowered his head to his chest, puffing out his neck. White scars could be seen on his dark skin. "Probably just as well. Where was I? Yeah. We were on this LV, I forget which one. Mining colony was losing miners and support staff. Turns out some of those eggs were found deep in the mine. Same eggs we have in the lab right now. We never did get the chance to see what the eggs looked like, just heard about them. Instead, we had full-on adult Xenomorphs. I'll never forget them. I watched them plow through six marines like the creatures were hot knives and the marines were butter."

Everyone's eyes were on him. Leaning forward.

Part of this story, and part of theirs.

"We didn't come down without firepower, though. We had a pair of M577 armored personnel carriers."

Buggy gave a low whistle.

Rawlings looked at him and nodded. "Yep. A pair of synchronized RE700 20mm Gatling cannons. We were able to back the Xenos into a corner of the mine and opened fire with all four cannons. We didn't care for shit about the flechettes. We gave them all we had in HE rounds. Imagine six thousand eight hundred high-explosive armor-piercing rounds slamming into the dozen Xenos that were preparing to charge. Brothers, we turned them into mush. They covered the walls, the floor, the ceiling. We fucking obliterated them."

"I don't get it," Chase said. "I thought you were going to tell us how you lost your hand."

"But wait… there's more," Rawlings said. "We waited, and once the thermal imagers and ultrasonic motion trackers gave us a consistent negative reading, we prepared to open the hatch and exit. I was the first out, opened the hatch, and as I did, some of their fucking Xeno blood fell onto my hand. Must have been dripping from the ceiling.

"The pain was immense. I watched as my hand just turned to liquid and fell away. I remember screaming and falling back inside the carrier. I ordered the driver to put it in reverse and get us the hell out of there. Once we were back in daylight, we got the medics to take a look. The wound had cauterized itself, which was good, but I had no hand. Gone. Just like that. From a few drips of blood. Now imagine what a whole pool of that blood will do to something—do to someone?"

All eyes were wide.

The smile on McGann's wide face was anything but friendly—more a grimace than anything.

Chase looked ready to bolt.

Buggy's jaw was set into a firm frown.

"And the M577s," Rawlings continued. "In the light of day, the armor had been pocked by the Xeno blood. It hadn't made it all the way through, but it might have, had we let the ceiling continue to drip on it. As it was, there were holes you could put a fist through."

Rawlings pulled himself up from the bed and went over to his dresser. He opened the second drawer and pulled out a bottle that was only a third full. He took a deep draught and passed it around. Each of the others took a deep draw, as well. When they passed it back to him there was enough for one more, and he took it. He held the empty bottle in his artificial hand.

"And that, gentlemen, is what we have in the laboratory. If any of those get out, not only do we need to kill it, but we need to watch after, because their blood is as deadly to us as they are alive."

24

Fairbanks hadn't eaten in three days. He hadn't drunk anything either. A container of his own urine stared back at him, begging him to take a sip. He'd read and seen planetary survival vids where people had been forced to drink their own urine in order to live, but he'd never thought he'd be one of them.

An hour or so ago—he'd lost the ability to keep track of time—he'd gone to it and lifted it to his face, but the smell had overpowered him and made him gag. With nothing in his stomach, it was little more than dry heaves, but the attempt had left him exhausted.

When he'd fled, he hadn't been sure where he was going to go. All he knew was he needed to get away. He needed to be able to think—to come up with a plan. After all, he wasn't a bad guy. He'd just been caught up in the middle of bad things. He'd been blackmailed, pure and simple. Was it his fault? No. He was a victim.

He'd go to the grave believing as much.

But he'd needed a place to plan. Because of his work in

Logistics, he knew where things were kept. He knew the layout of the storerooms, and knew which ones were never inventoried. Which ones were so inconsequential that they didn't have sensors. He'd chosen one of those, certain that he couldn't be found. He'd made himself a hiding spot behind some old bedframes and boxes of paint. What it lacked in the comforts of home, it more than made up for in its spartan qualities.

After he'd overcome his initial fear at being caught, he'd fallen into a deep pit of boredom. No vids. No games. No books. Nothing. Just him and his mind, replaying the events of what turned out to be a pretty pathetic life. Somewhere during the second or third replaying of his school years he'd decided that if he ever got out of this situation, he'd make a wholesale change. He'd find a way to leave Weyland-Yutani, maybe buy out his contract, then sign on to a terraforming mission or a pilgrimage. Life wasn't meant to be lived inside the cold steel walls of an outpost like Pala Station. Life was meant to be lived outdoors, under wide open skies. Life was to be lived with people.

He knew this last part was because of his loneliness. Ever since he'd come aboard the station, he'd found it hard to make friends. The idea of having a boyfriend or a girlfriend was even more ludicrous. The funny thing was, the one he was most drawn to was the blonde security guard. She could probably break him over her knee, but he'd enjoy her doing it. He'd once had a boyfriend in college who was twice his size. He'd thought he'd loved him, but it turned out that he'd become codependent. The guy was addicted to stims, and could be quite the bully. Eventually, Fairbanks realized that he'd spent more time trying to placate his partner than being with him on his own terms. Or were those his own terms?

His head jerked.

Was that a sound?

He stopped breathing and listened for the door to open.

Nothing came.

Maybe he hadn't heard anything.

Maybe it was all in his mind.

But there it was again. Not the sound of the door, but something smaller. Something like a scratching noise. What could it be?

He scooted so his back was in the corner where the urine container was. He glanced around for a weapon, scrambled toward one of the bedframes and grabbed a piece of metal that had been dangling. He gripped it and began to wrench it back and forth, making more noise than he believed possible.

The scrabbling came again, this time nearer to him.

He wrenched faster and managed to come away with the twelve-inch piece of metal just as a creature leaped onto the bedframe in front of him. He fell back, colliding with the urine container, the putrid liquid sloshing up, wetting the back of his shirt. He gaped at the creature.

It had been a rat once, for sure. But instead of small rat legs, it now had long segmented chitinous legs that held up an enlarged torso. And its face. Its face held a maw with serrated teeth that looked capable of shredding his arm. The entire creature was the size of a station cat, which meant it had to have increased in size no less than ten times. But how could that be?

A high-pitched laugh escaped him.

Was this something Hyperdyne created? Or was it something they wanted?

No. He couldn't believe it. More likely it was something that escaped from the lab. Hadn't there been a breach before the Leon-895? Either that or… or what if the regular rats had come into contact with the blood of one of the escaped specimens? Could that have done this?

The creature leaped to the ground, landing five feet in front of him.

Fairbanks let out an, "*Eep!*" and kicked out with a shoe.

The creature easily avoided the move and leaped atop the leg. Fairbanks bit back a scream as he began to shake his leg furiously, trying to remove the thing, but as hard as he shook, the creature wouldn't let go.

He managed to climb to his feet while still shaking his leg. The creature had its long legs wrapped around it and was trying to chew through the fabric of his pants. Shoving the length of metal against the creature's torso, he tried to dislodge it, but it wouldn't move. He tried again, this time poking harder. The creature looked up and snarled at him, then went back to trying to… bite him? Eat him?

Stepping forward he kicked his leg against the metal bedframe. It made a calamitous noise, but the creature still held fast.

"Fucking hell!"

Fairbanks kicked five, six, then seven times, pummeling the creature against the metal until it finally released. He fell back against the wall. His leg ached with the kicks. He held out the metal, this time prepared to defend himself.

The creature had landed on its back and it took a moment for it to right itself. When it did, it glared at him and bared its serrated teeth.

"Fucking hell," he repeated, this time his voice low and filled with dread. "Stay back you little fucker," he said, punctuating his words with the metal.

It took a step toward him, then another, then before Fairbanks could do anything, it leaped. He swung with the length of metal and missed. Instead, the creature landed on his arm. He was surprised by the weight, and even more surprised by the pain as it bit down on his hand, separating tendons and breaking bones.

He couldn't help himself as he screamed and dropped his makeshift weapon. He spun to the wall and began to smack his hand against it over and over. The creature seemed to become weaker and weaker with each battering, until finally it fell to the floor, knocking over the urine container.

Fairbanks didn't hesitate. He stomped the damn thing until he saw its guts come out of its mouth. Once he was sure it was dead, he backed away from it, chest heaving, out of breath from both exertion and fear. After a few moments, he looked at his savaged hand, and almost retched.

It looked as if a wild beast had just taken bites from it—which was true. He straightened and removed his shirt, but couldn't rip a bandage from it with one hand, so he used the entire thing to wrap his wound. When he felt the wetness, he remembered the shirt back had been soaked with his own urine. He could only hope it held some sort of antiseptic property.

With the creature dead, he sat and stared at it, resting in a pool of urine. Was that it? Had he become infected with the same thing that mutated the rat? Was he going to grow long legs and rollick about the station, trying to eat people? The idea made him giggle. The impossibility of it made him laugh—but what if it was true? He didn't know anything about science or biology, but wasn't that how it worked?

He sat thinking like this, losing track of time, when an idea came to him.

The longer he'd sat staring at the creature, the more he'd been reminded of his own hunger. And as far as he looked at the situation, it was a win-win. If the creature was infected, it had already infected him, so eating it wouldn't do any more damage. If he *wasn't* infected, then the creature couldn't infect him, which meant he could eat it and nothing would happen. Except he'd finally have something in his gullet.

But he'd have to get the guts out. He couldn't eat guts.

And he couldn't eat the skin, so he'd have to gnaw the meat.

He wished he had some way to cook it, but that would be impossible. The smoke alone would set off alarms. No, he'd have to eat it raw. Thinking about it, he realized he'd already made up his mind.

Using the ragged piece of metal, he crawled over and hacked at one of the spider legs. Once it came off, he sat back and began to gnaw on it. It tasted bitter and vile, but that was probably the urine. If he could get past that, the creature might actually taste good.

One thing was for sure. He wasn't going to starve.

Like he'd thought, this was a win-win.

25

Hoenikker hadn't said a word for the last four hours. Neither had Étienne, his efficient movements accentuated by the death stares he gave Cruz when the "chief" of the lab wasn't looking.

No one was happy to be there, but after all, they were scientists and needed to concentrate on the task at hand. At least, that's what Hoenikker said to himself, to make everything they were doing seem reasonable… ethical… moral. Because it sure hadn't felt that way.

Even as Kash quietly directed him to take samples from the exterior of the eggs and store them for further examination, he couldn't help but glance at the human test subjects who would soon be used as incubators to propel the alien's morphology along.

Hoenikker had tried to send a message back to Weyland-Yutani corporate, begging for a transfer, but Bellows had put a block on all outgoing comms while the Xenomorphs were on station. According to Buggy, the very existence of the Xenomorphs was supposed to be classified. That they'd only been rumored to exist demonstrated that there were active controls on the information.

Kash handed him another sample.

He took the metal tube, tagged it, logged it, then put it into cryogenic storage.

To keep sane, he'd have to concentrate on the scientific method. Used by scientists across the known systems, the method hadn't changed since the 1700s—conduct background research, construct a hypothesis, test the hypothesis through experimentation, analyze the data, draw conclusions, then communicate the results.

They had little knowledge regarding the pathogen and its interaction with organic beings. What they did know was that the goo tended to exacerbate naturally occurring characteristics of the test subject, and weaponize them. He'd read the data from when they'd created the acid-resistant armor. The goo was definitely the catalyst, but how it had been used was genius. Now they were going to try different levels of irradiation, as well as a serum developed from Leon-895. If they could give the armor a cloaking or chameleon quality it would make the wearer near invincible.

One of the questions they needed to address was, how did the Xenomorphs see? Was it through thermal imaging? Did they have some sort of motion detection? So many questions, with elusive answers on the horizon.

Truth be told, the scientific method excited him.

What didn't excite him were the prisoners.

Especially Test Subject #3.

Cruz had insisted that each of the human test subjects remain anonymous, so that the scientists could retain some semblance of objectivity. The problem was that some of the test subjects looked like people they knew from the past, which erased some of the subjectivity. Like Test Subject #3. She looked like an older version of Hoenikker's steady girlfriend during the first two years of university.

Her name had been Monica Enright. She was blond, introspective, but eager to please as if it had been drilled into her by her parents and she couldn't turn it off. In the end, that had been the problem. No matter how Hoenikker messed up his life or his grades or his relationship, she forgave him and wanted nothing more than to make him happy—in order to *be* happy.

It had been toxic for him, and just as toxic for her, he'd convinced himself. In the end, he'd walked out.

He'd always wondered if he'd done the right thing. Was it her fault that she'd loved so unconditionally? Was that something he deserved? It certainly didn't make her a bad person. The opposite had been true—she was a great person. He could still see her face as he left, not understanding, unable to fathom why he was leaving when she would do anything for him.

Perhaps that was the problem. A relationship couldn't exist without some degree of conflict. He'd *needed* her to be angry. He needed balance. Still, he wondered what his life would have been like had he stayed with her, married her.

Shaking his head to clear it, he glanced up at Test Subject #3. She was looking at him.

No, staring.

Could it be her?

He had to know.

He went to Cruz. "Can I have a moment with you, Doctor?"

Cruz paused at his workstation. "I'm a little busy now, Hoenikker. Can it wait?"

Hoenikker nodded and began to back away.

Cruz returned to his work.

Hoenikker stared at him for a moment. "You know what? No, it won't. I need that moment now."

"Fine then." Cruz sat back from his pad, eyebrow up at Hoenikker's intrusion. "What it is?"

"I need to know who the test subjects are."

Cruz gave him an impatient look, and prepared to get back to work. "I already explained. We're not doing that."

"Wait." Hoenikker surprised himself by putting his hand on Cruz's shoulder. "Wait. I—I think I know one of them."

Cruz stared at him, then the offending hand.

Hoenikker removed it and took a step back.

Cruz appraised him. "You've been nothing but trouble since you got here."

Hoenikker shook his head, thinking of all the specimen therapy Cruz had been doing off the clock. But he let that go. "That's not true at all. I was promised alien artifacts. I'm not used to live specimens. It's not my specialty."

"Take that up with Mansfield," Cruz said. Then he added, "Oh, wait. He's dead."

Hoenikker felt himself becoming exasperated. "What are you talking about? All I want to know are the names of the test subjects."

"Because you think you know one of them."

Hoenikker nodded. "I'm almost sure of it."

"Do you know what the odds are for that? Come on, Doctor. Do the math."

"Math be damned. I think I know Test Subject #3. I think she was my… was my girlfriend in college." Cruz glanced at the test subject in question for a long moment, then shook his head. "She's no one to you, Hoenikker. I'm not going to release the names."

Hoenikker opened his mouth to argue, but Cruz beat him to the punch.

"Enough of this. Get back to work. She's not who you think she is."

"But you don't understand—"

"I understand everything." Cruz stood, towering a full head above Hoenikker. "You want to save the test subjects. Everyone does—but the universe doesn't work like that. Those people signed a contract, much like *you* signed a contract. Weyland-Yutani owns your ass. Weyland-Yutani owns them. It's a contract. They get to be part of a complex experiment to try and help save the lives of Colonial Marines, and in turn Weyland-Yutani does something for them." He poked Hoenikker in the chest as he said the next words. "Just. Leave. It. Be."

Cruz sat, returning to his work.

Hoenikker stood for a moment, his hand rubbing where he'd been poked, then he turned and walked back to where Kash was working.

"What was that all about?" she asked.

Hoenikker stared at Test Subject #3 and she stared back at him. She cocked her head, shook it as if to say no, then looked away.

He gasped.

"Tim. What is it?" Kash asked, her eyes round with concern. "What's wrong?"

He opened his mouth to speak, but nothing would come out. He couldn't even breathe. The cocking and shaking of the head was pure Monica. She was the only person he'd ever seen shake her head that way. Twenty years had passed, and now they were back together, only to have her die in front of him.

For the sake of a Weyland-Yutani experiment.

When he could finally breathe again, he gasped. The room swayed around him. He put his hand out to grab the table to keep him from falling. He had to free her. He needed to get her out of there and to a place of safety. But how? How could he save her? Where could he take her?

The room snapped straight and he could suddenly breathe.
And think.
He knew exactly who to talk to.
Without comment, he hurried out.

26

It took him three tries to find Reception Tech Rawlings' room. If there was anyone who would know what to do, it would be the guy who knew everything.

The first time the door opened it was a female security guard who'd been sleeping in the nude. He'd barely processed her nakedness, apologized, then hurried away.

The second room turned out to be a storeroom and was devoid of human occupancy. The problem was the corridors. He still didn't know the layout of the station. His paths went from his room to the bathroom, the mess hall, and the lab. He really hadn't paid attention to what was in between.

As he approached his third try, two men and a woman came through the door. He recognized Buggy from Comms, but the others he didn't know. They nodded at him and he nodded back. Once at the door, he knocked and waited for it to open.

After a moment, Rawlings opened it wearing nothing but underwear.

"If you're looking for more hooch—" he began, then stopped talking when he saw it was Hoenikker. Rawlings glanced down at his naked black torso and Weyland-Yutani underwear. "You. What do you want?"

"I need your help." Hoenikker pushed past him into the room. He paced to the end of the room, then turned. Rawlings closed the door and scratched near his crotch.

"Can't you see I'm under the weather?"

Hoenikker spied the empty bottle on the desk. "Looks more like you've been drinking."

"Lots of things can make you under the weather," Rawlings replied. "Drinking is one of them." He went to the edge of his bed and sat on it. "I'd offer you something, but as you can see, we're fresh out."

"I'm not here to drink."

"Then what can I do for you, Doctor?"

"It's her. I know it's her." Hoenikker paced back and forth from the door to the wall and back again. His normally ordered thoughts were a jumble. "How do I make them understand? They can't kill her. They just can't. Maybe I still have a chance to make it all up. Maybe I can be there for her now."

"Whoa now, killer. I thought I was the one who'd been drinking. What's got you all juiced?"

Hoenikker stopped pacing. "Her. I told you. It's her."

Rawlings shook his head. "You haven't even introduced her."

"Monica. My girlfriend. She's here!"

"Well, that's great, my friend. You and her can get some nookie, and have a great old time."

"No." Hoenikker shook his head furiously. "You don't get it. She's in the lab."

"She's in the lab? But only scientists are in... the..." Rawlings blinked quickly. "She's one of them?"

Hoenikker threw up his hands. "That's what I've been

telling you. She's there in the lab. Test Subject #3. Containment Room Three."

Rawlings rubbed his face, continuing over the top of his skull. "Oh, Doctor." He shook his head. "You've got to be mistaken. It can't really be her."

"Oh, it is. At first, I was like you. 'It couldn't be.' But then when I saw her do some of Monica's mannerisms—mannerisms I haven't seen replicated in twenty years—"

"Okay." Rawlings patted the air. "Let's say that what you're claiming is accurate. Let's say that an ex-girlfriend of yours from twenty years ago somehow got crossways with Weyland-Yutani, and became a test subject at a science station at the ass-crack end of the universe. What do you intend to do?"

Hoenikker straightened. "Rescue her."

"Rescue her?" Rawlings stood.

"Yes." Hoenikker nodded. "Rescue her. With your help."

"My help?" Rawlings sat back down. "I picked a doozie of a day to start drinking again." He smacked his face several times, then closed his eyes and opened them. "Damn. You're still here." He paused a moment as if in thought. "So, what do you propose?"

Hoenikker shrugged. "I don't know. Hide her in a room? Steal a shuttle? Something. *Anything*. I mean, we have to do something, right?"

"We don't have to do *anything*. I know you want to do something, but look... We don't even know if it's her."

Hoenikker leaned in. "Can you check?"

"Can I check? Shoot. I have access to everything. I can even tell you what Bellows is reading right now." Rawlings got to his feet, went over to his desk, and sat down. He began to fiddle with his vid screen. Punching numbers and swiping until he got to what he wanted. "What did you say her name is?"

"It was Monica Enright," Hoenikker said breathlessly.

"So, here's what I have. I have no first names, just initials. Then I have last names. I have two Ms. One M. Russel and M. Trakes. Sorry, Doctor. It's just too vague."

Not to be defeated, Hoenikker asked, "What's the background on M. Russel?"

A swipe and a few moments later, "Okay. Gender is female. Forty-three years old. From Earth. One son. Not married. She was arrested for murder aboard a Weyland-Yutani space station six years ago."

Could that be her? "You say she has a son. How old is he?"

"Thirteen. Sorry, Doc. Can't see that it could be yours."

"Of course not." Hoenikker felt dizzy with the information. "What about the other one?"

"M. Trakes. Also female gender, but thirty-four years old."

Hoenikker nodded. "With cryosleep, she could be any age between thirty and forty-three." He nodded. "Go on."

"M. Trakes has two daughters." Rawlings punched a few digital keys on the screen. "Aw. I see it now. One of her daughters has a rare disease. Costs a fortune to get it taken care of. The company has offered to take care of it. They chose this one specifically because she's AB negative."

"That's the rarest blood type."

"Wait a minute." Rawlings punched a few more keys. "All of them are AB negative. Must have been difficult to track down that many volunteers with the world's rarest blood type."

"Any more information about M. Trakes?" Hoenikker asked.

"She's from Earth as well. Her daughters are with her husband." Rawlings shook his head. "I'm afraid this wasn't much help."

"I don't know," Hoenikker said. "She could be either of the two. The only way I'm going to find out is by asking her, it seems."

"And you think Cruz is going to go for that?"

"He won't have to. He won't be there." Hoenikker began to pace again. "We're going to need a distraction."

"And then what? What is it you're going to do? Steal a shuttle, you said? Hide her?" Rawlings picked up the empty bottle, tipped it upside down over his mouth, then grimaced and put it back on the table. "This is the Weyland-Yutani machine you're up against."

"I understand that, but I—"

"Do you really understand? We're talking *Weyland-Yutani*. They could disappear this whole station, and no one would even blink. They're probably the most powerful corporation in the known sectors, and you want to go against them. Even if I were to help you—and I'm not saying I will—how many others on the station would help? Because we're going to need a goddamn lot of them."

"Maybe when they hear my story—"

"They'll what? Be willing to lose their jobs? Be prepared to go to prison? All because Doctor Timmy Hoenikker found out that one of the *voluntary* test subjects used to be his girlfriend?"

Hoenikker stopped pacing and stared at the floor.

"Then what is it I'm supposed to do?"

Rawlings stood and placed his hands on Hoenikker's shoulders as he faced him, naked down to his underwear.

"What do you do? Nothing, Doctor. There's nothing to be done. This is merely the irony of the universe, that you two might have met near the end."

"I can't—" Hoenikker gulped. "I can't accept that."

Rawlings gave him a look a mother might give a child who'd just discovered he wasn't the center of the universe.

"You're going to have to. This is out of your hands."

27

The next morning was set for the experiments to begin. According to the plan, they'd remove the lower half of the cryogenic travel cases so the Ovomorphs would awaken. Then, sometime between ten and thirty minutes later, each Ovomorph would detect the presence of another biological organism, and would deliver the face-hugger, who would then find the organism.

Pitting human against face-hugger, there would be no winning for the human. It wasn't even a challenge, especially since there was nowhere for the humans to run.

Cruz insisted that all doctors be present to acknowledge the sacrifices the test subjects were making, but Hoenikker believed that was all a ruse. Cruz wanted them all there for cover, so he wouldn't be the only one gleefully observing the destruction. Still, Hoenikker couldn't deny that the lab was finally functioning like an actual lab, as if Cruz had been able to spin it into his own, as easy as running a Colonial Marine platoon.

Hoenikker would be there, but first he had something he had to do. At four in the morning, after a sleepless night, he entered the lab. The lights were in maintenance mode and cast the room in a barely lit gloom. He noted the two synths watching him, but ignored them. He wasn't going to do anything that would cause them to come alive.

He approached the workstation in front of Containment Room Three and sat before it. The chamber was dark, except for the blinking lights on the cryogenic travel cases. He dialed up the vid display and toggled infrared, noticing immediately that Test Subject #3 was sitting up on the rear ledge and facing in his direction. So, he wouldn't have to wake her up after all. He toggled the lights up to fifty percent to reveal that she was staring back at him.

He turned on the intercom. His mouth felt dry. He'd planned a speech. He'd practiced in the mirror.

All that came out was, "It's you, isn't it?"

She wore her blond hair short. The wide space between her eyes accentuated her features. High cheekbones made it seem as if she was always on the verge of a smile. Her green eyes mesmerized as they caught the light and changed.

She nodded.

He bit his lip.

"I knew it from the moment I saw you."

She cocked her head and shrugged.

"Will you talk to me?"

She stared at him for what seemed like forever, but was only thirty seconds.

"What is it you want me to say?" she replied, her voice as soft as he remembered. "That you broke my heart? That you walked out on me—on us?"

Twenty years and a hundred parsecs flashed through him. He remembered them holding hands in college, going to class, concerts, even the library terminals. Her kiss tasted sweet because she was always sucking on one candy or another.

Even the smell of her clothes burst through him in a timeless hurricane of scent memory.

She'd make him dinner most nights. Nothing special. They were students. But just the effort of someone making him instant noodles or instant rice was a convenience he'd taken for granted. And her smile. She always smiled at him as if not to smile would drive him away.

Now, looking at her, he could see her without a smile, yet she was still beautiful—and he'd left it all behind. Had he thought that it would be too much? That he'd end up behind a desk doing something corporate and meaningless? Had he been afraid that his dream of becoming a scientist would be lost, because he'd have to settle with her as soon as she became pregnant or decided she was done with school?

Or was it just that he'd been a selfish prick who didn't understand that he'd had it good.

"That was twenty years ago," he said.

She regarded him with side eyes. Then she stared at the egg resting in the cradle of the cryo travel case. She didn't seem to be afraid of it.

"Ever wonder if your life would be different if it wasn't for a single decision?" she asked.

Had his leaving started her on a path from which she couldn't return?

"Me leaving?" he asked.

She sneered. Then she stood and walked to the glass, putting her hands on it.

"I'm over that. I mean the decision I made when I decided to kill the man I was with, for his money."

Hoenikker, who'd been leaning forward, sat back hard. He'd hoped she'd been the one with the terminal illness, but she was the murderer.

"What? You didn't know?" she asked, adding a little vinegar

to her sugar. "I've killed many a man. Turns out I like it."

All he could do was shake his head.

"Turns out I've always been this way. My desire to please was nothing more than an emotional placeholder. When I pleased people, they would return the gesture, and it would fulfill something in me. But what I found is that a man begging for his life is even more of an emotional rush—the idea of pleasing them because I might allow them to live filled me with a certain ecstasy."

He couldn't parse her words with the memory of her. They didn't match. It was as if his old girlfriend had had her mind wiped clean and replaced. She couldn't have been like this when they were together.

"What are you saying?" he asked.

"I can see you there, feeling sorry for me, and wondering what would have happened had you not walked out. I'm not exactly sure. You might have become my first victim or you might have kept me from killing—although, I have to tell you, Timothy, murdering is *such* a fucking rush."

Hoenikker flicked off the intercom. This wasn't his memory. This was someone else entirely. Sure, it was Monica, but it was as if something had invaded her body, changed her.

He sat and stared for several moments as her lips continued to move, not even wanting to know what she said.

"Not exactly what you expected is it?"

The voice came from behind him.

Hoenikker spun.

Cruz sat back in an alcove, where Hoenikker had missed seeing him, his attention so focused on Test Subject #3. Cruz held a glass in one hand and an unlit cigar in another.

"I knew you'd come around," Cruz said. "I just wanted to see what you would do."

"I thought about trying to free her."

"Anyone with a scintilla of decency would do the same, if they were in your shoes." Cruz took a sip of amber liquid. "I'd expect nothing less."

"But what you said before—"

"Was absolutely right. We need to approach this as scientists. Not as regular people. We can't afford to be regular people. We have a responsibility to try and make the Colonial Marines safer. *Everyone* safer, and if it takes twelve people sacrificing themselves, then so be it." He held out the glass. "Have a sip of this. You need it."

Hoenikker stood and went over, accepted the glass and took an angry sip. He felt so manipulated. How was it other people had such a better handle on their emotions? He knew the answer, of course. Other people used their emotions more often. They practiced at it. Hoenikker had spent most of his life trying to avoid emotion. As the liquid burned through him, so did his anger.

"She's not the same person," he said, turning to regard her.

"Does that make any difference? Would you save her for the person she was?"

Hoenikker shook his head. "She just made me remember things. Regrets."

"Oh, Doctor Hoenikker, we all have regrets. We can look back and hear them following us like footsteps if we listen close enough."

"What's she getting out of being a test subject?" Hoenikker asked, passing back the glass. Cruz accepted it, made a motion for cheers, then took a sip.

"She was facing a life sentence, and bound for a terraforming prison work detail. Dangerous work. Nothing I'd wish on my worst enemy. This is her way out. This is how she is escaping her fate."

"Escaping her fate," Hoenikker repeated. "Just like I did when I walked out, all those years ago."

She knocked on the glass.

He thought about turning the intercom back on, but what was there to say? She was a different person. He stared at her for a long moment, trying to revitalize his feelings for her, trying to return to his need to save her, but that emotion was irrevocably lost. So, instead, he shook his head, turned, and left the lab.

Hoenikker needed to get some sleep. The testing began in the morning, and he needed to be there to record the data.

Once again, he retreated to the scientific method.

It was easy.

It was safe.

He couldn't get his feelings hurt.

28

Hypothesis #1: The pathogen, when irradiated and injected into the Ovomorph, will positively affect the Xenomorph morphology.

Hypothesis #2: The pathogen, when irradiated and injected into the human host, will adversely affect the Xenomorph morphology.

With the hypotheses in place, the scientists began their experimentation.

Hoenikker was asked to stand back and record data for this first group of tests. Étienne and Kash would be the primary researchers while Cruz supervised the process. Kash would be taking readings, as well.

Hypotheses one and two were tested on the subjects and eggs in Containment Rooms One and Two. Containment Room One saw the injection of the irradiated pathogen into the Ovomorph. There the test subject was an elderly female of African lineage.

Containment Room Two saw the injection of the irradiated pathogen into the test subject—a morose looking man in his forties or fifties who was severely overweight. The injection must have made the process seem more real, and he became agitated almost immediately.

After fifteen minutes, the remainder of the travel cases were removed, and the Ovomorphs began to approach room temperature. Hoenikker could tell immediately when they had recovered from the effects of the cold. The top of the egg structure began to twitch and quiver, as if it could smell the presence of the human test subjects.

The test subject in Containment Room One didn't run or act agitated. She merely sat with her back facing the egg, perhaps unwilling to face it. She appeared to have made peace with her situation, and was just waiting to play her part. Hoenikker considered her smart. If it had been him, he wouldn't have wanted to face what was coming next, either.

He stole a glance to Containment Room Three where Monica sat, watching them like a cat might, sitting in the window of a home. She wore a disinterested look, almost laconic, as she observed everything around her. Hoenikker wondered if, when the time came, she would be like the woman in Containment Room One, or like the man in Containment Room Two, who, even now, scrabbled at the glass, begging to be let free, his stomach bobbing as if it had been filled with too much jelly.

The intercom was turned off, but there was no mistaking what he was screaming. Hoenikker prayed that if he was ever in that position, he wouldn't behave the same way. But then, he couldn't be sure how he'd behave when faced with the inevitable prospect of being face-hugged by a Xenomorph. Although he'd rather be like the elderly woman, he feared he might end up like the fat man.

Each of the test subjects had been fitted with transmitters that provided live health data. Hoenikker made sure these were streaming as his vid display recorded the results.

Then, as inexorably as he'd been told, the top of each Ovomorph began to peel back, and a creature began to appear. At first it was the tail, whipping about, snapping, the end cracking the air. This he knew would eventually wrap around the test subject's neck to hold the face-hugger in place. He'd read the literature and watched the vid, but seeing it in person held him fast. Not only was he observing the morphology of an alien entity, he was also witnessing the impending death of a human being.

The face-hugger in Containment Room Two was faster—perhaps because of the behavior of the test subject. Although he had nowhere to run, the face-hugger didn't yet understand the parameters of its captivity. Not only did it whip itself free of the egg, moving in a blur, but it attacked the man's back, scraping him, forcing him to spin, thus making the job of the face-hugger that much easier.

The creature attached itself to the man's face, so Hoenikker couldn't see his expression, but he could imagine the wide eyes and the strangled scream, quickly silenced by the pressure of something entering the throat. The tail came around and wrapped itself once, then twice around the man's enormous neck. He clawed at the Xenomorph, but it was of no use.

Staggering to the center of the room, he spun one hundred and eighty degrees until he was facing toward them. His face was completely covered by what looked like the carapace of a large crab. He staggered again, fell to his knees, then onto his side.

Hoenikker checked to make sure the health data was still streaming, and shuddered.

The man was still alive.

Over in Containment Room One, things were moving a bit slower. The woman still sat with her back to the Ovomorph. The face-hugger had already crawled out of the egg and seemed to be regarding its imminent host. In no hurry, it moved to her. When it touched her back, she tensed, but otherwise made no move. She knew there was nowhere to go. Knew it was her end. She just didn't want to have to see it happen.

When it did, it happened fast. The face-hugger's tail latched around her neck and it propelled itself around in an arc, like a rock climber with a rope, landing on her face as if it were the face of a mountain it wanted to conquer.

She fell backward.

Her body twitched several times.

Then the tail tightened.

All the while, Hoenikker ensured that the data was recording. After a few moments, Kash approached.

"It's different seeing it in person," she said, wiping sweat from her upper lip. Hoenikker realized his mouth was dry. He swallowed and licked his lips.

"Sure is."

"Some believe they were made to do this," she said. "Others believe that it was evolution."

"That evolution could create something that needs another creature to survive makes the universe seem cruel," he said.

"Tapeworms, roundworms, and flukes have been invasive to humans since the dawn of time," she said.

"I don't see them busting out of their hosts' chests."

"They don't, you're right. But give it a million years. Who knows?"

"How long does it take?" he asked, then followed up by being more specific. "I mean, to go from face-hugger to chestburster."

"Not as long as you'd think. The gestation period is brisk. Far faster than one would believe. But then, the host doesn't need to survive the transition."

"I'm sure it wreaks havoc," he said. "Crash and burn the system."

"That's all we really are, just a bag of DNA," she replied. "The process doesn't care what's left."

He stared at the woman lying on her back, the face-hugger doing what it did, the tail wrapped around her neck.

"But for the moment it knows to keep the host alive. The evolution seems too impressive to be natural. It seems engineered. I couldn't imagine a better way to create an army. Gestate in the bodies of your enemies, then be reborn with acid for blood."

"Maybe that's why they're here."

"If they're part of an army, then who is the general?"

She didn't answer, nor did he expect her to. She moved on, recording data as it came.

"How are you holding up?" Cruz asked, stepping up beside Hoenikker. He glanced at the taller man, surprised at the attention.

"Better than I expected." He hesitated as he watched the body in Containment Room Two twitch and shudder. "I thought it would bother me more, but knowing they're doing this with intention helps mollify my apprehension."

Cruz nodded, observing both test subjects and their face-huggers. Then he turned to Containment Room Three.

"Will you still feel the same when we get to her?"

Hoenikker glanced over, then looked down. How could he know until they did it? He wasn't sure how he'd react. His feelings had changed since they'd spoken. He realized that so much of what he'd felt was like an echo of how he'd felt so long ago. He wasn't even sure if he still felt the same way—was the idea of loving her, or being in love, a force of habit he'd failed to break even after all these years? It was as if when he'd stopped seeing her, he'd just shelved his feelings, and never dealt with them.

"What is it we're going to do with her?" he asked.

"Irradiated pathogen for both her and the Ovomorph," Cruz said. "We're still in the data accumulation phase. We got lucky with the acid-resistant armor. We're hoping that after we accumulate enough data, we'll be sufficiently informed to use Leon-895 DNA to try and create some sort of biological cloaking mechanism to add to the acid resistance."

"That would be beneficial for sure," Hoenikker said, realizing how hollow the words sounded. "Have they found the missing Leon?"

"Not yet," Cruz said, frowning as he answered. "We never attached a transponder or a PDT to the creature. Had we done something as fucking simple as that, we would have been able to track it. We're not going to have that problem anymore. All of the test subjects have been tagged with PDTs, as will the chestbursters."

"With all the tech we have, I'm surprised it hasn't been found."

"You'd be surprised how big this place really is," Cruz said absently. Then he turned to Hoenikker. "Keep plugging in the data. Our algorithms will make sense of it, and we can move to the next step." Then he walked out of the lab, the door closing behind him.

Hoenikker stared after him, thinking of what the man had shared. Was the place bigger than it seemed to be? Kash had mentioned on several occasions that it was, but he'd never followed up. Why was that? Even as he asked himself, he knew the answer. He was Timothy Hoenikker. He toed the line, didn't ask questions, didn't buck the system. He did as he was told.

Well, maybe that all should change.

Maybe he should be a little more discerning.

Maybe he should ask a few more questions before he blindly followed directions.

Kash called for him, and he turned to assist.

In Containment Room Two, the woman's body lay still. At less than six beats a minute, her heart was barely functioning. The face-hugger itself had crawled away and lay dead in a corner. That meant the embryo was in place.

"Any time now," she said.

Hoenikker stared at the woman, and then the data, trying to see patterns in the numbers. Not knowing what to look for didn't stop him from his attempt to understand. He was a scientist through and through, and trusted in the process. He knew that eventually the pattern would reveal itself, but until then he'd record and push the data.

"On Earth, there is a wasp that lays its eggs in a live tarantula," Étienne said as he approached. "Most call it a tarantula hawk because of its size, but *pomplidae* is definitely a wasp. It first paralyzes the spider, then drags it to a hidden site for brooding. Once there, it lays a single egg on the underside of the tarantula—which isn't dead, mind you. It remains alive as the larva grows and then hatches. Once hatched, it burrows a hole into the tarantula's body and begins to eat its way through, avoiding the large organs until the very last. The idea is to keep the spider alive as long as possible, because it's the larva's only food source."

Hoenikker shuddered at the idea of being eaten alive from the inside.

"I often wonder which is worse," Étienne said. "Being eaten from the inside, or dying a quick death as an alien bursts from your chest." He gestured to the containment room with the man. He was sitting up and scratching the side of his head as if nothing was wrong. There, again, the face-hugger had crawled away to die. "Do you think he's being eaten from the inside, like he's a tarantula?"

"I think being eaten from the inside out has to be the worst," Hoenikker said. "Knowing that something is inside you has to be terrifying."

"But look at him." Étienne pointed at the man, who was now standing and peering into the empty egg. "Does he look scared?"

Hoenikker checked the data. "I show a doubling in serotonin production."

"Maybe that's the solution. Like a frog in a pot of water that slowly comes to a boil. Make someone happy that they have a parasite in their body, and they won't mind as much."

"Is that what the Xenomorphs are? Parasites?"

"What else would you call them?"

Monsters was what Hoenikker wanted to say.

The waiting seemed worse than the implantation had been. They remained at their stations for what felt like an eternity, but was in reality a little more than eight hours—tense the entire time with anticipation. Cruz didn't return, but Hoenikker, Kash, and Étienne didn't dare leave.

Then it happened.

More suddenly than he'd expected.

One moment, she was still; then she arched her back and her chest erupted as two sets of telegraphing jaws pierced free to the air. Claws gripped the pieces of ripped chest and the chestburster pulled itself free. The woman's blood pooled as the creature moved off and onto the floor, more tail and teeth than anything else.

Her vitals hit bottom as death overtook her.

Meanwhile, the creature moved to the back corner of the containment room and huddled there, a hatchling programmed to protect itself until it grew larger.

The man in his containment room remained unaware of what had happened to the woman. He'd finished idly inspecting the egg and had moved to the glass. He was in the process of testing it with his fingers when he suddenly got a look like he was about to vomit. He doubled over, then straightened.

Then his chest exploded.

Blood spattered the glass as the chestburster shot free. One moment the man was staring in surprise down at the hole in his chest, the next he was sagging to his knees, falling on his side as gravity stole his mobility, forever and a day.

29

The next day found them doing the same thing.

As well as the next.

And the next.

The scientific method and data modeling.

Hoenikker spent the nights watching one video in particular. The taking of Test Subject #3.

He'd been through the data dozens of times, but never tired in disassembling her destruction. Which was strange, considering what they'd once shared. At first, he'd felt concerned about his lack of emotional response. But then, after watching it, he'd felt as if she'd gotten what she wanted—some semblance of finality to her place in the universe.

Monica had never really been happy. She'd always needed someone else to make her complete. That she'd once chosen him to complete her showed her own inability to make the correct decisions. A broken bolt twisted by a broken tool into a broken system—doomed to failure.

In the end, her death had been more similar to the woman's than the man's, in that she never saw it coming.

Sure, when the egg had released the face-hugger, she'd stood her ground. Balled fists down at her sides, straight backed, she'd only flinched a little as the thing attached itself to her, wrapping its tail three times around her slender neck. Instead of falling, she'd backed toward the ledge near the back of the containment room and sat, resting her fists in her lap as she leaned on it for balance.

Her stoicism was what kept him coming back to the video. That she seemed so accepting of her situation demonstrated how much she'd changed in the intervening years. He'd rewatched the first half of the video no less than twenty times, trying to see if there had been any other reaction he could discern, but as often as he'd watched, he couldn't see any.

The second half of the video was hardest to watch.

She hadn't fared as well in the last three minutes and forty-seven seconds.

The face-hugger had been long gone and her serotonin levels were maxed when the thing inside of her began to move. She felt it, and tore her shirt away. Her breasts hung heavy, nipples pointed down and no longer in the bloom of youth. He'd known and mapped them when they were younger, but they weren't the focus of his attention. Instead, he stared at the lump that continually pressed against the inside of her chest and abdomen. Tentative at first, the chestburster wasn't ready for the full Monty. Instead, it pressed its face and jaws against the inside of her skin, revealing itself even before it broke free.

Each time it moved within her she'd shriek, then force herself to stand still. It was as if her single *fuck you* to the universe was to try not to panic, instead provide as much of herself to the witnesses as possible. For the sake of science? It had to be for the sake of science, because no one could possibly get off on the destruction of a human being in such a way. No one he'd ever want to know, anyway.

After three minutes and forty-seven seconds of it acting as if it wanted to be free, it burst out of her chest, falling to the ground where it lay stunned for long enough that they might have thought it was dead.

The first several times his eyes were on the chestburster, wondering if it was going to live, then somehow insanely pleased that it had. Later he'd watched her, and noted that she hadn't died immediately. She'd managed to live for almost thirty seconds longer, her hand coming up and feeling the gaping hole in her chest, her fingers feeling around inside. Then falling to her knees. Staring out the containment room window, her face pinched with pain but also angry, as if asking if this was what they wanted her to do—be a tool for someone's experiment, allowing an alien to gestate inside her all so a mega-corp could create something from which it could profit.

He told himself this and then he argued with himself, even knowing it was specious.

She died for a reason.

Monica died because she *wanted* to.

She died because she'd murdered someone, and had to pay the price.

It was almost as if she'd had the last laugh. He might have been projecting, but even if he hadn't known her, he would have understood her stance and wondered at his own morality—of allowing a thinking and breathing human being to be used in such a manner.

The corporation be damned.

The Xenomorphs grew amazingly fast. The first three had already reached full adulthood and stalked back and forth inside their containment rooms. The bodies and the vestiges of the previous morphology had been removed via mechanical means.

Cruz kept the temperature near freezing in those containment rooms. Although the Xenomorphs were seemingly impervious to extremes, he was hoping that if needed, they could reverse the temperature with superheated fire to shock their systems. Sustained fire would kill them, and repeated shocks to their exoskeletons might make them more docile.

At least, that was Cruz's hypothesis.

The creatures salivated profusely, ribbons and rivulets dripping from their mouths. Cruz mentioned that he'd seen some with the ability to spit acid, but as yet this hadn't been an issue.

The two Xenomorphs in Containment Rooms One and Two appeared normal, their torpedo-shaped heads immense on a frame that even at two meters tall seemed too small to support them. Likewise, the tails and extended vertebrae nodes seemed normal, based on the records from previous encounters.

Things began to change with Test Subject #3. Although she'd become a drone like the previous two, her skin was dark and leathery with an odd striping, the texture evident from many meters away. The overall effect was different, this Xenomorph seeming more malevolent.

Test Subject #5 grew an extra set of arms. These mostly hung down at its sides, but the hands seemed to face behind it, so when it raised them, it was capable of holding items in either direction. Étienne was especially excited about this, wondering if the duopolistic condition also carried forward to its senses.

Test Subject #7 was perhaps the strangest augmentation. Although the head was the usual smooth torpedo shape of the drone Xenomorph with nary a mouth or any other visible sense organs, the body was translucent. Almost white. What one might call an albino.

The body was more human-shaped as well, the knees and torso larger than a human's but functioning just the same.

Étienne wanted to introduce this test subject to the others, to see how they'd react. His hypothesis was that this could be a super-drone, capable of leading the others. But Cruz was adamant that security protocols should be observed, so no comingling of test subjects was possible. Still, Étienne worked on several ideas to accomplish his goals, and determine if his hypotheses were correct.

Four test subjects had been reserved for Leon-895 experimentation. Security had managed to procure one of the creatures on an approved hunt, and Cruz was determined to inject its blood, combined with the pathogen, into the four subjects, while incrementally increasing irradiation. His hope was that they could create a Xenomorph with chameleon-like properties, and then transition the science to armor, much as they'd previously done with the acid-resistance experimentation.

That breakthrough had been based on the Xenomorphs' resistance to their own acidic qualities. One of the strongest corrosives in the known universe, the creatures had it inside their bodies both as a defense mechanism and to carry nutrients. How something could eat through metal, and not eat through skin and organs, had flummoxed the scientists until the late Matthews had analyzed the Xenomorph DNA. He had been able to pinpoint the gene that made it possible.

Thus gene-splicing armor was made from the lab-grown skin of a Xenomorph.

If they could do that, Cruz proposed, why couldn't they then identify the genes that enabled chameleon abilities, and use them in the creation of a new and improved Xenomorph? Hoenikker, while appreciating the idea, thought that having a nearly invisible, utterly impervious killing machine was a perilous idea, and was reluctant to have anything to do with it.

Which was why he was happy to play transcriber, while his associates manipulated the most dangerous genes in the galaxy.

30

Cruz didn't like where the experiments were taking them. Sure, they were seeing results that they could manipulate, but not the results they *needed*. They needed something they could monetize.

Bellows had already called him into the office. The station commander stressed the success of the acid-resistant armor, and demanded that they continue in that direction. The problem was, that last breakthrough had been the proverbial lightning in a bottle, and trying to replicate it might prove to be impossible.

Still, they'd been working on gene mapping, and had ideas where to go.

Then everything was put on hold.

The missing Leon-895 had gotten hungry.

Folks had mostly forgotten about it, many hoping it had found a way outside, where it wouldn't be a problem. Ironically, Edmonds of Casualty Operations had gone mostly missing. His ID and a magnificent amount of his blood had been found on one of the corridor floors. Bellows had insisted that every operation come to a full stop, until they were able to find and sequester the predator.

Cruz strode down a corridor, flanked by a synth and two male security guards with pulse rifles. One of the guards had a motion detector that was pointed toward the ceiling. The other had an IR viewer pointed in the same direction.

The synth faced backward, protecting their rear.

"I'm still not sure why I need to be part of the team," Cruz said, not liking at all that he wasn't allowed a weapon. He also knew that they'd never have been in this position had he been in charge from the beginning. It was the ineptitude of the bureaucrat Mansfield that had allowed the creature to escape. Not that he'd paid with his life, but still. Cruz should have been in charge from the very first moment he'd appeared on station.

"Not my business," security guard number one said. "Bellows is the one who put the teams together."

"I get that," Cruz said, trying hard not to roll his eyes at the commands of yet another bureaucrat. "But what is it you expect me to do?"

"Whatever you think will help," security guard number two answered. Which left Cruz scratching his now bearded chin.

He'd created Leon-895, but wasn't keen on its hunting techniques. He'd never seen it in the wild, had never interacted with it outside of a containment room. His intent had been to enhance the creature's innate ability to blend into the background. Just a little black goo behind the ears and *poof*—invisible.

They moved a few feet and stopped. The idea wasn't to search, but to hold an area. Other teams like theirs were in other corridors, waiting for evidence of the creature. If this didn't work, they'd have the synths go from room to room while they held their positions. One way or another, they were going to find the Leon.

The radio chattered.

One of the security guards responded.

Nothing more than boredom.

Cruz had seen it enough during his time in the marines. Standing around and holding a rifle wasn't anyone's dream job. Guard duty sucked, pure and simple, no matter where you were, but it was something that had to be done. He'd just figured, with his improvement in paygrade, that it would no longer be him.

Fifteen minutes later the radio chattered again. This time the words were punctuated by the sound of pulse rifles.

"What's going on?" Cruz asked, again wishing they'd given him a weapon. After all, he was probably more familiar with one than they were.

"Sighting," security guard number two said. "Corridor. Over by Comms section."

More chatter.

More pulse fire.

"Is it headed this way?" Cruz asked.

As if in response, the security guards spun and aimed their detectors at the ceiling. Both devices went off, and began to wail. Cruz watched as the Leon appeared, rushed by overhead, using the metal beams of the ceiling to propel itself forward. As it passed, it reached down with one appendage and tore free the head of the synth, the body falling to the floor, nothing more than a pile of useless invention.

Then Leon was gone again. The security guards fired blindly, defeating the purpose of the detectors. If they hit anything, there was no indication.

Cruz shook his head.

Why couldn't they just have a platoon of Colonial Marines, instead of private security? Reaching down, he snagged the pistol the synth had been holding. At least now he was armed. He felt better.

"Did you hit it?" Number One asked.

"I think so," Number Two said. "What about you?"

"Definitely."

Cruz pushed them both aside, grabbed the motion indicator, and headed after the Leon.

"You boys didn't hit shit."

"Wait? Where are you going?" Number One asked. "We're supposed to stay here, in the event—"

"You mean if it comes this way? It did. It came, and it went." Cruz continued walking. "And I'm going after it."

"But we're supp—"

He turned the corner before he could hear any more of their bullshit. He'd never been good at guard duty because he could never follow directions. The idea of staying in one place and staring into a pre-described space seemed as interesting as sticking a pen in his ear.

Cruz bumped into another security team that seemed as clueless the last one. Hoenikker stood with them, looking as out of place as an ice cream cone in a gun factory.

"Did it pass?" Cruz asked.

Hoenikker nodded. "Didn't see it. Just heard it." His wide eyes betrayed his attempt at courage.

"Give me a pistol," Cruz said to the synth on the team.

The synth handed it over.

"Hey, wait a minute," one of the security guards said.

"Enough. Give me your radio," Cruz said. He didn't wait. He snatched it from the guard, who looked as if he wanted to fight for it, but Cruz was the larger of the two and a station scientist. He handed the extra pistol to Hoenikker, who stared at it like it was about to go off.

"Safety is off. Jut aim and pull the trigger."

"What am I aiming at?" Hoenikker asked.

"Oh, you'll know." Then Cruz spoke into the radio. "All stations this net. Listen, find something liquid. Paint. Blood. Whatever. When the Leon passes, cover it so we can spot it easier. Right now it's doing laps around us. Paint it with something that sticks, and we can take it down."

"What are we doing?" Hoenikker asked.

"We're going to stand by and listen. Stand back to back and aim at the ceiling. I'll tell you when," Cruz said.

Hoenikker did as he was told, and pressed himself against Cruz until their backs were touching. They stood there for a few moments, listening to the crackle of the radio.

"Sorry about the way I've treated you in the lab," Cruz said.

"What? Oh. It's okay," Hoenikker said. "Things have been… well… a little frightful."

Cruz listened to the chatter, tracking the action. "None of this is what you expected, is it, Tim?"

"I can't say I planned on this. Mansfield promised me alien artifacts."

"How about actual aliens?" Cruz asked.

"Not so fond of living creatures, no offense to them," Hoenikker said. "I was just hoping to apply my specialty."

"You do see the importance of our mission, don't you?"

"Of course." Hoenikker shifted his pistol to his other hand. "I mean, protecting people is important, but… well… never mind."

"No, what is it?"

"It's just that, knowing the history behind many of the civilizations that preceded us could better inform our way forward on both a macro and micro level. Imagine the advancements we could make, researching the successes and failures of those who've come before."

Hoenikker had made a valid point, but Cruz knew research of that sort wasn't what made Weyland-Yutani the corporation that it was. Discovery of the Xenomorphs, and their attempts to own the morphology, spoke volumes about the company. They'd monetize breathing the air if they could validate it in court.

Hell, given the filtration systems, they already had, he supposed.

"Hold on," Cruz said, hearing harried curses on the radio. "It's coming around again."

"Which way?"

Cruz listened, then spun so that he and Hoenikker were facing the same direction.

"This way."

"Is it coming?"

"Yes—and some brainiac actually listened to me."

Pulse rifle shots from around the corner.

Cruz held his pistol and began to fire even before he saw anything. Aiming for the ceiling rail because that was what the Leon would be using to propel itself.

Reports were that it had been shot. When it appeared, it almost shocked him. Someone had managed to cover it in pink paint, defeating its camouflage ability in a mockery of science. His rounds snapped into the Leon as it hurtled around the corner, blood mixing with the paint, splattering against the wall.

Beside him, Hoenikker turtled, hunching protectively inward, the pistol clutched in two shaking hands.

The Leon fell to the ground and began to crawl toward them. Slowly, on its last breaths. But Cruz was out of ammo. He dropped the hand holding the pistol and backed up a step.

"Shoot it," he shouted to Hoenikker. "Kill it."

The terrified archaeologist held out his pistol with shaking hands, and just as the creature reached him, pressed it to its head and pulled the trigger. Brains went everywhere.

Then Hoenikker threw up.

31

It wasn't all a loss. At least they were able to harvest mature stem cells from the dead Leon-895, which Cruz felt could better manipulate the Xenomorph morphology.

Hoenikker played along. He was so out of his element, he just wanted everything to be done so he could get back to his *real* research. Dealing with aliens hands-on wasn't what he'd signed up for. He wanted artifacts. He wanted models. He wanted constructs.

He wanted stone and metal and composite, and not the biological messiness that came with living beings.

Instead of losing a full day, they'd only lost a few hours. Bellows was beyond pleased. With one synth and two guards lost, he called it an unmitigated success. He'd lauded the effort over the intercom, boasting his idea for so long that people started to ignore it and went back to work.

Back in the lab, they finalized several variations of the stem cells to inject into the last three Ovomorphs. The other containment rooms all boasted grown Xenomorphs. Their menacing pacing and scratching against the glass served as reminders that only slim engineering protected the scientists from certain death.

The Xenomorph in Containment Room Five had already shown overt aggression. Cruz was having none of it. He spent an hour burning it with flame and freezing it with ice, until finally the hideous beast retreated to a corner and cowered beneath its four clawed hands. One set was pointed weirdly outward. Hoenikker had been afraid that Cruz might be borrowing trouble, but the results were undeniable.

Étienne and Kash asked him to join them at the examination table near the front of the lab. They had their vid screens laid out, displaying some data they'd been debating. They needed an impartial assessor, and he'd been their first, last, and only choice since asking Cruz was out of the question.

They all perched on stools. Étienne had his hands placed on top of each other, his eyes entreating. Kash sat sideways, as if she'd been forced into the conversation but felt she had to be part of it.

"We need interaction," Étienne said firmly. "We need to put two of them together." Hoenikker glanced at Kash, who rolled her eyes. He looked back at Étienne.

"What does interaction provide that you can't have now?"

"I want to test how their pheromones change when they are in proximity to one another."

"I still don't understand," Hoenikker said. He looked at Kash again, but she just shook her head.

"They were either developed or evolved to become prime hunters. Definitely the alphas at the top of the food chain," Étienne said, his French accent a little stronger when he became more assertive. "Yet they have no discernable eyes.

There have to be additional ways they can identify friend and foe. Some have hypothesized that echolocation is one means to identify prey, as it is with bats. Others believe they can see through the carapaces, and have a much wider view than we suspect."

"It's too dangerous," Kash said, interrupting. "What you plan is too dangerous."

"No. No. *Mademoiselle*, what I plan can surely be done. We need to shock their systems, then they will be—"

"We don't even have a handle on human pheromones," Kash said. "We've been studying those for centuries, and it's still pseudoscience."

"Then how do you explain some of the perfumes used to draw men or women? It's no longer just pleasant smells. I had a friend from medical school who was working on the idea of capturing sweat and recreating it in labs." Étienne rubbed his armpit, smelled his hand, then held it out for the others. "To someone, this is as sweet as the most expensive perfume. In it, there is a science of behavior we can finally understand."

Both Kash and Hoenikker leaned away from his offer.

"This is more than just the smell of sweat," Étienne continued. "It will tell you if I am afraid. It will tell you if I am in love. It will tell you many things—our problem is that we have an imperfect method of evaluating and translating the information."

Kash put her hand on his arm. "I get that, Étienne. I really do. Please, put your sweat away, and hear me out. Trying to evaluate the chemical properties of the perspiration on an alien is about as esoteric a concept as one can imagine." She glanced back to where Cruz sat at a workstation, and jerked her chin in his direction.

"Plus, he will never go for it."

Étienne grinned and smoothed his mustache. "*Ma cherie*, I have always been one to ask forgiveness first, and ask permission later."

Kash gave a sigh of frustration and almost turned away.

"What's the primary benefit that can be derived from this experiment?" Hoenikker asked.

"Primary benefit?" Étienne replied, his eyes off and into the distance.

"*Oui. Quel est le principal avantage?*" Hoenikker asked.

Étienne's eyes lit up. "*Oui. Oui.* I see what you have done here. Who knew you spoke French?" He waggled a finger. "You have been keeping this from me. *Le principal avantage*, hmm. If we are able to capture the scent of a Xenomorph in close proximity to another Xenomorph, perhaps we can create a chemical compound that is a deterrent? It could be replicated, and used as a protective spray."

"They can still tell that we are human, or at least not of their species," Kash said.

"If we look human but smell Xeno, wouldn't that give them pause?" Étienne asked. "Come on, Erin. This is all scientific method. This is a hypothesis. At least give me a chance to prove it before you dash it on the rocks of common sense."

"Do you really think you have the ability to break down the scent of a Xenomorph?" Hoenikker asked. Étienne stared at him for a long moment, then placed his hand on Hoenikker's shoulder.

"Yes. Yes, I do."

"Then let's do it," Hoenikker said. "But first, we have to clear it through Cruz."

Étienne's face fell. He threw up his hands.

"Then this will never happen."

He got up and walked away.

But Hoenikker had another idea. He felt that Cruz would

go for it. It was all in how he sold it. Even the worst pill could be swallowed if given with something sweet.

An hour later, they were preparing Containment Rooms One and Two. Like the other rooms, these had accesses in the rear and were joined by a common door. No Xenomorph would need to be removed. Instead, they would just open the door between them.

"How'd you get Cruz to go for it?" Kash asked as they prepared for the experiment.

"I made him think it was his idea. I also pointed out that if it worked—and if Weyland-Yutani could monetize it—every Colonial Marine, and miner, and settler in the known systems would want a spray bottle of Xenomorph Defender."

"Did you come up with the name?" Kash asked, her smile wide and appreciating.

"I did," Hoenikker said. "Think it's too much?"

She laughed. "No. I think it's perfect."

None of them were sure what was going to happen when they raised the door between the containment rooms. Would the Xenos attack each other? Would they see each other as allies? Given their source, the scientists believed that the Ovomorphs came from the same queen, so the adult Xenomorphs were essentially siblings. They *should* be able to interact without killing each other.

In fact, Étienne was sure of it, but the moment the door slid open and the two creatures turned to face each other, the lab was filled with tension. No one said a word. It wasn't until they rushed at each other, then circled like dogs might have, sniffing each other, that Étienne pounded a victorious fist into his palm.

"Yes!" he said.

The creatures moved together for a moment, then switched rooms, each Xenomorph investigating the newly opened space. Their movements were sudden, much like a display on a vid that jerked due to an irregular signal—stuck one moment, and then having already moved the next.

Having inspected their new surroundings they met again, touching each other, tails whipping, jaws drooling. The scientists watched while they continued in this way for an hour, then when each Xenomorph found itself in its original containment room, they shut the door between them.

What came next was unexpected. Each containment room boasted a suite of utility arms that could detach from the walls, floor, and ceiling. Whenever they tried to release one, the Xenomorph would attack it. The hypothesis was that once they became aggressive, the pheromones would change.

So it was with a deft hand that Cruz operated the workstation. He pumped in music that might be present in the mess hall or waiting in a med suite. Whether it was to calm the creatures or himself, he never said. Then he fired an arm from the ceiling of the room that wiped the torpedo skull of the Xenomorph with a length of cotton. The creature whipped around, some of its drool striking the wall, ceiling, and cloth. Then Cruz snapped the utility arm back into the ceiling.

He sat back and grinned.

"Okay, Étienne. It's time to get your science on."

Étienne looked surprised.

"Don't pretend this wasn't you," Cruz said. "I know Hoenikker, and he'd never think of pheromone sprays. Trust in a Frenchman to want to make a cologne."

"Oui." Étienne grinned. *"Oui*. Time for science."

32

Things were humming.

Kash was continuing her painstaking observations.

Étienne was working on his pet project that might actually *be* something.

And Cruz was doing what he wanted—supervising the team, and he had his own project with the Leon. All the Xeno eggs had hatched, including the last three they'd saved for the Leon-895 stem cells. Mixed with varying amounts of pathogen, each egg was injected with a serum in an attempt to see if they could replicate the chameleonic abilities in a Xenomorph.

The most difficult gestation to watch had been Test Subject #11. For a few days he had begun to exhibit a hope that had never been there. He'd been fed and kept comfortable for so long that he came to believe they might actually have commuted his sentence. But when they'd finally removed the bottom of the cryo case, he'd run to the glass and banged against it until his fists left streaks of blood.

When the face-hugger finally did emerge, he ran, then fought the creature, actually managing to grab the tail as it whipped around his arm. He began to beat the arm against the wall, hard enough to break it. Bone could be seen protruding from the injury. He tried to pry free the face-hugger, but the creature was having none of it.

Then the Test Subject did something completely unexpected. He placed the tip of the bone against the side of his neck and rammed himself into the wall. Once. Twice. Three times. Then on the fourth he managed to puncture his jugular. He went down, blood pumping furiously.

Cruz could have sworn that the man smiled, dying as he did, having outfoxed the face-hugger, who wouldn't be able to implant a chestburster inside a dead man. The face-hugger tried to attach itself to the dead man's face, but its own biological imperative wouldn't allow it. It needed something living, and there was nothing in the room to which it could attach itself.

It scrambled around, seemingly frantic, bouncing against one wall then another, plastering itself onto the glass that fronted the enclosure, until it slid miserably to the floor.

Cruz turned away. Unless they had a spare prisoner, Containment Room Eleven was a wasted opportunity. While part of him had rooted for the man to survive, and part of him had saluted the man for giving the big middle finger to Weyland-Yutani, the waste of an Ovomorph wasn't going to play well with the boss.

Bellows had handed him his ass, or at least tried to. Drill sergeants and commanders had handed Cruz his ass on various platters, so he took what Bellows gave and pretended he had enough hurt feelings to mollify the station commander.

Shit way to run an operation, he thought angrily. *Someone should show them how it ought to be done.*

Someone like him.

Hoenikker, meanwhile, was busy helping where he could. While Cruz hadn't really liked the man—probably because he was so entirely different from a Colonial Marine—he'd come to appreciate his work ethic. Even Étienne had backbone. Kash had backbone. Hoenikker... Cruz just wasn't sure.

Even now, the archaeologist carried samples back and forth for Kash, acting more like a third-year lab assistant than a fully credentialed scientist. What was a theoretical archeologist, anyway? Didn't really sound very scientific.

Étienne approached. "Remarkable. Do you know how complex these beings are?"

Cruz nodded. "However they came to be, they have some remarkable tendencies. What have you learned?"

"I examined not only the sweat you gathered from the carapace, but also the salivation we managed to capture. I think there's a sympathetic symbiosis between the two, as many of the cells I found were exactly the same."

Cruz grinned. "Can they be replicated?"

"I think so."

"Then what's the next step? Are you going to lather up and walk into one of the containment areas?" Cruz asked.

Étienne gave him a look. "That isn't funny," he replied. "We'll figure it out once we are able to replicate. Until then, I'm not even going to worry about it."

Cruz shook his head. "You can't go through your life being an inflight spaceship repairman."

Now it was Étienne's turn to grin. "Of course I can. It's worked for me so far." And then he was off, back to his microscopes. Cruz enjoyed the man's energy and his confidence. If only every scientist had the same.

He approached the Xenomorph in Containment Room Seven, observing the smooth, elongated head and reticulated jaws that continually snapped at the air. The human-shaped body was also intriguing. They'd been able to conduct scans and noted a biology that seemed to share components of both humans and Xenomorphs. With no eyes and no nose, it had to somehow detect the presence of others and note its surroundings through its mouth, using echolocation, or perhaps tasting the air.

Maybe Étienne was onto something. Perhaps pheromones were the missing link to understanding these complex aliens.

The longer Cruz stared at the creature, the more he wondered at its genetic origins. A static at the back of his brain started to rise, as if he'd tuned in to some new broadcast. The adult Xenomorph drones on either side of Seven began to spit acid at the glass. Their jaws launching forward, their tongues following like alien stilettos. Cruz felt a need to *do* something. He *wanted* to do something, but he didn't know what it was.

Cruz blinked and shook his head. The feeling remained, but it lessened a bit. Was he feeling contact from Seven? Had it told Six and Eight to attack the glass, and was he able to listen in to part of it? Or was he imagining it?

Hoenikker paused to stare at the glass of Containment Room Six.

"Should they be doing that?" Captain Obvious asked.

Cruz heard but didn't say anything. Instead, he listened and attended to the feeling. Was Seven communicating somehow with the others? Was the feeling inside his own head a broadcast of some sort, or was it literally inside his head?

Hoenikker approached him.

"Dr. Cruz, I don't think that—"

"Shut up and listen. Do you feel it? Do you *sense* it? Use your brain and embrace the science instead of the fear, Dr. Hoenikker. Seven is trying to communicate." Cruz looked past Hoenikker's hurt feelings and saw Kash working diligently in the front of the lab. "Erin. Do we have anything to measure frequencies?"

She paused and stared thoughtfully at one of the supply closets. "We don't, but I bet Comms does."

"Can you get us something, please?" he asked. She stared for a moment, then nodded.

Kash understood the need.

She wasn't scared like Hoenikker.

Then she left the lab.

Cruz's head buzzed with some sort of purpose he couldn't quite work out. He felt the energy. He felt a directive, but he lacked the translation to understand what it meant. He turned to Six and watched it spit acid repeatedly at the same spot. Over and over. Acid. On the glass. Then he turned to Eight and watched it doing the same thing. Directed. Focused.

Then Cruz understood.

Seven was smart.

Seven was the brain.

Seven wanted to escape.

It didn't have the capacity itself, but it did have a way to influence.

Cruz stepped over to Containment Room Seven's workstation. He sat and stared for a moment at the gray-skinned Xenomorph, so different to the others. Was it really a byproduct of irradiated pathogen—an accident of nature? Or was it designed to be this way? Had they unlocked something?

Kash had wanted to introduce this drone to the others, to see how they'd react. Her hypothesis was that this could be a super-drone, capable of leading the others. Cruz believed she might be right.

He watched as the other Xenomorphs attacked the glass for a few more moments, then he pressed a button. Fire rained down on Seven, causing it to flinch and fall back. And the other two Xenomorphs?

They stopped their attacks on the glass, instead investigating their demesne as they had been—in menacing whirls and jerks, tails whipping, no longer concerned at what they'd just been poised to do.

Cruz nodded.

Kash had *definitely* been right. Whether by design or accident, Seven was a creature to be watched.

33

Life in the lab continued anxiously, four scientists doing what eight should do.

Hoenikker was beginning to like this life a lot more since the chestbursters had turned into adult Xenomorphs. Even as he thought it, he felt bad for the thinking of it. For the adults to be present meant that humans had to have died, but he'd been working on coming to terms with it. He'd forced himself to accept it. He hadn't been in charge, and had no control over the process. Because of this, he'd been able to detach himself from the morphological step that required the incubation of humans.

Even the idea that Monica had now become an inglorious Xenomorph was an acceptable fact in the face of the idea that he finally had a race of alien entities for which he could create an archaeological model.

He pored over the data they had about the lifecycle of the Xenomorphs, curious about the relationship between the drones and the warriors and the queen. It was too easy for him to make comparisons to a beehive or an anthill because of the use of the term "queen." He needed to realize that the imperfect word was meant as a description for an unknown to adhere to a known, and wasn't truly identifiable. "Queen" was nothing more than a placeholder until a better scientific term could be found.

By using the term, he locked himself into a certain train of thought. The use of "queen" meant there was a sort of worship and respect. That all other beings of the same genetic model would intervene on her behalf, and do her bidding. But the term "mother" could also be used for that.

Or another term, not yet determined.

One of the issues with archaeological modeling was that unless he used the exact terms in the target species' language, he was doomed to be wrong. Bringing human terms to a model of Xenomorph anthropology was akin to bringing a knife to a gunfight. Sure, he might succeed, but there was so much he had to overcome to do so.

Not that they had a queen to study, which Hoenikker found himself wishing they had. He'd love to study the female Xenomorph, and its ability to control the males of the species. In that, the Xenomorphs were interesting because they didn't parallel carbon-based mammals as much as they mirrored an insectile sociological structure. Which brought him back to the bees.

With a female being at the center of all activities, and perhaps even directing them, how would the eleven Xenomorphs they held in their containment areas create their own sociological interactions, unless there was some sort of genetic marker that identified one as being superior to the other?

While examining Seven, Hoenikker couldn't help wondering if the Xenomorph might not have been genetically triggered *because* of the absence of a queen. Could nature be predisposed to fill a vacuum? He had been fascinated by

Seven's apparent ability to silently manipulate or direct the other Xenomorphs. But now, after three more days of having to flame Seven because the others were spitting acid on their glass containment fronts, the humanlike Xeno was becoming a pain in the ass.

Cruz wanted to get rid of it, but Bellows wouldn't allow it. They'd already lost Eleven, and Bellows didn't want to have to explain to Weyland-Yutani why they kept losing hyper-expensive corporate resources. So, Cruz was left with continually trying to stop Seven from influencing the others.

Meanwhile, the creature's reach had grown, and it became able to influence Four, Five, Six, Nine, and Ten, all of which would randomly begin attacking their glass barriers. Every time they started, one of the scientists would have to move to Seven's workstation and actuate the flame system.

Worse, there was no way to measure damage to the glass. Fabrications came to take a look, and their idea of help was to stand around with blank looks in their eyes, gaping at the Xenos, scratching their heads and saying, *"I don't know."*

When faced with this new problem, Bellows' solution was to have the two synths already assigned to the lab flame each of the Xenos whenever they started spitting acid at the glass. As logical as it sounded, the synths were suddenly in everyone's way, racing from one workstation to another as they tried to stop all the creatures.

What upset Cruz the most was that Seven seemed to be influencing the new Leon-895 he'd been able to create using the stem cells he'd mined from the original creature. At the same time as the Xenomorphs began to spit acid, the Leon would begin cycling through the colors of the spectrum in a dizzying display of camouflage. This ate into Cruz's experimentation time. His frustration was evident in the way he would take it out on the others. He'd begun to talk to Hoenikker as if he were a lab assistant.

"Give me a hand, will you?" Étienne said, jolting Hoenikker out of his reverie.

"What do you need?" Hoenikker asked, eager to do something. Étienne held up a beaker that had several ounces of clear liquid.

"Smell this."

Hoenikker hesitated, then leaned forward.

"There isn't any scent."

"No. Nothing that we can smell. However, watch this."

With an eyedropper, Étienne took a sample. Two cages rested on the table, a rat in each cage. He pulled the rat on the left free of its cage and placed two drops on its back. The rat squirmed for thirty seconds and almost got free, but went still. Étienne put it back into its cage. The rat circled a few times, then stopped.

"What am I supposed to see?" Hoenikker asked.

"Nothing yet. Wait for it."

Étienne then pushed both cages together. The other rat immediately ran to the side of the cage farthest from the first rat, and began to tremble visibly.

"We can't smell the liquid, but these rats can."

"Why didn't the first rat react?"

"Oh, it did. You saw it trying to get away. It wasn't trying to get away from me. It was trying to get away from itself. Somehow the pheromone merged with that of the rat, and it calmed. That's not unlike what happens when a face-hugger calms its victim. Or else the rat's brain sensed that there was no obvious threat. I'll need to experiment further to figure this out."

Étienne took the cage with the unchanged rat over to the workstation in front of Containment Room One. He glanced at the Xenomorph, who was prowling the other end of the chamber. Removing the rat, he opened a small hatch to the bottom right of the glass, placed the rat inside, and closed the door. Then he depressed a button on the workstation, an access panel slid to the side, and the rat fell into the room. It immediately found the nearest corner and started scratching where the glass met the wall.

The Xenomorph's torpedo-shaped head whipped around. It spun, impossibly fast, tail ripping through the air. In three steps it was upon the rodent, jaw opening, then telescoping out to snap the mammal in half. The alien rose to its full height and stared at Étienne, red and silver saliva dripping to the floor. It snapped its jaw out one more time, this time catching the glass, the teeth scraping it as a lance-like tongue tapped against the barrier.

Étienne grinned, got up, and returned the cage to the table. "That was fun," he said.

Then he grabbed the other cage, containing the rat that had been subjected to the pheromone. He took this to the workstation and repeated the process. In a moment, the rat was in the cage, just as frantic as the other, scrambling over the remains of the first as it tried to claw through the window.

Xeno One watched the whole thing, and in a single bound hovered over the rat, saliva dripping onto it, making it frantic with terror. Curiously, though, the predator didn't attack the tiny creature. Instead it crouched, reached down, and grabbed it in a clawed hand. It held it there as if examining it. Then it stood took two steps back and hurled the creature as hard as it could into the glass.

The rat exploded as its skin parted with the force of the contact and its organs burst forth. Hoenikker, who'd come forward to observe, backed away in horror. Meanwhile, Étienne clapped his hands and laughed.

"Isn't it wonderful?"

"What do you mean? The Xenomorph still killed the rat."

"Yes, but not for the reason it killed the first one."

"But they're both still *dead*."

"The second one lived longer than the first. Why is that, Timothy? Why would the creature let it live, even go so far as picking it up and examining it?"

Hoenikker shook his head with disgust. "And then throwing it against the glass."

Étienne turned. "You're letting your emotions get in the way, and missing it. The pheromone I reproduced had a definite effect. We've achieved something measurable." He hurried back to the workstation. "Now to record the data and see if I need to manipulate the strain."

Hoenikker remained in place, his gaze on the streaks of blood and guts that were slowly sliding down the vertical surface of the glass.

Archaeological modeling.

No blood in that science.

Just clean facts and clear suppositions.

He shook his head and turned away, wishing he'd never taken this job.

34

Rawlings would rather have been sitting behind his desk, drinking his third cup of coffee of the day. He'd already had two, one before breakfast and one after.

Or better yet, in the mess hall. Today was Salisbury steak day, one of his favorites, but he'd be lucky if he even got leftovers. Both he and Webb from Engineering had been assigned to find a missing box of data chips that were required to fix the air conditioning in the commander's quarters. Engineering swore they knew where they were, but as it turned out—not so much.

And Rawlings. Hell, he wasn't doing anything. Might as well get him to do something that's not his job because someone else lost a box of data chips. Sure. *"Get Rawlings. He's just here to take care of pretty much everything."*

They'd gone through two rooms thus far, and had twelve more to go.

He sighed.

"And you should'a seen the walls of the old deputy's quarters," Webb continued. "He has heads of creatures I didn't even know had heads. So much outside'a Pala Station. I understand people hate it inside, but the outside is hella more dangerous."

Webb was a little over five feet tall, with an immense chest and arms. Fabrications had to make special tops for his uniform so they would fit. He was a gym rat and was always asking Rawlings if he couldn't get them to requisition more exercise equipment. But as big as he was, he had a higher pitched voice than was normal, and was the station's center of gossip.

Rawlings nodded as he used his security card to open a third room. Webb hadn't shut up the entire time they'd been searching. This room had belonged to Comms Specialist Brennan, and had been filled with boxes of supplies brought down from the *San Lorenzo*. Each box bore the name of the ship from which it had come, along with a barcode. Made of composite metal-plastics, they were both heavier and lighter than seemed appropriate.

They had to move them aside as Webb used his scanner to find the box they were looking for. He'd scan, the device would beep, he'd look at the readout, and shake his head. All through it, he never stopped talking.

"This was Brennan's room, wasn't it? I heard he died. Some say he was murdered." He glanced at Rawlings, dimples on his face as he grinned. "What do you know about that?"

"Really not supposed to talk about it."

"Aww, come on. We're just passing time. You know you can trust me to keep a secret."

Now it was Rawlings' turn to grin.

Webb saw it and added, "When have you ever known me to share a *real* secret." *Beep.* "Sure, I might pass some info around about this or that." *Beep.* "What about that time there were bugs in the food? I was the one who broke the news and saved the station." *Beep.* "You act as if I'm never helpful." *Beep.*

"You're helpful," Rawlings said. Half the Salisbury steak was already gone. He was sure of it. "I just can't talk about it."

"Well, it's not as if Brennan wasn't going to get in trouble anyway." *Beep.* "Everyone knew he spent most of his work time playing a video game." *Beep.* "What was it called? Damn if I remember." He stood up straight. "Whelp, it looks as if this room is clear. Let's go."

They moved to the next room that was being used to store supplies. This one was farther away from the active corridors, and near the blockaded area where station personnel—other than security services—were unable to pass. Rawlings spied a rat scurrying down the edge of the corridor, but ignored it. He'd tired of the constant presence of the creatures, and was loath to report it. After all, he might be the one chosen to be on extermination duty. Searching for a missing box was bad enough, but that would be even worse.

He slid the security card over the door and it opened, sending a rush of putrid air that quickly surrounded them and threatened to make the coffee return for a second showing. Webb turned his head.

"Something die in here? Jesus." He pulled his collar over his mouth and nose.

Rawlings covered his face with his left hand. Surely they hadn't stumbled on something dead? He recollected that there was a thing called a King Rat, where rats in a nest got their tails so intertwined that they couldn't move, and ended up dying of starvation. Was that what this was? Had they stumbled upon the mother of all King Rats?

"You first," Rawlings said nasally, trying not to breathe.

"Hells no." Webb shook his head and backed up a step. "You want to go in there, then you go."

Rawlings felt a flare of anger. He was missing breakfast because the engineers lost a box, and now their chosen representative didn't want to go into a room because it stank. What the fucking hell?

Webb must have seen his face because he patted the air, palms out.

"Okay. Fine. Be that way. I'll go in first."

"You did lose the box," Rawlings pointed out, not willing to let it go. "I'm just along for the ride."

Webb gave him a sour look, but said nothing more. With a ham-fisted hand he pushed open the door. The room was like the others, filled with boxes nearly to the ceiling, except this one felt as if it was an animal's burrow.

"Jesus. What lives in here?" Webb asked.

Rawlings had no idea and didn't care. He expected there had been a carton or two of food that had been meant for the mess hall, but had either been mislabeled or mis-stored or both. Just thinking about it, he was reminded of the meal he was missing. Any goodwill he might have felt toward the pit bull of a man in front of him went away.

"What are you waiting for?" Rawlings asked. "Let's get this done."

Webb began scanning the inventory tags. He'd kept his T-shirt over his mouth and was breathing through the cloth, so he wasn't talking. Rawlings was thankful for the silence, but not thankful for the stench.

Webb hurried through the first two rows of boxes, then he and Rawlings had to move several aside to create a lane toward the back of the room. It was then that they noticed there was a large open space in the far-left corner. When they stepped through to continue scanning, they saw what appeared to be a dead thing lying in a large clump upon the ground.

Rawlings tried to make sense of it. What looked like giant segmented legs were folded in on it. Beneath them was a body, possibly human. He stepped closer and leaned in. There were arms, too, folded in on themselves. He didn't see any hands. Nor did he see a head.

"What the fuck is that?" Webb asked, stepping beside Rawlings.

"I have no idea. Looks like something with legs. Think it could be something from outside the station?"

"It sure could be," Webb said. "But the question is, how did it get in here?"

Rawlings examined the ceiling and upper corners of the room. He didn't find any openings or broken ceiling panels. Nothing to explain the presence of the dead creature in front of them.

"We should call this in to Security."

"What are they going to do?" Webb scoffed. "Need to get a maintenance crew to take out the trash."

Then the thing moved.

Both Rawlings and Webb jumped back a step.

They looked at each other and, after a moment, Webb laughed nervously.

"What do you think?" he asked.

Rawlings examined the ground around the thing. A pile of filthy blankets. Small bones scattered on the floor. A container stained yellow. Possibly from urine. Whatever the thing was, it had been here for some time. He surmised from the bones that it had either starved to death or died from dehydration. There were no water sources, so the latter was certainly possible. Then again, it could be both.

Then he stopped.

He backed away slowly.

A single eye stared up at him through the mass of legs.

"Webb," he whispered.

"You know, it looks like a giant spider of some kind," Webb said. He held his scanner out as if to prod it.

"Webb," Rawlings whispered a little louder.

The pit bull straightened and turned toward him.

"What? Why are you whispering?"

With a rustle like wads of paper being stuffed into a box, the thing rose on its feet to its full height. It wasn't dead. It wasn't even wounded. It was completely alive and terrible to behold. It was as if a human had sprung long chitinous legs from the hips. Its human legs had withered and were a third the size they should have been. They swayed as the thing moved.

From the waist up, the creature looked almost human, but the nose had disappeared because of the enlarged mouth that took up nearly half the face. Twin rows of jagged teeth rimmed the inside of the jaw. Oddly, the eyes remained human enough for Rawlings to identify the man.

Fairbanks. Or what was left of Fairbanks.

Whatever had happened to him, he'd become a monster.

Webb must have seen Rawlings' eyes widen, because he began to turn around—but he never made it. Before he could move more than a few inches, the Fairbanks monster grabbed him by the head and bit down on it, coming away with a round bit of skull and brain matter. The creature chewed quickly as the legs adjusted themselves to stay balanced. Standing on those new legs, the creature's head nearly brushed the ceiling.

Rawlings couldn't take his eyes off Webb's face. The eyes were wide and the mouth was open as if he were about to scream. Then the eyes narrowed and his lips curled down as if he were confused and about to cry. All the while the creature chewed mechanically.

Feeling his way backward, Rawlings used the boxes to help him navigate. Oh, how he wished he had a pistol at his hip, or a pulse rifle slung across his back. The monster watched him as he began his retreat, its hands still on the side of Webb's head.

Just as Rawlings reached the door, the Fairbanks monster tossed Webb aside and rushed, the four chitinous legs propelling it incredibly fast. Rawlings spun, keyed the door open, and sprinted left down the corridor, more afraid for his life than he ever had been as a Colonial Marine.

35

Too late, he realized he should have shouted a warning. He plowed into two maintenance workers, knocking them both to the ground. Instead of helping them to their feet, he spared a quick glance behind him and saw the monster closing fast. He turned and ran, leaving the two workers to the creature, hoping they would slow it down and condemning himself for feeling that way.

"Shit. Shit. Shit," he said under his breath, his cursing keeping time with his pounding feet. He came to an intersection. He hadn't been in this part of the station in a long while. He chose left, immediately saw a blank wall blocking his way, and knew he should have turned right. He backpedaled and peered down the corridor.

The Fairbanks monster was dragging one of the maintenance workers by her long black hair. Her arms hung limp. The creature eyed him and let out a scream that was eerily human.

Rawlings shot down the right corridor, feeling all forty-two years of his slightly overweight Colonial Marine veteran body. He saw a fire alarm and pulled it. The alarm immediately began to ring from every speaker in every corridor, hammering at all thought.

It was the least he could do.

He had to warn people.

But it backfired.

Instead of being fearful, the alarm made everyone open their doors and step out into the corridor. They looked around, concerned as Rawlings ran past.

"Where's the fire?" one asked.

"Monster," he yelled, out of breath. "Run."

"What about the fire?" someone else asked.

Then the creature turned the corner, moving rapidly and still dragging the woman by her hair. It screamed once, then lifted a leg and brought it down on the chest of a man, pinning him to the ground.

Rawlings had to stop. He stood with hands on hips, trying to get his wind as he watched the monster reach down, pull the man up, and bite his face off.

That was all it took.

Everyone in the corridor screamed as they turned and ran.

He started running again as well, allowing the wave to carry him along as they all funneled through the corridors. It was pure panic. Others joined them, not knowing what they were running from, but understanding the need. Those with more sense opened their doors, saw the stampede, and closed them again. A man tripped, sending those behind ass-over-elbows. Rawlings had to step on one to keep his balance, almost going down himself. He knew that if he had, he'd never be able to get up again. No. He needed his balance, so he took short running steps, his hand close to the man's belt in front of him.

A security guard appeared with a pistol drawn, but she was

flattened by the mob before she could even open her mouth.

Someone, somewhere, turned the alarm off.

As they came to various corridors, the mob began to dissipate, some taking the corridors, some continuing forward, some finding unlocked rooms. The problem with the station was that it was essentially a closed loop. A giant set of rectangles that had you turning and turning until you were back to the place you began. If the monster had only realized this, it wouldn't have tried to chase after its prey. It could just stand still and let them race toward it.

A stitch hit Rawlings' side like a stiletto driving into his lung. He lurched to a stop, his hand held to the place of greatest pain. He leaned against the wall as those few who remained behind him flowed past like water might go around a rock. He was done running.

Staggering back, he saw that the Fairbanks monster was about forty feet down the corridor. It had stopped. It had finally let go of the maintenance worker's hair and was busy eating the face of the downed security guard.

Rawlings gasped for air as silently as he could. It couldn't come fast enough. His lungs burned. He remembered when he could run five, even ten kilometers in full battle rattle. Now he couldn't run ten meters without the threat of passing out.

He spied the pistol on the ground about midway between him and the monster. He staggered toward it and managed to grab it before the monster registered his presence. The safety was off. Raising the pistol, he sighted down the length, aiming for center mass. Then, noting the legs of the security guard fighting for traction, he adjusted his aim, and pulled the trigger.

Blam!

Blam!

Blam!

He fired until she stilled.

Nothing worse than being eaten alive.

Probably.

The Fairbanks monster dropped its meal and glared at him.

Rawlings raised his pistol and aimed, but his hand was shaking from the adrenaline bleed. He brought his left hand up and steadied his aim, then pulled the trigger three times in succession. Two rounds hit, knocking the creature back several steps. The legs threatened to fold in upon themselves for a moment, then they righted, and the creature skittered backward and out of sight.

The sound of boots running toward him filled the silence.

"Put it down," someone commanded from behind. "Put the gun down now."

He relaxed his two-handed stance and let his gun hand fall to his side, but he didn't let go. He turned. Two security guards faced him. One with a pistol drawn and aiming at his face. The other rushed past to the downed security guard he'd just put out of her misery.

"I said put the gun down," the guard with the gun said. The name tag on his shirt read MAHMOOD. He had dark skin and even darker close-cropped hair. A scar tore through the skin under his left eye.

"She's been shot," the other security guard cried. "He shot Fredericks in the back."

Mahmood stepped forward and pressed the barrel of his pistol into Rawlings' cheek hard enough to click the teeth through the skin.

"Why the fuck you shoot Fredericks?"

"Tell the other asshole to look at her face," Rawlings said. Seeing the look of doubt in Mahmood's eyes, he said, "Ask him. Come on. *Ask him.*"

Mahmood shouted over Rawlings' shoulder. "This one says to look at her face."

After a few seconds, "Oh shit. Something's been eating it." The universal sound of retching came next. Mahmood's eyes went from what was happening behind Rawlings to his face.

"A fucking monster is loose and it was eating her face when she was still alive." Rawlings pushed the pistol away. "So yeah. I shot her. Wouldn't you have?"

Mahmood walked over and stared down at Fredericks. Rawlings joined him. Whatever her appearance had been, there was no trace of it anymore. One eye dangled free. The other was missing, along with the nose, lips, and cheeks, revealing open jaw, gums, and teeth as if someone had tried and failed to stuff a human skull into a flap of skin.

"What kind of monster did this?" Mahmood asked.

"I don't have a nomenclature for it. I've been calling it the Fairbanks monster because whatever it is now, it used to be Fairbanks."

"Fairbanks as in the missing comms specialist?"

Rawlings nodded. His legs felt like lead. "The same, except this one has giant fucking spider legs and a mouth with enough teeth to eat a cow."

"And it's loose in the station?" Mahmood asked.

Rawlings nodded and kept his snark in check.

Mahmood grabbed the radio from his belt and called to put the station on alert. Rawlings straightened and headed off in the direction the monster had gone.

"Where are you going?" Mahmood asked.

"There's a monster on the loose," Rawlings said without turning. "Don't you think we oughta be trying to kill it before it kills someone else?"

"Uh, yeah," Mahmood said, running up beside him. "Let's go get the damned thing."

Shoulder to shoulder they moved down the corridor. Finding the creature didn't prove as hard as it could have been. Rawlings had hit it squarely, and it had left a trail of blood. They found it two corridors to the left, munching on a fabrications tech. It must have preferred the soft skin of the face, or maybe brains, because once again the creature was concentrating on the head.

Mahmood called it in on his radio.

Rawlings leveled his pistol and began to pull the trigger, but he only fired two rounds before he heard an unsatisfying click.

The monster spun and ran.

Rawlings still felt the stitch in his side.

He wasn't going anywhere.

36

The ruckus was intense. The noise mind-blowing. Every single Xenomorph in every single containment area had begun attacking its glass with fervor. Acid spitting, hand clawing, tail banging, anything they could do to attack the glass.

The only containment rooms that were silent were the one with Seven and the one with Leon-895-B. Seven stood implacable, staring blindly outward. Étienne, Kash, Hoenikker, Cruz, and the synths were busy trying to stop the creatures from attacking the glass. Cruz privately feared they'd break containment at any moment, and was considerably worried that all of his security plans wouldn't be enough to stop whatever had gotten into Seven.

They'd heard a fire alarm, but then it had gone off.

Cruz got word through the command channel that some creature was loose in the corridors, and people were dying. In the meantime, they were on lockdown and had their own problems.

"When are they going to stop?" Étienne asked, shouting over the din.

"I don't think they're going to," Kash hollered back.

"But that means..." Étienne didn't have to finish the sentence. Everyone knew what that meant. Cruz cursed. He went over to Seven and stared at the damn thing a moment.

"You want to be the first one to die, you bastard?"

He opened the cover on the abort switch. The difference between the flames they'd been using and the flames from the abort was astronomical. Nothing could survive it, jets of fire firing from all angles, microwave beams designed to cook something from the inside out.

His hand hovered over the switch.

The Xenomorphs suddenly stopped.

The only movement was the constant drip of saliva from their mouths and the swaying twitches of their tails. Hoenikker leaned back in his workstation, out of breath. Kash stared wide-eyed at Cruz. Étienne leaned forward, draping his arms over his panel.

Just as he thought.

Cruz nodded at Seven.

"The next time you do that, I will begin with you, and work my way up." He replaced the cover on the abort button. "Heed my words." He had no idea if the Xeno could hear him, or understand.

The command channel on his vid beeped, indicating an incoming call. Cruz answered it. Bellows was on the other end. The station commander's face was beet red, his eyes wide and veined.

"What the hell have you done to my station, Cruz?"

"What are you talking about?"

"Your damn specimens. They're in my corridors." He looked away from the screen for a moment, then back. "Reports are that the dead and dying are everywhere."

Cruz put a hand up to the side of his head. What was the

man thinking? "I'm telling you, sir, that all of my specimens are present and accounted for."

"That can't be. You should see my station."

"There may be something out there, but it's not from the lab. I can show you if you—"

"You can stop right there." Bellows held up a hand, and looked at Cruz sadly, like a father might to a lying child who was caught in his falsehood. His chin lowered, and he stared down the length of his nose. "My synths have already reported that one of the containment rooms is empty. Number twelve."

"An empty..." he said. "There's no empty containment room. That's where Leon-895 is. He's not visible!"

Bellows shook his head. "You're not the right one to lead this, Dr. Cruz. Not only are you not to be believed, but you failed to warn us that a specimen escaped."

"Bellows. Seriously. Listen to me," Cruz said. He couldn't fucking believe he was having this conversation. "For the love of Christ, there is no escaped specimen. All my containment rooms are occupied."

"That will be all, Dr. Cruz." The station commander stared at him for a long moment, then shook his head. He moved to turn the vid off and paused. "Oh, and Dr. Cruz?"

"Yes, sir?"

"Don't take the Lord's name in vain, to try and explain away your incompetence."

Cruz blinked several times. "What? What do you mean?"

But the screen was blank.

Cruz looked up and noted that everyone was staring at him.

"What was that all about?" Kash asked.

"I think I've been fired," Cruz said.

"But why?" Hoenikker asked.

"Why would he fire you?" Étienne asked.

"That's just it." Cruz tossed the vid display onto the table. "I don't really know." He turned to stare at Seven, who stood silently in the middle of its containment room, arms hanging at its sides. The creature was as still as a statue. Was it looking at him? Was it *laughing* at him? Did it even understand what was going on?

Suddenly the two synths came to life. They'd retreated to the wall when the Xenomorphs had stopped harassing the glass, but now they moved to the workstations for Containment Rooms One and Two. Each of them opened the cover for the abort button.

"Whoa. Wait!" Étienne cried. Closest to them, he reached out for the synth at the workstation for Containment Room Two, and was thrown back as the automaton backhanded him. Étienne fell hard to his back, face bloody.

"Stop," Cruz yelled. "Don't!"

The synths ignored him.

Each of them depressed an abort button.

Flames from all angles poured over the Xenomorphs. They began to scream and flop, their arms and legs rattling on the ground as they were consumed. Invisible microwave radiation baked them from the inside. Their animal cries were almost human in their terror, the heat they were experiencing unimaginable. Their skin was on fire, causing the fluids in their bodies to boil, acid dripping into the flames.

The synths remained in place, their hands over the buttons, protecting them, finishing the job, not moving until the creatures had been aborted.

Cruz realized what was happening. Bellows wasn't taking any chances. Whether or not the creature loose in the station had originated from the lab, none would escape now. The station commander had ordered the synths to destroy them, knowing that the scientists would balk. What a fucking idiot.

On one hand, he refused to let Cruz abort Seven because of its value to the company; and on the other, he decided to abort *all* the Xenomorphs out of fear.

The synth who was sitting at the Containment Room One workstation stood and moved to the workstation for Containment Room Three.

Hoenikker was already there with a fire extinguisher.

"No!" he cried, and he brought the extinguisher around.

The synth deflected it, then pushed Hoenikker to the ground.

But Hoenikker wasn't done. As the synth gathered itself into the seat, Hoenikker climbed to his feet and brought the fire extinguisher down on the synth's head. The synth fell forward onto the workstation control panel. Hoenikker brought the fire extinguisher up again, but felt it ripped from his hands.

The other synth was up and protecting the first. Hoenikker spun and found himself being thrown into the air and onto the worktable in the center of the lab, scattering vid displays, beakers, and various scientific equipment.

Then all hell broke loose.

All the Xenomorphs resumed their attacks on the glass. If anything, their frenzy was multiplied. The glass fronts smoked with acid as each of the creatures spit and slammed their teeth over and over, each into a single space. They raked the glass with their claws so quickly that had they been attacking a human, the skin would have been flayed down to tendon and bone in a matter of seconds.

A crack appeared in the glass of Room Four.

The Xenomorph redoubled its efforts.

Étienne took up the fire extinguisher and began to hammer at the synth Hoenikker had hit before. Its head was canted as if it had lost the ability to straighten.

Kash helped Hoenikker to his feet.

Cruz stood in the middle of it all, watching as crack after crack appeared in the glass fronts, spidering, growing and running to the ceilings and walls and floors. A feeling began to grow in his stomach. A feeling he'd last felt when his squad had been overrun and torn apart.

The Xenomorph in Containment Room Four died at the hands of a synth; at the same time, the glass from Containment Room Five shattered. Cruz backed away and grabbed Étienne by the shoulder as he did. The Frenchman stopped hammering, noticed the broken glass, and let himself be dragged away.

Out stepped the Xenomorph known simply as Five.

But it ignored the scientists. Instead, it stepped tentatively toward the containment room holding Seven. It stood there, saliva falling from its jaw and the occasional twitch of its tail showing that it wasn't some hellish statue that suddenly appeared in the midst of the laboratory.

They watched as Seven and Five seemed to have some silent exchange. With the glass between them, it couldn't be Étienne's pheromone that allowed them to communicate. It had to be something else, and the only thing he could think of was some form of telepathy. He remembered the buzz in the back of his head. If his brain had been wired in the same fashion as the Xenomorphs', he'd have known what it had been trying to say.

Five moved to the workstation and depressed a series of buttons.

He's been watching, Cruz thought. Then another thought struck him. Seven might be better at management and organization than all the bureaucrats on Pala Station combined.

The surviving synth pulled its pistol and fired several rounds into Five. The creature turned, pushed one more button, and the glass front slid aside.

Damn. How had Seven known the complex combination of buttons needed to do that?

The synth fired again, approaching the Xenomorph. Its implacable expression didn't reveal anything. If it had been Cruz or any human approaching such a monster, fear—and perhaps determination—would have been plastered over his face. But the synth was eerily passive.

Five whirled and grabbed the synth by the side of its head, bringing it in close. Its jaw telescoped and scored the synth's metal head. The synth punched the body of its attacker, then brought a palm up, slamming it into the underside of the Xenomorph's jaw.

"Cruz!" Kash whispered urgently.

The Xenomorph threw the synth across the room, bending one of the wall lockers into Rorschach origami.

"*Cruz!*" she whispered again.

He snapped out of it. "What?" He glanced at the other scientists. All scared. All desperate to leave. Étienne was grabbing a container of some sort. Hoenikker looked like he wanted to cry.

"We can't leave."

More crashing from behind.

"They put us on lockdown," Étienne said.

Cruz glanced behind him.

Another Xenomorph had freed itself.

They were all going to die.

Still, they had to try. "There's an override," he said. "Try 198473 in the access panel. *Hurry.*" He turned back just in time to see Seven step from its containment room. It turned to face him, standing in the middle of the lab as chaos raged around it.

The synth had managed to kill the Xenomorph from Five, but it was surrounded by three more. Leon-895 flashed in the background. That meant all the containment rooms had been breached. Cruz laughed. Bellows would really be pissed now.

Fire roared from Containment Room Eight. The glass had already broken and even this far away Cruz could feel the heat.

Then the door to the lab *sssked* open.

Seven stood there. It didn't say a word, nor did he expect it to, but by the buzzing in the back of Cruz's head, he would swear it was smiling.

He turned and ran.

37

Hoenikker flinched as Étienne poured liquid from the beaker over his head, all the while giggling like a child. If the pheromone was going to work, it was do or die.

Kash pulled at Hoenikker's elbow.

"Come on," she said. "We need to leave, now!"

Now out in the corridor, Hoenikker stared into the lab. He had lost count of the Xenomorphs, but they all seemed to be swarming around the strange white-colored one known as Seven. Hoenikker found himself looking for Three—what had formerly been Monica. For a moment he thought she might have already died, but then he saw her, the light striping on her arms and torso so different than the others. She held the head of the last synth in her hand, before turning and hurling it toward him.

Both he and Kash dodged the missile.

Kash grabbed him one last time.

This time he followed her lead.

They ran into a pair of security guards, who grabbed Kash's free arm to stop her. They ended up swinging around so their backs were to the door of the lab.

"What happened?" one asked.

"The Xenomorphs," Hoenikker said. "They're all free."

"The fuck you say?" the other replied.

"Go see for yourself," Kash said. They turned to leave, and the first security guard stopped them.

"I wouldn't go that way."

"Why not?" Hoenikker asked.

"Another fucking monster is why," the second guard said. Hoenikker stared at him. How many monsters were out there? What had happened to the nice peaceful station they'd had?

Who was he kidding? The station had been infested since the moment he'd set foot on it. Once again, he wondered why the hell he'd left his cushy corporate job to come to this godforsaken place.

Just then a Xenomorph shot into the corridor, grabbed the first security guard, and jerked him back into the room. It all happened in the blink of an eye, and the man didn't have a chance to make a sound. The other guard turned and looked from side to side.

"Barron? Where the fuck are you?" He turned back around. "Where did he go?"

It had happened so fast that both Kash and Hoenikker stood like idiots with their mouths open. Then another Xenomorph grabbed the second security guard and jerked him inside the lab before he could even reach for his gun.

Kash and Hoenikker glanced at each other. They prepared to run…

"Frère Jacques, Frère Jacques. Dormez vous? Dormez vous? Sonnez les matines. Sonnez les matines. Din din don. Din din don."

Étienne came walking out of the lab. Somehow, some way, the Xenomorphs hadn't taken him, or even noticed him. The pheromones had *worked*.

A Xenomorph popped into the corridor in front of Étienne, who stood swaying gently from side to side as if he were on a ship.

"I once saw a man in India reach out and pet a King Cobra," Étienne said without a trace of fear. Hoenikker wondered if he'd gone insane. "The idea was to lull the snake into a false sense of security. He would sway from side to side and the snake would mimic him."

Hoenikker watched in horror as Étienne reached out with his hand. The Xenomorph wasn't swaying from side to side. It was leaning forward, saliva dripping, tail snapping the air, claws opening and closing. But Étienne wouldn't stop. He reached out and ran a hand down the side of the torpedo-shaped head.

"There now, *mon frère*." He waved jovially at Kash and Hoenikker, then turned and walked the opposite way, soon lost in the curve of the corridors. The ghost of the song leaving a trail of musical breadcrumbs behind him. *"Sonnez les matines. Din din don. Din din don."*

"God loves drunkards and fools," Kash said.

"And evidently Frenchmen," Hoenikker added.

Then they did run, but they didn't get very far.

They almost tripped over the first body they came across. Blood smeared the walls. The head was missing. One leg bent at an unnatural angle—but it couldn't be from the Xenomorphs. Those were behind them, or at least Hoenikker thought they were. Then he remembered the harried video call from Bellows, believing that it was one of their Xenos who had escaped. That was what had started it all. So then, what kind of creature were they going to encounter?

Screams came from behind them.

They both turned toward the sound.

Then came a roar from the way they'd been heading.

Hoenikker knew he was close to his room. He grabbed Kash's wrist and tore off down the corridor toward the roar, praying. When he approached the intersection, he saw coming the other way the creature that must have wreaked havoc in the corridors. With the face of Fairbanks and the legs of a giant spider, it came for them, nine feet tall and impossible fast.

Kash screamed.

Hoenikker jerked her hand as he pulled her the other way. When they reached his door, he palmed in, pulled her after him, and closed it behind them. Instantly Kash ran to the end of the room, fell to the ground, and pulled her knees to her chin. He joined her, and they sat staring at the door as scream after scream came and went, individual Doppler effects of terror.

Another alarm sounded, drowning out most of the screams.

They sat that way for several hours, anticipating that the door would burst open, one of the monsters from the lab coming to get them. Or worse yet, Three coming to give him a warm hug.

When the alarm finally silenced, so did the sound of screams.

"No one is ever going to know," Kash whispered.

"Know what?" Hoenikker asked.

"Everything. Nothing. What we've done here." She waved her hand around. "It's all going to be forgotten."

"Not if we survive," he said, not really feeling the hope he was trying to project.

"Survive?" She snorted. "We're not going to survive this. Even if we do, we can't be sure they got them all. Besides, this whole event will be a wart on Weyland-Yutani's success. They'd rather nuke us from orbit than expend the moral credits needed to save us, and explain how they failed."

"You're painting a bleak picture."

"It's a watercolor made of blood depicting the end of all things." She shook her head. "The first group of specimens we had were different. They hadn't been subjected to the pathogen. The black goo did something to Seven. Made it smarter. Made it more in control."

"I was thinking about that. Perhaps because there isn't a mother, some DNA we thought was junk turned on instead, to create a leader."

She nodded. "It was made to help them survive."

"I've been modeling what we know of their society. They need a mother. A leader. They *want* a leader. Without one they're nothing more than a wolf pack without an alpha. Renegades." He chuckled. "Ronin. Like the masterless samurai who used to roam feudal Japan."

"The Xenomorphs have a lot more weapons than a samurai."

"Don't be so sure." Hoenikker stood, cranking his neck until it popped. "Weapons weren't allowed in feudal Japan. The samurai were like modern tanks. To the common man, they were weapons of mass destruction. Which makes me believe more and more that these alien Xenomorphs were purpose-made. They're too perfect. A bipedal version of ancient samurai who spit acid."

Kash stood as well, putting two fists in the small of her back as she bent backward.

"I hate to break it to you, Tim. These aren't samurai. We *wished* we had samurai." She pulled her hair out of the bob and shook her head. She went over to his bed and lay down on it. "I'm just so tired."

He grinned. "Me too." He laughed.

"What's so funny?" she asked.

"I was thinking about that hard-ass, Cruz. Know what he'd say?" he asked. "Probably something like, 'No napping during Armageddon, Hoenikker.'" He bellowed, trying his best to imitate the man's voice.

Now it was her turn to laugh. "Do that again."

"There ain't no napping during Armageddon, Hoenikker," he said again, his voice a full-on parody of a military bellow.

Suddenly, there came a banging on the door.

Kash shot out of bed and stood near Hoenikker.

He stood still, staring at the door. He felt like a kid who'd just gotten caught making fun of their parents.

The banging came again.

38

A maintenance closet was the last place Cruz imagined himself. Wedged between cleaning supplies and a floor scrubber while others fought and died. It was as ignoble a position as he'd ever experienced. He'd never been one to turn tail and run, he'd always been ready to fight.

Or at least, he wished he'd been that person. He deserved to be that person, with all the hard work and dedication he'd put into being a Colonial Marine. But then LV-832 happened. Moose-sized xenomorphic quadrupeds with tentacles happened. Snyder, Bedejo, Schnexnader, Correia, and Cartwright happened.

He closed his eyes to calm himself, smelling the sharp tang of cleaning solution.

That was then. This was now. He could make up for it. He could save his crew. He'd run away leaving his previous crew to die, but now he had a chance to redeem himself. He had Kash and Étienne. He even had Hoenikker. Although he didn't like the man, this was war, this was survival. He was human and the damned Xenomorphs were not.

Plus, he had to get all of their research out, or it would be irrevocably lost.

Bellows and Security probably thought they could retake the station, but Cruz had heard and seen enough that he felt it was a fool's bet. The Xenomorphs were the universe's chosen killing machine. It was nature's way of ridding space of humanity. How dare humans assume that, just because they possessed something like an LV, it was theirs? Bellows would learn. His security guards would learn, and in the meantime, Cruz would help his team escape. There were a shuttle and the *San Lorenzo* orbiting above. They still had hope.

First, Cruz needed to find a way to get back into the lab. So, he waited, and began to prepare himself. He spent ten precious minutes hacking his vid display into station security using one of his command controls. He needed to know what was going on.

At first the screams came fast and furious, matched by the sounds of running feet and what could only be humans being ripped apart. A pool of blood seeped beneath the door. He moved back as far as he could, but the puddle reached and surrounded his feet.

He searched through the station vids until he found one near his door, where he saw several station personnel running, while being chased by a juvenile.

Eventually the sounds became fewer and fewer, long stretches of silence punctuated by occasional screams of the dying. After hour three had passed he put his ear to the door and, upon hearing nothing, palmed it open, hoping that the vid display showed him the door to the maintenance room he was in. The sound of it opening seemed impossibly loud in the silent corridor.

He looked down and saw Comms Chief Oshita lying in a pool of her own blood. Or what was left of her. Her hair had singed away, leaving her scalp raw and ugly. Her face was locked in a grimace, probably from the intense pain from exposure to Xenomorph acid. Her chest cavity was empty, and her body still smoldered, thin curls of smoke wafting upward. The Xenomorph saliva that had dripped on her gave her an unholy sheen.

He glanced at the vid display and saw an image of himself. He looked up, then down, then nodded. This would come in handy.

Stepping over her, he frowned as his feet squelched in her blood. Looking left, then right, he gripped the steel handle of a floor mop, the only weapon he could readily find, and took three steps down the corridor, squelching less and less with each step. He had about thirty meters to go to get back to the lab. The mop would do little as an offensive weapon, but it might just give him a chance to flee. He was hoping to find a dropped security weapon along the way.

Cruz kept his back to the wall as he slid sideways down the corridor, clocking each door in case he had to find a place to hole up.

The dead were plentiful.

A maintenance worker, gutted from stem to stern.

A fabrications tech, chest hoved in, neck sliced, lying in a lake of blood.

He recognized former Colonial Marine Fields from Logistics, his head crushed and separated from a body that looked as if the Xenomorphs had had an end-of-the-world rave on top of it. Then, finally, a literal pile of security guards, each owning their own version of death by alien monster.

He set aside the mop, overjoyed he hadn't had to use it, and gathered three pistols and a pulse rifle. The pistols he shoved into his belt and pockets. The rifle he shouldered after checking to see if it was loaded and had power. The ammo counter read 99, which meant the poor schmuck hadn't even had a chance to fire. Must have been surprised either rounding the corner or coming from behind.

Yeah, Bellows was full of shit if he thought that he could retake the station.

Then a thought hit him that made him worry. What if Bellows already knew that and had decided to leave? What if the shuttle was already gone? He glanced back the way he'd come. The shuttle bay was at the far end of the station. He should check first, but the lab was closer, as were his team. He shook his head. He'd have to chance that the shuttle would still be there.

Sliding sideways several more meters, he came to an intersection. He searched left, then right, then jerked his head back. A Xenomorph stood down the corridor, munching on something that looked remarkably like a human heart. The problem was that he had to go that way to get to the lab.

He checked the rifle again, set it to four-round bursts, then eased the barrel around the corner and sighted over the top of the carry handle.

The Xenomorph was no longer there.

Which meant it either went in the other direction, or was…

He pushed the barrel all the way around and saw the Xenomorph coming toward him along the wall. Blood dripped from its left hand where it had gripped the organ. Pink-colored saliva bubbling from its maw.

He aimed and fired at the side of the carapace and grinned as the bullets punched through. But the creature kept coming. He fired twice more, eight explosive-tipped rounds finding their mark in the side of the Xenomorph's head.

It fell to the floor, propped on a knee, but continued toward him, making a hollow sucking sound as it came. He aimed again and it leaped at him.

Cruz was barely able to get back around the corner.

The monster sailed past, hitting the ground and rolling to its feet, already facing him. He put a four-round burst into its chest, creating four neat little acid-dripping holes. The alien went down with a single loud squeal.

He turned and ran. No telling whether or not the sound of the pulse rifle would draw any others. He made it to the door of the lab, which was held open and continually trying to close on the body of a synth whose head was missing. He pushed the synth out of the way with a boot, then slid inside as the door closed. He breathed a little easier, but only a little. He still didn't know if there were any creatures left in the lab.

Which was trashed.

He went to the mainframe, grabbed the backup drive, and slid it into his pocket. Then he switched the rifle to full auto. If he encountered something in the lab, he wouldn't have the luxury of picking it off from a distance. It would be full-on close quarters combat, and he'd need to overwhelm a Xenomorph with the sound and fury of an M41A pulse rifle on full automatic.

Lucky for him, there was no need. The lab was clear. Even Leon-895 was gone. Or at least, he thought it was.

Setting aside the rifle, he grabbed two things. The first was the prototype acid-resistant body armor, which he put on. The helmet was a little tight around his large hair, but with a little shoving he got it to fit. Based on an M4X body armor frame, the acid-resistant polymer coating was an upgrade to the limited acid-resistance of the old M3 vest. The armor provided full body protection with sleeves, gloves, and a full-face helmet capable of withstanding light velocity rounds. The armor was augmented with a complete body frame to help with balance when the wearer was struck by tremendous force.

The second thing he grabbed was the flamethrower, or M-240 Incinerator Unit, comprised of a large capacity napthal backpack tank and attached firing nozzle. It felt heavy, and he had to adjust the shoulder webbing to allow the tank to sit higher on his shoulders.

Now he felt better prepared.

Grabbing the pulse rifle from where he'd left it, he slung it over his shoulder. He'd use the Bake-A-Flake for now, trying for wet shots at first for distance, and flamers for anything close in. He exited the lab, taking one last look at the place he'd called home for three years, a place he'd been put in charge of, now destroyed because of events that were beyond his control.

There was a noise from the way he'd just come. He couldn't place it for a moment, but then it all came together. Singing.

Someone was singing.

He strode down the center of the corridor, stepping over and around the occasional body or piece of one until he saw the Xenomorph he'd shot. Inexplicably, Étienne was rubbing himself against the ruined torpedo-shaped carapace.

"Frère Jacques, Frère Jacques. Dormez vous? Dormez vous? Sonnez les matines. Sonnez les matines. Din din don. Din din don."

Cruz approached. "Étienne? What are you doing?" The man kept singing and rubbing himself against the alien skin. Cruz couldn't fathom what the man was doing, unless…

Pheromones.

"Étienne? *Ça va*?" Cruz asked. "What's going on?"

"*Mon ami*, isn't this wonderful?" Étienne grinned from ear to ear as he climbed to his feet. "I am invisible to them. I can walk through them. I can move past them. They do not see me."

Had it really worked? He'd have to see it to believe it. To all appearances, it looked as if the Frenchman had experienced a break with reality.

"Étienne, come with me. I'm going to get everyone out."

The scientist shook his head. "I am not done yet with my field study. I need more data."

"You have enough data," Cruz said. "This is too dangerous."

Étienne grinned again. "Not for me." He made a shooing motion with his hands. "Now, you go. I am busy. I will catch up to you." Then he turned and walked down the corridor, singing the old children's song about Brother Jack. Over and over. Crazy like a scientist holding a hypothesis in a death grip…

Cruz stared for a long moment, then turned and headed back, past the lab and toward their rooms. Twice he spied a Xenomorph, but they were all moving the other way. Once he saw something totally unexpected that looked for all the world like a person with giant spider legs, but by the time he'd shaken his head and closed and opened his eyes, it was gone.

Reaching the corridor with all the scientists' rooms, he went to Kash's door first, but then moved on when he heard a loud voice coming from Hoenikker's room.

That's not smart.

"There ain't no napping during Armageddon," the voice said, somehow sounding similar to Cruz's. Smiling, he banged on the door.

He could only imagine what they were wondering inside.

When they didn't answer, he banged again.

"Who—who is it?" Hoenikker said.

"It's Cruz. Open up."

The door opened and Cruz pushed his way inside. When the door closed behind him, he turned to stare at Hoenikker, well aware of what he looked like in the power armor and with the flamethrower.

"Now, what's this about Armageddon and napping?"

39

Hoenikker about peed his pants. Cruz looked more like a battle robot than a scientist.

"How'd you get through?"

Cruz began removing his gear and putting it on the desk. "The corridors are mostly clear. I don't know where the Xenomorphs have gotten off to, but I did see a few. I also saw something else."

"That would be Fairbanks," Kash said. "I posit he was somehow exposed to the pathogen."

Cruz frowned. "That's not advised."

"No." She shook her head. "Not at all. What are you doing here?" she asked, then added hurriedly, "Not that I'm complaining."

"I came to save you."

"Me?" Hoenikker asked. "Us?"

Cruz placed his large hands on Hoenikker's shoulders. "I might not like you at times, Timmy, but you're one of us. You're on my team, and I need to take care of you."

The gesture incited the warmth of belonging combined

with the smarting of not being liked. But then, Hoenikker never really cared about being liked anyway. Science wasn't about liking things. Liking things was about emotion. Still, he'd prefer to be liked than not, at least by his coworkers.

"Thank you?" he said, the words sounding more like a question.

"What's the plan?" Kash asked.

"We'll need to make a beeline to the shuttle bay." Cruz pulled out three pistols and laid them on the table, then sat in the chair. "Assuming it's still there. But Étienne is a problem."

"Last time we saw him, he was singing French and heading down the corridor in the opposite direction," Hoenikker said. He eyed the chair Cruz had taken and sat on the edge of the bed instead.

Cruz nodded. "He's still doing that. He was also rubbing himself against a dead Xenomorph. Know anything about that?"

"During the chaos, he poured a beaker of pheromone over his head and lathered himself up," Hoenikker said.

"And did it work?"

"Yes," Kash said. "We watched as a Xenomorph approached him, and then moved on."

"Fascinating." Cruz scratched the side of his head. "If only we'd had more time to study."

"The containment rooms weren't solid enough to hold them—" Hoenikker began, but a sharp shake of Cruz's head stopped him from continuing.

"There's never going to be a containment room that will keep them, as long as there's something like Seven. Each of the Xenomorphs is its own boss, determining how or when to fight. They don't coordinate with each other. They don't plan. There's no strategy. Unless they have someone to lead them. In the absence of a queen, it has to be a mutation."

"Do you think that's what they're doing now?" Kash asked. "Organizing?"

Cruz looked critically at both Kash and Hoenikker. "There are things you aren't aware of. For instance, there are a lot more eggs that we have in cryo travel cases."

"More eggs?" Hoenikker asked, eyes widening. "How many?"

"Dozens. Maybe as many as a hundred," Cruz said. "And each egg begets a face-hugger, which begets a chestburster, which begets a full-blown adult Xenomorph killing machine."

"We haven't heard any screams in a while," Hoenikker said. "Do you think…" His eyes widened.

"Go ahead and finish the sentence," Cruz said.

"I was going to say, do you think that they might be collecting people to create Xenomorphs? Do you think Seven is that smart?"

Cruz stared at the floor as he smiled grimly. "Either that, or all the Xenomorphs are dead, and I just can't believe that."

"We have to do something." Kash looked at Cruz in horror. "We can't just let them all—"

"What is it you would have us do?" He grabbed a pistol and tried to shove it into her hand. She wouldn't grab it at first, so he closed her hand around it and let go. "Do you want to go face down a Xenomorph, or a dozen or two dozen, to save the lives of the few remaining humans on the station? Then go ahead. Be my guest." He leaned back in the chair and stared at her down his nose. "But I'll tell you this. You'll die. You'll die horribly, or you'll be an incubator for a Xenomorph."

She stared at him for long grim moment, then carefully laid the pistol on top of the bureau.

"So, your plan is to run? To get to the shuttle then call for help from space?"

"Damn skippy," he said.

"I remember you telling me about the last time you ran. You have the names of your team members tattooed on you, is that right?"

"Careful where you are going."

"Let me just say this," she said. "I don't have enough skin on my body to tattoo the names of everyone we're going to leave behind. So, when we do, can I borrow some of yours?"

Hoenikker stared at Kash, and Cruz for the longest. He didn't know what Kash was talking about, but it hit home. Cruz had gone from red to pale, his frown deepening. For a second he thought the man might strike her.

"What you're saying," Cruz began slowly, "is that our team is bigger than us four. You're saying that all the humans on Pala Station form a team. Is that what you're saying?"

She nodded slowly.

"You're right," he said. "I can't run again. My conscience couldn't survive that. We'll see if we can save them first. We'll do what we can. But if we find out there's nothing we can do—that we'd die trying—then we go back to the original plan. Is that good for you?"

"Damn skippy," she said, reaching for the gun.

Hoenikker wasn't sure what just happened, but it felt like things just went from bad to worse.

"First, we need to go back to the lab, to get our work," she said.

Cruz grinned slightly. "Got it right here," he said, patting his side pocket.

"Then all we need to do is grab a gun and head out. We're certainly not going to save anyone dicking around here," she said. "Hand me that pulse rifle." When he just looked at her, she added, "What? You get the flamethrower *and* the rifle? I don't think so."

"Can you handle one of these?"

"I dated a Colonial Marine once. His idea for a first date was to go out shooting."

"Sounds like a Colonial Marine." He handed it to her.

"What about me? Hoenikker asked.

Cruz raised an eyebrow. "You date a Colonial Marine, too?"

Hoenikker snarfed. "No. I mean, what does that have to do with anything?"

Cruz handed him a pistol. "Point and shoot. Just keep your finger off the trigger until you're ready to fire. Understand?"

Hoenikker accepted the pistol, and the first thing he did was examine it by looking down the barrel.

"Tim. Stop," Kash said. "That's where the bullet comes from."

He looked at her and cocked his head. "Oh. Of course." Then he looked back at the gun and hurriedly turned it away. He should have known better.

Before this week, Hoenikker had never fired a gun. He'd never even held a gun, but he'd seen the popular movies and knew the basics. Hold, aim, point, shoot. It couldn't be brain science. After all, if Colonial Marines could do it, so could he. He practiced aiming down the barrel at his bureau, which he figured was about as wide as a Xenomorph.

"You don't need to squint," Cruz said, standing. He took two quick steps and took the gun away from Hoenikker. "Try it this way." He held the gun with two hands, chest high, arms thrust out in front of him. "If you hold it like this, you will shoot whatever you're facing."

Hoenikker studied the man's grip, then nodded.

Cruz gave him back the pistol.

As best he could, Hoenikker imitated the way Cruz had held the gun. His fingers fought to find a place to rest, but eventually he realized that one hand's fingers fit neatly into the spaces between the other hand's fingers. Yet as he imagined actually using it, butterflies began to crash into the sides of his stomach, bouncing to and fro. He felt sick and light at the same time. He was going to have to shoot something.

Shoot or be dead.

Even if he did manage to shoot a Xenomorph or, God forbid, that monster Fairbanks had become, he might still be killed. After all, his handgun couldn't possibly have the stopping capacity of a rifle or that flamethrower.

"Is everybody ready?" Cruz asked as he began putting his armor back on.

"Does Weyland-Yutani fuck people over?"

Cruz gave Kash a raised eyebrow.

"I used to date a VP at Weyland-Yutani," she muttered. Then looking up, she said, "What? You never dated anyone?"

"Whoa there." He held up his hand. "Not judging." He finished putting on the armor, including the gloves, then used the table to support the backpack tank and bent down and slid into the straps. When he stood, he let out an *oof* before adjusting the straps and the placement of the tank on his back.

He noticed Hoenikker staring at him.

"What? Never seen a man in combat armor before?"

"No. It's just that I feel so underdressed." Hoenikker grinned.

Cruz laughed and patted him on the back. "Funny, Timmy. Very funny."

40

Rawlings wanted nothing more than to drink himself into oblivion. Some nice whiskey to soothe his shattered soul. Maybe just a little bit of go juice to make his jitters dance away. Perhaps a few shots to soothe the savage beast inside of him, screaming to come out.

The bottle on the table in front of him had a devil doing a jig on its artsy label, the artwork reminiscent of a French advertisement. The more he stared at it, the more he could have sworn the devil was staring back at him.

The memory of his right hand being burned away by acid thrashed once again through his head. The pain had been so intense he'd fallen to the ground and rolled to try and get away from it. Then it was gone as the acid seared the nerve endings, the absence of pain a black hole to his soul in the shape of a hand that had loved and hated and created. A bright image of the hand cradling his mother's cheek right before she died.

He reached for the bottle.

The door opened. McGann and Buggy slid inside.

McGann's black hair was tousled like she'd just gotten out of bed. She held a pulse rifle in one hand and a pistol in the other.

Buggy's bald pate was slick with sweat. He had a pistol jammed into a holster, one he'd clearly stolen from the Colonial Marines when he'd been in the service. But then, hadn't they all. Rawlings had weapons he'd made sure to procure before he left the service. He was about to say something to Buggy, but the guy went straight to Rawlings' bottle and grabbed it by the neck.

"Got no time for this shit," he said, shoving it into the trash compacter and pressing the button.

Rawlings' eyes went wide. The finality of the trash mechanism struck him in the gut, and he sat back in his chair. He wanted to bitch. He wanted to complain. But he knew Buggy had done the right thing.

Damn him.

"Come on," Buggy said. "Get your ass up. We need to plan."

"There's too fucking many," Rawlings said. "Did you see what they did to the mess hall?"

"They're organized as fuck," McGann said, pacing back and forth in the small space of the room, talking mostly to herself. "I thought these were like drones. The way they lined up those men and women, and fed them one by one to the face-huggers, it was too much." She stopped and stared. "Who knew they could do that?"

Rawlings had found a place to hide and watch as it happened. The scientists had called the Xenomorph leader Seven. Standing in the middle of the mess hall, Seven had commanded the others to do things he was pretty sure they shouldn't have been able to do. Rawlings had watched at first in fascination and later in terror as the other Xenomorphs first moved the tables and chairs against the wall, then brought out egg after egg. All the while a gaggle of humans was herded into a far corner and guarded.

Then, after a time, a Xenomorph would grab a human one by one and force its head to face into the egg until a face-hugger wrapped its tail around the neck and found a home.

The victims were then stacked like cordwood on the other side of the mess hall, which was what eventually sent him to his room for a last and final date with his bottle of Scotch.

"I don't think this is normal," Buggy said.

"We need to get out of here before the juveniles hatch," McGann said, pacing.

"They're already hatching," Rawlings said. "Not in the mess hall, but from somewhere else. I saw them."

"We need to do something," Buggy said.

"What?" Rawlings asked. "What is there to do?"

Buggy smacked Rawlings across the face. "Get the fuck up. You were the one who brought us all together. You were the one who warned us bad shit was coming. Well, bad shit paid us a visit, and it isn't leaving anytime soon. You need to decide whether you want to sit here and feel sorry for yourself, or join us and see if we can't ride this out."

Rawlings snapped his head around and stared at Buggy, then at McGann. The comms tech was right. He needed to get up. He needed to do something. He got to his feet.

"What's the plan?"

"Right now, Security is spread thin," Buggy said. "They have a cluster of security techs around Bellows, and another group of external security techs in the landing bay, pretty much keeping everyone from taking the shuttle and getting the hell off the rock."

"So, we can't escape even if we wanted to," McGann said.

"I have to admit, the shuttle looked like the best choice," Rawlings said. "Without it we really don't have much choice… unless…"

McGann stopped pacing. "Unless what?"

Rawlings wiped the side of his face where he'd been smacked. If Buggy was going to say he was sorry, the moment had passed. Anyway, they were marines. It didn't matter.

"Well, there's one possibility, and for the life of me, I don't know why Bellows didn't take it."

"If you have an idea, then share," Buggy said.

"What about Thompson's hunting lodge?" Rawlings asked.

"Hunting lodge?" Buggy asked.

McGann wrinkled her eyebrows. "Yeah, what lodge?"

Rawlings nodded. "I thought you'd know, Buggy. After all, they had major comms set up in there—or at least, that's what I read on the installment order."

"I have no idea what you're talking about."

"Well, unless it's a lie—I've never actually seen the place—Thompson wanted a place to stay outside of station so he could spend more time hunting. He had a lodge built. One of the reasons we were so short on tungsten. I'm not sure where, but in addition to the communications array, I'd imagine it has everything we'd need to survive. So all we'd have to do is find it, get there, and lock the fucking door until help comes."

Buggy shrugged. "Sounds like a plan to me."

McGann nodded. "Who do we ask where it's at?"

Rawlings shook his head. "We *don't* ask. If we start spreading the word that there might be a safe place outside of the station, we'll be lucky if there isn't a riot. We don't know about the food and water stores in the lodge. I'm assuming it'll have enough for the three of us. Four, if we can find Cruz, but that's it. No more."

"Then how do we find out where it is?" Buggy asked.

"That's a good question," Rawlings said.

McGann scratched her head. "If it's getting power, then Engineering would have electrical schematics, showing where it attaches to the main power grid."

Rawlings nodded. "That's a great start." He grabbed his own pulse rifle from where it leaned against the wall. "Then all we have to do is make our hundred-meter dash to freedom." He held his rifle at the ready. "Who's first?"

"It was my idea." McGann headed toward the door. "I'll go first."

"Then lead the way," Rawlings said, almost happy he hadn't drunk his courage, like he'd planned.

He, McGann, and Buggy posted at the door in that order. They'd done this a thousand times, although never with each other, but that didn't matter. Every Colonial Marine did it the same way. There was only one technique to conduct CQB, and they'd all learned it in the same bloody crucible.

Each of them held a pulse rifle at the ready, trigger fingers disciplined to stay off the trigger until needed, lest they shoot each other in the back. McGann palmed the door open and they moved like a three-coiled snake through the corridor, hugging the right side. Dead body to the left. Pieces of a dead body to the right. Rawlings' universe was sixty degrees of nothing.

Until there was something.

The Xenomorph couldn't have been five feet tall—a juvenile by all accounts. It snapped at him and twitched its tail as it exited a room, almost oblivious to their presence. Rawlings opened fire, giving it seventeen free automatic bullets, more than half of them finding a home in its chest, a spray of blood and acid in their wake.

It died and they continued to move, three becoming one, muscle memory taking them over. Rawlings felt the fear of the unknown, the fear that they might all die, but he also felt the comfort he'd known only as a Colonial Marine. They'd had the same training, the same experiences, the same shit-cloaking tear-shedding training, each of them emerging better than when they'd begun. Their civilian skins forever shed, to be replaced by the pride and capacity of a Colonial Marine.

McGann cornered into a corridor and opened fire.

Buggy fired from behind.

For now, Rawlings didn't need to fire. He had no targets. His sector was clear.

41

Cruz liked the hug of the armor against his skin. It made him feel invincible, even though he knew he wasn't. He held the pulse rifle ready. Hoenikker and Kash huddled behind him, hiding behind his size.

They'd come to a place in the corridor where they couldn't go any farther. Furniture had been piled in the middle from floor to ceiling to block all traffic, whether alien or human. A few rifle barrels sprouted out of the available openings, hints of movements behind them.

"Let us pass," he said to no one in particular.

"Where'd you get the armor?" a voice responded.

"Stay where you are," another voice said.

"The armor is mine," Cruz said. "What the hell is going on here? We need to talk to Station Commander Bellows."

"He's not talking," the second voice said.

"Who am I talking to?" Cruz asked, deepening his voice like a Colonial Marine non-commissioned officer would to a misbehaving private.

A pause. "Security Tech Francis. Security Tech Hardon is with me."

"Francis. What's the deal with the station commander? Why won't he speak with us?"

There was another pause, the sound of whispering.

"He's locked up in his suite with most of the external security personnel."

"Jesus. What's he doing there? Hiding beneath his bed? I have information I need to give him."

"He won't listen," Francis said. "He's not listening to anyone."

"How much you take for your armor?" Hardon asked.

"Not for sale," Cruz said flatly. Then he added, "Try and take it, and I'll make you wish you were facing a roomful of bugs."

"Easy, big fella," Francis said. "It was just a simple question."

"Where's the rest of Security?" Cruz asked. "Why aren't they clearing the corridors?"

"That's beyond my paygrade," Francis said. "I was just told to guard this point."

Fucking paygrades. Being an enlisted soldier, or a security technician, was just like being a mushroom. You were kept in the dark and fed shit. Cruz didn't respond to Mr. Paygrade. Instead, he backed away and around the corner, keeping Hoenikker and Kash protected. When they were safe, he found a supply room and ushered them inside. Once the door was closed, he removed his helmet and placed it on a shelf near some floor cleaner.

Kash lowered her pistol.

Hoenikker did the same with his, holding it uneasily in two hands.

"Things are worse than I expected," Cruz said. "We might have had a chance if it wasn't for the commander."

"What do you mean?" Hoenikker asked.

"If we could do a sweep of the corridors, we could create safe zones. The problem, though, is that we have islands of efficiency. The commander has turtled up in his suite and decided to wait out the infiltration. Same thing happening in the shuttle bay. Security locked it down and are keeping us away from the one way off the rock." Seeing the look of surprise in their eyes, he said, "There are things you don't know—things I was briefed about after Mansfield became fertilizer, and I was promoted. We're worse off than you think we are, especially now that the security staff have been OPCON'd directly to the commander."

"OPCON'd?" Kash asked.

"Sorry," Cruz said. "Operational controlled. Yeah. This means he's either taken over the role of security chief, or the security chief is dead. The commander could do his job and we could rid ourselves of the Xenomorphs, or at least keep them locked in the mess hall."

"Wait?" Hoenikker asked. "What's going on in the mess hall?"

"Seven is what's going on." Cruz shook his head. "They've turned the mess hall into a Xenomorph factory."

"What?" Kash's mouth dropped open. She glanced warily at Hoenikker.

"Here," he pulled out his personal vid display from where he had it secured under his armor. "I patched it into the security cams. Just take a look how organized the Xenomorphs are. It's going to blow your fucking mind." He handed it to Hoenikker.

The screen clicked on. The Xenos were still at it. Only a few humans remained in one corner of the mess hall, kept there by a twitchy adult alien that snapped and drooled at them every few seconds. They cowered, hugging each other, and even though the display had no sound, it was obvious they were crying and begging the universe to save them.

Even as they watched, a Xenomorph held a red-haired young man over an Ovomorph, its wide-clawed hand on the back of his head, locking it in place. They watched in horror as the Ovomorph opened like the petals of a terrible flower, then the snap and twist as a face-hugger launched out of it, wrapping its tail around the man's neck, its claws grasping the man's head for purchase.

"Jesus," Hoenikker said, jerking back. "This is terrible." Then he leaned back in. "How do you think it's communicating?" he asked, turning to Kash.

"I don't even care," Kash said. "We have to stop it." She turned to Cruz, her eyes pleading. "We have to stop it. Can we go stop it, now?" Her lips tightened and trembled as she spoke.

"What's to stop? Look at the others, stacked over there like logs. They've been at this for hours. It's as if Seven and the other Xenomorphs knew where the other eggs were—but that was a well-kept secret." Cruz shook his head. "Best we can do is lock the doors to the mess hall, and keep them trapped inside."

"And then what?" Hoenikker asked. "Then what do we do?"

"We need to hook up with Rawlings and the others. There's several of us Colonial Marines who planned for something like this. I have an algorithm running that will let me know when they show up on one of the security cameras."

A subdued *ding* came from his vid screen. He grabbed it from Hoenikker, punched up a different view.

"Just as I said." He saw two men and a woman moving down the corridor, then into Engineering. The last one in line turned to check the team's six, revealing the face of Buggy. Cruz turned to the others and grinned. "We're heading to Engineering."

Pulling up a schematic of the station, he found that there were two routes they could follow. One would take them near the mess hall, though, and he wasn't sure he wanted to get that close to the breeding ground. He glanced at Hoenikker and Kash. No, not with two civilians.

"Alright, you two. Stay on my six. We're going to join the others, and we're going to be moving fast, so keep up." Cruz slid the vid display back under his armor.

The other two scientists stared at him, terrified.

"Nod if you understand," he said.

They both nodded.

Hoenikker licked his lips.

Cruz put his helmet back on and checked the ammo counter on his rifle. All was good. He palmed the door open, looked left, then right, then left again. After a moment, he turned right and took off at a small jog. The body armor was heavy, but he'd run in much worse conditions. He could be running outside. At night. In the mud and rain. Enemies firing at him. This was nothing more than a jog down the—

He ran full tilt into an adult Xenomorph.

Before he could bring up his rifle, the beast turned to him and shot forth its multiple jaws, spraying him with acid and knocking him to the ground. The armor bore the brunt of the acid. He tried to scramble to his feet but the Xenomorph whipped around, the barb on its tail catching him in the side and throwing him into the wall. He lost his grip on the rifle, which twisted out of his hand.

The Xeno turned to face the scientists.

Both backed away, pistols aiming at the floor.

"Shoot the damn thing!" Cruz bellowed.

The Xenomorph took three quick steps toward them and began to open its mouth.

"I said shoot!"

They raised their pistols so slowly it was like they were moving through water. Cruz knew right then they were going to die. First the other scientists and then him, because like a raw recruit he'd lost control of his rifle. *Fucking damn it all to hell.* He twisted into a sitting position and reached for his rifle. It was his only chance.

Someone screamed.

Then the sound of two pistols opening fire.

He spun to the sound. The scientists had finally done it, sending dozens of rounds into the face and chest of the Xenomorph. Its body jerked and twisted with the impacts. Acid and spittle flew from its face, landing on the walls and ceiling. Where it hit, the surfaces sizzled. Finally, it fell backward, its blood blistering the ground beneath it. Had the floor been made of metal or something less solid than concrete, he was sure it would have melted through. Even so, pockmarks appeared.

Cruz kicked out to get away from the spreading pool of acid, then managed to get to his feet. He checked the armor, which didn't seem worse for wear, snatched his rifle off the floor, and nodded at the pair.

They both stood wide-eyed and open-mouthed, staring at the dead Xenomorph. Cruz approved. They might be good for something after all. Chances were they were going to get killed pretty quickly if the shit hit the fan, but at least they'd been blooded, and knew the working end of a pistol.

"Good job." He turned and stepped around the dead predator. "Okay. Let's go." He started his jog again, this time slowing down a little at blind corners. About a minute and a half later they were at the door to Engineering.

He palmed open the door.

Three hard-looking persons turned to greet him with their pulse rifles.

Then they all grinned.

"Howdy, Marine," Buggy said.

Cruz mock saluted, made sure the two scientists were in

the room, then palmed the door shut.

Rawlings pointed to the scorch mark on the chest plate of the body armor.

"Ran into a little trouble, did you?"

"Score one for the scientists. Thing took me by surprise." He cranked his neck. "Damn those things are strong." He noticed that McGann was studying a particularly confusing schematic. "What is it you all are doing?"

"We need some place to turtle," Rawlings said. "Shit's going to get a lot worse before it gets better. Not to mention we can't even get to the food storage now."

"Wait until those assholes in the commander's suite run out of food. They'll start eating themselves, sooner or later." When Rawlings shot him a questioning look, Cruz related what he knew, and the conversation he'd had with Security Tech Francis.

"So where's the place you think is such a good candidate to hide?" Cruz asked.

"Thompson's hunting lodge. I heard there was one off station," Rawlings said. "And 'off station' means we get away from the Xenomorphs. Even better"—his face brightened—"it's supposed to be fully stocked."

"If I remember right, there were enough dangerous things outside of the station to keep us on lockdown," Kash said, joining in.

"That was before the Xenomorphs," Cruz said. "Plus, if it belonged to Thompson, then it probably has a lot of firearms. Something tells me we don't have enough."

Rawlings nodded, pointing at his scorched armor.

"Something tells me you're right."

4 2

Hoenikker felt the shaky aftereffects of the adrenaline rush. He'd never fired a pistol point blank into an alien that could kill him in the blink of an eye. At first, he'd frozen and couldn't move. A voice screamed from the inside, telling him to lift the pistol, but the only muscles working had been his leg muscles, propelling him backward.

Then his scream became real and his arms unlocked. He could still hear the sounds of gunfire and see the rounds impacting the Xenomorph's head and chest. The way it stiffened and fell back with each impact.

Realizing he was still holding the pistol in a shaky hand, he set it down on one of the desks. He wiped sweat from his forehead, bewildered that a body could produce so much, and glanced over at Kash. She seemed to be processing the same emotions, but was taking it better. Still, he could tell by the slight tremble in her shoulders that her adrenaline was bleeding away as well.

And Cruz? He seemed to be impervious. Daunting in his power armor, his dark skin, sharp features, cutting the perfect image of a Colonial Marine. He stood with one leg jutting out, one hand on his hip as he spoke confidently with the others. Moving from the maintenance closet to Engineering had been a walk in the park for him.

Hoenikker straightened his spine. If he was going to survive this, he needed to emulate the man as much as possible. Cruz noticed his movement, glanced at him, nodded, then returned to his conversation.

Evidently former Deputy Station Chief Thompson, prior to being unceremoniously removed from his position by Bellows, had used station assets to build his own hunting lodge about two kilometers from the station. His own outpost where he could play safari. If what the others said was right, they'd have enough food and weapons to last until a company of active Colonial Marines could come.

"Does anyone know if there's been an SOS?" McGann asked.

Buggy, who was a comms tech, responded, "Here at Pala, we don't have the capability for deep space transmissions. We sent SOSs to the *San Lorenzo*, but we have no idea if their radio systems are set to auto-forward, or if there's a comms tech doing the work. We can't raise anyone, and have no way to go find out unless we take the shuttle up."

"The shuttle is out of the question," Cruz said, "for now."

"That means no one knows what's happening here," Hoenikker said.

Buggy nodded. "That's exactly what it means."

"All the more reason to get out of here," Cruz said. "Let Security fight the Xenomorphs until either one side or both are dead." He pulled out his personal vid and groaned. The screen had cracked in two places. He tossed it onto a desk. "It's all about water and food now. Napoleon knew that an army traveled on its stomach. It's why he almost conquered all of Europe. He didn't have to master warfare—he only had to master logistics. The two groups that are holed up are probably experiencing hunger pains. Infighting is going to follow."

Kash began to rummage through the desks and the lockers.

"What are you doing, ma'am?" McGann asked.

"I don't know of a single office that doesn't have munchies. Snacks. We should gather up what we can, when we can—don't you think?"

Hoenikker agreed. He began on the other side of the room. Let the marines make their plan. At least he could be of use.

Before long they had several bags of chips, some crackers made from some sort of seaweed, and nuts. Then Hoenikker hit the motherlode in Engineering Chief Dudman's office. Dudman had a minifridge that contained a bunch of food ranging from fruit to some sort of mystery meat in gravy. Hoenikker left it in the fridge, but grabbed a pad and a pen and made a note of what was there. Then he returned to Kash.

"Looks like with the six of us, we have about two days of food," she said. "Three if we ration even more."

"That gives us enough time to get to the lodge," Hoenikker said.

"About that…" McGann began.

Hoenikker recognized the tone, and worry immediately set in. Everyone turned toward the engineering tech.

"Might as well tell us," Cruz said, a frown already deepening in his face. "News is like a dead body. It don't smell better with age."

"As it turns out, there's… one of three ways to leave the station," McGann began slowly. "The first is the shuttle bay. There's an exit by the venting system."

"That's out," Cruz said. "Unless we can talk our way in."

"Then there's the mess hall. Backside of the kitchen is an exit door."

Hoenikker shuddered. That was the last place he wanted to go, no matter how intriguing their interaction was from a scientific point of view.

"Might as well lay down and get face-hugged," Cruz said.

Everyone nodded.

Buggy shuddered.

"Then there's the command suites. They have an emergency hatch that allows for them to escape." She pointed at the screen of the desktop vid. "Good news is that it hasn't been activated, and it does have power."

"So you think the commander doesn't know about the lodge?" Hoenikker asked.

"When he kicked the commander and deputy commander off station," Buggy said, "I doubt there was an exit interview. External security would know about it, because they were the ones who guarded Thompson while he was outside. They must not have told Bellows, for some reason known only to them."

Everyone stared. The best guess Hoenikker could make was that the security personnel wanted the lodge for themselves.

"So no matter which way we go, we have to fight," he said, putting words to what they all must be thinking. "Either the security forces or the Xenomorphs. Am I getting this right?"

"Afraid so." McGann nodded.

Cruz leaned over and stared at the screen. He tapped it thoughtfully. Hoenikker wondered what was going through the man's mind. His critical thinking skills might be sharper even than his sadistic tendencies.

Cruz pointed. "Can we shut down power to various doors from here?"

"Sure," McGann said. "But what good will that do?"

"Well, first thing we can do is secure the doors to the mess hall. That will keep Seven and his merry band of killers in there for as long as it takes him to figure a way out. Hopefully, that will be long enough for us to blow this popsicle stand."

"And second?" Buggy asked. "You said first, so I figure there must be a second."

"Second, we lock down *all* the doors. We're in Engineering. We have special access. Perhaps we'll get to the point where we have something we can trade for safe passage out of here." He turned to Kash. "How much food did you say we had?"

"Two days. Three days max."

"So, we have seventy-two hours to figure this out. They should be good and hungry by then." He tapped the screen. "My guess is that the guards in the shuttle bay will blink first. The command suites probably have decent food storage. But the shuttle bay and loading docks? Naw. They're going to get hungry."

Hoenikker looked askance at the food on the table, and thought about the stuff in the fridge. He'd never had to ration before—never been told there wasn't enough food to eat. He glanced at the other men, all bigger than him. Surely they'd need more calories than he would to survive. They'd have to eat more food.

What would happen in three days if they couldn't negotiate their way out? Things were going to get worse. Would they actually draw straws, like he'd read about in old books, or would they just kick him out the door? Certainly, he'd be first. After all, what good was he in a firefight, compared to them?

Times like these, one's ability to survive trumped any other academic or God-given skill.

Cruz noticed him looking at the door.

"I know what you're thinking," he said. "It's not going to come to that."

Hoenikker stared at him, blinked several times, and wondered how the man could possibly know what he was thinking, unless he was thinking the same thing—only from his own point of view.

That wasn't reassuring.

"We're going to get this handled," Cruz said. "First step is to remove power from every door. That'll keep them from being able to rewire. Then we sit back for a day and let them freak out. At the end of that day, we get on comms and let them know what their choices are."

Kash shook her head. "The longer we wait, the more time the Xenomorphs have to breed. Right now we're facing seven or eight. Soon there will be several dozen."

"Well, let's hope that's the station's problem. We'll let the security forces sort it out if and when the Xenomorphs are able to leave the mess hall," Cruz said.

"I'd say *when*, not *if*," Kash replied.

"I'm afraid that you're right."

"Say? Anyone seen Étienne lately?" Hoenikker asked.

Everyone looked at him.

"I can't see how he survived," Cruz said. "I guess he went out like he wanted to."

Hoenikker thought of the man singing, walking down the hall past the Xenomorphs. He couldn't help but smile at the sheer lunacy of it, and hoped Étienne *had* found a way to survive.

43

The first day seemed longer than normal.

It was nothing to remove power from all the doors. Rawlings imagined that for the first few hours, people were trying to figure out why the lights and the air systems were still running, yet the doors wouldn't open.

By midday, someone tried to hack into the engineering systems. Buggy stopped them in their tracks and sent several Trojans into the computers, shutting them down. He was gleeful in his ability to outthink and outmaneuver them.

Rawlings was happy for him.

Hell, he was happy for all his new best friends. Cruz had become a scientist. McGann had become an engineer. Buggy had become a communications specialist. A lot of people never found a life after the marines. Far too many couldn't take civilian life, ending up on a penal planet or eating the barrel of their own gun. To see some vets achieve success was a testament to their drive and desire.

Which also made him sad. All their efforts, all their training, would be ruined because some of them weren't going to survive. It was the law of combat. You go in thinking you'll probably die, and come back happy to be alive. Those who go in not wanting to die made mistakes or were too slow to react.

His eyes went to the two scientists—Hoenikker and Kash. *They'd* hesitate. They'd go in wanting to live, and die for it. But him and the others… sure, they might die, but they had a better chance of living because they accepted the possibility of death. They were ready for it. Hell, they'd gladly do it, if it meant they could save their fellow marines.

By that afternoon, Rawlings was bored to tears. More importantly, he wanted a drink. He began pacing around, eyeing the desks and the layout, wondering where the best place would be to hide a bottle. Kash had been right that every office had snacks hidden in desks—and every office had liquor hidden somewhere.

The office was divided into four rooms: the bullpen, the project room, the water closet, and a private office. All three desks used by the engineering techs were in the bullpen, which was the large space next to the exit. The desks faced each other, so if anyone was to drink, the others would see him. So then where?

McGann lounged at her desk, looking like she was about to fall asleep, head back, eyes almost closed. Behind her was a storage area with shelves and cabinets. Rawlings went through each one of these, careful not to make much noise. He searched the best he could, but didn't find what he was looking for—just cables and couplers and everything in between. He even checked behind each one for spaces in the wall.

Nothing.

How could an office not have any booze?

He turned around, frowning and a little bewildered. McGann was awake and staring at him.

"How long?" Rawlings asked.

"Long enough," she said. "Do you really think this is a good time?"

So, she knew.

"Is there ever a bad time?" Rawlings countered.

"When we're about to go into battle," McGann replied. "I'd call that a bad time."

"But we're not." Rawlings grinned. "We have more than two whole days. A few nips now, and by the time we need to be sober, we will be."

McGann gave him a long look, then shrugged.

"Fuck it. You're your own man. You want to get shit-faced, then get shit-faced. Bottle's in the chief's office, bottom right drawer of his desk."

Rawlings winked. "Thanks, pal."

He passed by the project room. Cruz had laid his armor, weapons, and flamethrower on the table and was asleep beneath it. Kash had pulled two chairs together and was curled up on them, her elfin arms and legs drawn into themselves. He walked softly past them and into the office.

Hoenikker was fast asleep on the couch that sat in front of the desk, his body turned facing the cushions. He'd taken off his shoes and placed them in front of the couch. His knees were drawn up and his right hand rested on the side of his face.

The office was spartan. A map of the facility was hung on the wall behind the couch. Open shelving housed several dozen actual books, each of them antiques. Their topics ranged from astrophysics to non-Euclidian topology. Wedged within them was a book of poetry. Leaning in to get a closer look at the name, Rawlings noted that it was by Walt Whitman.

That name was familiar, though all he knew of the man was that he lived in the 1800s back on Earth, and wrote the poem 'Oh Captain, My Captain', which he'd heard spoken at too many Colonial Marine funerals. How did the end go?

My Captain does not answer, his lips are pale and still,
My father does not feel my arm, he has no pulse nor will,
The ship is anchor'd safe and sound, its voyage closed and done,
From fearful trip the victor ship comes in with object won;
Exult O shores, and ring O bells!
But I with mournful tread,
Walk the deck my Captain lies,
Fallen cold and dead.

It always had been a miserable damned poem.

He turned, gingerly pulled out the chair, and sat in it, noting the softness. *Must be good to be a section chief.* Then he reached down and pulled open the bottom right drawer. Sure enough, a liter flask lay there. He plucked it from the drawer, opened the lid, and sniffed. His head jerked back. It might as well have been paint thinner. Jesus, but it smelled strong.

Taking a tentative sip, he sat back as a nuclear holocaust occurred in his mouth before searing his throat and then slamming into his stomach.

McGann stood at the door, grinning.

"What the hell is this stuff?" he asked, whispering.

"Shine," McGann whispered back. "Dudman bought it from a guy in Fabrications."

"What percentage alcohol is this?"

"All of it," McGann said. She strode over and took the flask. She took a swig and her face turned instantly red. "Jesus. How can anyone drink this?"

"Practice," Rawlings said, accepting it back. He took a sip and then set the flask on the desk. "Something tells me this is our last hoorah." He touched his mechanical hand and flashed back to when he'd lost it.

"Probably." McGann nodded. "But then I've had a good run. I've had my share of women. I've been places I'd never dreamed of—done things I'd never thought possible."

"I've had my share of women, too," Rawlings said, eyeing the one in front of him.

McGann sneered. "I bet I've had more than you."

Rawlings shook his head. "I won't even touch that bet." He paused a moment, then asked, "Don't you want to do just one more thing?"

"Like what? I mean, sure, it's nice to be alive, to taste something wonderful, watch a vid that stimulates. But haven't we really done everything?"

Rawlings considered. He had done more than he'd ever thought. He'd shot, fucked, and fought across a galaxy that seemed to be getting larger by the day. Maybe he should treat this as sport. Maybe killing the Xenomorphs should be a final game, one in which the loser *really* loses.

At least that way he'd be motivated.

McGann was turning away and about to leave when Rawlings spoke.

"I bet I nail three of them before I bite it."

McGann turned, grinning like a fool. "Three, you say? Then I'll bag four."

"Adolescents count as much as an adult," Rawlings added, swigging.

"Adolescents count as much as adults." McGann nodded. "Sure."

"We get to call our shots, too," Rawlings said.

"Well, if one of the creatures is a danger to all of us, then we're all opening fire." McGann nodded again. "But I get your point. If we see one at distance and you want to call it, you just have to say it ahead of me."

"What about Buggy? Think we should get him involved?"

McGann shook her head. "He's way too serious for all of this. We'll just make sure he has our sixes."

Rawlings took one last drag, noting there was still plenty more for later, and leaned back. Yeah. Shooting Xenomorphs at the end of the world. This was going to be hella fun. He imagined killing Xenomorphs until the flask was empty. Then he turned around and puked in a waste basket. He wasn't feeling very well.

Hoenikker was sitting up when he turned around.

"Was that you?" the scientist asked.

"Whuth? You nether saw pipple puthing?" Rawlings vaguely realized that he couldn't move his tongue.

Hoenikker stood suddenly, covering his nose and mouth with a forearm.

"Oh. The smell." He hurried out the door.

"Gud riddith," Rawlings said, then he staggered toward the couch.

He had passed out before he even hit it.

44

Cruz keyed the audio. Thirty-six hours had passed since he'd put everyone on lockdown, so he imagined they were eager to get out. He glanced at those around him, then began.

"People of Pala Station," he said. "By now you've figured out that you can't move from where you are. All doors have been locked. There are no drop ceilings. There are no secret passageways. What you see is what you get. Many of you might be hungry and or thirsty, as well.

"The problem is that Security have hunkered down, and aren't doing what Security are supposed to do," he continued, "which is clear the station. I will open the doors for the next hour, and observe through the security cameras, to see if Security are doing their job. If not, then I will close the doors again."

He glanced at McGann. She keyed in a command.

"The doors are open."

He sat back. "Now let's see the chaos."

They had five vids running—outside the command suites, outside the shuttle bay, outside the mess hall, outside

Engineering, and inside the mess hall. They counted three distinct Xenomorphs roaming the corridors. The rest were in the mess hall pretending to be wet nurses for the humans who had woken after being face-hugged.

Security techs with pulse rifles poured out of the shuttle bay, searching this way and that for targets. They looked scared and confused. Their hair and uniforms were in disarray. Much different to the security techs coming out of the command suite, who looked professional and military. They moved with purpose and allowed Cruz and his companions to view them for exactly five seconds before someone shot out the camera.

Cruz hadn't unlocked the mess hall doors. He wasn't *that* crazy. But he wanted to see what the security forces would do. Word would spread, and shortly everyone would know about the activities in the mess hall. So, it was either turtle up in each end of the station, or become proactive and kill the monsters in the corridors. In addition to the three Xenomorphs outside of the mess hall, there was the missing Leon-895, as well as the Fairbanks monster. Neither of them had been seen or heard from.

"Someone's trying to access the escape hatch in the command suite," McGann said.

Cruz nodded. As he'd suspected. He'd turned on power, but had locked the door. He just wanted to see what they had planned.

"Remove power," he said.

McGann did as she was told.

Hoenikker and Kash hovered over the vid display showing the inside of the mess hall, murmuring to each other. It was all they could really do. Cruz might have liked to have joined them, but he'd partitioned that part of his brain and was now firmly once again a Colonial Marine. He had to be, or else they would all die.

Buggy was furiously warding off attacks on the comms servers. They were becoming more and more sophisticated, but he seemed to be up to the task.

And Rawlings?

He was passed out on the couch in the chief's office. The old warrant officer had needed to blow off steam. Two good things came from his bender. The man had been able to voice his issues so he could get right in the head, and they were now officially out of alcohol.

The others had argued with him about whether or not he should have let them out. They were afraid everyone would make a beeline for Engineering and try to take them out. But Cruz needed Security to patrol the corridors and remove the threats. He also knew it was a matter of time before Seven would figure a way out of the mess hall. That Xeno had an agenda, and Cruz hoped he wasn't playing checkers while Seven played three-dimensional chess.

If that was the case, then they were all doomed.

Several security guards from the shuttle bay reached the mess hall. They tried to palm open the doors, but found themselves locked out. Cruz watched as they argued amongst themselves. Then he leaned forward. Either it was a trick of the light, or the wall had moved.

Then the wall moved again.

Or something the same color as the wall. Just as he was about to form the words "Leon-895," it partially materialized and grabbed one of the security guards. The creature took a huge bite from the top of the man's head, and then dropped the body.

One of the remaining security guards turned and fled.

The other fired blindly—once, twice, then turned to run.

He didn't get but ten feet before he was jerked off his feet.

The top of his head disappeared, as did his brain, in a shower of blood, bone, and gore. A fleck of gray matter landed on the security camera bubble, creating a blind spot until it dripped off, leaving a wash of red film to see through. Clearly the Leon preferred brain matter over any other body parts.

A security force appeared outside the Engineering section door. He'd anticipated that. Curiously, they didn't shoot out the camera that covered the entryway.

"McGann, want to get suited up?" Cruz suggested. She nodded, ran to the project room, and shrugged on the power armor and the flamethrower.

Several security techs from the command suites were trying to palm the door open. One pried open the control panel and began to work on it. He jerked backward onto the floor as if pulled by a rope, a line of electricity following him from the box. McGann had made it so that the only thing hooked to the panel was the main power line. Although it was genius, it could only work once. The circuitry inside the access box was completely fried, but it would deter others from trying.

Cruz grinned and keyed the microphone. "You're going to have to do better than that," he said, his voice booming throughout the station.

The comms console buzzed.

It was an incoming call, and the ID flashed **COMMAND**. He guessed Bellows was ready for a parlay, and opened the line of communication.

"What the hell are you doing, Dr. Cruz?" Bellows demanded.

"What needs to be done," Cruz responded calmly. "Are you finished hiding in the corner, or are you ready to get Security out so they can do their job?"

"Hiding in a corner?" Bellows blustered. "I'm doing nothing of the sort. I'm conferring with the head of Security to identify the best way to deal with the problem, while you're playing evil overlord and locking down all the doors so we can't get anything done."

"So, you hatched a plan?"

"Of course we hatched a plan. That's our job. To protect the station."

"I noticed the Weyland-Yutani company personnel inside the mess hall weren't part of your plan," Cruz said, a grim note entering his voice. "Had you done something sooner, they might be alive."

Bellows paused. "We took that under consideration. Security felt the situation was untenable."

"You mean you couldn't convince them to put their asses on the line," Cruz said. "Or didn't try." Another pause. This one longer. Cruz wondered if perhaps Security Chief Rodriguez wasn't beside him, listening in.

He decided to press it.

"Are you safe, Station Commander Bellows?" Cruz asked. "Are they holding a gun to your head?"

"No one is holding a gun to anyone's head, Dr. Cruz," Cynthia Rodriguez said, each word tightly enunciated.

"That's good to know," he replied. "Because when help eventually arrives—and it will—you need to make sure you've been acting aboveboard and for the benefit of the station, and not for yourself and your security technicians."

"They'll understand why I did what I did."

"History judges decisions in a far harsher light than the present. You'd better hope so." Then he said, "Commander Bellows?"

"Yes."

"If the Xenomorphs manage to get outside the mess hall, without Security having a plan to keep them in or kill them, all that's going to be left of the rest of us is piles of smoking acid. They're breeding, and soon there will be a lot more of them. Do you really have a plan?'

Silence.

"Bellows?"

Silence.

"Bellows?"

"I think he disconnected," Buggy said.

"Just as I figured." Cruz turned. "Okay, it's time for round two."

"What's that?" Hoenikker asked.

"We turn off the lights."

"How does that help us?" Kash asked.

A few seconds later, the security techs in front of Engineering found themselves in the dark. None of them had thought to bring night-vision devices like the one on the camera in the corridor.

Cruz pointed at the three milling bodies outside their door, now illuminated in green night vision by the cameras. "They've made their points clear. They want what we have. The only way to get that is to kill us."

"But won't they die?" Kash asked. "What about the Xenomorphs?"

The security techs fumbled around for several minutes, then panicked and began to open fire. The terror in their faces was lit by the strobes from their pulse rifles.

Then there were two.

The flash of a whipping tail and fangs.

Then there was one.

Then silence.

As the Xenomorph marched on.

It was truly every man and woman for themselves.

45

Six hours later, Cruz turned the lights back on.

His chin rested on his fist as he stared at the screen. There had to be a reason they hadn't shot out the camera in front of Engineering. If it had been his plan, Cruz would have shot out *every* camera, blinding those who had control over power and the doors. So, what was the reason? What were they planning where they needed to be seen? What subterfuge was in play that he couldn't recognize?

If he didn't figure it out, he might fall victim to it.

Then it happened.

A woman.

She arrived breathlessly at the door, glancing back fearfully, banging on the composite metal as if her life depended on it.

Cruz knew immediately what it was, and was disappointed. It was as if they thought he was stupid. She had to be a Trojan horse. They should have known that he'd know, too. Was that it? Were they counting on him to double-think?

He leaned forward, intrigued.

Twisting the camera around, he checked to see if there was anyone else down the hall. It was empty. Then he hit the control and let her in, the door *snicking* open fast enough that she fell forward.

Three security techs rushed into sight.

He closed the door. They weren't fast enough.

McGann grabbed the newcomer by the back of her neck and pressed a pistol to her head.

"What's your name?"

"Susan," she said breathlessly. Medium build. Mousy brown hair. Brown eyes. A face that had probably been pretty when she was younger, but had fallen victim to middle age. She wore a blue jumpsuit. Interesting. No one on the station wore blue jumpsuits.

She glanced feverishly around the room—or was she taking inventory? Making a map of everything, so she could go back and inform Bellows or Rodriguez or whoever was in charge.

"Last name," McGann asked.

"McCune. Susan McCune. What the hell's going on with the station?"

Cruz raised an eyebrow. "What do you mean?"

"We just arrived on Pala Station. The security techs in the shuttle bay said you have control of the whole facility. They refused to escort us, and something took down my copilot. I never saw it. One moment he was here. The next… nothing."

So, that was their ruse. An unplanned shuttle.

Interesting.

"Buggy, get Rawlings up," Cruz said. "I need him. Meanwhile, McCune, you just sit there."

"No can do," Buggy said. "I need to monitor comms. There are incoming like you wouldn't believe."

Cruz growled. "Will someone wake Rawlings the fuck up?" Kash nodded and stood, then went into the office.

"What's your copilot's name?" Cruz asked.

"Ernest Withers."

"What type of vessel do you hail from?"

"Merchant ship. We received an emergency hail from the *San Lorenzo*."

"We did get the word out!" Hoenikker's normally dour face lit with excitement. Cruz shot him a look.

"Are you Weyland-Yutani?" he asked McCune.

"Private contractor. We've worked with Weyland-Yutani before, but not currently."

"What's your cargo?"

"Ore. Primarily magnesium and cesium."

"What's your compliment?"

"Sixteen. The others are in cryosleep. Withers and I were awakened when the emergency beacon contacted our ship. Listen, what exactly is going on here? Why the interrogation? I'm just following the rules of open space. If we hear an emergency beacon, it's our duty to investigate."

Rawlings staggered into the bullpen. "My mouth feels like a family of rats took a shit inside, and then smeared it everywhere." He looked like hell. Bloodshot eyes brimmed with liquid atop a bulbous, red-veined nose. His dark skin was the color of old clay.

"Rawlings, I need your full attention," Cruz said.

"Yeah?" He blinked several times and rubbed his hand on the back of his neck. "What is it?"

"Do you recognize this woman?"

Rawlings peered at her through bleary eyes, then shook his head.

"Never seen her before."

"So, she's not from the station?"

"Nope. I know everyone. It's my job. She's not from here."

"Can you please explain to me what's going on?" McCune asked.

Cruz held up a hand. "Run her face through biometrics," he said, handing Rawlings a personal vid unit. The reception tech fumbled with it for a moment, then keyed in instructions. He held it up to her and took her picture, then ran it through biometrics.

Everyone looked at one another in the silence, no one really wanting to be the one to break it. The only sound other than breathing was Buggy punching his monitor, his hands moving fast enough that he could have been playing a piano.

Finally, Rawlings shook his head. "No record of her being on the station. No record of her being in Weyland-Yutani. Looks like we have a certified stranger."

"What about her PDT?" McGann asked.

Rawlings shook his head again. "I remotely scanned everyone's in this room. We all have one. She doesn't."

"Does that mean she's really here to help us?" Hoenikker asked.

Now Cruz *really* was intrigued.

"Who were the security techs outside?" he asked, meaning the three who had rushed the door. "Did they bring you here?"

She shook her head. "I don't know what you're talking about."

Either salvation had just appeared at their doorstep, or she was a great actress and somehow had been working on the station like a ghost. Still, it didn't entirely make sense. If there had been a shuttle landing in the bay, then command would have wanted access to both the pilot and the shuttle.

And there wasn't any way to check out her story. He was blind in the bay and in front of the command suites. Then again, he *wasn't* blind, was he? Every door and access point on the station could read a personal data tracker, and everyone on the station had PTDs implanted in their bodies.

"McGann, I think it's okay to lower your pistol," Cruz said, then he turned to the engineer. "Follow me." He and McGann walked into the office, and outlined his idea. McGann nodded, grinned, and confirmed that it was definitely possible. Then she sat down behind the desk.

Cruz called in Buggy, who joined them. They chatted for a moment, and Buggy disappeared into another room. Cruz returned to his seat in the bullpen.

"What do you know about Xenomorphs?" he asked McCune.

Her eyebrows twisted. "Xenowhats?"

"Xenomorphs. Brought to us care of the *San Lorenzo*, which towed a facility that was infested with them. Creatures capable of using a human as a gestational host from which to transition and grow. They enter the human host through the mouth, then burst from the chest, then grow at an alarming rate until they become full-size killing machines." He grinned flatly. "What do you know about them?"

She shook her head, but displayed no emotion. "This is the first I've heard of them," she said evenly.

"The security techs in the shuttle bay didn't warn you about them when they let you into the station?"

"All they said was that there were monsters," she replied. "I thought they were nuts."

"So you and your copilot—"

"Withers."

"Yes, you and your copilot Withers just entered the station, and made a beeline to Engineering rather than the command suites."

"The shuttle bay techs said that the people in charge were in Engineering," she replied. "They gave us directions."

"You came unarmed."

"We're a private ore hauler. We don't have weapons."

"And you've never heard of Xenomorphs."

"That's what I said."

Cruz stood and went over, gesturing to shake her hand. She held hers out automatically as she stood.

"Excellent," Cruz said. "I'm going to let you be on your way, then—I'll provide you with directions to the command suite, and you can talk with them regarding assistance."

"I don't understand," she said. "I was told you are in charge."

"Only the lights and power," Cruz said. "McGann? Are we ready?"

"We're on it."

"Let's hit the lights before she leaves."

"Lights off," McGann said.

"Excellent." He turned to their visitor. "Well, are you ready?"

"It's too dangerous," she murmured.

"I have good news," he lied. "Xenomorphs need light to survive. They hibernate in the dark. Just don't bump into one, and you'll be perfectly fine." Hoenikker stood and was about to say something, but Cruz snapped his fingers to shut him up. Buggy came over with a flashlight. He snapped it on and off in his face.

"This should get you there." He handed it to her. "And hey, thanks for saving our asses. We really appreciate it." Wearing a confused expression, she looked from one to the other, her hand on the flashlight, her thumb turning it on and off absently.

"Will one of you come with me?" she asked, her voice small and breathless.

"Sorry," Cruz said, returning to his seat. "We've got too much work to do. But like I said, you'll be okay. The Xenomorphs hibernate. They're usually against the walls—they do that to keep from falling down. So walk down the middle of the corridors, and you'll be alright."

"I heard there might be other monsters."

"That's not what you said," Cruz replied, adding a curious note to his voice. "You said, 'all they said was that there were monsters.' You never said anything about there being more than one type."

She glanced from one to the other including Hoenikker and Kash, then she frowned, her face going ugly.

"You fucking sonuvabitch."

"Just as I thought." Cruz nodded. "McGann, what do you have?"

"Four of them around the corner."

Cruz got up and went into the project room. He returned thirty seconds later wearing the flamethrower.

"You can't possibly," McCune said, staring wide-eyed at the lick of flame dancing at the end of the barrel.

"Oh, I absolutely can," he replied. "What did you think you would do to us? Have one of us follow you, or find a way to open the door? I knew you were a Trojan the minute I saw you. How you're on the station without us knowing about it is another thing entirely. For now, though, we'll let the station understand we mean business." He adjusted his shoulders and spoke to Hoenikker and Kash. "You two might want to get over there," he said, nodding to where the storage was to the right of the door. "McGann, when you're ready."

The door *snicked* open.

"Here they come," McGann called.

Cruz depressed the actuator just as they came into view. Instantly the four men were consumed at the entrance to Engineering. One managed to get a shot off into the ceiling, but the others became flaming imitations of men, their arms waving, legs dancing, then crumbling as each one of them tried to scream, sucking flame and superheated air into lungs that burned from within.

They never made it inside.

McGann closed the door, leaving only the smoke and the smell of human flesh to remind them of what had occurred. They were still visible on the vid, which showed a smoldering pile of would-be attackers.

"I can't believe you did that," McCune said breathlessly. Cruz turned toward her.

"Don't go getting sanctimonious on me," he snarled. "You would have done the same to us, given the chance." She seemed unable to stop staring at the display.

Cruz left her there, took his flamethrower back to the project room, and set it on the table.

46

"Who *are* you?" Cruz demanded, his face stone cold with purpose.

Hoenikker felt as if he was an outsider looking in. He'd thought they were fighting against the monsters, but as it turned out, they were *all* monsters. The Xenomorphs, the Leons, and the humans. Their capacity for killing could not be underestimated, nor could it be ignored. There was no safe haven here. There was no place to hide. Enemies were all around, some of them fleshed in the bodies of "friends."

"I gave you my name," she said, tight lipped, sweat beading on her brow. She sat in a chair, her hands bound behind her with cable straps.

"Susan McCune, why aren't you on the station rolls?" Rawlings asked.

She turned to him and frowned. "That's above your paygrade, Warrant."

Rawlings grinned at that. "So, you know I was a Colonial Marine, and you know my rank. Good for you."

"Nothing is above *my* paygrade," Cruz said. "Answer the man."

She seemed to consider the question. "Let's just say there are doors you can open, and doors you can't." She paused. "And there are doors you don't even know exist."

"Does that even make sense?" Buggy asked.

She just sneered.

"You know you're going to prison, right?" she said to Cruz. "You killed them in cold blood. I'll be a witness at your trial."

Cruz laughed hollowly. "There's never going to be a trial. You're not going to survive what's coming. Fuck. *None* of us might survive what's coming, except Rawlings and Hoenikker here. After all, God favors drunks and fools, and those who don't understand what's going on."

"Hey," Hoenikker said. He certainly didn't feel like a fool. For the most part.

"No offense, Doctor," Cruz said, nodding in his direction, then he addressed McCune again. "My point is that if the two groups of security techs don't get together, to plan a way to defeat Seven and his Xenos, then we're all screwed. You'd be lucky to make it ten feet by yourself, much less all the way to a corporate court."

"Chief Rodriguez assured me we have this handled," she replied. "She has a plan. We just need access to Engineering."

"And how much experience does Cynthia have with Xenos?"

"She's dealt with them before. She knows their weakness."

"Their weakness? Susan, you're talking to a group of scientists who have been studying them for weeks, trying to find their weaknesses." He pointed at the door. "Those things have no weaknesses. They have no natural enemies. They were created to attack a host, gestate, explode from a chest, and become a battle-raging acid-spitting machine." He laughed. "You and yours. You think you know more about these creatures than the scientists—and I get it.

"I was a Colonial Marine," he continued. "I felt like there wasn't anything I couldn't fight, fuck, or kill. Then I ran into something none of those verbs worked against. Yes, there's shit out there in the universe that we don't ken, and we should run from it as fast as we can. Xenomorphs are at the top of the list, only Weyland-Yutani wants to 'monetize' the impossible."

No one spoke for a moment.

Finally, Kash broke the silence.

"Susan, what's the plan?" she asked.

"I'm the one talking to the prisoner," Cruz said.

"The hell you are. I've sat back and tried to convince myself that you all are doing this the Colonial Marine's way." Kash said the last like it left a horrid taste in her mouth. "But I doubt their way is to kill four Weyland-Yutani security techs in cold blood."

Cruz began. "But you don't underst—"

She whirled on him. "Listen to me, Buster. No more killing station personnel. Not unless they try and kill us first."

"You might not get that chance," Cruz said, his voice low and carefully controlled.

"I—*we'll* take that chance." She pointed at the vid screen. "Better to die a human than a monster."

Cruz was about to say something, when Kash turned back to Susan. "Again, I'm asking. What's the plan? Right now, ninety percent of the threat is in the mess hall. Have they considered setting up units at the doors?"

McCune stared, then seemed to come to a decision.

"Rodriguez believes that we can induce stasis in the creatures by alternating the frequencies of light," she said. "According to her, it worked before."

"Disco lights?" McGann said. "She wants to use *disco lights* to defeat the monsters?"

Hoenikker considered. It might actually work, but they hadn't tested it. What Rodriguez had seen in the wild—outside of a controlled experimental space—might have been the result of anything. Not being a scientist, she could have applied the vector inaccurately. It didn't pass his logic test, but that didn't mean it wasn't possible.

"Hoenikker, you might be the smartest of us," Cruz began, avoiding eye contact with Kash. "You look like you're working this out in your head. What do you say? Is it possible?"

He stared at Cruz, and couldn't shake the image of him setting afire the four living human beings who had tried to burst in.

"We don't have enough data, but we could always conduct a controlled test," he suggested. "After all, the Xenomorphs are in a single space. We could create an algorithm to adjust the light variance, and record what effects they might have on the ability of the Xenomorphs to conduct regular activities."

"What did he just say?" Buggy asked.

"He said we can test it out," Cruz said.

"Then why didn't he just say that?"

"He did, doofus." Rawlings took a swig of water from a jug.

"Easy on that," McGann said. "We don't have much left."

"Cottonmouth. I can't help it."

"Last cottonmouth you're ever going to have," Buggy said.

"Fuck, I hope not."

Cruz leaned forward to talk to the prisoner, but looked to Kash first, who gave him a hard nod. "McCune, did they even consider attacking the mess hall?" Cruz asked.

"Not once," she said. "They don't want to be directly involved with the creatures. As Weyland-Yutani employees, they—we—don't feel like it's our responsibility. After all, that's what Colonial Marines are for."

"I'm not sure if you've noticed," Rawlings said, "but there's a current shortage of Colonial Marines."

"They'll come eventually," McCune said.

"Oh, really—and how will they come?" Cruz asked. "Has anyone called them?"

"That's above my paygrade."

"You and your fucking paygrades," Rawlings said.

"Easy, Warrant. You'll blow a gasket," she said.

Just then the power snapped off. A couple of them shouted their surprise, and a couple more swore. Darkness surrounded them all, and Hoenikker was afraid to even move. Finally, it was Cruz's voice that rose above the rest.

"Everyone fucking shut up." Once the chaos ebbed, he added, "Rawlings and Buggy, grab rifles and attend the door."

A light blinked from a desk.

"McGann, what's that light?"

"Master control. We have a direct line to a single power cell, in the event of an EMP or anything that disrupts the main power feed. It's shielded."

"Can you get on there, and figure out what happened?"

"I think so." A dim figure in the near-absolute blackness, she hurried to the blinking light. There was the sound of a chair being moved, followed by a halo of light shining on her face as a screen lit.

"Hoenikker, Kash, find flashlights. Check the shelves."

Hoenikker could barely see, but he knew where the shelves were, so he zombie-walked in that direction, hands out to be his eyes as he used his fingertips to sort through the detritus of the Engineering department.

Kash was the first to find one. She snapped it on and handed it to Hoenikker, then she grabbed three more. She passed one to Buggy and the other to Cruz, and held onto the third, snapping it on and flashing the beam over everything, including their prisoner, who was still in place but struggling to free herself.

"I don't think that's a great idea," Kash said to her.

"Make sure her bonds are secure, please," Cruz said.

Hoenikker walked over to the screen where Cruz stood with McGann.

"Looks like a power node was disrupted here," McGann said, pointing at the screen.

"Disrupted how?" Cruz frowned.

"With the exception of the master, all of our power comes from solar cells on the roof and a massive solar array we have on the south side of the station."

"So, the node is an intersection?"

"Yes. I can reroute the power, but it will take a bit of programming."

"What could have caused the outage?" Hoenikker asked.

"Yeah, what he said," Cruz added.

McGann furiously punched in commands. "I can't be sure." She shook her head. "It could be anything."

"Where's the node located?" Hoenikker asked.

"Near the south side of the station."

In his mind, Hoenikker mapped what he knew of the station. When he thought he had it figured out he turned sharply to Cruz.

"It's the mess hall. That's on the south side."

Cruz's eyes narrowed in the glow of vid light. "Where are the nodes located?"

"On the roof," McGann said. "Only way to access them is from outside."

"Can you go through the roof to access them?" Hoenikker asked.

McGann answered. "Sure, but you'd have to—fuck."

She glanced at Cruz, then Hoenikker. "Do you think that's what happened?"

"What else could it be?" Cruz asked.

"I suppose, depending on their ability to detect ion energy, they might have been able to detect directional energy." Hoenikker looked up as he continued talking. "I mean, being close to a power conduit might be the same as being next to something that's magnetized. If they have, or have developed, the ability to detect power, and understand what it is, then perhaps they could track and destroy it."

Perhaps this is one of the mutations Seven has acquired, he thought. *Given his heightened sensory capabilities, like telepathic communication. Even if the rest aren't so advanced, he could direct them.* The thought made him shudder.

"Ever wonder if what we've done here might be the doom of the entire universe?" Kash asked, joining them. "The experimentation with the pathogen, combined with the irradiation, might have helped create even better killing machines."

"My thoughts exactly," Hoenikker said.

"Enough of what we shouldn't have done," Cruz growled. "We did it. We were paid for it. We wanted scientific advancement at any cost." He shook his head. "Just look at what we did to our fellow humans. We allowed them to become victims of the creatures. Despite what I said, I was as disgusted as the rest of you. But Bellows had put me in charge. If I didn't follow his instructions, it might have been one of you, or some front-office flunky."

The lights suddenly came on again, dimmer than before.

"Okay," McGann said. "We have power, but it's not full. Something's siphoning what power I have, and I don't know the reason why."

"Hurry. Check the mess hall," Cruz ordered.

McGann dialed up the cameras on her vid display. She gasped and showed it to the rest in the room. They gasped.

"What's wrong?" Rawlings asked from the door. "What do you see?"

"They're gone." Cruz ran a hand over his face. "Every last Xenomorph is gone. All that's left are the bodies, and the husks from the face-huggers. I don't know how they did it, but they found a way out."

"What about the other cameras?" Buggy asked. "Like the one in front of our door?"

McGann punched the screen a few times.

"There are no other cameras," she said. "We're blind."

"That devious bastard," Cruz said.

"What's devious? Who bastard?" Kash asked, her face still red from their previous interaction.

"Seven. He killed the screens. He's mocking us. He's warning us, because he doesn't think there's anything we can do. He's saying, *ready or not here I come*." He shook his head. "We had him trapped in a cage, and now he's returning the favor."

Hoenikker stared at him, knowing that what he said was true and wishing that it wasn't. He glanced around, and found where he'd laid his pistol. It seemed so small and pathetic. Was it going to be enough? Would it keep him from being killed? Dear God, why had he ever come here? He backed away from the desk on two stiff legs.

"And now we are the hunted."

The sound of claws scraping against metal came from the door. Hoenikker spun and stared, just like the rest.

He had an overwhelming sense of having to pee.

47

"Alright. Everyone get geared up," Cruz said. "This is the end game—both humans and monsters are going to be coming at us. I don't know which is worse, so we have to be ready."

Kash handed Cruz his helmet. "Sometimes humans *are* the monsters. This is your chance not to be one."

"Humans are always the monsters," Cruz said, not meeting her gaze, "but there can be monsters more dangerous than us, and we've just spent weeks making them better." He fit into his gear and then turned to the others. He knew how he looked. A Colonial Marine in full battle rattle was a bad enough sight to behold, but one carrying a flamethrower was enough to send them running.

Rawlings, Buggy, and McGann all had pulse rifles, with pistol backups. Hoenikker and Kash had pistols, which was about as much as they could handle. Then there was McCune, the invisible resident of Pala Station.

"What's it going to be?" he asked.

She crossed her arms and tried to look brave, but he could

see the nervousness in her eyes and the way she tapped the toe of one foot. Probably meant it to show her impatience, but he'd seen enough people about to go to battle that he knew what it really indicated.

"What do you mean?" she said.

"Well, you came all up in here with a handful of lies that fizzled when the Xenomorphs took your queen."

"You're mixing your metaphors like a drunken AI that's been head-smashed at a Humans First rally," she said.

"Maybe I feel like mixing them, especially since I need to decide whether to tie you up and leave you here as alien food, give you a pistol and ask you to join us, or send you packing to find your own fate."

"Will you give me a gun if I want to go back?" she asked, foot tapping double-time.

"You can pull one off a dead body on the way," he said. "Besides, we need all our guns and ammo. Not sure what's going to happen, and we need to have our contingency plans at the ready."

She stared at him, the corners of her mouth curling. She was close to tears, but she controlled it. Held it back and swallowed hard.

"Would you trust me with a gun if I joined you?"

"Would you really choose to shoot us over the Xenomorphs?" he countered. "Your safety rests in our numbers. The fewer of us there are, the greater chance you'll die."

"You didn't answer my question."

He knew the answer. He just didn't want to have to voice it.

"Probably not."

She raised an eyebrow. "Probably?"

"Okay." He grinned tightly. "No. I wouldn't."

"Then I know what I have to do," she said.

He nodded. "I suppose you do." He turned to the others,

wiping her from his concern. "Order of march is me up front with Buggy alongside. Behind us will be Hoenikker and Kash. Rear guard will be McGann and Rawlings. Watch your rate of fire. Count your ammo. Don't shoot anyone in the back." He stared pointedly at the two doctors. "And for God's sake, watch out for their blood. Even a little will burn through you until it finds daylight."

Everyone adjusted themselves. Hoenikker and Kash nodded to each other, as if sharing courage.

Another scratch came from the other side of the door.

"This is it," Cruz said.

He nodded to Buggy, who palmed the door open, revealing an adult Xenomorph. Its head in profile, saliva dripping onto the floor, sizzling where it landed. It made a sound of heavy breathing as the head began to turn toward them. Cruz lit it up with a gout of flame and Buggy opened fire, putting ten rounds into its chest and torso. Then he palmed the door closed.

Cruz turned and grinned at Buggy.

Two former Colonial Marines working as a team, wordlessly understanding what was needed to complete the mission. This was the way it should be.

After a thirty count, Buggy palmed the door open again. They were greeted with the stench of burning carapace.

The alien lay off to the side, curled in on itself, half burned, blood eating at the floor beneath. More importantly, it wasn't moving.

"With me," Cruz said. He stepped into the hallway, turned right and moved out. Buggy strode a little behind him, not wanting to be in the range of the flame, but ready to use his pulse rifle at anything within a 120-degree forward arc.

They didn't get ten meters before a juvenile Xenomorph popped out of an open door. Compared to the adult, this one could have been a toy at an amusement park. Something a kid could ride. Tempting to think it wasn't as deadly as the full-sized version. Then it leaped toward them, arcing through the air.

Cruz caught it in a plume of fire, then backed up to give the cute little monster space to land. But he didn't have much room to do so. Fire from two pulse rifles sounded from behind him. Rawlings yelled for them to move. Cruz kicked the smaller Xenomorph against the wall, regretting it immediately. Acid poured onto his foot. He tried to shake it off, but the pain was so intense he couldn't help but cry out. He didn't dare look, though, to see how much damage he'd done to himself.

He needed to move forward.

Two more juveniles appeared up ahead, probably drawn by the sound of gunfire and his scream. Buggy opened fire, rounds ripping into both of the Xenos. Blood and body parts sprayed the corridor until pieces of the nasty little monsters clung to every inch of the walls, floor, and ceiling.

"This isn't so hard," Buggy said, turning to Cruz and grinning.

Then the comms tech was jerked into the air and began flying down the corridor. He screamed, trying to shoot his invisible attacker.

"Let me go. Let me go, you fucker!"

They couldn't see how he was being held, but it had to be the escaped Leon. Cruz raised his nozzle to fire, but then lowered it. He couldn't do it without frying Buggy. As best he could, he began to run after them, pulling his pistol from its holster.

Buggy managed to get his rifle around and pulled the trigger. The Leon let go and he fell to the ground, landing with a loud grunt. The rifle skittered away.

Cruz saw blood on an otherwise blank surface, raised

his pistol, and fired seven times. The Leon screamed, and disappeared around the corner.

Hoenikker ran up to Buggy. "Are you okay?"

Buggy had claw marks on his back and shoulder, but otherwise he seemed fine. Hoenikker helped him to his feet.

"Son of a bitch," Buggy said.

From behind them came a scream.

Punctuated by another.

And another.

They were the screams of a woman.

No one needed to ask whose they were.

McCune, the mysterious woman who shouldn't have been on the station, was no longer on the station. Cruz wondered where she'd come from. Surely there were places here they knew nothing about?

How many more of her type were there?

48

Rawlings didn't like pulling rear guard. Facing that direction, it meant he was backing into unknown danger. He had to trust in those behind him, but it had been a few days since he'd been a Colonial Marine. He was no longer used to having his life depend on someone else.

Back in the marines, the idea of partnership had been ingrained through exercise after exercise, until it was muscle memory. On Tuesdays during one training phase, instead of doing the morning runs like normal people, they ran backward. The first time they'd tried it, it was a clusterfuck extraordinaire.

They couldn't keep their spacing, tripping and falling blindly over one another, each unable to see the rest—and it was because they didn't trust their fellow recruits. The space was constantly changing, and they were constantly looking over their shoulders.

Until they accepted that nothing bad was going to happen. Then it started to work. Still running backward, each stared at the next person, who stared at the next, peripheral vision keeping track of the person to the left and right, maintaining the spacing.

Trust was what would keep them alive.

But could Rawlings trust the scientists? They'd never been through training. They were civilians through and through, and didn't know how to operate in sync.

Sync.

Synth.

What about the synths? Where were they, and why weren't they clearing the station so that the humans didn't have to. They were probably guarding the command suites, which made Rawlings wish he was there. Not only would he be safe and sound, he'd probably have access to top shelf liquor.

Abruptly they came to a halt. Buggy had been skied by a Leon, which seemed to want to take him to its nest, wherever that was.

Rawlings didn't like being at a halt.

He wanted to move.

"I don't know what's taking them so long," McGann said beside him.

"Picking their nose or something," he called back over his shoulder. "Hey up there. We moving, or what?"

"Easy back there," Cruz called. "We're moving in one mike."

McGann cursed.

As did Rawlings.

A lot of shit could happen in a minute.

A juvenile appeared, this one grabbing ceiling pipes and pulling itself above them.

"Like fucking cockroaches," McGann said. They both opened fire, each plugging it with a handful of pulse rounds. The creature hung on for a moment, then fell to the ground.

Rawlings stepped forward and put two more rounds into its brain pan, careful to avoid the spray and glad he did as it sizzled and popped the paint on the walls. This was actually easier than he'd thought it would be. He was afraid it was going to be wall-to-wall Xenomorphs, but as long as they came at them one after the other, it was a shooting gallery.

What was the old term?

Easy peasy—

"Oh, shit," McGann said, grabbing Rawlings' collar and pulling him back.

An immense creature came skidding around the corner, slamming into the wall. Huge chitinous legs supported it so the head almost touched the ceiling. One of its four legs looked broken, and it walked with a limp. The central figure was human, with withered human legs dangling uselessly beneath it. Twin rows of jagged teeth took up most of the face—except for the eyes, which remained disconcertingly human.

Rawlings' eyes widened.

Fairbanks.

Or rather, the Fairbanks monster. He'd forgotten completely about it.

The creature roared. Reaching out with its claw-tipped human arms and hands, it rushed them.

Rawlings and McGann opened fire, but it was as if the creature was fast enough to dodge the pulse rifle rounds. Its legs propelled it along the walls and across the ceiling in the blink of an eye. Wherever they fired, the monster wasn't.

There wasn't enough time to call for help before the monster grabbed McGann by the head, slamming her into the wall and dislodging the pulse rifle. She managed to hold onto it with one hand, but the left hand released. Then the creature backed away and folded in on itself, using McGann as a shield.

"Shoot it," Buggy cried.

But he couldn't. Like one of those long-legged house spiders that looks impossibly large, it was able to fold itself into a smaller size, virtually hidden behind McGann. The battering had all but rendered her unconscious. She held onto the grip of the pulse rifle, probably automatically. Not knowing what it was. It might as well have been a stick.

"What do we do?" Hoenikker shrilled.

Rawlings tried to find the right angle, but it was as if the creature knew and adjusted each time, spoiling the shot.

"Shoot!" Buggy called again.

"Just watch our six!" Rawlings shouted back. "I got this."

McGann woke screaming.

"*Ohmygod*. OHMYGOD."

Then the scream of someone being eaten alive. Her eyes were all whites and her mouth was all red. Her neck strained as she screamed, over and over.

"It's *eating* her," Kash cried.

By God if it wasn't, while still using the body as a shield. Rawlings fought the urge to shoot, just to put her out of her misery, but he wasn't sure if it was too late to save her.

Fuck it.

He ran forward, zigzagging as he tried to get an angle.

One of the monster's legs wasn't all the way hidden—the broken one.

He fired and scored a hit. The monster brought its leg in, and as it did, its left shoulder hove into view. Rawlings shot two rounds into it, the impact sending the monster back. He moved in for the kill, but the monster righted itself impossibly fast, and continued eating.

McGann was screamed out, glass-eyed and staring, but still alive.

Rawlings felt a presence next to him.

Cruz.

He had a pistol in his hand, and fired into McGann's head until the glass eyes turned dead.

Rawlings jumped with each impact. When he realized that his friend and comrade was dead, he raised his pulse rifle and put twenty rounds through her. The first five ripped a hole through her chest. The second five found the monster behind it. The final ten created a flesh-and-bone free-for-all as pieces of McGann and Fairbanks exploded outward in all directions.

What was left of McGann sagged to the right, revealing the monster. It was gasping through its twin rows of sharp teeth.

Buggy raised his rifle again, but Cruz put his hand on the carrying handle and gently pushed it down. Instead, he holstered his pistol and raised the tip of the nozzle. First he gassed the flamethrower, letting out a stream of wetshot, thickened fuel misting both McGann and the struggling creature. After a few seconds of that, he clicked on the burner in the nozzle and the stream became a gout of flame.

When the flame touched the targets, they erupted in a *whoosh* of fire, reaching all the way to the ceiling and walls.

Then Cruz turned and glanced once at Rawlings.

"You need to do a better job at watching our six."

He pushed through Kash and Hoenikker, both of whom were ogling the sight of the burning beings, and resumed his place at the head of the squad.

"If y'all are ready, we still might make it out alive."

4 9

Cruz was trying not to limp. He sure didn't want to see what the acid had done to his foot. Even if he looked, it wasn't as if he could do anything about it. They still needed to get to the lodge or—if they could—the shuttle. By now, he didn't know which one was safer. What was it called when the shit hit the fan after the shit had already hit the fan?

Whatever it was, this was it.

They'd lost McGann. They'd probably lose more before it was over. As it was, they'd been lucky. The flamethrower was like a weapon of mass destruction against pretty much everything biological. As soon as he'd learned that the deputy commander was going out hunting, he'd arranged through an associate in Security to, at a steep price, slip this last-generation M240A1 flamethrower into a requisition.

Problem was, he was down to a third of the requisite napthal fuel. He shouldn't have flamed McGann and the monster, but he'd been so frustrated by the loss that he couldn't help but wetshot the whole clusterfuck.

Moving through the corridor was easy for the moment. Soon they'd be in a much more vulnerable position. By his estimation, they were less than a hundred meters from the shuttle bay. There was a junction of corridors ahead that he'd expect to be occupied by at least one Xenomorph. So, he'd held the squad back, waiting to hear sounds of movement.

It wasn't long before they heard screams and the sound of pulse rifles. He couldn't tell if it was human on human, human on alien, or a combination thereof. Whatever the case, something was going on. There was dying, and that was going to help them get past, so it was to their benefit to wait.

The firefight was long by marine standards. A few stray rounds scored the corridor walls in front of them, but they were in no danger. A piece of Xenomorph and a human arm skidded to a stop in front of them, swirls of smoke coming from the arm, acid-splashed and skin melting.

Human on alien, then.

Kash and Hoenikker whispered behind him.

Then Rawlings opened fire.

Cruz glanced back. A juvenile had skidded around the corner and slammed against the wall, scrambling on the slick floor to get back to his feet. Rawlings evidently wasn't taking any chances. He opened fire and laced the beast, so that when the next one slammed into it, its skin and carapace were splashed with acid. But then it stood, unfazed.

It regarded them, torpedo-shaped head pointed their way. Its tail whipped absently behind it as it took a few tentative steps toward them. Rawlings fired.

Nothing happened.

"Oh, fuck me," he said. "Jammed."

It was as if the Xenomorph understood English. The words were like a switch and it went from zero to homicidal in 2.2 seconds.

Kash and Hoenikker both began to fire. Hoenikker's trigger discipline made his barrel jerk all over the place. If the ceiling had been the enemy, it would have been dead. But Kash stood with a two-handed grip and fired round after round, catching the Xenomorph in the chest with each round.

At the last moment, before it plowed into them, Rawlings cleared his jam and opened fire, catching the juvenile in the side, throwing it into the wall.

Acid rained down and caught Kash on her wrist and Rawlings in the face. Both of them gave sharp intakes of breath, but refused to scream. Kash vigorously wiped her hand on the wall next to her.

Rawlings pulled out a water bottle and leaned forward, dousing the area to clean out the acid. Then he checked his pulse rifle. Cruz approved. It would do no good if it jammed again. Regrettably, when Cruz had flamed McGann, he'd also ruined the dead woman's pulse rifle. Melting it was a rookie move.

The firing in the junction had stopped, but the screeching sounds of the Xenos continued. Cruz tapped Buggy on the shoulder, then made the sign instructing him to move ahead and recon. Buggy nodded, lowered himself into a tactical stance with the barrel of the pulse rifle pointed to the floor. He would be able to raise it quickly in a time of need. The butt of the rifle was deep in his shoulder. His trigger finger lay across the trigger well, not in it.

He inched forward until he reached the corner. Once there, he glanced back, then did a quick snoop around the corner before he jerked his head back. He turned to the group and made a fist, palm forward. Then he held up three fingers and shook his head.

Three.

They could take three.

The idea was to get past them and hit the lab, where they should be safe for a time. Cruz could have kept the group where they were in Engineering, but he was afraid that they'd be OBE. Overcome by events. He also didn't want anyone to take the shuttle or the lodge before they could, so he had to gauge where and when the pleasant folks from the command suites would make a break for it. His hope was that they'd make a run for it and get cut down by the Xenomorphs commanded by Seven. Some were bound to get through, but it was relatively unlikely that those would have the shuttle code.

It was a wild guess, but one based on hundreds of military operations, wargame scenarios, and an understanding that humans wouldn't allow themselves just to stay in one place. The oft-asked question was, "Why did they do it?" It's because they had to. Their DNA forced them to.

Only Colonial Marines were capable of resisting their genetic urges, because it was trained out of them. Where others would run away from danger, marines would run toward it, because they knew they had to eliminate the danger on their own terms, before it came at them on *its* terms.

"Okay," he said softly. "Buggy and Rawlings. Lay down fire into the intersection. Controlled bursts. Five seconds total, then back away and get behind me. We'll see what happens with whatever you don't take down."

Rawlings made his way forward and exchanged hand signals with Buggy. Buggy took high, and Rawlings took low. On their silent count, they cornered with their barrels, then fired into the intersection, controlled bursts of four rounds each. After a five count, they stopped firing and backed away until they were behind Cruz. Rawlings faced the rear. Buggy continued facing forward.

"I think we got two," Buggy said.

Cruz waited for the third.

And he waited.

And waited.

A minute went by.

Fuck it. He edged forward and peered around the corner.

And was attacked for his efforts.

A full-sized adult Xenomorph had been waiting for him. It lashed out with its tail, catching him in the legs. Cruz went down hard on his back, the naptham reservoir making him cant to the left. The creature mounted him, acid and saliva dripping onto the armor. Cruz couldn't help but feel the terror trying to creep its way from where he'd hid it. That the armor worked was a testament to their science. The appreciation aside, he was in grave danger.

The Xenomorph's mouth telescoped once, then twice, trying to get through the acid-resistant prototype helmet to the soft spot of Cruz's face. Still, Cruz twisted and jerked at each attack, unwilling to trust a recent development against a creature that had been made eons ago to destroy the universe.

Suddenly the sound of pulse rifles and the impacts of the rounds sent the Xenomorph thudding off him. Cruz rolled to his left, and was able to get up on one knee before he was slammed face first into the floor.

The sound of pulse rifles continued. Still two, then only one.

The Xenomorph continued its attack.

What *was* this thing?

Then it stopped.

Cruz glanced up just in time to see the alien grabbing Buggy's arm and ripping it free. The sloppy wet sound was compounded by a short, slushy *crack* as the bones snapped. Tendons and sinews trailed from the top part of the arm, and ribbons of red blood gouted thickly from the hole in his shoulder. The arm still gripped the pulse rifle, and the alien threw it aside.

Hoenikker and Kash rushed forward and fired point blank into the Xenomorph's mouth. The alien shrieked and fell back, its tail lashing, knocking both of them down. Its movements were frantic, as if it knew it was going to die.

Then it was still, and the only sounds were Buggy's screams.

As Cruz scrambled awkwardly to his feet, his chest dripping acid onto the floor, Rawlings grabbed Buggy and tackled him. The alcoholic comms tech forced the blood-pulsing stump into a pool of acid. Buggy's scream rose so high it couldn't be heard. The blood burned away in a singe of disgusting redolence that made everyone want to gag.

Hoenikker did, turning as he hurled. Still, Rawlings held the stump in the acid until finally Buggy was able to kick free. But the acid had done its job. The wound had been cauterized. The communications tech slumped to the wall as the adrenaline bled off, communing with a pain he'd never imagined.

Cruz clambered to his feet and checked the dead alien to make sure it was indeed dead, then glanced over at the intersection. For now, it was empty. He'd have loved to stay where he was and lick his wounds, but they needed to move. They needed to get to the lab, so they could reassess and plan for their next phase.

"We're going to move, and move quick," he said. "Everyone stick behind me. We're going to the lab. Pick up any ammo or weapons you find along the way. We can make it in thirty seconds if we move out. On my command. Are there any questions?"

Hoenikker wiped spittle from the side of his face, and shook his head. Kash's eyes were wide with the rush of her adrenal glands. She shook her head, as well.

Rawlings slung both his and Buggy's rifles on his back. He helped Buggy to his feet. The wounded man moved sluggishly, but moved nonetheless. For one traitorous moment Cruz considered leaving him, but knew he couldn't. The mantra of *don't leave anyone behind* was too ingrained in his martial DNA.

"Okay. Then follow me."

And he was off, his nozzle ready to spray hot wet death at whatever got in his way.

50

As they tumbled into the lab, Cruz and Kash immediately cleared the central table so they could lay Buggy on it. Hoenikker ran to the first aid station and pulled out bandages and searched for morphine, but couldn't find any. Then he remembered that there was little or no difference in the analgesic response and safety of intravenous morphine versus fentanyl for adult trauma patients. So he snatched up some fentanyl lollipops.

At first the injured man resisted the medication, but the outside of the lolly became slick with the man's saliva, and became easier to administer. After a few moments of the analgesic taking hold, Buggy allowed it to stay.

Meanwhile, Kash addressed the cauterized wound that still smoked from the acid.

Rawlings and Cruz grabbed several carts and stacked them at the entrance. It wouldn't stop any intruder, but it would slow them down long enough that they could grab their pulse rifles and deter them with rounds.

Hoenikker stood back and surveyed the scene. He was

beyond wishing he'd never come here. He'd shot and killed things he never knew existed. He'd run and fought like some hero from a docudrama. All he cared about now was the next few minutes. To care any farther into the future was a luxury he couldn't afford.

In their thirty-second rush to freedom they'd passed piles of dead station personnel and Xenomorphs, and a few ripped-apart synths. They hadn't seen anyone living, so Cruz's strategy seemed to be working. Everyone else was doing the fighting.

They'd managed to pick up several pulse rifles and bandoleers of ammunition, so they might be able to make it to the shuttle bay after all.

He turned to survey the lab. He'd spent so much time here—more than a place of work, it had become a place of inspiration. A place of *perspiration*. He'd loved and hated coming to work here. Sure, he wished he could have stayed with computer modeling, but by being forced to live outside of his comfortable box, he'd learned so much more about the scientific method, and about himself. He'd actually *miss* the place. Coming to work to find out what craziness Cruz had done during the night, or the constant wonder that Étienne tried to project, or the confidence that Kash owned in everything she did.

Buggy moaned from the table.

Kash made soothing sounds.

And then a sound came so unexpectedly, his eyes went wide. He spun, and waited to see where it was coming from.

"Ami Mark, lève ton verre. Et surtout, ne le renverse pas!"

Friend Mark, raise your glass, but definitely don't spill it.

"Ami Timothy, lève ton verre. Et surtout, ne le renverse pas!

"Amie Erin, lève ton verre. Et surtout, ne le renverse pas!"

Étienne was there, just out of sight behind some equipment. In the rush to address the wounded, they'd missed him altogether. Kash rushed over to him.

"*Mon ami*. You're alive."

Étienne laughed. "Yes. It is me. Alive like a walking ghost."

The Frenchman looked worse for wear, however. The hair on one side of his head had burned away. The face beneath it was pocked and scarred from contact with acid. His clothes were covered in someone else's blood. Still, his eyes were bright, and he held a beaker of something liquid in his right hand.

"The pheromone worked?" Hoenikker couldn't help grinning from ear to ear.

"Eh, my friend." Étienne put an arm around him. "It worked until it didn't. Looks like it had a time limit before it wore off. My estimate is that it was about two hours. Still, what a discovery, no?" He took a sip, and offered it to Hoenikker.

Hoenikker accepted, and almost fell down with the strength of the liquor.

"Ack. What is this? Embalming fluid?"

"Just some hooch I found in Fabrications when I was hiding there."

Hoenikker held him at arm's length. "What's all the blood from?"

"*Alors*, once the pheromones wore off, I was forced to hide underneath some bodies. There was one hell of a firefight. Acid flew everywhere, which accounts for my new look." He turned to show his mangled face. "You like, yes? I look, how you say, rakish?"

Hoenikker frowned. "I'm sure it's lovely."

"Enough of the hugging and kissing," Cruz said, stepping over. He'd removed his armor and flamethrower. The clothes beneath were sodden with sweat and stank of battle. "You still crazy, Étienne? What was all that *frère Jacques* nonsense?"

Once again, the Frenchman grinned. "It was, how you say, ballsy, yes? I wanted to see if they detect each other through sound, or if the sound might counteract the pheromone. As it turns out, it didn't matter what I said. They left me alone until the pheromone wore off." Then his face turned serious. "We need to get this out. We need to make sure that Weyland-Yutani can replicate it in their labs. Just think how we can better protect the Colonial Marines."

"I'm picking up what you're laying down, Étienne, but we need to survive the infiltration first," Cruz said. "We're a three-minute sprint to the shuttle bay from here. We need to find a way to ascertain where everyone is, and what they're doing."

"Would a radio help?" Étienne asked, his face as innocent as a babe's.

"All the comms are down," Rawlings said, joining them, his eyes immediately going to the beaker.

"Then why are they still talking?" Étienne asked, pointing behind him.

Rawlings glanced at Cruz, then hurried to one of the empty containment rooms. He returned with a portable comms unit that was abuzz with conversation.

Cruz frowned, and pointed at Rawlings. "Monitor what they're saying. We need to know where everything stands." To Étienne, he said, "Where'd you get that?"

"There was a battle. Security from the other end of the station tried to get to the shuttle bay, and didn't make it. One of the dead security guards had this, so I took it. I thought it might come in handy, *ça va*?"

"Drunks and fools," Cruz said, shaking his head, the shadow of a grin appearing beneath his mustache. "Drunks and fools and Frenchmen."

Étienne saluted him with the beaker, and took a sip.

Cruz took it from him, took a sip, then shook his head and made a sound somewhere between satisfaction and dying. He handed it back. "Definitely embalming fluid." Then he turned. "Come with me, Hoenikker."

Hoenikker followed, as did Étienne.

Buggy looked no worse on the table. His eyes were glazed from the fentanyl, but it was helping him with the pain. The stump of his right arm no longer smoked. Kash had wrapped it in a gauze bandage.

Cruz looked at her and said, "I need you to look at my foot."

She paused for a moment, then motioned him to one of the workstation chairs, which had a back. A stool would have been too difficult for balance. Cruz sat in the workstation for Containment Room One and spun it so that she could have access to his foot. He tried to remove the boot, but it had melted to his skin. He tried to peel it away, but it was as if the rubber and the skin had molded into a new element. He glanced to where his toes should have been and didn't see any.

Leaning back, he groaned.

"Tell me what you see," he said.

Kash leaned in. Hoenikker stood over them and stared at the vile mess of the man's foot.

"I don't know how you've been walking," Kash said after a few moments. "You've lost all of your toes and the front third of your foot."

"What you're saying is I now have a pod," he said humorlessly.

"Does it hurt?" she asked.

"Now that the adrenaline has worn off, fuck yes."

"We're not going to be able to do anything about it here. We need a proper medical suite. I'm sure there's one on the *San Lorenzo*, but for now, all we can do is treat the pain."

Hoenikker was already on it, and handed him a fentanyl lollipop.

Cruz pushed it back. "I don't want to—"

Kash pushed it toward him. "You asked for my help, and

this is it. We need you to get us out of here. None of us are equipped. Sure, we'll point and shoot at whatever you tell us to, but without you, we don't know what to do. We have no strategy. We have no tactics. Our way of surviving is to follow the Great Cruz. So, you *will* take this this fentanyl and you *will* suck on it! It'll make you a bit high, but it will also allow you to function."

Cruz stared at her for a moment, then took the fentanyl in his mouth. "You had me at 'the Great Cruz.'" Then softly, "I'm sorry for the way I acted before."

She shook her head. "You'll have to answer for it if we survive. I won't forget."

He stared at her for a long time and then just nodded, looking away.

"There's something going down." Rawlings ran up, excited. "What's left of the command suite security forces are making a final push to the shuttle bay. The synths seem to have abandoned them. They don't know or they won't say why. So, there's only nine security techs left, and Bellows.

"Here's the thing," he continued. "They're going to have to pass by the lab to get to the shuttle bay. We can invite them inside, and then go as a larger force, or we can just stand by and see what happens."

Even though he wasn't a tactician, Hoenikker understood the pluses and minuses. Having more targets for the enemy would increase their chances of survival; but then again, if they got themselves killed, and took out more Xenomorphs in the process, then it would be better for Cruz and his crew.

It was both a win-win, and a lose-lose.

"What'll it be?" Rawlings took a swig of the beaker, which he had commandeered. It was half empty.

Cruz sucked on the lolly for a moment. "If they're all moving forward, who are they speaking to?"

"Seems as if there's a contingent of security forces forward of the command group, trying to clear the way. Bellows is there and he may have some security with him, I just can't be sure."

Cruz nodded. "Let's listen in, and see what happens."

As if on cue, the sound of gunfire came out of the tinny little speaker, accompanied by screams.

51

Cruz asked for the radio. He depressed the call button.

"Break. Break. This is Cruz. We have safe harbor in the laboratory. Repeat, we have safe harbor in the lab." Then he handed the radio back to Rawlings, stood a bit unsteadily, and asked for help clearing the door.

They moved the blockage, and then Cruz drug-fumbled his way into his body armor. He left the flamethrower sitting on a side table, but checked the ammo in the pistol at his waist.

The sounds of screams and pulse rifle fire began to diminish until it was only a single scream and a single rifle firing. Then there was silence. Pure and utter silence.

"What do you think happened?" Hoenikker asked.

Cruz knew exactly what happened.

"Let the cowboys and Indians fight amongst themselves," he said. "There's less we have to deal with between here and our objective. As for the station commander, he had a choice he decided to ignore. Now, he's run out of resources—and guess where he's going to be coming."

There was a banging at the door.

"This is Station Chief Bellows." The voice came through the radio, as well as through the door. "I demand that you open this door."

Rawlings looked at Cruz. "Doesn't he know it's unlocked?"

Cruz grinned around his lollipop and spoke into the radio. "We don't accept any demands. If you want a rescue, we might be able to accommodate."

Buggy moaned and tried to sit up. Kash asked Hoenikker to help her, and they held him down.

The banging came again. "*Let me in.*"

Étienne laughed. "Not by *zee* hair of my chinny chin chin." Cruz couldn't help but smile. Goddamn but he loved the Frenchman.

He paused.

Where did *that* come from?

He pulled the fentanyl candy out of his mouth. Yeah. That was it. He popped it back in and sucked on it. He couldn't feel his foot, which was all he cared about at the moment.

"Fucking hell." Rawlings took a swig, handed the beaker to Étienne, then strode to the door. Just as the commander began to pound again, he opened it, jerked the commander in, and closed the door behind him. Bellows fell to the ground, his jacket still smoking from an acid burst. He scrambled to get up, but Rawlings put his foot in the middle of the man's chest and drew his pistol.

"Now, tell me what the fuck you think about us now?"

Before the half-drunk warrant officer could shoot the station commander, Cruz stood. He figured the only reason the security techs hadn't taken the shuttle was because they didn't have the access code. Now that he had the commander, they could get the code and get the fuck off this rock.

"Ease off, Rawlings," Cruz said. "Let Bellows get to his feet. After all, his men are all dead or dying, so all he has is us."

Rawlings glared at him, then sighed and backed away. He holstered his pistol and walked around the table next to Étienne.

Bellows huffed as he got to his feet, opened his mouth, and seemed about to launch into a diatribe. Then he saw the looks on the faces that surrounded him. He closed his mouth, his confidence fled. He looked like a deflated old man, his once bright, confident eyes engulfed in fear and self-doubt.

"How'd you survive?" he asked.

"Skill, planning, and luck," Cruz said. "What about you?"

Bellows shifted his feet and put a hand on his lower back. "We didn't fare as well."

"It's because you had a larger force," Cruz said, and the commander shot him a confused look. "You didn't consider conservation of resources. You chose to try and bludgeon your way through, rather than strike at sensitive areas of the enemy until it could no longer fight."

"How do you..." Bellows laughed hollowly. "That's right. You're one of the Colonial Marines." He looked at Rawlings and Buggy. "They were, too. Smart. You got together."

"It was Rawlings who got us together. At first, I thought it was going to be nothing more than a club where we reminisced about old times. Rawlings had a gut feeling, though."

"A gut feeling?" Bellows asked, staring at the reception tech as if for the first time.

"Yes," Rawlings said. "A gut feeling that the station was so poorly run that it was only a matter of time before everything went to shit, and it was every man for himself."

Bellows jerked back as if slapped. "Well now. Don't hold back."

Enough of the small talk, Cruz thought. "What's the disposition of your forces?"

"What forces? Everyone's gone. Or if not gone, in hiding."

"What about the group at the shuttle bay?"

"They might be there, or not. We lost contact with them an hour ago." Bellows' eyebrows creased as his eyes narrowed. "What *is* that thing you created? How did it know what do to? Did you see the mess hall? Did you see the death factory it created?"

"We saw. We don't understand it, but we saw."

"If it wasn't for that piranha-headed Xenomorph, we might have been able to retake this station," Bellows said. "It has more than animal instinct. It has intellect."

Cruz liked the piranha-headed comparison. It fit.

"How many Xenomorphs did you see?" Hoenikker asked.

"At the end, none. I was too far back. But your head alien is holding the area in front of the shuttle bay." He glanced at the vial, and licked his lips. Étienne passed it to him and was thanked with a nod. "Honestly? There can't be that many left. Four. Five. Seven tops."

"Is that thesis supported by evidence?" Kash said.

Bellows pointed at the door. "Well, missy, the evidence is out there. You want to find it, I assure you, I won't stop you."

Hoenikker stepped forward, grabbed the commander by his lapel, and pushed him up against the wall. Cruz didn't know who was more surprised at the move, Hoenikker or Bellows. He was about to jump in, but wanted to see it play out.

"What? No threats?" Hoenikker asked. Bellows tried to disengage, and he pushed him against the wall again. "You think it's as easy as all that? You think it's our fault?" He leaned in. "Who's the asshole who brought in human beings to be experimented on?"

Bellows glanced toward Cruz, who just shrugged.

"I was just doing what corporate told me to do," Bellows mumbled.

"Just doing what you were told to do?" Hoenikker's voice rose a pitch. "You think that's a fair excuse to kill people? And what about the threats you made—to *all* of us?"

"Threats?" Bellows asked, his voice small.

"You were going to tell everyone about my sister. Do you want me to tell them now? My sister is a drug addict. We've been trying to cure her, but she steals to get money for drugs, and is on a prison planet." Hoenikker waved his fingers in front of Bellows' face. "Oooooh, that's so *awful*."

Cruz had to laugh.

"Hell, she might have been one of the people you made us kill," he continued. "And then you called Dr. Kash—one of the finest humans and scientists I have ever worked with—the Angel of Death. What the fuck was that about? And our friend Étienne? You said he should be in prison?"

Hoenikker pushed Bellows hard into the wall, released him, then backed away.

"And now you want our help. You want us to forget all the terrible things you've said and done, because your guards are all dead and you're *scared*. You are pathetic. No, you're *worse* than pathetic. You're what looks up to pathetic, and wants to be pathetic."

The station commander didn't reply. No one spoke.

"Enough," Cruz said, finally. To Hoenikker he said, "You're what looks up to pathetic?"

Hoenikker's gaze went to the ground.

"It was all I could think of."

"No, no." Cruz put a hand on the archaeologist's shoulder. He liked it when members of his team stood up for the others. Hoenikker had come a long way. "What you said was good, and it was needed." He pinned Bellows with a look. "But now, it's time to leave. Everyone gun up and be ready."

"Am I coming with you?" Bellows asked, glancing at Hoenikker.

"Only if you don't want to stay here," Cruz said. "But before you go, what's the command code to release the shuttle."

The room went as silent as a tomb.

"If I tell you, you'll leave me behind," Bellows said evenly.

Cruz shook his head slowly. "I'm a Colonial Marine. We never leave anyone behind."

Bellows seemed to consider. "But you're a *former* Colonial Marine."

Rawlings stepped forward. He wobbled a little, but Cruz didn't think Bellows noticed.

"Once a marine, always a marine," Rawlings said.

Bellows frowned. "Is this the condition for me coming with you?"

"It is," Cruz said.

"Fine." Bellows sighed. "Fuck it. One-nine-seven-five-three."

"Alrighty then," Cruz said. "Let's go."

52

As they prepared to leave the lab, Cruz moved to the back. He insisted it was because he was concerned about the amount of fuel he had left for his flamethrower. Hoenikker studied him with a frown. The man's foot was basically gone, though if they survived this, he could probably obtain a prosthesis much like Rawlings had for his hand.

They put Bellows next, giving him a pistol. Hoenikker wasn't sure of the logic—they hadn't trusted McCune, after all—but by the way he held it, it seemed as if he knew how to use it. That might prove to their advantage. Étienne stood next to him, a pistol in his hand, an expression of joy on his face.

Then it was Hoenikker and Kash, next in line. They were given the choice to carry rifles or pistols. Kash chose to take the rifle. Hoenikker thought about it. He'd fired one before, thanks to Cruz, but ultimately decided that he'd be better off carrying a pistol. He was more familiar with it, and felt that changing weapons might be to his detriment.

Buggy and Rawlings were in the front. Hoenikker didn't know why either of them should be there, but they'd insisted on it. Rawlings was eight-ways-to-Sunday drunk and could barely speak. Buggy was as high as he could be after two fentanyl lollipops, and only had one arm—his firing arm.

Even so, they'd argued and Cruz had decided that if they wanted to go first, then they could go. Buggy held a pistol in his good hand. Hoenikker realized that it meant he and Kash were the *de facto* front line, but they were almost to the shuttle, and they had the command code. All they had to do was make it there, lock themselves in the craft, and they'd be home free.

In the instant before going out the door, Hoenikker remembered Stokes' comment when Hoenikker had asked whether he should take the job.

"You might never get this opportunity again. Sure, you could stay here at your nine-to-five, going out for dinner on Fridays, seeing your therapist on Wednesdays. Or you could travel to the edge of the known universe, discover wonders no man has ever seen, and be better for it. Be boring and stay here. Or be dangerous and travel far."

Once again, he wished he could opt for "boring." If he ever got out of this, he was going to go back to his friend Stokes and punch him in the gut. The image of it made Hoenikker smile. Yeah, he was ready.

Let's get this show on the road.

Rawlings reached for the door, and they all tensed, ready for an attack.

Nothing was there.

Turning left, they kept a tight formation. They couldn't go a foot without stepping over the corpse of a human, or that of a Xenomorph. It was as if the floor was carpeted with the dead. Had it been his first week on station, Hoenikker would have found himself on his hands and knees, vomiting at the sight and stench of it. But the weeks he'd been here had made him into sterner stuff.

They didn't have far to go before they saw the enemy.

Seven stood in the middle of the corridor. It was as if he was staring into the distance. His jaws worked furiously, dripping saliva and acid. Around him crouched eleven juvenile Xenomorphs. Seven didn't seem to be looking at them, but finally it turned to them, and as it did, so did the eleven monsters. Their tails twitched and their jaws worked. Saliva dripped like waterfalls of death and sizzled onto the floor.

Beyond them lay the shuttle bay doors, and freedom.

Hoenikker could taste it. He could almost imagine lying down in a cryo-sleep cradle and drifting off, only to wake up to a place that had a paucity of Xenomorphs and an abundance of great wine. His own personal heaven.

"Hoenikker," Étienne said from behind.

"Yes?"

"It was nice knowing you, *mon ami.*"

Hoenikker gulped.

Then the juveniles attacked.

Buggy began firing with his left hand, one round after the other. Rawlings, who had a hundred rounds and another hundred to load, began firing full-automatic in what Cruz had referred to as the "spray and pray" method. Rounds flew by the dozens, catching Xenos in midair and on the ground.

Only there were too many of them. Hoenikker tracked a juvenile who walked the walls and then the ceiling as it raced toward them. He fired, and Kash did as well. She caught it in the head, but as it died it rained blood.

Buggy and Rawlings both screamed as the acid fell on them. Buggy went down hard, his skull melting as the majority of it landed on him. Rawlings reeled into the wall, still pulling the trigger, but went down on one knee.

Kash and Hoenikker kept firing until the juvenile fell to the ground in front of them.

It twitched once.

Then twice.

Then stilled.

Rawlings glanced back, his face running as the skin sloughed off. He tried to speak, but his lips burned away before he could. He fell face first into the dead Xenomorph and continued melting into it.

Hoenikker looked away, and was stunned to see that the other Xenomorphs had stopped attacking. In fact, they'd moved back to protect Seven, squatting next to him like children would their parent. He counted four more dead or dying juveniles on the ground. Which mean it was now seven against five. But half of their firepower was now gone, with Rawlings and his ruined pulse rifle down for good.

Staring at Seven, Hoenikker began to feel the familiar buzz. The Xenomorph was broadcasting something. What it was, he didn't want to know. He just wanted to see it dead.

Then he became aware of a new sound.

Crying.

It was Bellows behind him, blubbering. He was like a child, all tears and snot and not wanting to be here. Hoenikker glanced at Étienne, who was all business. The look on his face was one that Charlemagne probably wore when he faced the Byzantine Empire.

"Fuck me to tears," Cruz said from behind.

"What?" Kash asked. "What's going on?"

"I'm going to have to charge," Cruz said. "You all stay where you are."

"What exactly do you mean 'charge,' *mon frere*?"

"Exactly what I said. Listen, when I get close, fire at the

reservoir on my back. Trust me. It's our only hope. I can take them all out without issue."

"But that's suicide," Hoenikker said. He didn't like this at all. He'd rather continue the firefight, and let the chips fall where they may.

"I was never meant to make it off this rock. My entire job was to lead you scientists. I know, I know, I'm a scientist too—but at heart, I am a Colonial Marine. I want to go down fighting. Sometimes to survive isn't enough. If you're the sole survivor, it means that everyone you've loved has died. They're in a place together, and you're alone. Every day I wish I'd died with my friends. Every day I hate myself for surviving. Every—single—day. I don't want to outlive you all.

"In fact, I refuse. So, this is my choice."

"But you can't," Kash said.

"You can't stop me."

Kash growled. "I wouldn't even try."

"Thank you, Erin."

Cruz pushed Bellows aside and edged between Kash and Hoenikker. He glanced down at Rawlings and Buggy, and shook his head. Then he toggled off the igniter and prepared to run.

"Ready or not, here I come," he said, just loud enough for them to hear. Then he sprinted, spraying wet napthal out the end of his hose, shouting, "This is for you, Snyder, Bedejo, and Schnexnader. This is for you, Correia and Cartwright. I'm coming home.

"Flame on!" At the last, he flicked the ignitor and all the fuel he'd been spraying suddenly exploded into flame. He stood in the middle of it, in front of Seven and his *children*, who were burning. They screeched, but could do nothing.

"Shoot now," Cruz cried.

Seven reached out for him, grabbed him, and pulled him in.

Cruz let go of the nozzle and fought the creature, but even from where he stood, Hoenikker could see that the big man was overmatched. He glanced at Kash, who was locked in a trance, and grabbed the pulse rifle from her. She let it go without a struggle. Hoenikker planted the butt in his shoulder and stared down the sights, just as Cruz had shown him. Then he took a breath.

Cruz began to scream.

Hoenikker fired at the reservoir of fuel. When it exploded, they were knocked off their feet.

53

He climbed to his feet, using the rifle as a crutch. The explosion had left him fuzzy. Hoenikker flashed back to his arrival at the station, then to the Rat-X going free, then to the Leon-895 chasing him, then to the memory of the girlfriend he'd once had.

To Cruz sacrificing himself. It was funny how the man he'd once thought of as a sadist had shown the most humanity of them all.

He coughed, the air thick with smoke.

The corridor ahead of them was completely in flames. There was no evidence of Cruz, or Seven, or the juveniles. Just a flaming pyre of death that the air scrubbers couldn't diminish. He was forced to kneel and get down low so he could breathe.

Hoenikker glanced around.

Étienne and Kash were rising slowly, rubbing their heads where they'd hit the ground. He helped them and pointed to the dark haze of smoke near the ceiling. They nodded, understanding that they shouldn't stand.

Bellows was already up. He gave Hoenikker a hate-filled grin, then pushed him aside as he raced toward the blaze. To the left side there was a section free of fire, and this was what he was aiming for.

"Stop him," Hoenikker cried.

Kash unholstered a pistol and aimed at the fleeing man.

But she didn't have to.

A burning arm came out of the fire—a Xenomorph arm—and it pulled him in. His screams came fast and repetitive, until they stopped completely.

No one would mourn the man.

"What now?" Étienne asked.

"We escape to the *San Lorenzo*," Hoenikker said.

He felt weird. He felt like the *de facto* leader. Up until now, he'd looked to others to make decisions, but now—now he couldn't help but notice the way that Kash and Étienne looked at him. They wanted his guidance. They wanted his approval. How the hell did he earn such a position? Was it merely survival?

"Follow me." He crouched and held the pulse rifle like he'd seen Rawlings do it.

Moving quickly but carefully, he went toward the left side of the blaze. When he was near enough, he opened fire and sprayed the flames with twenty rounds, just in case another hand was waiting to grab them. When he made it around the pyre, he waited for Kash and Étienne, who followed without a problem. Then the three of them approached the shuttle bay.

On the other side of the door was an abattoir. Blood and acid mingled in smoking pools. The bay floor was carpeted in bodies. Hoenikker could almost relive the battle by the size of the clumps of humans and Xenos.

"Be careful. Be ready," he said. There could be survivors.

They turned a corner, and there, like a religious icon, sat

the stubby frame of the shuttle. All their hopes and dreams had rested on it, and now they were here.

Hoenikker turned to Kash.

"What about the lodge?" he asked.

"We don't even know if it really exists," she said. "We have this in front of us. I say the shuttle."

"Oui. Oui," Étienne said.

Then it was settled.

Hoenikker checked the outside of the craft, underneath it as well as on top. All seemed clear. He entered and found it empty, except for the single dead body of a woman in the hold. They pulled her free and left her on the bay floor. Once the three of them were inside, he figured out the toggles and closed the door.

He asked Kash to punch in the command code.

One-nine-seven-five-three.

She did and the engines responded. Before long they were ascending. He felt like cheering, his grin from ear to ear. They'd made it. Thrilled to be alive, they held hands.

"I can't believe I made it," Étienne said.

"Drunks and fools and Frenchmen," Hoenikker said, mimicking what Cruz had said earlier.

"Thank you," Kash said.

Hoenikker shook his head. "I didn't do anything but what I was told."

"I thought about running so many times," Kash said.

"I did as well," Hoenikker admitted.

"If it wasn't for Cruz, we'd all be dead," she said.

"I will buy everyone a drink, once we return to civilized space," Étienne said. "We will raise a glass to him." Abruptly the shuttle lurched, and they all froze for a moment, then broke into laughter.

"Probably leaving the ionosphere," Kash said.

Hoenikker was laughing when he saw death appear. More precisely, he saw the Leon-895 change its camouflage appearance so it could be seen. He was about to cry out when it snatched Étienne and hauled him backward. Before Hoenikker could even scream, the creature bit down upon the Frenchman's head, ripping free the skull plate with a sickening crunch. Then it dipped its face into the skull and began to chew.

"No!" Hoenikker screamed, finally able to move. He raised his rifle and fired until there was nothing left to fire, the pulse rifle clicking over and over and over as the battery tried to find a round to fire.

Both the Leon and Étienne were riddled with bullet holes. Neither had a chance at living.

"What have I done?" Hoenikker asked, falling to a knee. "I killed him."

"No, you saved him," Kash said.

Hoenikker folded in upon himself until he was sitting on the deck, the empty rifle beside him. Étienne had come so close to freedom. It wasn't fair. It could *never* be fair. He sat that way for a long time, staring at his friend, the look of utter surprise on the Frenchman's face that had appeared as his brain was being eaten by a creature they'd created from the fauna on the planet's surface.

"Why did you say what you said?" Kash asked eventually.

Hoenikker looked at her, feeling drained.

"That I was the best person and scientist you've ever known," she added.

He shrugged. "I don't know. The words rang true."

"But you don't even really know me."

"I know you well enough."

"You never asked why I was called the Angel of Death."

"I figured if you wanted to tell me, you would have."

"This wasn't the first time I was involved in human experimentation," she said, looking away.

He shrugged. "We all have things in our past."

"Oh, yeah? What was yours?" she asked. "You're about as clean and pure as the best of us. Hell, you might *be* the best of us."

"Don't count on it," he said.

"*Prepare to dock with the* San Lorenzo." They jumped at the computerized voice, then both took their seats. Just as the docking sequence commenced, the shuttle rocked as if with a blow.

Hoenikker looked toward the place where they'd been hit and saw that it was the broad front window. Instead of space—which is what he expected to see—he saw a fully adult Xenomorph with light stripes along its arms and torso.

Monica. How had she—

Even as he watched, she brought her clawed hands up and pounded a windshield already weakened by her acid. She chewed at the glass, and drooled on even more of it as she pounded.

"Will it never end!" Kash screamed.

Hoenikker glanced behind him at the body of the Frenchman and noted that it was completely alone. The Leon was nowhere to be seen. Either it had camouflaged itself in death, or it wasn't as dead as he'd thought it was.

There was a *thump* as the docking sequence concluded, and the rear door opened. They raced inside. Hoenikker headed left and Kash followed. He bypassed several doors and found the bridge. There the door responded to his palm, so the place wasn't on lockdown.

Still, it was deserted.

"Watch my back," he said. "I'm going to send a distress signal." He found the communications array and looked for a way to send a signal. It took a few moments, then he found it. A switch underneath a red protective cover that said **EMERGENCY**. He lifted the cover and pressed the switch. The screen in front of him came to life with several choices.

1 – Evacuate Ship
2 – Vacuum Ship
3 – Send Emergency Message
4 – Destruction Sequence

He selected number three. Waited. When he saw what looked like a microphone flashing green, he spoke.

"Anybody out there. Anybody. This is Dr. Timothy Hoenikker from Pala Station. Everyone is dead. Please come. I am on *San Lorenzo*. We have an infiltration of—" He noted that the microphone was no longer flashing, and had switched to red. The message would have to be enough.

He turned and said, "Okay, let's find us a place to—"

Monica had Kash, a claw over her mouth.

The Xenomorph had made it on board.

He reached down and discovered that he was weaponless. He'd left the pulse rifle in the shuttle—but that had been emptied.

Kash squirmed free, fired several times at her captor, then screamed as the acid washed against her, cascading her chest.

"Run, Tim!" she gurgle-screamed. "Save yourself."

The Monica Xeno hissed as it twitched toward him. Acid-laced saliva slapped Kash's face, and she screamed. Then it cocked its head, just as Monica had done what seemed like eons ago.

Hoenikker didn't know what to do.

Kash managed to fire again, and the shot was a wake-up call.

Hoenikker stepped backward, then found a way around the struggling pair, and bolted through the hatchway. He watched the walls for guidance and was soon aft. His only hope was to find a place to hole up until help arrived. He noted a pedestrian tunnel that said **TO KATANGA**. The place where they harvested the Xenomorphs. *Oh, hell.* He hesitated, but then heard another of Kash's screams.

Katanga might be dangerous, but the thing that had been Monica was right behind him.

Racing down the tunnel, he reached the door and palmed it open. Behind him there were more shots, and more screams. He considered going back, but what if Monica was still alive? He gave an insane little laugh at the idea that an old girlfriend had turned murder machine, and wanted to kill him.

He ran down one corridor, and then another, not paying attention to where he went. Eventually he was out of breath and the screams came closer. They clearly weren't human. He stopped at a random door, palmed it open, then closed it and threw himself into a corner. He was almost to the point of hyperventilating, and forced himself to slow his breathing. Concentrated on the act until it was back to normal, his mind still racing at how he was going to survive.

He thought of Kash, and wondered if she'd been killed. But then, when he remembered the acid that had bathed her bosom, he knew better.

A claw scraped the outside of his door.

Was it Monica?

Was it something else?

He waited for it to repeat, but it didn't.

As quiet panic set in, he reminded himself that he'd made it. He'd survived. Against all odds, he'd somehow been the one to live at the end. But that thought was squashed by Cruz's words right before he'd made his mad dash to suicide to save them.

"If you're the sole survivor, it means that everyone you've loved has died. They are in a place together, and you're alone. Every day I wish I'd died with my friends. Every day I hate myself for surviving. Every single day."

And then he'd called out the names of his comrades.

Was that what Hoenikker was destined to do? Was he going to go out like Cruz, calling the names of his own dead?

Prior.

Matthews.

Lacroix.

Cruz.

Kash.

Monica.

A claw scraped across the door again, making him jump.

Sometimes to survive wasn't enough.

He'd never wanted to die more than the moment he thought he was going to live.

ACKNOWLEDGEMENTS

Being part of the *Aliens* universe had always been a dream of mine. My dream was first realized when I was invited by Jonathan Maberry to write a story in *Aliens: Bug Hunt*, an anthology of Colonial Marine stories. The dream was fully realized when Titan editor Steve Saffel contacted my agent, Cherry Weiner, and asked if I had time in my schedule to write an original *Aliens* novel that was not only to be canon in the universe, but also to be a prequel to a new video game. What a dream. What an honor.

As most of you know, I am best known as a horror author. Even when I write science fiction, it's dark-as-hell science fiction. But that's okay, because *Aliens* has never really been science fiction. It's always been horror. The terror of losing control of one's own body. The fear of becoming something impossible. Ridley Scott said it best in the tagline of his 1979 groundbreaking movie, *Alien*. *"In space, no one can hear you scream."* So, thank you to Jon, Cherry, and Steve.

Thanks also to the Titan crew, Nick Landau, Vivian Cheung, George Sandison, Davi Lancett, and Dan Coxon.

I'd also like to give a shout out to Carol Roeder and Nicole Spiegel at Fox, and the hardworking gamers over at Cold Iron Studios, including Craig Zinkievich, Jared Yeager, Chris L'Etoile, and Sylvia Son. Finally, I'd like to thank the fourteen-year-old version of myself, my date, and her brother, for braving possibly the scariest movie of the 1970s and creating the embryo of a young man who would later xenomorph into a horror author.

ABOUT THE AUTHOR

The American Library Association calls Weston Ochse, "one of the major horror authors of the 21st Century." His work has won the Bram Stoker Award, been nominated for the Pushcart Prize, and won four New Mexico-Arizona Book Awards. A writer of more than thirty books in multiple genres, his Burning Sky duology has been hailed as the best military horror of the generation.

His military supernatural series SEAL Team 666 has been optioned to be a movie starring Dwayne Johnson, and his military sci-fi trilogy which starts with *Grunt Life* has been praised for its PTSD-positive depiction of soldiers at peace and at war.

Weston has also published literary fiction, poetry, comics, and non-fiction articles. His shorter work has appeared in DC Comics, IDW Comics, *Soldier of Fortune* magazine, *Weird Tales*, *Cemetery Dance*, and peered literary journals. His franchise work includes the *X-Files*, *Predator*, *Aliens*, *Hellboy*, Clive Barker's *Midian*, Joe Ledger, and *V-Wars*. Weston holds a Master of Fine Arts in Creative Writing and teaches at Southern New Hampshire University. He lives in Arizona with his wife and fellow author, Yvonne Navarro, and their Great Danes.

ALSO AVAILABLE FROM TITAN BOOKS

ALIEN™

ISOLATION

KEITH R. A. DeCANDIDO

The official video game adaptation—
and much more!

The product of a troubled and violent youth, Amanda Ripley is hellbent to discover what happened to her missing mother, Ellen Ripley. She joins a Weyland-Yutani team sent to retrieve the *Nostromo* flight recorder, only to find space station Sevastopol in chaos with a Xenomorph aboard. Flashbacks reveal Amanda's history and events that forced her mother to take the assignment aboard the *Nostromo*.